To Na

No News is Good News

Maggie Cammiss

All good things

Maggie x

Published by Accent Press Ltd 2014

ISBN 9781783757039

Copyright © **Maggie Cammiss** 2014

The right of **Maggie Cammiss** to be identified as the author of this work has been asserted by the author in accordance with the Copyright, Designs and Patents Act 1988.

The story contained within this book is a work of fiction. Names and characters are the product of the author's imagination and any resemblance to actual persons, living or dead, is entirely coincidental.

All rights reserved. No part of this book may be reproduced, stored in a retrieval system, or transmitted in any form or by any means, electronic, electrostatic, magnetic tape, mechanical, photocopying, recording or otherwise, without the written permission of the publishers: Accent Press Ltd, Ty Cynon House, Navigation Park, Abercynon, CF45 4SN

Acknowledgements

My thanks to Tori Howell for reading various drafts and giving invaluable feedback; to the Cutting Edge Writers and Ruby Ormerod for their advice, suggestions and encouragement; to everyone at Accent Press and to Nick, for his unfailing support and enthusiasm.

Chapter One

The insistent vibration under the pillow brought Eleanor into bleary consciousness and, groping under her pillow, she squinted at the tiny letters of the text message.

Daniel's been in touch. He's coming back for the party. Gx

Eleanor was suddenly fully awake. She blinked, rubbed the sleep from her eyes, and read it again. A seed of disquiet lodged in the pit of her stomach.

She checked the time: 4.50 a.m., stupid o'clock. Her friend must be at the airport to be texting so early. Off on yet another overseas jaunt, she thought, though Grace was the only person she knew who piloted herself.

She fell back, exhausted. Despite six hours' sleep, it felt like she'd only just left work. The days merged into each other, like being trapped in a revolving door; early starts, late finishes; night shifts, weekends – the job would take up as much of her life as she was willing to give.

There'd be no dozing off again this morning. Her mind was full of Daniel: his abrupt departure; where he'd been; why he'd stayed away so long, and what she'd say to him when they met again.

Pushing the duvet aside, she leaned over to kiss Toby's cheek. 'Sorry, babes, gotta go,' she whispered. 'See you later.' Toby grunted and burrowed deeper. It was far too early to even contemplate pleasantries.

At least they'd managed to make up last night, she thought, remembering with a shudder yet another row over nothing that seemed to be a feature of their lives at the moment.

Last night her boyfriend had arrived on her doorstep clutching a bunch of flowers which looked as if he'd swiped them from a grave, and a gift-wrapped CD.

'I bought you a present,' Toby had said happily. 'You like Michael Bublé, don't you?'

'Whatever gave you that idea?'

'You told me.'

'I never did. I hate Michael Bublé.'

'No, you don't. You said …' Toby had frowned at her. 'Well, anyway, it was just a gesture.' He'd thrust the exhausted flowers into her hand on his way to the television. 'I'm going to watch the footy. Chelsea are playing tonight.'

The remark had provoked an evening of tetchy niggling, neither willing to give any ground. Eleanor's argument that this was her house and she didn't want to watch yet another football match had fallen on deaf ears until a 2-0 win for his team had smoothed Toby's wrinkles. Full of bonhomie, he'd suggested that they have dinner the next day at the new Japanese restaurant that had opened close by Eleanor's work.

She reached for her dressing gown at the end of the bed, surprising Mabel, curled inside its silken folds. Her striped silver body thumped to the floor in a flurry of indignant fur. She followed Eleanor down to the kitchen, sniffed the biscuits in her bowl, and stalked back upstairs.

Eleanor squinted uncomfortably in the sunshine streaming through the thin blind. The contrast between the complete darkness in her blacked-out bedroom and the intense light of a summer morning always took her by surprise. She flicked the radio on to find out what the day had in store for her; John Humphreys and a female cabinet minister were arguing about immigration numbers. Eleanor zoned out, contemplating a slice of toast, but the sick feeling in her stomach was occupying all the available space.

While waiting for the kettle to boil, she tried Grace's number. No network coverage. She was probably already in the air.

In the shower she lingered under scorching water and swore as the last squirt of shampoo shot out of the bottle and slithered down the plughole in a gelatinous blob.

Back in the dark bedroom she threw on jeans, top, and cardigan, all black. She'd long since refined her wardrobe down to this one colour, to avoid having to make any decisions in the early hours. She hurried distractedly through her minimal make-up routine, grabbed her keys and bag, and left the house.

She walked into the UK24 newsroom thirty minutes later.

'Morning.' Ashok Kumbal greeted Eleanor as she approached the newsdesk. He was dressed in his usual crisp white shirt and immaculately tailored grey suit that emphasised his tall, lean frame. Only the loosened tie and open collar betrayed the labours of his past twelve hours as duty editor. Night shifts hardly seemed to bother him at all.

His eyes widened as she drew closer.

'What's the matter?' Eleanor's hands raked through her hair. 'I ran out of shampoo. This is my badly-fitting-wig look. It's not too bad, is it?'

'No, no,' Ashok replied, tapping his keyboard busily. 'You look fine.'

She logged on, sat back, and looked around as she waited for the computer to gather its wits.

From her desk at the far reaches of the Forward Planning group, handily situated between water cooler and photocopier, she surveyed the familiar scene – the clusters of work stations equipped with the usual computer hardware, TV monitors, and telephones radiating from the centre like a molecular diagram; the multi-screen video wall showing a selection of muted news feeds from foreign stations and breakfast programmes from rival outfits. Journalists, producers, planners, and researchers were drifting in to start their shifts.

Except for the on-air talent, who favoured designer clothes in bright block colours and were theatrically made-up for the studio, most people were casually dressed. Jackets hung from the backs of empty chairs, giving the impression that their occupants would be back shortly, after a sly puff outside the back door.

Eleanor switched on her small television monitor and quickly took in the news headlines crawling along the bottom of the screen. Nothing untoward there, no *Breaking News* strap. 'So, what's occurring?' she asked Ashok.

'Some flooding in the South-west, but nothing epic,' he replied. 'No worse than usual; things have calmed down a bit now. Did someone call you in? You could have stayed in bed. No one's died.'

It was a truism that a newsroom flourished on others' misfortunes: death, war, natural disaster, or public humiliation – these claimed undivided attention until more interesting events occurred, when the spotlight dimmed and the news caravan moved on to the next catastrophe.

'No, nobody called,' said Eleanor. 'I got some rather startling news, then I couldn't get back to sleep. Thought I might as well come in.'

Belle Fenton sauntered over. 'I hate these early starts,' she complained. Belle's shifts always seemed to start in the middle of the night. 'I didn't have time to get dressed properly this morning.'

'Really?' Eleanor regarded her latest outfit sceptically. Every day brought a new challenge and today the newsdesk assistant was Doris Day from her bangs to her bobby socks. Belle maintained that she was bringing cinema to life in the newsroom. How, Eleanor wondered, did she afford all these fashions on her meagre salary?

'Looks like you had the same problem,' Belle observed.

Eleanor paused in the adjustment of the height of her chair and looked down at her black garb. 'Why? What's wrong?'

'You'd better check your face.'

Eleanor delved into her handbag for her mirror and saw that she had two bright patches of unblended blusher streaked across her cheeks.

'Why didn't you tell me?' she stormed at Ashok. 'I look like Lady bloody Gaga! You'd have let me stay like that all day, you tosser!'

He shrugged innocently. 'Sorry. I assumed it was intentional.'

Belle nudged her arm sharply. Following her gaze, Eleanor hastily rubbed at her face as she watched the Home News editor chat his genial way across the newsroom towards her. Julian Bedworthy was quite good-looking, she reflected, if you liked blond, floppy-haired boys with twinkling blue eyes and infectious grins. But today the effect was spoiled slightly by the shrimp-coloured jacket he wore, which gave him the look of a seafood stall-holder.

As he approached a waft of expensive aftershave preceded him, tickling Eleanor's nostrils with a familiarity she couldn't quite place. He moved a folder to one side and perched on the edge of her desk, eyeing her through black-framed spectacles. 'Have you sorted out your screen test yet?'

She looked at him blankly. 'No. I ...'

'We discussed this in your annual review, Eleanor. You seemed quite keen then: a change in your career path. Are you having second thoughts?'

'No, of course not.'

Eleanor had been pleased at Julian's reaction to her request for a screen test. She didn't really expect to pass muster, but she wanted to test herself, to see if she'd be any good in front of the camera. If she could conquer her fear of performing for an audience, albeit an invisible one, it might help with her singing ambitions. And they might just use her on overnights.

'How can we make a decision without seeing you in action?' Julian was saying. 'Arrange it,' he commanded. 'I think you'll be good at it. I mean, it's only reading out loud, isn't it? How hard can it be?' His eyes swept from her face to her feet. 'We can sort the rest out later,' he added.

'Oh. Right.' Eleanor nodded. 'OK. I'll see if they can fit me in after my shift tomorrow.'

'Are you coming to the editorial meeting?' Julian threw over his shoulder, walking off. 'We'd better get going if you want a seat.'

Eleanor followed him to the already-packed meeting room and they stood for a moment at the back, pressed up against each other like commuters on a Tube train. She tried to edge away from the too-intimate contact, again conscious of that familiar scent.

Julian shoved his way through and sat down in his reserved seat at the head of the table. 'Can I have some quiet for a moment, everyone, please?' He had to raise his voice over the din. 'Either we've got too many people at this meeting, or this room is too small.' He looked round. 'Only those directly involved need stay.'

No one moved.

'OK. We need to book a bigger room in future. Though,' he looked pointedly at Belle's petticoats, which almost needed a chair of their own, 'if some of us wore rather more understated clothes, we might fit more people in.'

Seemingly unbothered by the implied criticism, Belle carried on scribbling in her notebook. Probably designing tomorrow's outfit, Eleanor thought.

After the daily specifics had been covered, Julian continued to some forward planning. 'The features schedule is looking pretty bare at the moment,' he announced. 'Let's get some ideas going.' Blank faces gazed back at him from round the table. 'Come on, doesn't matter how stupid they seem at this stage.'

He cocked a speculative eyebrow at Eleanor and for a second she wrestled with the maxim that it was better to keep quiet and be thought stupid, than open her mouth and prove it. But Julian's expectant stare was boring straight into her forehead. 'Come on, Eleanor,' he said. 'I thought this was your area of expertise. Any daft ideas from la-la land?'

She wilted under Julian's gaze, feeling her confidence draining away. 'Well, I've got a couple of possibilities. They're not finalised yet, though,' she qualified.

But Julian wasn't about to give up. 'Try us,' he said.

She hated being put on the spot. 'OK. I'm lining up a woman who had risky chemotherapy while she was pregnant. Went on to give birth to healthy twins. Health issues always get good viewing figures,' Eleanor continued, getting into her stride.

'I'm well aware of that, thank you,' Julian said sardonically. 'But one case history won't fill the summer schedule. 'Look everyone, I won't patronise your collective intelligence,' he carried on, 'but this is the time of year when we need some good material to keep the viewers interested. We can't manufacture a natural disaster – today's floods don't count – or rely on someone important dying, or another stupid directive from the EU. You're all intelligent people. Think!' He got up and burrowed his way to the door. 'Same time tomorrow, please. And bring some bloody ideas!'

Eleanor's phone was ringing when she got back to her desk. She grabbed it hopefully.

'I have to cancel dinner tonight,' Toby blurted. 'Sorry.'

She'd been really looking forward to tonight. So much for Toby's promises. 'Oh,' she said, waiting for the explanation that didn't come.

'So I'll see you later in the week instead. Is that OK?'

'I suppose so. I don't think I've got anything planned. I'll have to check my diary. Will we still be eating at Sushi Sushi?'

'Dunno. Probably not. Sorry, I've got to rush. I'll text you when I can make it. We can have a takeaway and watch the footie.' And then he was gone.

'Thanks for that,' Eleanor muttered to dead air. He was getting worse, she thought.

She turned to the pile of newspapers and magazines threatening to avalanche off the side of her desk and pulled it towards her. She leafed through several glossy magazines and started to make notes about a woman who'd been strangled by her gastric band. But Grace's early morning revelation kept intruding.

Daniel was coming back.

She glanced down at the heart-shaped loops she'd been unconsciously doodling on her pad and hastily covered them with illegible scrawl.

The seed of disquiet grew.

Chapter Two

Eleanor and Sam had been best friends since secondary school. Arriving late on her first morning, Sam had tripped over the laces of her clumpy shoes and landed in an untidy heap at Eleanor's feet. Looking down, Eleanor saw an abundance of dark, unruly hair tinged a brassy copper by too much henna and held precariously in place with a scrunchie which, on closer inspection, turned out to be a lacy black thong.

'Shit!' the new girl had exclaimed loudly as she'd pulled herself and her huge bag upright, bright red and glowering.

Eleanor looked round nervously. Swearing wasn't allowed on school premises, but she didn't relish being the one to caution this large, flamboyant creature.

'So, is this your first day?' she'd asked instead. 'What form are you in? I'm in 3b.'

Sam bent down to pull books, cassettes, two packets of chewing gum, a pair of raffia sandals, and a sweater out of the cavernous bag. Eleanor was beginning to expect a Mary Poppins standard lamp complete with shade to emerge when Sam dredged a grubby sheet of paper out of the depths and smoothed it on her skirt. She traced a finger down the page. 'Ah, here we are. I'm in 3b too.' She frowned at Eleanor. 'That's good, you can introduce me to everyone.' She held out a hand. 'Hi. I'm Sam Somerton.'

'Short for Samantha?'

'No,' she'd replied flatly. 'Samarinda, would you believe?'

'Oh, that's really lovely. I've never heard that name before.'

'It's a city in Borneo,' Sam had explained, rolling her eyes. 'That's an island ...' she waved a casual hand, 'somewhere near Africa. It was where I was conceived, apparently. And this was before Posh and Becks made it trendy!'

Eleanor had been impressed; here at last was someone whose name had an even more esoteric ancestry than hers. Her parents had been unable to resist hijacking the eponymous heroine of a popular Beatles song to name their only daughter. 'Don't talk to me about trendy parents,' she'd said wryly. 'My name's Eleanor Wragby.'

Sam's angry face had broken into a huge, empathic grin. They'd linked arms, their friendship sealed.

So Eleanor had to tell Sam about Daniel. Sam would know what to do.

Sam answered her mobile on the first ring. 'Hi. Everything OK?' She had an unsettling ability to divine even the slightest upset in her friend's mood.

'Daniel's coming back.'

There was a small silence. 'Oh shit. When?'

'Grace texted this morning. He'll be at her thirtieth.'

'That makes sense,' Sam said grudgingly. 'He is her brother.'

'Yes, and I'm supposed to be singing. Remember? I promised, after Grace heard my rendition of that Adele song at that karaoke party.'

'Oh God, yes, I'd forgotten about that,' said Sam. '"Someone Like You", wasn't it? You'll still do it, though, won't you?'

'I can't really cry off now, can I? It's too late. But how am going to face Daniel?'

'Let me think about it. Are you doing anything tonight?'

'I was, but I've been subbed. Toby's had a better offer, apparently.'

'I'll be over. See you about eight.'

'I'll get some wine in.'

Daniel's return was not entirely unexpected. Grace's landmark birthday was obviously going to attract the attention of her older brother, Eleanor told herself. But it was the fact that she hadn't heard from him in over four years that was causing her heart to beat crazily.

She thought back to the last time she had seen Daniel. They'd been staying with her parents for a few days; a break from the summer heat of the city in their cottage deep in the Pennines. She loved the early morning and they'd gone out walking on the crags before the rest of the household had risen.

She could still recall every aspect of that walk; how her legs had ached after the long climb up the mountain path and the way the wind had stung her cheeks.

She remembered the tiniest details of what they'd talked about: what their plans were for when they got back home and how their various commitments would impact on them. She'd mentioned an unavoidable shift change that meant supper with some of Daniel's colleagues would have to be rearranged. He seemed rather preoccupied – she'd had to prompt him about their names – and then, 'I have to tell you something,' he'd said. 'I'm glad I've got you on your own.'

Eleanor's heart had lurched. He was going to propose.

'I don't want your family to know,' Daniel had carried on. He'd struggled to find the words. 'I've fucked up, Eleanor. Really badly.'

'What do you mean?'

'I wanted to ask you to marry me. I even brought …' He'd fumbled in his pocket, pulled out a small blue box and showed her the exquisite solitaire diamond. 'It was my grandmother's.' He'd flipped the box shut immediately. 'But I can't give it to you. I can't let you become involved. I've … I've done something really stupid, El.'

'What?' Eleanor's mind was racing. What could he

possibly have done? 'Talk to me Daniel. Tell me. *What* have you done?'

He'd shaken his head. 'You'll never forgive me.'

Anxiety had fluttered in her stomach. 'I will. Trust me. I love you. Whatever it is we can get through it. But you have to tell me. Is it about your family?'

'No, it's ... it's work.' He'd rubbed his face with his hands. 'God, I can hardly bear to even think about it.'

She'd caught his hands and held them steady. 'Daniel, you're frightening me,' she said. 'What have you done that is so terrible?'

'I can't tell you. I can't tell anyone. The bank has sworn me to secrecy.'

'I don't understand.'

He'd shrugged helplessly. 'Don't you see? I can't ask you to marry me in these circumstances. We can't start married life with a huge secret between us.'

'So tell me. It can't be that bad, surely?'

'Eleanor, please believe me. It's very bad and I can't tell you! Not with your job and everything.'

'My job? I don't understand,' she'd repeated. 'Oh. You don't trust me. Is that it?'

Daniel had turned away. 'It's best if I just go. I'm so sorry. I love you, but –' He'd started to scramble down the hillside and his last words were lost in the rattle of loose pebbles.

She'd hurried after him but he was too fast for her.

'Be careful!' she'd shouted. 'I'll see you back at the house ...' The wind had tossed the words back in her face like a reprimand. Tears of frustration had filled her eyes as she'd watched him recede further from her.

By the time she'd got back to the cottage, he'd left. He'd rebuffed all her attempts at contact, had never acknowledged her calls. He had left England and not even his sister Grace knew where he'd gone.

The shock at being so unceremoniously dumped was

profound. She carried the loss around like a burden she couldn't put down. The excoriating grief had eventually diminished, but it had left a residual disappointment that had leached into every area of her life and tainted all its aspects with the whiff of failure.

She had little idea where Daniel had spent the intervening years. She knew that he'd left the job he hated at the merchant bank where he'd made his mysterious, but still unexplained error, and begun a new life as a fledgling investigative journalist. He'd kept up a blog, Facebook page, and Twitter feed to help his newly launched career and had gradually built a following for his human interest stories from trouble spots the world over. But personal communications had been minimal; for all the contact he'd maintained with friends and family, he may as well have joined the Foreign Legion.

It was as if he'd been running away from his life. They'd been together for five years, through the final year of university and on to working life afterwards in London, and she'd thought they had something really special. She'd been wrong, obviously. She'd gathered her hurt around her like a cloak and stumbled on with her life. She'd long since given up any hope of speaking to him again; he'd clearly forgotten all about her.

But now he was back.

Putting Daniel firmly to the back of her mind, Eleanor opened a new email. It had been a long morning and she still had lots of contributors to contact. The lack of any newsworthy items was always a problem at this time of year.

'Bloody Silly Season,' she muttered.

'I've heard that expression before,' piped up the intern who was picking his nails at the desk opposite. 'What's it mean?' He had a Sideshow Bob haircut and Eleanor imagined him stuck on the end of a pencil.

'It means,' she said, 'well, it's the summer months, Parliament will soon be in recess, not much news around ...'

'So we have to make it up?' he asked eagerly.

Eleanor shook her head. 'Not exactly. But rolling news is a hungry beast and, with politicians on their holidays, there's no one else around opening their mouths to change feet on a regular basis. So it means we have to work extra hard to fill the bulletins.'

'Oh, I see.' The boy was clearly disappointed.

'What's your name?'

'Fraser.'

'Well, Fraser, are you doing anything at the moment?'

'Nah.' He looked around guiltily. 'I'm zero tasking.'

Eleanor snorted in amusement. 'Right then, I'll give you something to do, but first can you make yourself useful? What time is it in Beijing?' She indicated the bank of clocks on the far wall showing the time in various international zones. 'I've left my long-range specs at home.'

'Oh, hang on a minute.' Fraser peered at the clock. 'Sorry, I can't quite make out ...'

Eleanor sighed. 'Could you get a little closer, please, if you can't see either?'

Fraser looked uncomfortable. 'It won't make any difference,' he muttered. 'They've all got hands.'

'They often do. So?'

'I can only tell the time if it's digital. I've got a Binary,' he added proudly, showing Eleanor the chunky space age timepiece on his wrist.

She studied the complicated array of coloured lights. 'You geek,' she said. 'How come you can decipher this but you can't read a normal clock face?'

Fraser shrugged. 'It wasn't taught at school. Everything's digital now, anyway. I didn't think it'd matter ...'

Eleanor turned back to her screen. Next time I have to be responsible for anyone on work experience, she promised herself half-seriously, I'm going to insist on someone very clever and very good looking. 'Go and get some lunch,' she said to Fraser. 'I'll have some printing for you to do when you get back.'

'I thought this was a paperless office,' he complained, mooching away with his hands in his pockets.

Eleanor busied herself with something non-intellectual – dumping all her carefully researched articles into a new computer folder. The printing would keep Fraser occupied and she could present everything to Julian for his summer features schedule. That might win her some much-needed brownie points

Her phone rang. 'I'm really sorry I texted you so early,' Grace began, 'but Daniel phoned just as I was doing the final checks and I wanted to tell you before I took off. I've just flown in to Paris for the weekend; thought the old Islander needed a bit of an outing.' Before Eleanor could say anything, she went on, 'He sounded really chilled.'

'Good for him,' Eleanor said frostily. 'Did he say where he'd been all this time?'

'Sort of. He's given me all the major plot points, but he's still got to fill in the finer details. There's lots of catching up to be done.'

After a short pause Eleanor asked hesitantly, 'Did he – did he mention me?'

'No, as a matter of fact, he didn't. But I'm sure everything will be fine,' Grace carried on airily.

'He left me, remember,' Eleanor reminded Grace pointedly. 'I think I'd better be the judge of that.' She paused, then asked, 'Did he ever tell you why he left so suddenly, what he did that was so terrible?'

'No, he never has. I would have told you. We're none the wiser, any of us. Though I think he might have told Dad. Hopefully all will be revealed at the party.' Grace's breezy tone took on a more serious note. 'Actually, talking about Daniel, there's something I need to tell you …'

'Eleanor!' Julian bellowed across the room. He beckoned her over with a flick of his head. 'When you've got a moment.'

'Shit. Sorry, Grace, I'm being summoned. I'll speak to you later.'

'Wait a minute, El, this is important. Daniel has …'

'Sorry, I've got to go.' Eleanor put the phone down and hurried across the newsroom.

Chapter Three

'You are *soooo* still in love with him,' Sam teased. 'You say you're over him, but you're not. You're still holding that candle. Go on, admit it.'

'I am not!' Eleanor protested. She twisted the ring on the middle finger of her right hand; Toby had given her the trinket for her last birthday. 'But we were soul mates, or so I thought. I was devastated when he dumped me like that.'

'I know,' Sam said sympathetically. She poured red wine into two glasses and handed one to Eleanor.

'But it's been more than four years. He's obviously over me and I'm over him, too. He's probably married by now and she'll be wearing that fabulous ring. No,' she added firmly, 'the candle's well and truly burned out.'

'Don't give me that. You sound like bloody Elton John! I know you too well.' Sam took a large slurp of her wine. 'There's absolutely no conviction in your voice. Anyway, never mind all that. What are you going to wear for the party?'

Eleanor brightened. 'Oh, I picked up a brilliant bargain the other day. I'll go and put it on.'

The dress, in emerald green raw silk, was stunning: a simple shift that fitted perfectly. Eleanor slipped on a pair of scarlet stilettos and twirled around the room. 'What do you think? It doesn't emphasize my tummy, does it?'

Sam stared. 'It's green!'

Eleanor's heart plummeted. 'You don't like it!'

'It's absolutely fab,' Sam said hastily. 'It's just not black, that's all. But I love it. And those shoes! Where did you get them?'

'You won't believe it. A tiny little shop on the high

street. They were calling to me from the window.' Eleanor looked down at her frock. 'It's not too short, is it? Only Toby thought ...'

Sam sighed. 'Never mind what Toby thinks, you look lovely. That is really your colour. You should wear it more often.'

Eleanor looked doubtful. 'You don't think I've bitten off too much, do you?'

'Oh, here we go again! Is this about singing the solo? Of course you can do it. You've got a beautiful voice.'

'Yeah,' said Eleanor dismissively. 'What if it goes all croaky? It's done that before. Remember that solo I did in the church at Christmas? I was terrible.'

'Yes, but it was winter, the church wasn't properly heated, and you had a cold. You're too hard on yourself. You should have cancelled.'

'I couldn't. I'd promised. I can't back out now.' She took a sip of wine. 'Pity Grace wasn't at the carol concert instead of the karaoke party. If she'd heard me make a mess of "In the Bleak Midwinter" rather than singing those Adele songs we wouldn't be here now.'

Sam nodded enthusiastically. 'That was great. *You* were great. But you could still have refused. Why didn't you?'

Eleanor raised an eyebrow. 'Probably because it was the Chablis speaking, not me.'

The party was in two weeks' time. Eleanor had already been regretting her impetuosity; now she was totally panicked.

'Will you please stop worrying!' Sam exploded. 'You'll be brilliant! Anyway, you can't fool me. This isn't about the singing. This is about Daniel, isn't it?' She took another gulp of wine and refilled their glasses. 'Has Grace told him you're going to be there?'

'She must have, surely? God, I'm so bloody nervous, I feel like a schoolgirl again. And I've got that screen test tomorrow, too. I thought it might help but now I'm not feeling so confident.'

'Just pretend you're doing karaoke,' Sam advised airily. 'You'll just have to ignore him, like all professionals. Sing your heart out to a complete stranger, isn't that how they do it?'

'How would I know? I don't spend all my spare time in a karaoke club.'

'Anyway,' Sam added. 'Daniel will be willing you on. He'll want you to succeed. It's his sister's birthday party. Why would anyone want you to fail?'

The next day Eleanor was in the standby studio for her screen test, facing an enormous camera and wondering what on earth she was doing there. She wasn't front-of-house. She was back office. She made sure everything ran smoothly. She brought order to chaos, she didn't contribute to it. And besides, everyone knew that a studio camera added an extra ten pounds to even the skinniest frame.

When she'd told Toby about her conversation with Julian, he'd laughed out loud.

'You don't look like a newsreader,' he'd said, with the authority of one whose television was permanently tuned to Sky Sports News. The comment hadn't made her feel any better.

'Ready?' Phil, the studio director's disembodied voice boomed in Eleanor's earpiece.

'Hang on.' She hunted through her handbag and pulled out a small brown phial. She put a couple of drops of Rescue Remedy on her tongue and breathed deeply, peering into the mirror the make-up lady had left for her. She looked like she'd fallen head first into a vat of fake tan. She knew the studio lights would make her appear a little more human, but even so there was enough foundation and bronzer on her face to ice a cake. At least in this small backup studio there was no chance of being observed.

Phil murmured reassuringly in her ear. 'All right, ready to roll. Just ignore the camera.'

'Easier said than done.' She watched the remote-controlled lens as it glided up and down on its telescopic pedestal, eventually coming to rest on her face.

'Don't look down, it gives you a double chin and makes you mumble.' Phil issued a series of simple instructions to calm her nerves. 'Nothing to it, really,' he added. 'It's only reading out loud.'

Julian had said the same thing, she remembered. Did everyone have the same manual? She sat up straight, tucked the back of her jacket under her bottom, and tried to imagine the top of her head being gently pulled upwards and backwards, a tip from one of the proper newsreaders.

'That's better,' Phil whispered in her ear. 'Don't worry if you make any mistakes, just carry on. I'll keep recording and edit them out. I'll count you in from 5. And don't forget to smile!'

Eleanor swallowed hard. Smile? She was clenching her teeth so hard her jaw ached and her face was set in a grimace. Too late, the red light came on and Phil was counting down. She stared into the camera, feeling a blush rising up her neck, and attempted to arrange her expression into one of practised authority. 'Good evening. I'm Eleanor Wragby with the seven o'clock news from UK24,' she croaked.

'Not too bad,' Phil growled. 'Carry on.'

Taking a gulp of water, she looked steadily into the camera and started again, eventually getting into her stride. She read the three news reports that were littered with deliberate tongue twisters and foreign place names she had no idea how to pronounce, but at least she didn't stumble over them. At the end she smiled shakily, waited until the red light blinked off, and got up from her seat.

'Sorry. That was rubbish,' she said to Phil, when she

joined him in the gallery.

'You were fine,' he reassured her. 'A couple of mistakes, but you were nervous; you'll get better.'

'I don't expect to get the chance.'

'Want to have a look?' He gestured towards a small screen. 'It'll playback on that monitor. Any minute now.'

'I'm not sure I –' The giant newsreader that appeared, dressed in a much larger version of Eleanor's clothes, almost took her breath away. She gazed at the screen with morbid curiosity. 'I knew the camera put on a few pounds, but not a couple of stone. Hell, I look enormous. And that's without widescreen or high def.'

'Calm down,' said Phil. 'Everybody says that. Maybe you are a bit chubby on screen but your delivery was fine …'

'Chubby?' she echoed. 'I think *that*,' she pointed at her frozen, smiling image, 'gives a whole new meaning to the word. And anyway, who are you calling chubby?'

Phil shrugged. 'The camera never lies,' he said darkly.

'Well, I think the sooner we draw a line under the whole sorry experience, the better,' Eleanor said. 'Now, if you'll excuse me, I've got to get this gunk off my face. I feel like an iced doughnut.'

'You were fine,' Phil persisted. 'And I'm sure Julian will agree.'

Eleanor stopped halfway across the room and wheeled round. 'Oh, I forgot about that. Have you really got to show it to him?'

Phil nodded. 'No choice. He insists on seeing all the tests.'

'Couldn't you just wipe it? Delete it, lose the tape, or something?'

He shook his head. 'I told you, you were fine. Don't worry. You'll be doing the graveyard shift like an old hand before you know it.

Chapter Four

A large cup of industrial-strength coffee materialised in front of Eleanor as she was struggling to stay awake at the end of the night shift.

'You look like you could do with it,' said Belle. She was wearing jeans, boots, and an over-large chunky sweater in deference to the enthusiastic air conditioning, and looking like no film star Eleanor had ever seen.

'Sorry, I was miles away.' Eleanor looked up. 'Not dressing up today?'

'I'm trying to keep a low profile,' Belle confided, obviously unaware that her modest outfit was like a beacon in the fog – such a departure from her usual exuberant outfits that she may as well have been sporting a red *Baywatch* swimsuit.

'Why? What've you done?'

Belle checked her watch theatrically. 'How long have you got?'

'Sounds bad.' Eleanor patted the chair beside her. 'Sit down and tell me everything.' Listening to Belle would at least ensure she didn't fall asleep. It would also put all thoughts of Daniel out of her mind, if only temporarily. She took a huge gulp of coffee. 'Thanks for this. Just what I needed. So what's happened?'

Belle went on to recount a guest booking of the previous evening, who had presented himself at the studio wearing an enormous snake round his neck like a *Doctor Who* scarf. 'He was just there to discuss an increase in the adder population,' Belle explained. 'I wasn't expecting him to bring the ruddy creature in with him, I swear! And it wasn't even an adder. More like a python.' Belle giggled. 'It all got a bit *Snakes on a Plane* after that, to tell the truth. It managed to slither under the desk –' she shuddered dramatically, '– everyone was running round like headless chickens. Very unprofessional. Ashok was muttering about risk assessments and Health and Safety. They eventually found the damned thing coiled up in the computer cabling, fast asleep.'

'I bet Julian wasn't impressed. What did he say?'

'I haven't had that pleasure yet. I've heard rumours that he wants my head on a stick.' She looked down at her sweater. 'Hence the disguise.'

Eleanor yawned and rubbed her eyes. 'I'm ready for bed,' she confessed.

'Too many late nights?' Belle asked.

'No,' Eleanor replied, shaking her head. 'Quite the opposite, in fact.'

'Ooh, I could do with some juicy gossip. Do tell.' Belle settled herself into the chair beside Eleanor and made some encouraging gestures.

'It's nothing like that.' Eleanor began, 'I'm not sleeping well, that's all.'

'That's what they all say. Who's keeping you awake?'

Eleanor shrugged. 'Someone I was very close to. He's just reappeared and I'm not sure how I feel about it yet.'

'Reappeared? Where's he been? He didn't leave you in the lurch, did he?' Belle was agog. 'Typical.'

'No, no, nothing that dramatic,' Eleanor said wryly. 'We weren't actually at the church …'

Belle's eyes widened and she scooted her chair closer.

'He said he wanted to marry me,' Eleanor continued. 'In the same breath as he told me he couldn't.'

'Eh?'

'He even showed me the engagement ring.'

'Shit. What a –' Belle frowned. 'So, why did he go? Has he been in contact since he left?'

'Not a peep. It was like he'd died. But now …' Eleanor

sketched in the details about Grace's thirtieth birthday party then her phone rang again. 'Sorry, I'll tell you the rest later.'

Belle pointed to her third finger. 'What was it like?'

Eleanor put her hand over the mouthpiece. 'The biggest diamond I've ever seen,' she whispered miserably. 'But I never got to wear it.'

Daybreak was well underway by the time Eleanor climbed into her car at the end of the night shift. As she negotiated the narrows streets on autopilot her thoughts turned once more to Daniel as she recalled the time before he'd cut himself so completely out of her life.

After their finals, the three friends had moved to London; Daniel joined Grace in a spacious apartment in a mansion block in South Kensington, courtesy of a maturing trust fund; Eleanor and Sam rented a shoebox in a more central location, which Sam had found through her numerous and questionable connections. Sam had immediately begun working for a graphic design company and had seen her artistic efforts promoting new bands and websites all over the country.

Two years Daniel's junior, Grace had joined a photographic agency rather than waste precious time at university and found herself, several years later, exclusively accompanying a famous photographer, Felix Goldman, wherever his assignments took him. He called her his minder; she thought of herself as his babysitter. Grace might have looked more model than minder but her languid good looks and laid-back attitude hid a steely temperament. Her pilot's licence and a contacts book that read like *Burke's Peerage* were two attributes that opened many doors in her line of work.

Daniel had followed in his father's footsteps, joining a merchant bank in the City, as expected. He'd hated the high-octane environment with a passion but had stuck at it until the error of judgement that had caused the split with Eleanor and the termination of his employment. This was conjecture, of course. She had no real idea what had actually happened, or where he'd been.

In the wake of Daniel's departure Eleanor had drifted from one magazine contract to another until she'd had landed the job at UK24 and found that she loved the hectic atmosphere in the newsroom.

It was probably too late for them now, she thought now. Too much water under the bridge. Daniel would be a different person. Probably in another relationship; he wouldn't want to know her at all.

She drove past the park, deserted except for a single jogger and his dog circling a statue of some ancient local dignitary. A man from the council was watering hanging baskets and the pavement outside the little parade of shops was wet from a recent hosing. On impulse, she pulled in to the kerb and dashed into the bakery.

At home, she slammed the front door and listened for the rubbery *thwok* of the cat-flap signalling Mabel's return.

She put the TV on and switched to UK24 – she was a news junkie like the best of them. As she peeled a tangerine she watched a bulletin, noting that some idiot in Graphics had put up the wrong caption. An earnest charity representative would be for ever known during his fifteen seconds of fame as *Manuel and his Music of the Mountains*. Eleanor resisted the temptation to ring the newsdesk and point out the mistake: rolling news was never wrong for long.

She laughed with sympathetic satisfaction as the early morning anchor mucked up her lines. 'Everyone's a critic,' she said to Mabel, as she snapped the television off. 'And you never know, one day that might be me.'

Eleanor considered the apricot and almond Danish she'd just bought. After seeing the horrific results of her screen test, she doubted whether she'd ever look a carbohydrate in the face again. Putting the pastry back in the paper bag, she consigned it to the rubbish bin with a sigh.

Her phone rang.

'El!' chirped a ridiculously cheerful voice. Sam didn't keep normal hours; she probably hadn't been to bed yet, either. 'How are you? How did the screen test go?'

'Awful. For once I think Toby was right.'

'Did you fluff your lines?' Gales of laughter flowed down the line.

'Let's just say I'm unlikely to be the next UK24 autocutie. God, I looked huge on the playback!'

'I'm sure you didn't. Have you got a recording of your performance?' Sam asked. 'I want to see it.'

'No, I have not,' said Eleanor, shuddering. 'In any case, apparently Julian looks at every test, so I don't have a hope of ever being on-air. Don't know why he even agreed, really. He likes his talent to be skinny and blonde, and I'm neither. I'd be much better off on the radio.'

Sam laughed. 'You might beguile him with your voice.'

'Yeah, right. Still, no point in getting into a state about it. I haven't got the headspace at the moment. I'm stressed enough as it is.'

'You're not still worried about the party?'

'What do you think?' Eleanor snapped. 'Oh, sorry, I didn't mean … Sorry.'

'Never mind,' Sam soothed. 'Sounds like you need to chill. Relax. Have you got any chocolate? That might help.'

'No, I haven't,' Eleanor said. 'But … actually, I've got to go. Speak to you later.'

She ended the call and strode into the kitchen where she retrieved the Danish pastry from the bin, pulled it apart meticulously, and stuffed the entire thing into her mouth, morsel by delicious morsel.

Chapter Five

Eleanor's heart sank as she entered the gym; she'd been so keen to work off the effects of the morning's pastry that she'd forgotten that the place would be crowded at this time of day. Clumps of sweaty men wearing enormous trainers (never mind the myths; in her experience big feet only ever meant one thing ... big shoes) hung around the equipment like teenagers round a lamppost. Music videos blared from the huge screen mounted in the corner and the air was heavy with male pheromones and eau de fart.

She was doing stomach crunches on a floor mat when Jim Paget passed by on his way to one of the rowing machines.

Jim was the only gym user that Eleanor actually knew by name. She'd first met him when a conversation with one of the attendants had given her an idea for a story.

Jim had been morbidly obese until his doctor scared him into a strict diet and exercise regime by telling him he risked not meeting his grandchildren. He had plunged into the exercise programme and, at Eleanor's suggestion, UK24 had followed his progress for the first few weeks for a feature about couch potatoes. A year later, Jim was six stone lighter and the fittest man in the gym.

'Less foot-tapping, more effort,' he encouraged now. She grimaced and tried to nod when he made a T gesture with his hands; since she'd turned him into a minor celebrity they'd often met for a quick cuppa after their workouts.

They took paper cups of the scalding liquid that might have been tea to the seating area by the side of the club's swimming pool. A tall, extremely attractive boy wearing a

T-shirt that declared 'girls fuck you up' approached them smiling good-naturedly; Eleanor was immediately conscious of her post-gym complexion – beetroot face was so not a good look.

'Hey, how's it hanging?' the stranger asked, plonking himself down without waiting for an invitation. 'Mind if I join you?'

'Sure,' said Jim, grinning. 'How are you doing? Sorry, Eleanor,' he explained, 'this is my son, Nick. I've told you about Eleanor haven't I, Nick? She's my mat-mate,' he added proudly.

'Hi.' Nick smiled, his eyebrows raised, grasping Eleanor's outstretched hand.

Jim chuckled. 'Eleanor is the first woman I've laid next to for ten years!'

'Dad!'

'Well, your mother died a long time ago.'

'Well, I know, but …'

'Do you use the gym too?' Eleanor asked politely.

'I'm usually here first thing in the morning,' Nick said. 'I've just graduated.'

'Most students I've known are still in bed at midday,' said Eleanor.

'Dad never lets me lie in,' he grumbled. 'Not even at weekends.'

'Tea or coffee?' Jim interrupted. He gestured to his son to stay seated. 'I'm getting us refills.'

When his father was out of earshot Nick leaned across to Eleanor. 'You're in television, aren't you?'

Eleanor glowed. 'Oh, well, in a small way, I suppose. Only in the background.'

'I know what you do,' Nick said. 'Dad told me. Anyway, there's something I'd like to talk to you about. You might be able to help me and,' he looked around furtively, 'it's a great idea for a programme.'

She shook her head. 'But I don't …'

Nick waved his hand. 'Not here. I don't want Dad to know.'

'Can you give me a clue? I'm really not …'

'Can we meet?' Nick whispered urgently. Jim had begun his return trip.

'I'm not sure I … yes, I suppose so.'

'Red Lion. About nine thirty?'

'What? Tonight?'

'Sorry, is that too short notice?'

'Er, well … yes, it is.' She grabbed a pool programme. 'What's your mobile number?' She scribbled it down and folded the sheet into her pocket. 'I'll call you tomorrow and we'll sort something out.'

Nick narrowed his eyes suspiciously.

'I'm not giving you the brush off,' Eleanor protested. 'I've got plans tonight. It's all right, you can trust me. We'll talk tomorrow, when I've got my diary.'

'OK. So, what's your favourite bit of the gym experience?' he asked, changing the subject neatly as Jim deposited the drinks on the table.

Eleanor thumped her thighs critically. 'Oh, the tea and chat at the end, without a doubt.'

By the time she got home, Eleanor was looking forward to catching up on the American crime shows she was addicted to before Toby showed up. Her heart sank for the second time that evening as she walked up the path; a light was on, which could mean only one thing: Toby would be sprawled on the sofa, bottle of lager in hand, watching some sport or other that he'd recorded on her Sky+ box.

Damn the man. He was far too early.

Mabel came mewing down the stairs at the sound of the front door and wound herself round Eleanor's legs; the cat always kept her distance when Toby was around and now she headed for the garden.

Toby was glued to the television. 'Chelsea versus

Arsenal,' he pronounced by way of greeting.

'What happened to our agreement?' Eleanor asked. 'I thought we could go and –'

Toby gestured with the bottle. 'Cup match, El. Can't miss that.'

'Right. Fine, I'll go and watch something upstairs,' she said, mildly annoyed at being made to feel like an unwelcome visitor in her own home. Why bother coming round if he didn't want to talk to her?

In the spare room sheet music lay open on a metal stand beside an electronic keyboard with a volume control. Eleanor plonked herself on the stool and jammed the headphones on her head. She turned the volume setting to mute and played a few scales, but there was no way she was going to attempt any singing exercises. Not with Toby in the house. There was no volume control on her voice and he would soon be shouting up the stairs, asking her to please shut up.

Frustrated at not being able to practise, she tidied away some paperwork, wrote a cheque for the window cleaner, and hunted for something to put it in.

The folder where she kept her envelopes was unaccountably empty. She rifled through drawers stuffed with assorted batteries, post-its, memory sticks, and printer cartridges, assuming she'd put them somewhere else. Swearing softly, she went downstairs and into the living room where Toby was squinting at the final stages of the football through one half-closed eye.

'Daft question,' she began, 'but have you used any of my envelopes lately?'

'You're right,' he muttered sleepily. 'Daft question.'

'Only, there aren't any left and I could have sworn …'

'Oh, actually,' Toby held up a hand in admission. 'I may have used a couple last week, writing to the bank and stuff.'

'That solves that mystery then.' Eleanor was

exasperated. 'Why didn't you tell me you'd used the last one? I could've bought some more.'

He pressed the pause button on the Sky+ just as the Chelsea striker was lining up for a penalty. 'Didn't think. Sorry. Can't you cadge some off work?'

'Well, of course I can, but I need one now.'

'Whatever.' Toby shrugged and pressed play.

In bed later, Eleanor was restless but the book she was reading wasn't capturing her attention. Beside her Toby scrolled annoyingly through the channels as if the television in the bedroom offered a different selection to the one downstairs. He eventually clicked the set off and dropped the remote control, leaning across to give her a perfunctory peck on the cheek before turning away. 'Sorry, babes,' he apologised, 'I'm really tired tonight. Must have drunk too much at lunch.'

'Oh, thanks,' Eleanor said. 'That doesn't usually ...'

'Leave it out, El,' Toby moaned. 'I'm just too tired, OK?'

She couldn't sleep. She was exhausted but every time she closed her eyes the same vision of Daniel scrambling down the scree away from her replayed itself. She could almost taste the bitter hurt. Leaving Toby snoring loudly, she picked up the book and slipped out of bed. Downstairs she made a cup of milky hot chocolate and, snuggled in a throw, settled on the sofa with the lacklustre paperback. She was joined immediately by Mabel trying to nudge the book aside and curling onto her lap for some blissed-out purring.

Eleanor turned pages but registered little. She tried to concentrate on the storyline, stroking Mabel absentmindedly, but her mind wandered. Giving up, she replaced the old envelope she was using as a bookmark with a junk mail invitation to join a casino. She would scribble her name out and use it for the window cleaner's cheque. But it had dislodged a memory and she stared at it for a long moment, tapping it with her fingertips.

The last proper, handwritten letters she'd received had been love letters from Toby. She'd loved them, looking forward to their regular plop on the doormat with all the nervous anticipation of a teenager on Valentine's Day. Toby had written them with a fountain pen, in navy blue ink, and she had kept them all.

The realisation sprang into her head fully formed and without a scintilla of doubt. It lodged there like a seed in a broken tooth. She tried to tell herself that the suspicion was unfair. The fact that Toby had never written a letter to a bank in all the time she'd known him shouldn't necessarily condemn him.

She reminded herself that he actually used an online bank.

She didn't need to convince herself, the signs were all there, presenting themselves for examination like a series of tick boxes on a survey: hastily ended phone calls when she walked into the room – check; all that annoying texting that he'd said was work-related and so important – check; implausible excuses and ridiculously expensive presents by way of apology – check. She couldn't even sneak a look at his mobile; Toby kept his phone on his person at all times, he was never parted from it. It was always switched to silent and she even suspected it was waterproof, so he could take it into the shower.

Eleanor wandered into the kitchen and zapped the mug of now tepid chocolate in the microwave. She had a sudden recollection of her mother confessing that she suspected the 'separate interests' that her husband protested he had every right to pursue included some extra-curricular activities of the female persuasion. Sylvia had added that it had probably gone on for most of their married life.

She'd felt queasy listening to this catalogue of betrayal

but the revelation had answered a lot of questions. She remembered a father who'd been absent more than he'd been there. He'd never attended school concerts or sports days like her friends' fathers and she'd struggled to understand why he didn't seem to want to be close to her. By her teens she had stopped trying to attract his attention.

Toby was seeing another woman; of that she was now absolutely certain. His attention was elsewhere, as Sylvia used to put it so quaintly. Her mother might have grown to accept the situation, but Eleanor couldn't do the same. She couldn't sit by filled with suspicion that Toby was having an affair. She would have to do something.

But, knowing that Daniel was coming back, suddenly it didn't seem that important any more. She waited for the big emotional breakdown but it didn't come. All she felt was overwhelming disappointment and an increasing annoyance at his boundless cheek.

She crept back to bed and slept for what seemed like ten minutes before Toby turned over and began nuzzling her breasts.

For a sleep-filled moment Eleanor felt her body melting under his familiar touch, taking pleasure in the stroking and teasing of his expert fingers. His hand cupped her buttock and he pulled her closer. Abruptly, the night's suspicions swam back into focus and she rolled away, berating herself and her treacherous body for so enjoying the sensations he awoke.

'Wasamatter?' grumbled Toby, reaching for her again. Waves of antagonism radiated from him like heat.

'Nothing,' she replied, sliding smartly out of bed. 'I'm going to be late.'

He groaned, pulling back the duvet. 'What am I supposed to do with this?'

'I'm sure you'll think of something,' she snapped, stalking into the bathroom and locking the door, something she couldn't remember ever doing previously. This morning she couldn't bear the idea of exposing her nakedness to Toby's lascivious eyes. Let him suffer, she thought, as she turned the shower on full blast.

Chapter Six

At nine thirty that evening, Eleanor walked into the Red Lion to find Nick waiting for her at the bar. If anything, he was even better looking than she'd first thought.

'Hi,' he said. 'How are things?'

Grateful for the anecdote to break the ice, Eleanor gave him a quick rundown of Belle's snake incident. By the time she'd finished his eyes were round as saucers.

'Do things like that happen a lot?'

'More often than you'd think,' she replied.

'Brilliant,' said Nick, shaking his head. He pulled out his wallet. 'Now, what're you drinking?'

'No, let me,' Eleanor said, waving the note aside. 'Your dad tells me you're on limited funds at the moment.'

He nodded as she ordered the drinks. 'Student loan up to my ears, overdraft and credit card maxed out. You name it. I need to get a job for the summer, soon.'

'So, what do you need me for?' Eleanor asked. 'I can't do much about a job, I'm afraid. I could just about wangle some work experience. Unpaid, of course,' she added hastily.

'No,' he shook his head. 'It's not about me. Well, not directly.'

'Shall we sit down?' Eleanor gestured towards a battered old leather Chesterfield under the window. 'Now, tell me all about it.'

He was terribly attractive, she couldn't help thinking. He looked a bit like Daniel. His hair was mousy brown, highlighted by the sun in that natural way women paid a fortune for at the hairdressers, and he constantly flicked it out of his eyes unconsciously. She gave herself a mental shake.

'To cut to the chase, my grandparents have disappeared,' Nick said bluntly. 'We've no idea where they are.'

'Who's we?'

'All the family. Me and Dad, as well as Dad's sister, and …'

'I'm sorry, Nick,' Eleanor cut him short. 'I'm a planning editor, not a detective. What do you think I can do about this?'

'Wait a minute,' Nick carried on. 'Let me finish, then you'll have a better idea.'

As he talked, Eleanor's mind began whirring, weighing up the possibilities. Her palms began to sweat – a sure sign she was on to a winner. This could be so good, she thought.

'Does your father know you're talking to me?' she asked suddenly.

'No, I haven't said anything to him yet.'

'How do I know you're telling the truth?'

'What? Don't you trust me?' Nick said huffily.

'I don't trust anyone these days, Nick. Not when my reputation's at stake.'

'But I really am telling the truth.'

'OK, I believe you. What were you studying at university?'

'Current Affairs and Media Studies. Why?'

'So, you can handle a camera, then?'

'Of course I can,' he said, prickling with indignation.

Eleanor laughed. 'I think we might have the makings of something here, Nick,' she said. 'I can't go into details yet; I'll have to speak to my boss. But,' she smiled at him, 'if I get the go-ahead, you'll need to be ready to go at the drop of a hat.'

He perched on the edge of his seat. 'Go where?'

'To the ends of the earth, if necessary.' She winked at

him. 'Your turn to trust me.' She pointed to his empty glass. 'Another drink?'

'So tell me about the newsroom, then,' Nick cajoled after Eleanor had set fresh drinks on the table. 'I've always wanted to work in television, preferably on a newsdesk .'

'It's not all glamour, you know,' said Eleanor, laughing. 'Well, except for Belle.'

'Who's Belle?'

'The snake lady. She dresses up as a movie star every day.'

'What? Which one?'

'Different character every day,' said Eleanor. 'I think she's secretly yearning to be an actress.'

'It sounds like a riot.'

Eleanor took a sip of her drink. 'Yeah, laugh a minute. Actually, it's a great way to earn a living. These people definitely know how to party. But it has its serious side, too,' she added defensively.

'I'm sure,' agreed Nick. 'It's the way it changes all the time that attracts me. Not knowing from one day to the next what's going to happen.'

'Oh really? Eleanor smiled wryly. 'How come you know so much about it?'

'Well, I ... Two weeks work experience in a regional newsroom,' he admitted. 'Not very hands-on, though. I only got to watch.'

'Oh, well at least you've had a taste,' she said. 'But real life is a lot more stimulating.'

'So, do you think we've got something?' Nick asked eagerly. 'Will they be interested?'

Eleanor tapped her finger on the side of her nose and smiled. 'Don't tell anyone I told you, but this little project might be just what the doctor ordered.'

As she walked to the mezzanine coffee shop the next morning, Eleanor debated whether she should approach

Julian with Nick's story, or try Sara Cassidy first. Sara produced a weekly half hour programme and on the face of it, Nick's scenario was tailor-made for a feature. But Eleanor would have no say in how the search for the Pagets was executed. She would have to hand over ownership, something she didn't want to do just yet.

She dismissed the idea and began to marshal her arguments as she passed Fraser struggling with the newsroom's antediluvian photocopier.

'Fucking fucker's fucked,' he protested, kicking the machine and causing a flap to fly open and a part of the mechanism to shoot across the floor. Eleanor stooped to pick up the offending piece and handed it to him, marvelling at his imaginative use of the same expletive as a verb, an adjective and a noun, all in one sentence.

She would have to wait for the right moment. The incident with the snake had left Julian in a foul mood and Belle had only just managed to hang onto her job after the studio fiasco.

'He was absolutely furious,' she'd told Eleanor later. 'Hauled me into his office for a post mortem. He went potty, called me an incompetent.' She'd smiled ruefully. 'He wanted to sack me on the spot for gross negligence, but he couldn't because no one had actually been hurt.'

When Eleanor arrived at the top of the stairs she saw the man himself already there, tapping his foot in the queue. She joined him, hoping he'd calmed down.

'Hi, Julian,' she said. 'Have you got a minute to chat? I'd like to run something past you, if you've time.'

'Sure,' said Julian. They took their drinks to a window table and sat down. 'So, what's the problem?'

So far, so good, Eleanor thought. No sign of any temper yet. 'Not a problem exactly, but it might be a good story,' she began. 'I've got a couple of runaways.'

'Really?' He didn't sound very interested. He frowned at Eleanor. 'Hardly something to concern ourselves with.

Who are they and why should we be bothered?'

'Eric and Dora Paget, late seventies, totally disappeared off the radar. Nick, their grandson, is worried,' Eleanor persisted as Julian began swiping the screen of his tablet.

'So?'

'Hang on, there's a bit of a twist. Dora found out a while ago that she had some inoperable form of cancer.' Julian grimaced. 'But there's more. Yesterday, Nick was round at Eric and Dora's house doing a bit of gardening and houseplant watering. He found a letter.' Eleanor paused for dramatic effect but Julian just stared at his screen. She ploughed on. 'He opened it because it was from the hospital and he was worried that his gran might miss an appointment or something.'

Julian raised a disinterested eyebrow. 'Have you seen the letter?'

Eleanor nodded.

'And? Come on, Eleanor,' he said tetchily. 'I haven't got all day. What did it say?'

'Sorry. It seems that Gran's records got mixed up with someone else's. She hasn't got cancer after all. It's been an almighty cock-up. The consultant wants her to go in so he can apologise and set the record straight in person.'

'Cock-up in the NHS,' Julian repeated darkly. 'This is getting slightly better,' he added with admirable professional detachment. He suddenly frowned at Eleanor. 'What would you do if it was you? If you thought your days were numbered, that you'd been told by an expert to go home and get your affairs in order?'

'Go on the holiday of a lifetime, probably.'

'Exactly. So Dora and Eric are on the vacation of a lifetime. Thinking it'll be her last, spending all their savings. That would be my take on it.'

'Mine too, initially. But Nick thinks –'

Julian smiled slowly. 'Nick thinks that if Dora thinks she's got something serious, potentially painful, and also terminal, there's a possibility that she'll end it all. Doesn't he?'

She stared at him. 'How did you know that?'

'Too many years on the tabloids,' Julian explained. 'Always think the worst and work backwards.'

'Well, you're absolutely spot on this time,' Eleanor marvelled. 'That's exactly what Nick thinks. He remembered watching a TV programme with Dora about assisted suicide. He said she was convinced it was the most humanitarian thing to do.'

'Do the family know about any of this? The letter?'

'Not about the letter, no. Nick's only told me so far, I think. They know about the cancer ... I don't think they've discussed anything else. I'll double-check.'

'So, the question is, how long does she think she's got before it all goes pear-shaped?' Julian was in business mode now, making notes on his tablet and growing more animated as Eleanor's proposal developed.

'I'm not sure. Nick said – well, before he read the letter, he'd thought it wasn't progressing too fast. At this stage it could be managed with medication.'

Julian didn't say anything for a while. Eleanor resisted the urge to fill the silence; she wanted Julian to convince himself.

'Hang on, though,' he said eventually. 'Dora hasn't got a virulent form of cancer has she? The letter proves that. So what *has* she got?'

'The letter mentions some bacterial condition in the bowel that can be cured with a simple course of antibiotics.'

'How prosaic,' said Julian. 'So they might be heading to Dignitas, or something similar, therefore time is of the essence?'

Eleanor nodded. 'We know they haven't gone to Switzerland, their passports are still at home. But who knows what they could be planning after Dora has had enough of living the high life. We have to track them down, Julian. And we can, with Nick's, help. He's extremely articulate and photogenic, by the way. We have to find Dora in time. Before she ... she ...'

'Before she tops herself,' Julian said gleefully. 'Come on, Eleanor, you can't be squeamish about this. It's a matter of life or death!' He tapped some more notes. 'Now obviously we don't want a death on our hands, but this could run and run,' he added. 'It's not the sort of thing we would normally get involved with, but I can just about see the potential.'

'If we give Nick a camera,' Eleanor added excitedly, 'he could go on the road, pick up the trail, and report back every day at regular time-slots, to give the viewers something to look forward to. It would be like an epic poem. Like *The Iliad*, or was it *The Odyssey*?' she added.

'Let's not get too carried away.' Julian took a final gulp of coffee and set his empty cup back on the table. 'I mean, playing devil's advocate here, what's to stop the old couple seeing our first report on a telly in the pub or a B&B and coming straight home?'

'Nick reckons that Eric and Dora don't watch much telly, and they're teetotal, so they don't go into many pubs, either. But even if they saw a report, doesn't mean they'd act on it straight away, would it?'

Julian was suddenly serious. 'How come the kids don't know where their parents are?' he asked. 'Haven't they checked their credit card statements, that sort of thing?'

Eleanor shook her head. 'Nick checked all that. He discovered that their bank only sends hard copies of statements every three months, and they had one just before they disappeared.' She laughed. 'He thought we could track their movements by asking the bank for assistance, but I put him right, told him we couldn't go around tracing people's whereabouts from bank and phone records.'

'He's been watching too many detective programmes,' Julian agreed. 'We're not the police. We've got no authority. And there's the Data Protection Act.'

'And I also told him that we couldn't hack into anyone's phones and listen to their voicemails, not under any circumstances.'

'Christ!' Julian cried. 'Absolutely bloody not! If he can't find them without resorting to that kind of nonsense, he's no good to us.'

'I know,' said Eleanor, nodding. 'I told him all that. Anyway, in his search, he discovered that they don't have a credit card between them, which isn't unusual for their age, and they're not online either. So no email or social media. Oh, but Nick bought his gran a pay-as-you-go mobile a while ago, for her birthday.'

'So why hasn't someone called it?'

'They've been trying for days. Nick thinks that Dora's forgotten that it needs to be charged up periodically. She's probably thrown it away because it doesn't work any more.'

'The compensations of getting old,' Julian said. 'Brilliant.' He smiled widely. 'Let's do it. It could even be fun. Write me a proper schedule,' he continued. 'I want all the details filling in: dates, locations, timings, overnight stays, all the usual guff.'

Newsrooms could be completely pitiless in the face of a good story and Eleanor hoped she'd got the stomach for this. All the same, she'd done it. She could hardly contain herself. 'Will do,' she beamed.

I'll have to run it all past Britney, of course,' Julian added. 'But I think she'll be fine. It'll be a nice filler for the summer.'

"Britney" was Daphne Hewitt, the channel's head of news. How she had earned this tag was lost in the mists of time, but everyone assumed it had something to do with her reported predilection for shouting 'Do it to me one more time!' when in the throes of passion.

'You'll have to oversee everything.' Julian lectured. 'And we'll need to decide what to do about the letter from the hospital. We don't want to give the news on-air, or do we? Need to think about that. But we want Eric and Dora to get in touch or give themselves up to us. Nick will need some guidance. Maybe you should join him on the road from time to time. You'll be better at that than anchoring.'

Eleanor blinked. She could think of better ways of delivering bad news. Her news reading days were seemingly over before they'd begun.

'How is he with a camera, by the way?' Julian carried on blithely.

'No problem. He did Media at uni.'

'Brilliant. When can you get him in here?'

'Sometime next week, probably.'

'What about Monday?'

Eleanor thought quickly. 'I've got a ... an engagement over the weekend. I'll be out of town so I won't ...'

'Let's strike while the iron's hot,' Julian said, ignoring her. 'Monday morning it is.'

Chapter Seven

Eleanor was meandering aimlessly up and down the aisles at Waitrose when her mobile rang. She wasn't expecting any calls from the newsdesk; she'd only left there an hour ago. Hoping there wouldn't be a breaking news story that required her presence, she pulled the phone out of her pocket. There was no number displayed.

'Hello?'

'Hello,' said an unfamiliar voice. 'You probably don't know me. My name is Jemima Winstanley.'

Eleanor waited. The mystery woman was right; she had no idea who Jemima Winstanley could possibly be. 'Sorry?' Eleanor had no time for cold callers, particularly those who had managed to get her mobile number. 'Sorry,' she repeated, keeping a polite tone just in case the call was work-related. 'What did you say your name was? Whitstable? You have me at a disadvantage. Am I supposed to know you?'

Jemima Winstanley chuckled down the phone. 'Probably not,' she said. 'But I think you soon will.'

'I beg your pardon?' Eleanor was indignant. If she hadn't been so curious she would have hung up. 'Who *is* this?'

'Perhaps I should explain,' offered Jemima.

'I'm waiting. And get a move on, I'm at the checkout.' Eleanor had a sudden sinking feeling that she wasn't going to like what Jemima Winstanley had to say. She manoeuvred her trolley out of the queue and parked it next to a pyramid of watermelons.

'I found your name on Toby's mobile and I'm just ringing to –'

'What are you doing with Toby's mobile?' Eleanor asked. 'It's practically welded to – oh my God, he hasn't been in an accident has he? Is he OK?'

'He's absolutely fine,' Jemima reassured her. 'I just wanted to tell you that Toby and I are engaged now. I don't know quite what his relationship is with you, but I don't want you sending him any more lewd text messages.'

Eleanor was shocked into momentary silence. She looked at the phone in a parody of disbelief. 'I beg your pardon?' she repeated.

'I'm asking you, woman to woman, to stop –'

'I heard what you said,' Eleanor interrupted. 'I just didn't believe it. Lewd messages, did you say? And what was the other bit? Engaged?'

'Yes,' said Jemima. 'We thought it was about time.'

Eleanor struggled to get her thoughts in order. After all the time she and Sam had spent dissecting her relationship with Toby, this would be hilarious if it wasn't bordering on the tragic. The bastard had managed to get in first.

'Let me get this straight,' said Eleanor. 'You are getting married to Toby?'

'I am.'

'And you want me to stop texting him?'

'If you wouldn't mind,' said Jemima, mildly. 'I'd be terribly grateful.'

How very bloody British, Eleanor thought. I'm going to have some sport with this. 'It would be my pleasure,' she said. 'But would you mind if I sent him just one more? As a farewell gesture, you know?'

'Absolutely not!'

Eleanor held the phone away from her ear as Jemima exploded. 'Please,' she cajoled. 'Just one more. The last one. Promise.'

'No!' Jemima shouted down the phone. 'I, I forbid it.'

'Whatever.' Eleanor gave in. 'But he'll probably want

to meet me again, anyway.' she added.

'Why would he want to do that?'

'He's a regular at the club where I'm a lap dancer,' Eleanor improvised, articulating the last two words so loudly that shoppers cast curious glances in her direction as they moved reluctantly towards the tills. 'I can't see him giving up an expensive membership like that just because he's got engaged. He's been paying for private dances for a while now,' she added provocatively.

The ensuing silence was so profound Eleanor thought she'd been disconnected. She could hear wind whistling down the airwaves.

'Well, he'll just have to,' Jemima blustered eventually. 'He can't –'

'You can't start married life with a list of things he can't do,' advised Eleanor. 'Toby won't like that.'

'How would you know?' Jemima retorted. 'You don't know him like I do.'

Eleanor took a deep breath. She made an effort to lower her voice. 'Does he send you love letters written in navy blue ink on cream paper?' she asked. 'Does he buy you expensive, extravagant bunches of exotic flowers, or are you making do with the garage forecourt variety by now?'

'I … er … how do you …?'

'Does he watch too much football and golf and cricket on television?' Eleanor persisted. 'Or spend hours, days in fact, on his Xbox?'

'Well …'

Eleanor suddenly felt immensely sorry for the young woman.

'Sorry to do this to you, Jemima,' she said gently, 'but Toby and I have been practically living together for the past two years. I'm not a lap dancer; I have a perfectly respectable job and a nice little house, where, incidentally, he's left many of his personal possessions.'

'I …'

'If you don't believe me, you're quite welcome to come round and have a look. Before I bag everything up and put it out for the bin men. You could take it all away with you. You'll need some of the stuff for your new life.'

'I'm not sure there's going to be a new life,' Jemima snapped, anger raising the pitch of her voice a couple of octaves, 'if he's been lying to me all this time. How could he? The absolute bastard!'

'How long have you been seeing him?'

'About seven months. I know it's not long but we're so in love. He told me he was single,' she added defensively. 'He never said he was seeing someone else all this time.'

'Well, he wouldn't, would he?' said Eleanor dryly. It figured. Toby's strange behaviour had begun around Christmas, but she'd been blind to it. And since she'd heard about Daniel's imminent return she'd practically ignored him. 'How did you meet?'

'At a Christmas party. My company threw a bash for all its clients. Toby was there.'

'Never one to miss a party,' said Eleanor ruefully. 'That's my, sorry, *our* Toby.'

'What are you going to do?' asked Jemima. 'Are you going to tell Toby about this conversation, I mean?'

'I'm not sure.' Eleanor decided she could afford to be magnanimous. 'I'll let you into a little secret,' she carried on. 'I'd already decided to finish it.'

'Oh. Why?'

Eleanor hesitated. Should she show some mercy? No, she couldn't resist. 'Well, if you must know,' she sighed theatrically, 'the very last straw was finding another woman's knickers in my bed. Last week, actually, so your call is quite timely. Pink, sort of lacy and frilly. Not my thing at all. I presume they're yours?'

'No!' cried Jemima. 'They absolutely are not! I've never been to your house. I don't even know where you live! I didn't know anything about you until just now.' She was silent for a while. 'But that means that Toby's being unfaithful to both of us,' she said eventually.

'That's about the size of it,' agreed Eleanor, feeling only slightly guilty about the fabrication. 'And now, if there's nothing else, I really must get on with the rest of my life. Good luck, Jemima.' She was about to disconnect when a thought occurred to her. 'Oh, by the way,' she said, 'do you like Michael Bublé?'

'Yes. Why?'

'Oh, no reason.' Without waiting for a reply Eleanor ended the call, took a large crimson slice from the mountain of watermelons and pushed her trolley back into the checkout queue.

As it turned out, it was all over rather quickly.

'I told you I had to do some overtime,' Toby protested when Eleanor confronted him over dinner the next evening.

'Horizontal overtime, was it?' she asked acerbically. 'No one in the City works overtime at the weekend, Toby. Give me some credit.'

Toby assumed a butter-wouldn't-melt expression. 'But I was! I had to get the monthly figures to the boss. It took hours.' He peered at Eleanor suspiciously, sipping lager from a bottle. 'You don't believe me, do you?'

'You've used the overtime excuse four times in the last four weeks,' Eleanor explained patiently.

Toby narrowed his eyes. 'What're you getting at?'

'Oh, nothing.' Eleanor shook her head vaguely. 'It's just that Jemima gave me a rather different version.'

'Who?' he spluttered, spraying beer all over the table in a display of such outraged indignation that Eleanor almost believed him. 'Who's Jemima?'

'According to her, she's your fiancée. She rang and told me, you see.'

'Oh fuck.' Toby seemed to shrink before her eyes. The

fight left him abruptly. 'It's all your fault, you know,' he accused. 'You've been on a different planet these last week or so.'

'That doesn't explain why you've been seeing Jemima since Christmas.'

'Don't start splitting hairs,' he carried on, waggling the bottle at her and spilling more beer. 'God, you can be so superior, sometimes. Like you never looked twice at another –'

'I never did!' Eleanor protested.

'Maybe not, but there was always someone else in this relationship, wasn't there? It's no wonder ...'

'What are you talking about?'

'Oh come on, Eleanor! Did you think I hadn't noticed? You never want to make love any more. You –'

'Me? *I* don't want to a make love? You're the one who comes home too drunk to stay awake!' She was outraged.

'Well, maybe if you were a bit more welcoming. These days I get the impression I'm barely tolerated ...'

'Are you writing this down?' Eleanor exploded. 'You could write a bloody handbook. *50 Ways to Make Your Lover Feel Inadequate*. It'd be a bestseller.'

'He's back, isn't he?' Toby said quietly.

'Don't change the subject. Who's back?'

'Daniel.'

Eleanor was speechless.

'Your silence speaks volumes. Just as well I'm out of here, isn't it?' Toby carried on. 'Clear the decks ready to welcome the prodigal back.'

'Don't be so melodramatic. It's not like that at all. I –'

'It's true though. He's back, isn't he?'

Eleanor nodded in defeat. 'He's come back for Grace's 30th.' She smiled weakly. 'At least now you don't have to come to the party.'

'And I was so looking forward to it,' Toby said sarcastically. 'Such lovely people.'

'They're not all –'

'I didn't mean Sam, she's great. I meant Grace and the rest of those Hooray Henrys at Mensum Bottom. Mensum Arse, more like.'

'You can be so childish, sometimes,' Eleanor said caustically. 'I hope Jemima knows what she's letting herself in for.'

'Enough,' Toby sneered. He stood up unsteadily. 'I'll get my coat.'

'Don't be stupid. Where are you going to go at this time of night? It's almost midnight.'

'I'll get a cab. I can't spend another night with you in that bed.'

'Thanks for that,' Eleanor sniffed.

'I'll come and clear my stuff out another day. Don't worry, I'll make sure you're not around.'

'You can leave it here as long as you need to.'

'Gee, thanks. But no thanks. I'll manage.'

'What about Jemima? Will you move in with her, eventually?'

'Unlikely,' he spat. 'But thanks for the suggestion.'

Toby wrenched the door open and swayed into the hallway. 'I'll just grab some overnight stuff,' he gestured up the stairs, 'then I'll get lost.'

'Toby –'

A few minutes later Eleanor heard him stagger down the stairs and let himself quietly out of the front door. She sat at the kitchen table for a long time before leaving the dirty dishes in the puddle of beer and going to bed.

Chapter Eight

The day of the dreaded party and the equally unsettling meeting with Daniel dawned. Eleanor had practised the three pieces she was going to sing so many times she felt as if she'd written them herself, but she was still sick with apprehension, not all of it directly connected to her performance.

She carefully hung her green silk frock in its transparent travelling cover from the handle behind the driving seat, put her weekend bag into the boot along with the karaoke machine she'd borrowed on impulse from Belle, and set off on the long journey west. A summer downpour was just starting, the torrential rain soaking the few pedestrians brave or stupid enough to venture out.

She was waiting at the traffic lights on the High Street when, during a brief clear spell, she noticed a figure who looked suspiciously like Sam's boyfriend, Rob, sheltering under an awning outside a local department store. He had three bulging carrier bags at his feet and was looking expectantly up the street as if he was waiting for someone.

Eleanor couldn't begin to imagine what Rob might be doing patronising such an establishment. In fact, she couldn't imagine him shopping at all. She decided that she must be mistaken, given the quantity of rainwater obscuring her view. She put him out of her mind, concentrated on the traffic, and drove on.

She swept up the slip road onto the A40, then past the Art Deco Hoover building, now a Tesco superstore. Living on the west of the city, it was relatively easy to kick off its shackles and soon she was sailing along the M40. She pressed the shuffle button on her iPod and Joni Mitchell's crystal voice filled the car.

Eleanor sang along to 'Ladies of the Canyon', glad that Toby wasn't with her; his preferred choice of music was chaotic jazz of the where-shall-I-put-this-note variety, which did nothing for Eleanor's equilibrium or concentration and usually resulted in a tense and ultimately silent journey.

The road narrowed as she left the built-up areas behind, winding through small villages and hamlets, with their churches, ponds, and greens, then out into open countryside. The rain stopped and the sun broke through. Under a perfect Simpson's sky, the ploughed brown fields looked like gigantic Kit-Kats. The verges glistened with raindrops and a rainbow arched overhead. How apt, she thought – maybe there'd be some reconciliation after all.

Her nerves were jangling as she approached the village of Mensum Bottom. She slowed down and scanned the hedgerows for the finger post directing her down the valley to Mensum Hall. It was such a long time since she'd been here she'd forgotten where the turning was and almost missed the entrance amidst the tangle of hawthorn.

She negotiated the pitted track slowly; losing her exhaust in this part of the world would not be very clever. She came to a halt at a bend in the lane and gazed around at the familiar vista. The architect had surely planned what the view would be like in two hundred years' time, when the trees had matured and the lake was properly established. The late afternoon sunlight glinted off the water, the surface reflecting the magnificent oaks and beeches.

Sitting in a shallow valley surrounded by formal gardens and woodland, Mensum Hall had the sort of solid, reliable character that radiated comfort and well-being. The house was an elegant Georgian villa built of mellow grey stone, overlooking a gravelled circular courtyard with a fountain at its centre. Tall, mullioned windows looked out onto manicured lawns and shrubberies and the pillared portico was draped in an ancient, precarious wisteria that all but obliterated the door every spring. At the back, beyond the kitchen garden, a line of yew trees partially obscured an orchard.

The Hardwick family had made its money in textiles, importing cotton from India and building a successful empire. But the only son, Peter, had shown a marked ability for numbers instead and had sold the family business he disliked in favour of a very successful career in the City. The family owned the land as far as Eleanor could see. Farmland, woodland, streams, and hillside would all come to Daniel eventually.

Eleanor's mother had been particularly disappointed when the relationship had ended. Not merely because she was being done out of a society wedding – Daniel's father was expecting a baronetcy at the very least in gratitude for services to New Labour – but that she wouldn't have to worry about her daughter any more; Daniel and his money would have taken care of that.

Eleanor continued slowly down the long drive ribboning through fenced paddocks that had always contained horses, though there were none in evidence today. The pebble that had been lodged in her stomach for the past two weeks morphed into a large, immoveable rock. Sam had a last-minute job to attend to and wouldn't be coming down until later; there was nobody to hold her hand.

Get a grip, she chastised herself. Only the next twenty-four hours to get through and she probably wouldn't see him again for another four years. She couldn't decide if that was the best thing that could happen, or the worst.

The tyres crunched on the gravel in front of the house as she drew up outside the huge front door. It creaked open on cue and Daniel's mother appeared on the threshold.

Gwen Hardwick was from solid working-class stock and hadn't found the transition to a life that included a butler and a cook particularly easy. The women had liked each other instantly and their relationship had survived the shock of Daniel's abrupt departure, sustained by their mutual loss. At the time, Gwen had no more idea about the catastrophe that had stricken her son than Eleanor herself. They hadn't seen each other for over two years. Perhaps she'd be better informed now.

'Hello, Gwen.' She pasted a grin on her face as she got out of the car. 'Is it Hedges' day off?'

Gwen Hardwick was a formidable woman. Taller and slimmer than Eleanor, she possessed the most remarkable bosom Eleanor had ever encountered. It seemed to defy gravity, even in middle age. She hadn't been able to stop herself staring when she'd first met Gwen; the way her breasts entered the room before her and took centre stage.

Today Gwen was wearing jeans and a sweatshirt, her long dark hair swept into an untidy bun at the nape of her neck. She had streaks of dirt on her face, as if she'd just come from the garden. She smiled uncertainly.

'I wanted to welcome you back myself.' She opened her arms and drew Eleanor into her embrace. 'I'm so glad you could come,' she said warmly. 'It's been such a long time!'

Eleanor could only nod dumbly. She hadn't realised until this moment just how much she'd missed this family.

Gwen held her at arm's length and looked over her shoulder in a pantomime of expectation. 'All alone? Grace said ...'

Eleanor shook her head. 'We've just split up.'

'Really? I'm so sorry –' Gwen looked at her appraisingly.

'It was for the best, and don't worry, I didn't dump one because I was hoping for a reconciliation with the other.'

Gwen looked at her sharply. 'I didn't think that for a

moment.' Her face broke into a grin. 'I never did know when you were joking.'

Eleanor hugged her again. 'I'm sorry. I didn't mean ... I just didn't want you to think I have an ulterior motive.'

'No, I didn't, and besides ...' Gwen broke off.

'Besides what?'

'Oh, nothing. By the way, Grace is at the salon, so she won't be joining us until a bit later, I'm afraid,' Gwen apologised. She leaned into the car. 'Here, you take your beautiful dress and I'll grab your suitcase. I'll show you where you'll be sleeping.'

She ushered Eleanor up the steps into the circular entrance hall. A wide stone staircase rose on both sides, curving upwards in a grand sweep to the gallery. Doors opened to the left and right of the staircase and a wide passageway intersected the house, running from front to back in an uninterrupted line of chequered black and white marble flagstones.

'Daniel has just popped into the village,' Gwen continued. She led the way upstairs and opened the door of a bedroom at the end of the hall with a window that overlooked the stables. 'I hope you'll be comfortable in here. Now come downstairs – Peter's dying to see you.'

'Gwen.' Eleanor touched her sleeve. 'Before we go down ... I've got to ask ... I never found out what Daniel did that was so terrible, at the bank. Did he ever tell you?'

Gwen's mouth tightened. 'No, actually, he never did. He told his father eventually, who has remained ridiculously silent about the whole thing ever since. Honestly, I know as much as you do. I suspect it might have been a financial thing, which is why he confided in Peter and not me. Probably lost the bank a fortune,' she added flippantly. 'It's absolutely unforgiveable that he left you in the dark all this time. I'm so sorry.'

'There's no need to apologise, really. Is everything

sorted out now?'

'As far as I know, yes. He's put it all behind him as only the truly unconcerned can. That's why I think it's a money thing; Daniel was never that interested in finance. Anyway,' she led the way down the stairs. 'Let's go and find Peter. He's dying to see you.'

Daniel's father was reading that day's *Financial Times* in a large sunny room at the back of the house, his face a picture of misery.

'Peter,' said Gwen, 'look who's here.'

'Eleanor, my dear!' he cried, folding the newspaper untidily and getting up from his armchair. 'How are you? How lovely to see you.'

Daniel's father was a tall, powerfully built man with a head of closely cropped grey hair. He strode across the room in shabby slippers and a comfy old cardigan and Eleanor couldn't help thinking how incongruous he looked. She's never seen him in such casual clothes before; he'd always been suited and booted. She presumed he was having a rare weekend off to celebrate his daughter's birthday, and Daniel's homecoming.

He bent and kissed her on the cheek. 'How long has it been now, Gwen?' He looked at his wife and his eyes twinkled in the familiar way Eleanor remembered. 'Too long. But you're back now, to greet the prodigal son? I hope we'll see a bit more of you than of late, eh?'

Eleanor shuffled her feet uncomfortably. 'Well, let's see how things go, shall we?' she managed.

'Quite,' said Peter. 'And besides, there's the little matter of –' Gwen shot him a look that could have curdled milk and he closed his mouth abruptly.

'Anyway,' Gwen said brightly, as a car skidded noisily to a halt outside the open front door. 'I think that's Daniel now.'

Eleanor was quaking as they moved into the hallway. She stood behind Peter, hovering nervously in the chequered passageway; she wanted to get a good look at Daniel before he saw her.

But the person who sprang up the steps wasn't Daniel at all.

Chapter Nine

Angie Gold waltzed into Mensum Hall with an air of overwhelming entitlement that would have put a Tory cabinet minister to shame. As her name implied, she positively oozed opulence. She was wearing a butter-soft tan leather jacket over a white vest with jeans tucked into cowboy boots, showing off a perfect size ten body. Hair the colour of golden syrup bounced in shimmering waves around her shoulders and a long rope of polished amber beads hung round her lightly tanned neck.

She looked happy and relaxed and a pang of envious irritation reminded Eleanor how little she had liked her.

Angie had infiltrated her knot of friends at university. Attracted by rumours of Daniel's family's wealth, she had beguiled him for a while, before she'd found out that his family hadn't inherited their estate several centuries previously. That small fact wasn't going to assist her life plan at all. It had been an open secret that Angie had been intent on snaring a husband who would give her riches and a title; intelligent and well-educated as she was, she had no intention of spending more than the bare minimum of time actually working for a living.

But she was only interested in old money. When she'd discovered that Daniel's father was a New Labour supporter, with a past set firmly in a gritty northern mill town, she'd moved swiftly on to a different course and sniffed out a whole new set of friends who could help her relentless social mountaineering.

They hadn't met since their graduation and the last Eleanor had heard Angie had been scaling the dizzy heights of corporate management in the United States.

Angie had never taken the time to get to know Grace very well, so her presence at Mensum Hall was a mystery.

Eleanor shot Gwen a quizzical glance. Gwen shrugged apologetically, her mouth a moue of discomfort. Eleanor looked beyond Angie to the door, but Daniel didn't appear.

'Sorry, everyone,' announced Angie. 'Daniel got delayed by the vicar. He wanted to talk about some boring old festival in the church. I had to leave him in the village.'

'That would be the Summer Festival,' Gwen explained frostily. 'We always get involved with the preparations at this time of year.'

'Yes, well,' Angie said dismissively, 'he'll be along later.' She finally noticed Eleanor standing awkwardly at the bottom of the staircase and she opened her arms in greeting. Her brilliant smile was just as Eleanor remembered – inclusive and exclusive at the same time. It embraced her; drawing her inside its beam and making her feel as if she was the sole object of Angie's attentions, whilst temporarily shunting everyone else into the hinterland beyond the spotlight.

Eleanor was bathed in the megawattage for several seconds.

'El! How *are* you?' Angie asked. 'It's been such a long time!'

Eleanor bristled. Certain individuals were allowed to use her diminutive. Angie wasn't one of them.

'Gwen told me you were coming,' Angie gushed. 'You're going to sing at the party, aren't you? How quaint.'

Eleanor ignored the barb. 'Hello, Angie. I'm surprised to see you here.'

'Ooh, lots to tell you on that front.' She smiled secretively. 'But it'll keep.'

'So how will Daniel get back?' she asked. 'It's miles to the village.'

'Oh, don't worry about Daniel, he's used to walking. Isn't he, Peter?'

Peter nodded uncomfortably. 'He'll be fine. The walk will do him good. And he's got Doodle with him.'

Angie linked her arm through Eleanor's and led her towards the kitchen. 'We've got so much to catch up on! Come with me.' She shook the milk carton. 'Coffee, anyone?'

The kitchen at Mensum Hall was enormous. The ancient stone-flagged floor and butler sink contrasted with a battery of gleaming modern appliances, a huge stainless silver refrigerator and a range cooker. A large preparation island added to the contemporary feel. Eleanor had expected the kitchen to be bustling with staff making preparations for the party, but the room was deserted.

Angie saw her confusion. 'Don't worry, it's all being outside-catered. A really good little firm I found locally,' she boasted. 'I think Gwen was glad to hand it all over.'

Angie filled in the intervening years with a series of bullet points as if she was addressing a conference. '… and it was while I was in Paris last autumn, working my tits off for that lousy company that I ran into Daniel again. Total coincidence! Anyway,' she continued, 'I stayed on, worked my notice like a good little girl. Not that they deserved it, the bastards. Still, every cloud …'

Eleanor wasn't listening. The realisation sat like a lead weight in her stomach; suddenly she knew why Angie was here. Her heart thumped in her throat. 'Right,' she said slowly, 'so how long have you and Daniel …?' She felt slightly unbalanced.

'About nine, ten months now,' Angie said gleefully. 'Marvellous, isn't it?'

'I'm … I'm very happy for both of you,' Eleanor managed. 'A second bite at the cherry,' she added.

'Well, I suppose it is,' Angie agreed. 'I'm surprised you remember that. I'd almost forgotten myself.'

Yeah, right, Eleanor thought nastily. She realised that Angie was eyeing her, a quizzical expression marring her otherwise perfect features. 'Eleanor,' she said, 'I hope you don't think ... Daniel told me that you and he were over a long time ago. That's right, isn't it? I'm not treading on any toes am I?'

'No, no, of course you aren't.' Eleanor smiled weakly, feeling unaccountably guilty. 'That's all finished.'

'Exactly. Anyway, no hard feelings, eh? Let's just enjoy the weekend.' She put her hand on Eleanor's shoulder and leaned towards her. 'I'm looking forward to the future already.' She looked pointedly round the kitchen, laughing gleefully. 'I could get used to this, you know.'

'You've changed your tune,' Eleanor shot back, unable to help herself. 'I remember when this particular family's jewels weren't quite good enough for you. What's so different now?'

Angie had the grace to blush. 'I think I've grown up a bit,' she said. 'I don't mind admitting that I like nice things.' She gathered the amber beads into her hand and fondled them. 'I like getting presents. And,' she leaned towards Eleanor conspiratorially, 'since I've been jetting across the Atlantic on an expense account, I've found that I really like turning left when I get on an aeroplane.'

Eleanor sneaked a look at Angie's left hand. The ring finger was bare.

'Believe me, El,' Angie carried on, her voice charged with sincerity, 'I do love Daniel, and his family.'

Eleanor felt sick. No, she thought, I find it very hard to believe, actually. The Angie I used to know only loved Angie. She was silent for a moment.

'It must have been quite a surprise meeting Daniel in Paris,' she said eventually.

'Pure coincidence,' said Angie, smiling and nodding vigorously. 'We hadn't been in touch much, just the odd postcard here and there.'

This was news to Eleanor. She'd been under the impression that Angie hadn't communicated with Daniel since the day she'd ended their relationship at college.

'I'd been in the States, like I said,' Angie continued, 'and the firm sent me on a year's secondment to the Paris office. Too good an opportunity to miss, I thought. Then I was invited to a party and Daniel was there too. Neither of us knew the other would be there.' She sighed theatrically. 'Only in Paris,'

'How nice,' said Eleanor icily.

'And we've been together ever since. I still have to watch him, of course.' She noticed Eleanor's frown. 'But everything's fine now,' she added obliquely.

'Why?' Eleanor asked stupidly. 'What happened?'

Angie lifted the kettle and poured boiling water into a cafetière. 'I don't think I should say anything,' she said mysteriously. She perched the filter on top of the jug and started putting cups and saucers onto a tray. 'If he wants you to know, I'm sure he'll tell you. It's all water under the bridge, now, anyway,' she added, ignoring Eleanor's curious expression. 'So anyway, when I was given my marching orders, Daniel decided to come back to England too.'

Eleanor decided to leave it for now. 'How convenient,' she said dryly. 'I had no idea.'

'You know how it is. Things change so quickly, you don't have time to think, you just jump. And of course there was Grace's birthday, which gave us the perfect excuse.'

'So what are you doing now, work-wise?'

'Oh, nothing much at the moment. But then we'll be ...' She looked thoughtfully at Eleanor. 'I'm sure I'll find something soon. What are you up to these days? You still a jobbing journalist?'

'No, not any more. I'm a Planning Editor with UK24.'

Eleanor smiled across at Angie's frozen expression. 'Got into telly after all. Just like I said I would. I'm surprised Grace –'

'Can you bring the coffee pot?' Angie picked up the tray and nodded towards the counter. 'I'm so clumsy, I don't want to spill it.'

Eleanor followed her into the drawing room and set the pot down on the sideboard. No one seemed in the least concerned about Daniel, toiling up the valley.

She grabbed the opportunity to meet him without an audience. 'Actually,' she said, 'I'm getting a bit worried about Daniel. Should I go and meet him?'

'I don't think there's any need to do that,' said Angie hastily. 'You've only just got here, Eleanor. Sit down and relax, he'll manage. There's not much shopping to carry.'

'All the same,' Eleanor insisted. 'It's quite a way. And it's getting very warm. He might need a lift.' She stood up defiantly. 'I'll be back soon.'

She was half a mile down the lane into the village when she caught her first glimpse of him, striding along, a plastic carrier bag swinging from each hand, Doodle plodding along beside him.

Her heart jumped into her mouth, her gut twisting in a mixture of pleasure and angst. She pulled onto the verge and scrabbled through the glove box until her fingers closed on the phial of Rescue Remedy. Bolstered by a few calming drops she got out of the car and leaned against the bonnet to watch his approach, hoping she was projecting the air of relaxed insouciance she certainly wasn't feeling.

Chapter Ten

Eleanor was beyond nervous. Doodle capered up the hill towards her and she bent to stroke the black standard poodle, a large, athletic animal, not the customary canine companion for the country set. He looked as if he regularly ate Labradors for breakfast.

'I didn't think you'd be still alive,' she murmured, tickling his greying muzzle to hide her anxiety. The lump in her throat threatened to choke her. 'You must be getting on a bit now.'

'Just had his eleventh birthday,' gasped Daniel, as he came to a halt beside her and dropped the plastic bags on the ground. 'That's seventy-seven in dog years. He's an old man now.' He smiled self-consciously, squinting into the sun and shielding his eyes with his hand.

'Hi.' He touched her hand and they leaned together in a clumsy ballet of air kissing. 'It's good to see you. How've you been? Sorry I haven't been in touch, I …'

Eleanor avoided his eyes as she batted his easy apology away. 'It's OK. You were probably very busy. Your mum's been filling me in.'

'Oh?' He hefted the shopping into the boot. 'Anyway,' he said gruffly, 'best get back. Thanks for the lift. Do you mind if –?'

Doodle seemed poised to jump into the back seat.

Eleanor looked from the large scruffy dog to the cream leather upholstery of her car. 'Well, I'd rather he didn't,' she said stiffly. 'Can't he –?'

'It's only because he's old and it's so warm. He gets a bit out of breath on these hills, you see,' Daniel explained. 'I tell you what – he can sit on my knee. Would that be

OK?'

Eleanor laughed despite herself. 'Don't worry. Put him in the back. There's an emergency picnic blanket in there somewhere.'

She watched as he fussed with the dog and the blanket. She could hardly believe the transformation. Daniel was wearing a dark blue polo shirt, fawn chinos with creases that were still razor-sharp despite the long, hot walk, and Timberland boots, looking like he'd just walked out of a Sunday supplement advert for country clothing. It was completely at odds with what she remembered. The old Daniel had favoured a worn and battered leather jacket, T-shirt and shabby jeans, with at least three days of stubble on his chin. She wondered if he still rode his ancient Triumph Bonneville motorcycle.

He looked leaner, stronger. He was clean-shaven, his sun-bleached hair just starting to curl over his collar. He caught her appraising look. 'I've got a permanent job at *The Post*,' he said. 'I'm having to smarten up a bit.' He heaved Doodle into the back and got into the passenger seat. 'Let's go, Mum will be wondering where we've got to.'

Eleanor got into the car beside him. 'Wait a minute.' She couldn't believe that he wasn't going to apologise, at the very least. She reminded herself that she wasn't in the wrong. Four years of ignorance, of wondering what she'd done to deserve such treatment suddenly crystallised her thoughts. She wasn't going to let him get away with it any longer. 'Haven't you got something to tell me?' she demanded. 'Quite a few things, in fact.'

Doodle chose that moment to push his head between them and rest his nose on Eleanor's shoulder, panting hotly.

'Come on,' she persisted. 'May as well address the elephant while we've got the chance.' They sat in silence, Doodle's panting the only sound in the otherwise perfectly still afternoon.

'There's certainly nothing for you to apologise for,' Daniel said awkwardly.

She gaped at him. 'I hadn't intended to,' she snapped. Something came adrift inside her. Annoyance gave way to anger as years of pent up-rage, disappointment and humiliation bubbled up like caramelised sugar, clogging her throat in a scorching gout of vitriol.

'You left me, remember?' She struggled to keep her voice under control. 'With no explanation, no … You just upped and went without even leaving me a note! Have you any idea how that made me feel? Have you?'

Doodle pulled his head back abruptly, like a well-mannered friend giving the arguing couple some space. He stuck his head out of the open window, resting his head on the sill as if the tone of the conversation was upsetting him.

Daniel had the grace to look shamefaced. He stared out of the windscreen, unable to meet her eyes.

'Well?' she spat. 'At the very least, you'd have to admit it was cowardly. And I still have no idea why.' She tucked her hair behind her ears and adjusted the rear view mirror minutely. 'You humiliated me, Daniel. If you don't think that deserves an explanation, we may as well give up now.'

'It was unforgiveable,' he said eventually, unconsciously echoing his mother. 'And I don't expect forgiveness. I know that's too much to ask.' He paused. 'There was a reason I didn't wait around. And you're absolutely right, I should have explained. You don't know how much I've regretted that, El. I really do. It was my pride and my stupidity that got in the way. I don't know what I was thinking except that I was under a lot of pressure.'

She wondered fleetingly if this admission had anything to do with what Angie had been about to say in the kitchen earlier. She dismissed the thought as familiar feelings threatened to swamp her. 'Have you forgotten about the four years in between?' she asked. 'Never thought to phone or send an email? You might as well have died, for all the information I had. Did you tell your mum and dad and Grace not to say anything, too?'

'They didn't know anything. I wasn't in a good place. I didn't want to involve anyone else. Particularly you.'

'I might have been able to help.'

He shook his head vehemently. 'No, you couldn't. That was the whole point. I was beyond help. I'd got myself into all kinds of trouble and had to sort it out for myself. It took a long time and going away was part of it. I needed the distance.'

He lapsed into a silence that expanded like smog to fill every crevice of the tiny car. Eleanor had been anticipating this moment for four years, endlessly rehearsing what she would say and how she would say it. But now the moment had arrived she was gripped by an almost overwhelming irritation with herself. Why had she allowed this moment, this man, to loom so large in her life? It was time to make a choice. She didn't need to continue the half-life she'd inhabited since Daniel's abrupt departure. She could just let go of the feelings of anger and humiliation and move on. She could forgive him.

There was really no choice at all.

She broke the uncomfortable silence. 'You're the only journalist I've ever known to be lost for words,' she said. 'Well, all in good time. Let's leave it, shall we? We have a party to enjoy.' She held her hand up to stem his protests. 'No, you don't have to explain. It's obviously still too difficult for you. I don't need to know anything else,' she added glassily. 'It probably wouldn't have worked anyway.' She gestured out of the window. 'I never could see myself as lady of the manor.'

Daniel's shoulders slumped. 'Maybe you're right. It's

been a long time. Lots of water under the bridge. I know we're not the same people, but seeing you here, I remember what we had and … ' He tailed off, leaving the unspoken words hanging in the air between them. 'Still friends, though?'

Eleanor was silent for a while. Then she nodded.

'Still friends.'

He relaxed back into his seat. 'Did you bring Toby with you? Grace told me about him. Life and soul of the party, she said.'

'No,' Eleanor said bluntly. 'We've split up.'

'Oh, Eleanor,' he said. 'I'm so sorry. How insensitive of me. What happened?'

She shrugged. 'Nothing much. I think that was the problem. We were just boring each other. It's for the best, really. But never mind about me and Toby, what's going on with Angie?'

Daniel smoothed his chinos awkwardly and pushed his hands through his hair in a gesture so familiar it made her stomach flip. 'Not much,' he said carefully. 'We've become closer over the past few months, after we met again in Paris.' He rubbed his hand across his forehead and looked away. He seemed to sense Eleanor's reservations. 'You'll warm to her, I'm sure.'

Christ, thought Eleanor. He's only gone and fallen in love with her. She gazed unseeing through the windscreen as she absorbed the unpalatable truth, any hope that things might have been different fading like early morning mist. 'She seems pretty keen,' she said eventually.

Daniel shrugged. 'I owe her a lot, actually. She helped me when I was in Paris,' he added, ignoring Eleanor's questioning look. 'Now she wants something more permanent. She's made it clear that she wants to be the new Mrs Hardwick.'

Eleanor's insides clenched at the words. Mrs Hardwick. 'Well, we always knew she wanted a rich husband,' she reminded him.

He shrugged. 'Angie is convinced I came into some vast trust fund when I turned twenty-one. We both know that isn't true, but she won't listen. She thinks I'm joking when I tell her I haven't got much money. That I need to work.'

'Oh, come on! What about that flat you had with Grace …?'

He nodded sheepishly. 'Yes, I've still got that. There's nothing else left, though.'

'Well you've got two choices, haven't you?' she said in her best agony aunt voice. 'Either you marry her and Angie finds out for herself later, or you give it to her straight and risk her running out on you. Seems pretty straightforward to me.'

Daniel looked at her. 'Maybe you're right.'

'And what about Grace? Won't you have to buy her out?'

'The flat's all mine. She spent her trust fund elsewhere, remember?'

'Of course.' She recalled Grace's excitement when she passed her flying exams. 'She bought the plane.'

'Anyway, I'm going to sell the flat to release some money, and because Angie, we, would prefer something a bit more modern. We've settled on a new build near the river. You'll have to come round when we get organised.'

The suggestion was absurd. 'Oh. Maybe. I'll have to …'

'Angie's staying here until it's all organised,' Daniel carried on as if she hadn't spoken. 'Then the paper's sending me to Frankfurt. It's all go,' he said excitedly. 'Who'd have thought it?'

Eleanor turned the ignition and concentrated on manoeuvring the car back onto the lane, looking round for somewhere to turn.

'You'll end up in the ditch if you try and turn here.'

Daniel pointed down the lane. 'You'll have to go down to the bottom. You need a 4x4 out here, not a girly little thing like this. You look fantastic, by the way,' he said, deftly changing the subject. 'Your hair's different and,' he glanced at her hands, 'you've had your nails done.'

'I'm surprised you noticed,' Eleanor remarked dryly. She spread her fingers for him to admire. 'I'm a grown up now; they're all my own.'

'And you've lost weight. It suits you.'

'Thank you.' Eleanor couldn't help basking in the compliment. 'I had a screen test a while ago and –'

'Really? How did it go? I haven't seen you on the telly yet.'

She waved a dismissive hand. 'Not a hope. I think Julian is blocking my career path. He's my boss and he wants to keep me in my place, on the newsdesk. Actually, between you and me, he prefers spray-tanned skinny-minnies with poker-straight blonde hair and legs up to their armpits. God knows why he even agreed to my test. Anyway, I haven't heard anything so I assume I'm on the cutting room floor.' She shrugged. 'Still, at least I've got in shape, so it's not all bad. I even go to the gym now,' she added.

'Yeah, me too. Angie makes me.'

'Good for her,' Eleanor muttered. She scowled in concentration as she wrenched the steering wheel to avoid an enormous pothole. 'So how do you think Angie will take the news?' she asked. 'About the money, I mean.'

Daniel shrugged. 'She'll be fine. It's all bluff, really. Just because I've given her those amber beads she thinks I'm David Beckham. But she's not stupid,' he added uncertainly. 'Please don't tell her, I picked them up in Lebanon for peanuts. I hadn't even met her again when I bought them.'

Just as well you haven't given her that diamond yet, Eleanor thought; that would be all the proof she'd need.

'I'm sure she knows, really,' she muttered. 'And even if she doesn't, she'll find out soon enough.' Couldn't happen to a nicer person.

Chapter Eleven

How she'd managed to get through it she'd never know.

She'd allowed herself to be taken in by Daniel's non-committal remarks about his relationship with Angie, so she'd been completely dumbfounded when Grace had dropped the bombshell.

'What do you think about Daniel's news?' she'd asked carefully when they'd been together in the kitchen later that afternoon, washing up coffee cups.

Eleanor's stomach had plummeted. 'What news?' she'd asked.

Grace had looked at her sharply, then continued drying a china cup with exquisite care before she'd put it gently on the counter. Her hair was laced through with ribbons and tiny silk flowers and she'd looked every inch the birthday girl except for the frown. 'Shit. He said he was going to tell you at the first opportunity. I thought ... Now I've put my foot in it.' She'd hesitated then, uncomfortable, before carrying on. 'Oh well, too late now. I think you should know, anyway. Daniel proposed to Angie last week. She's living here with us until their new flat's ready. I'm amazed she didn't tell you.'

The disappointment she'd felt at Daniel's earlier tactlessness had been bad enough, but this news had really crushed her. The prospect of having to then sing for her supper had made her feel sick.

But she'd done it; she'd drunk a couple of gin and tonics to calm her nerves, taken a deep breath, and walked out onto the small stage as if she owned it. Taking Sam's advice to sing her heart out to a total stranger, she'd chosen the bashful teenage son of a Mensum Bottom neighbour and addressed him as though he was the only person in the room. The backing provided by Belle's karaoke machine had been a big plus and she'd sung the crowd-pleasing songs with a heartfelt passion that surprised even her.

She'd intended to sing the final number à cappella but she'd no sooner launched into the tentative opening bars of 'Over the Rainbow', than the guitarist in the band Grace had booked to provide the disco for the evening's entertainment had picked up his acoustic instrument and accompanied her with understated sensitivity. As the final chords faded away, the audience had gone wild, asking for encore after encore.

She had intended to stay the night, but now all she wanted to do was put as many miles as possible between herself and Mensum Hall.

But escape wasn't on the cards just yet.

She went out onto the terrace to look for Sam, who had arrived with Rob with minutes to spare before the party had begun, but it was Daniel she found on the floodlit terrace.

He took her hands, pecking her formally on the cheek. 'You look stunning,' he said admiringly. 'That colour really suits you. Brings out your eyes. And you sang beautifully. Good choice of tunes. That last one, particularly.'

Eleanor didn't know how to react. 'Thanks,' she muttered.

'Do you get much chance to practise? I mean, do you sing with a choir or anything? I remember you –'

'I joined a choir a while ago, actually,' she interrupted. 'But it didn't work out. You know how it is. Awkward shift patterns; I just couldn't commit the time regularly. These days it's … well, it's a bit complicated.' She looked down and plucked nervously at the bracelet encircling her wrist before she asked quietly, 'Why didn't you tell me?'

'Tell you what?'

'About the wedding. Grace let the cat out of the bag.'

'Oh.' He had the good grace to look embarrassed. 'Sorry, I ... I was going to say something in the car this morning but ... I ... That is ... Angie and I ... Oh, here she is now.'

They watched as the object of their consideration teetered across the lawn. Angie was wearing an orange dress that fitted where it touched and was so short that Eleanor hoped she'd remembered to wear matching knickers. Her shoes were a similar shade of tangerine, the spindly heels enhancing the impossibly long, tanned, and perfect legs.

Angie looked fabulous, Eleanor grudgingly admitted, but she still wished the ground had been a little softer; she would have liked to see those stilettos sink into the grass like a pair of tent pegs.

Angie leaned towards Daniel and kissed him on the cheek. She linked arms with him possessively, leaving her left hand free to gesticulate flamboyantly; her body language might be confused, but no one could miss the diamond on her engagement finger, flashing like fire in the lamplight.

Eleanor felt a sharp pang in the pit of her stomach. The ring proclaimed it: their upcoming nuptials were official.

'Absolutely lovely singing, El,' Angie said. She nudged Daniel. 'In fact ... darling,' she emphasised, 'have you asked her?'

'Er, no, not yet,' Daniel blustered. 'I haven't had chance.'

'Ask me what?' Eleanor looked from one to the other. 'Come on,' she urged. 'You have my full attention.'

Daniel looked uncomfortable. 'Maybe this isn't the time ...'

'What's the problem?' Angie asked. She turned to Eleanor. 'What Daniel can't seem to bring himself to ask is ...'

'Angie ...' Daniel put a warning hand on her arm.

She shrugged him off. 'Would you sing at our wedding, Eleanor?'

The question hung in the air between them like a cloud of poisonous gas.

'Pardon?' Eleanor asked stupidly. She couldn't quite believe what she'd heard. She stared at Daniel. He was silently studying his shoes.

'I said –'

'I heard what you said, Angie,' Eleanor said. 'You took me by surprise, that's all.' All the hurt, resentment, and, there was no getting away from it, jealousy, that she had been storing up all weekend suddenly emptied out of her like water from a bath, leaving her feeling hollow and deflated. She smiled determinedly as a group of guests walked past.

'I, I'll have to think about it.' Hot tears threatened to ruin her mascara and she made to move away. 'There's your mum and dad,' she muttered. 'I'll see you later.'

'I'm sorry to hear about the split,' Angie called after her.

Eleanor turned slowly. 'Sorry?'

'Toby, wasn't it? Still, plenty more fish in the sea, aren't there? I'll make sure you catch my bouquet.'

The large drawing room was cool and mercifully empty. Eleanor closed the door, dropped into an over-plump armchair and put her head back. She didn't know quite what to think. Daniel seemed to be completely besotted with Angie, but he also seemed to have lost the warmth and compassion that had been such a big part of his personality, along with his heart. The Daniel she'd known and loved all those years ago would never have behaved like this. She would have expected him to at least make sure that Angie didn't ask that insensitive question today of all days.

Her peace was interrupted all too soon. The door opened and Angie strode in. 'I knew you'd be in here,' she cried. 'Look, I wanted to ...'

'There's no need to apologise, Angie,' Eleanor said wearily. 'I wouldn't have expected anything less from you. It was just a bit of a shock, that's all.'

'Sorry?' Angie asked. 'Oh, never mind all that. I wanted to show you my ring. Look.' She advanced across the carpet, brandishing her engagement ring. 'Isn't it absolutely beautiful?' she crowed. 'I've been learning all about the 4 Cs,' she gabbled on excitedly. 'Cut, colour, carat weight and c ... I can't remember the other one. Anyway, it's a family heirloom. Daniel's grandmother –'

'I know,' Eleanor interrupted without thinking. 'I mean, it's *clarity*, the other C,' she added hastily. She examined the stone briefly. 'It's lovely.'

Thankfully it didn't seem to occur to Angie that Eleanor might already be familiar with the ring. She carried on listing the marvellous qualities of the diamond until Eleanor muttered an excuse about needing some fresh air. 'I think I'd better get back outside,' she said, heading for the door.

'Everything all right?' Daniel had appeared from nowhere and was blocking her route out of the room.

Gwen was right behind him. 'Are you all right?' she asked, pushing past Daniel. 'You look rather pale. The singing wasn't too much for you, was it?'

'No, it was fine. *I'm* fine, really,' Eleanor replied. She looked at Gwen, debating whether to tell her the reason for her distress.

Peter barged in at that moment carrying a plate heaped with food from the buffet in the dining room. 'Sorry, sorry,' he apologised. 'Just looking for a refill.' He jiggled his empty wine glass. 'I'll get out when I find another bottle. There's nothing left in the other room.'

Gwen pushed the remains of a bottle of burgundy across the table to him, giving him a meaningful look. 'I didn't put too much out,' she explained. 'I didn't want any to go to waste.'

Peter gave his wife a very old-fashioned look. 'Waste?' he asked. 'When was the last time we ever wasted any –' He stopped in mid-sentence, caught in the beam of Gwen's warning glare. 'Sorry,' he repeated. 'You have the last of that bottle. I'll grab a beer instead.'

Eleanor watched as Peter crept out of the room. The moment had passed and she was glad she hadn't unburdened herself.

'I'll just go and check that everyone's all right,' Daniel said, hustling Angie out of the door.

'Sorry about that,' Gwen said. 'This party has been quite a strain, one way and another. That silly woman,' said Gwen when they were alone. 'Interfering with the catering. Cost an absolute bloody fortune, those people she brought in. I don't know why I let myself be talked into it. I really can't warm to her.' She filled a tumbler with water and regarded Eleanor over the top of her glasses. 'There's no need to worry, you know,' she advised. 'I know her sort. It won't last.'

'But she's wearing his grandmother's ring,' Eleanor protested.

'Yes,' agreed Gwen. 'Stupid boy just wouldn't have it. His father and I have tried to tell him. He certainly won't see that again, when it all ends in tears. As it undoubtedly will.' She shook her head. 'Such a waste. Sorry, I seem to be taking in clichés.' She glanced at the door and lowered her voice to a whisper. 'Between the two of us, we were so much happier when he was with you. Though …' she paused. 'I don't know, maybe it's just a mother's sixth sense, but I … he seems to bend to her will a little too much. Silly really.' She shrugged. 'But, if that's what he wants …'

Eleanor didn't know whether to laugh or cry.

She left the room in search of Sam and found her sitting on the edge of the fountain drinking champagne with Rob. Sam's boyfriend was the kind of man who read cookery books in bed and discussed wine choices with the sommeliers in posh restaurants. He was a pleasant enough bloke with good manners and nice hair, but Eleanor couldn't figure out what Sam was doing with him; he wasn't enough of a challenge for her friend. She was on the point of asking him why he'd been standing outside a cheap department store in the rain, but she swallowed the impulse.

'Hello, Rob. Nice to see you again.'

'We came looking for you, but you'd disappeared,' Sam said. 'Where were you?'

'Being given an exclusive preview of the ring,' Eleanor said despondently.

'Ah, the diamond rears its ugly head again.' Sam frowned into her glass. 'Well, that's that then. The family will never see it again. Unfeeling bitch,' she added uncompromisingly. 'How do you feel about it?'

'Gwen reckons it's not going to last,' Eleanor said glumly. 'She said they tried to talk him out of the engagement, her and Peter. She agrees with you: she doesn't think Daniel will get it back when it all falls through. And she's certain that it will. She's also got this ridiculous notion that Angie's got some sort of hold over him.'

'Really? Did she say what?'

Eleanor shrugged. 'Not in so many words.'

'Anyway,' Sam continued, 'did you get to see much of wonderboy? On your own, I mean?'

'Hell, no. Apart from when I gave him a lift back from the village earlier, Angie's monopolised him the whole time. She probably thinks she can't trust him around me. I don't know what she's going to do when he's away.'

'Why? Where's he going?'

'The paper's sending him to Frankfurt for a while, so he can to get some political experience in the Eurozone.' She smiled ruefully. 'This'll make you laugh,' she continued. 'Though I don't think it's that funny, actually.'

'Oh, go on. Tell me.'

'She actually asked me if I would sing at their wedding.'

Rob had been listening intently. 'What an absolute cow,' he muttered.

Chapter Twelve

The god of parking was obviously smiling when Eleanor got into her car on Monday morning because she hadn't got a ticket; it was a risk she ran every time she had to leave her car a couple of streets away. One of these days her luck would run out.

At 10.30 a.m. she was sitting opposite Nick Paget in a glass-fronted office overlooking the newsroom. She was full of nervous anticipation, which wasn't helped by Nick constantly getting up and going to the window to watch the activity below.

'It all looks so exciting,' he enthused, wriggling around in his seat like an excited schoolboy. 'Where do you sit?'

'Depends what I'm doing,' Eleanor said. 'Mostly I'm over there with the other planners.' She indicated the pod of desks below. 'But sometimes I get to sit up here away from the mayhem.'

'Tell me who's who.' Nick was still gazing downward.

'Later, we've got too much to do.'

'You sound like a jaded old pro,' joked Nick.

'I am,' she said. 'Three years of early starts and late finishes does that to a girl.'

'Don't spoil it for me!' Nick protested.

'Sorry. You'll learn soon enough. But you'll absolutely love it.' Eleanor marshalled her thoughts. 'Right, let's think about this. Julian will be along in a few minutes, so let's get some sort of itinerary sorted out before he arrives.'

'Who's Julian?'

'He's our managing editor on Home News. My boss,

the great ME. He has power of veto. If he doesn't like it, it ain't gonna happen.'

'I thought ...' Nick looked crestfallen.

'Don't worry,' Eleanor soothed. 'I've been through it all with him and he's very interested. You've just got to make a good impression on him.'

'Oh.' He glanced at the door, as if weighing up how many seconds it would take for him to reach it.

'It's OK. I've done all the groundwork. All you need to do is convince him that this is a brilliant idea that will bring in loads of viewers who will be hanging on your every word, night after night for several weeks.'

'Is that all? Oh good,' he said weakly. He was looking increasingly anxious when the door opened and Julian walked in.

'Ah, here you are,' he said, shaking Nick's hand firmly. 'Eleanor's told me a lot about you.' Julian's eyes twinkled as he considered him. 'And all of it true, I see.'

Nick glanced uncertainly at Eleanor.

'Nick,' she began, 'why don't you take Julian through your plans while I go and get us all some coffee?' Nick's eyes widened in panic. Eleanor smiled encouragingly as she handed Julian several sheets of paper.

'It's all down here. Nick will fill you in on all the details.' She winked at Nick as she left the room. 'Back soon.'

'Well, what a find he turned out to be,' Julian marvelled as they sat over another coffee some time later.

Eleanor had given Nick a guided tour of the news operation and sent him off to do some packing, with instructions to present himself at the office first thing – yes, that really did mean 6 a.m. – the next morning to get the paperwork sorted out and have a trial run with the camera. She was almost hugging herself with glee. 'Told you, didn't I?' she said.

'You did,' Julian agreed. 'But he's even better, he's pure gold. And what a looker, too. How old did you say he was?'

'He's just finished his final year, so twenty-two, possibly twenty-three, I suppose. He did a gap year.'

'Marvellous. The viewers will love him.'

'We could do some good here, too.'

'What do you mean?'

'A fund. You know, set something up in the Pagets' name. Cancer research, that kind of thing.'

'What a great idea. I'll speak to the IT guys and get them to sort it out.'

Nick arrived yawning but right on schedule the next morning.

'It's still the middle of the night,' he complained. 'How do you do it?'

'You get used to it,' said Eleanor. 'Plays havoc with your sleeping patterns.' She looked closely at Nick's bleary eyes. 'Though I think you're too young to even know what they are.'

She took him round the newsroom and introduced him to some rather sceptical key people and stood by as he experimented with the camera, taking a few panning shots to demonstrate his shooting technique.

'Cool,' he said as he hefted it onto his shoulder. It was small and lightweight and came with a supply of discs and a mobile phone.

'You'll report to me, most of the time,' Eleanor explained. 'If that ever changes I'll let you know. Call in first thing every morning and again in the evening. In fact, whenever you have anything to report. Keep the mobile charged and switched on at all times,' she instructed. 'Here's my home number too, just in case.' She handed Nick a business card with a number scrawled on the back.

'Do I get expenses?' he asked cheekily.

'Of course you do, within reason,' said Eleanor. 'Keep all your receipts. Most important. Oh, and I forgot to tell you. I'll be coming with you.'

Belle's was the only dissenting voice when Nick's odyssey was introduced to the newsdesk at the morning's editorial meeting.

'Isn't it a bit, well, red-top for us?' she ventured.

'Yes, of course it is,' Julian agreed. 'But if we play this right, we'll have all the tabloids *and* the broadsheets *and* our competitors wanting some of our action.' He glanced at Eleanor. 'Remember the Tamworth Two? The entire country was electrified.'

'Yes, but that was because there wasn't any other news arou …' The words died on Belle's lips.

'Precisely!' Julian looked round the room triumphantly. 'We're not exactly beating off world exclusives with a stick at the moment, are we? This is a dead time of year. It's perfect. And we might make some money, too.' He outlined the cancer fund idea and dismissed Belle's doubtful pout. 'Anyway, here's how we'll play it. Nick will have a car, a camera, and a laptop. He'll be able to edit, and he'll use his ingenuity to get his material to us whenever he can.'

'How often will he send stuff in?' asked Belle.

'We'd like a twice-weekly report,' said Julian, 'but it depends on Nick.' He looked across the room at Eleanor. 'He's Eleanor's protégé and she'll have to do a certain amount of babysitting, so she'll be on the road with him, particularly during the early days.'

Belle nudged Eleanor in the ribs. 'If Nick is that lovely-looking teenager I saw you with earlier, you're a very lucky woman,' she whispered.

'He's not a –'

'Thank you.' Julian shot both women a sharp glance before continuing. 'If Nick's near any of our regional offices he'll be able to use their facilities. And when it looks like he's closing in on the Pagets, we'll send a satellite truck and do the thing properly.' He paused and looked round the room. 'Right. Any questions? I can see that some of you are rather doubtful.' He put his hand up to discourage any opposition. 'No? Good. One last thing. This should go without saying, but no, I repeat, no, leaks to the press or other broadcasters throughout this exercise. I will take a very dim view if any other bugger gets to the Pagets before we do.'

'I think I should start in Scotland,' Nick suggested. The two of them were huddled round Eleanor's computer. Nick had already found out that the two runaways had hired a motor home and that they had taken the dog with them, but not the cat. He told a concerned Eleanor that he thought the cat would be well provided for by neighbours. 'That cat has about five homes anyway,' he said. 'And they all think he's *their* cat.'

Nick had also discovered that his grandparents were lifetime members of the National Trust. He was convinced that they would be visiting various architectural or historical sites and his plan was to zigzag the country until he eventually caught up with them.

'I think they'll make for Scotland first. Maybe we could ask the National Trust for information.'

'Sorry,' said Eleanor, shaking her head, 'we can't do that. They aren't criminals. This comes down to good old-fashioned detective work. So let's start by checking the Trust website for possible locations.' She opened up a search engine and soon discovered that the National Trust didn't own any properties north of the border.

'I know they love that part of the world. I still think that's where they'll go first,' said Nick, refusing to be put off his hunch. 'Aren't the Scottish National Trust a separate thingy?'

'Quite possibly,' said Eleanor, busily clicking on her keyboard. 'Yes, here we are. Right, we need a map.'

'Here's one I prepared earlier.' Nick produced a map book out of his pack with a flourish. Quickly turning to the relevant pages, he traced what he expected the outbound journey to be with his finger.

'I reckon they'll head for the Kyle of Lochalsh and then Skye, but they might stop off at Loch Lomond. But they won't want to bypass Glasgow and Edinburgh,' he said, nodding decisively. 'I should make the east coast my first destination.'

'Well, you know your grandparents best,' said Eleanor. 'I'll leave it up to you and the great British public.' She lapsed into a thoughtful silence.

'Is there a problem?' asked Nick.

'No ... I was just wondering if they had any nicknames, besides Gran and Pops? We can't carry on calling them Mr and Mrs Paget, we need something a bit more user-friendly.'

Nick looked thoughtful. 'I know!' he said eventually. 'We should call it the Doric Imperative. You know, *Do*ra and E*ric*?'

'Hmm. Sounds like something Jason Bourne might enjoy. Could work, I suppose,' said Eleanor, privately thinking that Julian would make sure it didn't. 'By the way, I won't be able to join you until later this week; I've got a lot on at the moment. But keep in contact and I'll drive to wherever you are.'

'Look forward to it,' said Nick, smiling. 'Better get myself organised, hadn't I?'

Chapter Thirteen

'*Good evening.*'

Nick smiled into the camera. UK24's intrepid new reporter was standing at the head of the Skell valley with the impressive ruins of a twelfth-century monastery forming a picturesque backdrop. '*I'm Nick Paget and I'm here at Fountain's Abbey, in North Yorkshire, hoping to find some clues as to the whereabouts of my grandparents, Eric and Dora Paget, and their dog Prince.*'

'He's a natural,' said Julian, visibly relieved. He leaned back in his chair and linked his hands behind his head. The camera panned round the ruins. 'He can even frame a picture properly.'

'*The vaulted ceiling of the Abbey behind me escaped Henry VIII's dissolution of the monasteries in the sixteenth century, and it seems that my grandparents have masterminded an escape of their own,*' Nick went on. '*I'm appealing now to any viewers who may have information as to their whereabouts or any actual sightings.*' Photographs of Eric and Dora flashed onto the screen as Nick continued with a brief explanation about his appeal. '*It's really most important that they get in touch with the family as soon as possible. I have some very good news for them. I'll be back later this week with an update on my search. We're calling it the Doric Imperative; I hope you'll be watching,*' he concluded. '*Prince, by the way, is a very excitable Airedale terrier. You know, the sort of dog you used to have on wheels when you were a kid.*'

'Brilliant,' said Eleanor. 'He'll even get the dog lovers on board.'

'Who's writing his reports?' asked Julian.

'He is. He wanted to do them himself,' replied Eleanor. 'Though they'll all be checked back here before transmission, of course. Pretty good, so far, don't you think?'

'I'm impressed. What a great idea of mine this was,' said Julian smugly. 'Though I think we should drop that Doric Imperative nonsense.'

They walked across to the newsdesk where Belle was wearing a creation that seemed to have been fashioned from a pair of velvet curtains. Eleanor raised a questioning eyebrow. 'Can't you guess, darling?' Belle drawled. 'I'd have thought it was obvious. I'm –'

'I don't care,' Julian interrupted. 'Let's get down to business.' He began snapping out instructions. 'We'll put this first report out tonight during the five o'clock bulletin, with an invitation to send in photos and videos from mobile phones.'

Belle tapped furiously on her keyboard and copious notes soon filled her screen.

'And e-mails,' Eleanor added.

'And e-mails,' Julian repeated frostily. 'Scarlett O'Hara here will make sure they're monitored, won't you?'

Belle nodded, sweeping her hair over her shoulder and glowing with unspoken delight.

'And the website,' Julian carried on. 'For any uploaded photos and whathaveyou. We'll need to react if there's any news on the wrinklies' whereabouts and get Nick on the move to his next location.'

Julian turned to Eleanor. 'This is your baby. You should go and check up on him, make sure he's OK.'

'Maybe I should,' said Eleanor.

Eleanor set off for Northumberland the next day. Never one for breakfast, or even, on this occasion, lunch, her stomach felt as if it was being gnawed by a small animal by the time she pulled into the deserted car park on the coast at Beal. The tide was in and the causeway connecting the island of Lindisfarne with the mainland was completely under water.

A chilly wind swirled in from the sea as she got out of her car. Pulling her padded coat tightly around her, she walked towards where Nick was panning round the countryside with his camera. He turned slowly and the large lens came to rest on her face.

Eleanor held up a hand and grimaced. 'I hope that's not running.'

'Always,' Nick said. 'Never miss a shot that way.' He laid the camera carefully on the passenger seat of his SUV. 'Good journey?' he asked.

'Not too bad, except for the traffic after Birmingham. It just takes such a long time.'

Nick nodded in agreement. 'I took two days over it. Stayed overnight with some old uni friends in Leeds. Where're you staying?'

Eleanor already knew where Nick was staying; she'd found out from the newsdesk. 'I've got a room at the Kings Arms in Berwick.'

'Cool,' said Nick. 'I'm there, too.'

'That's lucky,' said Eleanor. 'I only booked one night. I presumed you'd be on the move again tomorrow.'

'I will.' He spread an enormous map over a flat rock and beckoned Eleanor over. 'Look,' he said, tracing a winding road with his finger. 'Someone has emailed a sighting here.' He stabbed the map north of the Scottish border. 'So that's where I'm heading.'

'Hmm,' said Eleanor doubtfully. 'We'll check more recent sightings on the laptop when we get back to the hotel. What I've seen so far seems to indicate possible locations anywhere from Land's End to bloody John O' Groats.'

'That's what I feared,' said Nick. 'But I have a system of sorts.'

'I'm waiting to be impressed,' said Eleanor. 'What is it?'

'Gran and Pops covered the south and west of England pretty well last year, so I think we should disregard any sightings in that part of the country. They're here.' He prodded the map again. 'I can feel it.' He smiled at her confidently. 'And I have something else up my sleeve.'

'Oh? What's that?'

'Gran's a Catholic. They'll have to find a church for Mass on Sunday morning. She'd never miss it.'

Eleanor looked at him closely. 'I thought suicide was against their religion. Catholics, I mean.'

Nick hesitated. He turned away, rubbed his index finger deliberately back and forth along a crease in the map. 'She said ... she told me ...' He brushed at his eyes with the back of his hand. 'Sorry.'

Eleanor felt a sudden pang of guilt for intruding on Nick's private anguish. He was obviously struggling with a difficult memory. She put a comforting hand on his shoulder. 'No, I'm sorry,' she said. 'This must be hard for you.'

'Sorry,' Nick repeated. 'Gran told me that she'd already had a chat with Him. God, that is. She's convinced that He wouldn't want her to be in pain; that He'd forgive her if the worst came to the worst.' He smiled wanly. 'Thank God He won't have to, so to speak.'

'Quite a personal relationship,' Eleanor observed. 'I've always envied people with a faith like that.' She stared out at the sea for a while. 'I'm sure we'll find them in time. Maybe we can recce a couple of likely venues tomorrow.'

Nick frowned. 'I thought you were going back tomorrow. Won't it muck up your weekend?'

Eleanor reflected briefly on the days stretching out in front of her at home. With Toby gone, Daniel in Frankfurt, and Sam preoccupied with Rob, she would be at a loose end. Mabel had plenty of food and water; the cat wouldn't starve.

'Yes,' she said brightly. 'But nothing that won't keep.'

'OK.' He smiled, his eyes crinkling at the corners. 'Well, there can't be that many Catholic churches on that side of the border, can there? Isn't everybody a Calvinist or something?'

'Probably,' agreed Eleanor. 'Shouldn't be too difficult to check.'

'Should we announce this little nugget to the public?' Nick asked.

'No, I don't think so,' she replied. 'Too much of a risk, even at this stage. There'd be people gathering outside church gates, posing in their Sunday best, as soon as they saw a television camera.' She shuddered. 'Can you imagine? And,' she pointed a finger at Nick for emphasis, 'we have to try and respect your grandparents' privacy.'

They looked at the map in silence for a while. Eleanor spoke first. 'There's always the possibility that Eric and Dora will leave Scotland before we catch up with them.'

'That's quite likely.' Nick frowned at her. 'How long have you scheduled this adventure for?'

'Ideally, two to three weeks. Long enough to keep the viewers involved, not long enough for them to get bored.' She paused. 'Hang on, are you thinking what I think you're thinking?'

Nick grinned boyishly and Eleanor was struck again by how good-looking he was. 'Can't you manipulate the timings?' he asked. 'Make things last a bit longer?'

'Nick!' She pretended to be shocked. 'Julian warned me about this. It has to be completely above board. No messing about.'

'I know, but …'

'If the trail goes cold,' Eleanor interrupted, 'we'll postpone your reports until you catch up with them again. Create some suspense, that's the most we can do.'

'Real time, then?' Nick pulled a face.

'Real time,' she repeated firmly.

'Well, at least Gran won't be deteriorating like she'd be expecting to,' Nick said. 'So they'll probably take more time over the trip, anyway.'

'Don't even think about it,' Eleanor warned.

They folded the unwieldy map like a married couple folding the laundry. Their fingers touched and Eleanor felt a sharp tingle of electricity shoot up her arm. She stepped back smartly. 'Right,' she said, hugging herself against the wind. 'We should pack up and get back to base. It's damn cold up here and I'm bloody freezing.'

'There's a flask of coffee in the truck.'

'Dib, dib, dib,' she laughed, putting two fingers up to her forehead. 'Proper boy scout, aren't you?'

'I don't like being cold either,' Nick replied reasonably.

They sat for a time in the car, sipping strong black coffee in a companionable silence, taking in the magnificent view through the gradually misting windows as they warmed their hands round the plastic mugs.

'That's better.' Eleanor shuddered as the caffeine hit her empty stomach. 'You don't happen to have anything to eat, do you? I'm absolutely starving.'

Nick scrabbled about in a side compartment and produced a couple of KitKats. 'Didn't you have any lunch?'

Eleanor nibbled delicately at the chocolate, savouring each bite. 'I didn't want to stop. All I've had today is a cup of tea and a chewable calcium tablet.'

'Nice,' said Nick. 'No wonder you're so skinny.'

'How kind of you to notice,' Eleanor said. 'OK. Let's get this show on the road.' She handed her mug to Nick and climbed out of the car. 'I'll see you back at the hotel. My room at …' she looked at her watch, calculating the journey time, 'seven?'

'Fine. See you there.' He waited. 'Have I got to guess which room?'

Chapter Fourteen

The water was hot and plentiful and Eleanor took a long shower, sloughing off her travel weariness and making use of all the free toiletries. She slathered on a miniature bottle of body lotion and combed her hair back from her face, deciding to let it dry naturally as she dressed quickly in jeans and a clean T-shirt.

She remembered the frisson of excitement she'd felt when her hand had touched Nick's. Don't be ridiculous, she thought; Nick was very sweet, good-looking, and terrific company, but she couldn't imagine getting involved with someone so very young. Sam would say he should have a 'look but don't touch' warning sticker. And anyway, she lectured herself, Toby wasn't very far into the past, and there was still the idea of Daniel hovering in the background; a memory that steadfastly refused to fade. She didn't need another relationship.

Nick knocked on Eleanor's door, freshly shaved and wearing a clean, if crumpled, shirt and chinos. His hair was still wet from the shower and he smelled delicious.

'Hmm.' Eleanor sniffed appreciatively as he walked into the room. 'You smell nice. What is it?'

'Erm ... eau de something. YSL, I think. My Auntie Julie gave it to me for Christmas.'

'Good taste.'

'Nah,' said Nick dismissively. 'She just works on a cosmetics counter. Gets a staff discount.'

'Come and sit down.' Eleanor had her laptop open on the desk and had already located the folder containing the emails and mobile phone footage sent in by members of the public.

'Citizen Journalism,' she said. 'Don't you just love it?'

'First things first,' said Nick. He produced a bottle of gin from the pocket of his chinos. 'Got any tonic?'

'Oh, excellent.' Eleanor retrieved two small cans of tonic water from the mini bar. 'No ice, I'm afraid, but at least the tonics are cold.'

They spent the next hour scrolling through a disappointingly meagre amount of photographs and videos of unlikely suspects.

'There aren't not many, are there?' Nick complained about the muted response. 'I thought there'd be more.'

'Don't worry,' Eleanor reassured him, 'we're just getting started. The great British public love a crusade; word will get round, you'll see.'

They clicked through the pictures, Nick getting progressively more morose at the parade of people accompanied by poodles, spaniels, and small terriers. There were couples of such disparate heights as to be laughably wide of the mark; couples so fat they could have qualified for corrective surgery or so thin they could be advertising the benefits of a no-food diet. There were even some snaps of children pushing toy dogs on wheels.

'You'd never think we showed photographs of the real people, would you?' he grumbled. 'I'd assumed the public would be a bit more savvy. These people couldn't be mistaken for Eric and Dora in a million years. And look at that dog! There's no way that's an Airedale.' He shook his head. 'It's going to be more difficult than I thought.'

'Don't lose heart so soon,' comforted Eleanor. 'This is the first day.' She smiled at him. 'You've got to admit it's quite funny, though, isn't it?'

Nick smiled wryly. 'Suppose so. Can we go and get something to eat now?'

'Let's decide where we're going to head tomorrow, first.'

'OK.' Nick looked pensive, then started typing on the

laptop. 'There must be a cathedral in Edinburgh,' he said. 'Gran loves cathedrals and ruins and stuff. That's why I started at Fountain's Abbey.'

'It's as good a place as any, I suppose,' Eleanor agreed.

Look,' he said, reading from the screen. 'St Mary's RC Cathedral, York Place. Mass is at 9.30 and 11.30 on Sunday morning. Sorted.'

'So we'll head towards Edinburgh tomorrow, then?'

Nick nodded. 'We can take our time; it's only sixty miles.' He closed the laptop, looking immensely pleased with himself. 'Food, now, please?'

Over a bowl of pasta and a bottle of Chianti in the small hotel restaurant, Eleanor discovered a lot more about Nick and his grandparents.

'When Mum died,' he began, 'I was only thirteen. Dad did his best but Gran had a lot to do with my upbringing. Dad was out at work all hours and I used to go to Gran and Pop's every night after school for my dinner. Dad would pick me up later, after he'd finished work and I'd finished my homework. Pops made sure I knuckled down, otherwise I'd have spent all my time playing with my mates in the streets.'

'It must have been difficult for you all,' said Eleanor.

'It was, for sure.' Nick shook his head. 'I wasn't a natural student and I argued with Pops all the time. I wanted to leave school, but he wouldn't hear of it.'

'What would you have done if you'd left?'

'Nothing. Just dossed around. That's just it. I had no plans. I just wanted out, like my friends. None of them were at work or studying. I suppose Pops thought I needed guidance, some kind of structure.'

'And now?' Eleanor ventured. 'How do you feel about it now?'

'It was definitely what I needed,' Nick said. 'I certainly wouldn't have done it on my own, and Dad was too busy to notice.'

'Do you feel bitter? You know, towards your dad? For not being there for you?'

'No, not at all. He was just doing what he knew. We both were.' He smiled sheepishly. 'It all worked out OK, though, didn't it? Look at me now.'

'Hmm,' laughed Eleanor. She toyed with the remains of the generous plateful of pasta as she listened to Nick. He's very appealing, she thought. In a Brad Pitt in *Thelma and Louise* sort of way. Same beguiling good looks, same easy manner. Probably broken a few hearts already. She'd have to ask him about that.

She tuned back into the conversation.

'Anyway,' Nick was saying, 'that's why I feel so strongly that Gran and Pops should spend their money however they want.'

'Even if it means that there'll be none left for you?'

'It's not mine, though, is it? They earned it through their own hard work. They've made enough sacrifices for me already. I don't care if they spend the lot!'

'But your dad and his brother and sister don't agree?'

'Well, up to a point. They'll come round. Dad was quite laid back about everything until Auntie Julie started going on at him and Uncle Jack about their inheritance. And she's only an in-law. So bloody insensitive! Then it all went pear-shaped. Gran and Pops found out about the cancer and then they disappeared.' He spread his hands on the table. 'Can't say I blame them for disappearing. I hope they have a bloody good time.' He paused to swallow a mouthful of pasta. 'But we need to find them quickly,' he added. 'To avert disaster.'

Eleanor changed the subject. 'So what about your love life? Sorry, you don't mind me asking, do you?'

He shook his head. 'Very boring, actually,' he replied. 'No one special at the moment. Concentrating on my career.'

'But at uni there must have been –'

'A couple, yeah,' he agreed. 'But none that meant anything. Nothing survived, if that's what you mean.' He took a swig of wine. 'I was a bit of a treat 'em mean and keep 'em keen sort of bloke in those days.'

'In those days?' Eleanor echoed. 'You make it sound like it was a hundred years ago! Don't tell me, you just weren't ready for commitment.'

'No, I wasn't,' Nick admitted. 'Far too young. Probably always will be. Love 'em and leave 'em, that's me,' he joked.

'A cliché for every occasion,' Eleanor observed, aware that she sounded like a prissy maiden aunt.

'But enough about me, as they say,' Nick continued, tapping her hand. 'What about you? I don't know anything about you, except where you work and that you go to the gym.' He refilled Eleanor's glass and sat back. 'Your turn.'

Eleanor picked at the wax crusted round the candle stuck in an empty wine bottle. 'Not much to tell, really,' she prevaricated.

Nick raised an eyebrow. 'Call me old-fashioned,' he said, 'but you work in the media. People on my course would commit murder for the sort of job you've got. You must have some tales to tell.'

'And here's me thinking you wanted to hear about me.' Eleanor commented wryly.

'I do. I'm sorry, I didn't mean …'

Eleanor waved away his apology. 'I was kidding.'

'No, really. I'm interested. Tell me about yourself. What's your boyfriend called, for instance? What does he do?'

'Haven't got one. It's just me and Mabel.'

'Mabel? Sorry, I didn't realise …'

'Mabel's my cat.'

'Oh.' He smiled. 'But there must be someone in your life.'

Eleanor shook her head. 'Seriously. No boyfriend. Well, not any more.'

'Ouch. That sounds recent, and painful.'

Eleanor shrugged. Was she really going to bare her soul to this attractive young man she'd known a scant few days? 'Well, once upon a time ...' she began. It seemed she was.

She could almost hear Sam cawing with laughter.

'We should watch some UK24,' Nick said as they walked back after their meal. 'Just in case there's been some developments.'

'Sounds good,' said Eleanor. She smiled to herself. Nick's company was very soothing and she was reluctant to bring the evening to an end. 'We could grab a bottle of wine from the bar ...'

'Your room or mine?'

'Yours,' she said decisively. It was easier for a woman to get out of a tricky situation if she was the one who had to leave. Not that Eleanor was expecting a tricky situation, but she'd rather have the upper hand.

Nick's room was almost identical to hers. Same enormous bed, different linen. She switched the TV on while Nick poured the wine into two tumblers from the bathroom and raised his in the air. 'To Gran and Pops,' he toasted. 'Let's hope they're watching.'

'Amen to that,' said Eleanor.

They settled incongruously on the bed, propped up by pillows and carefully avoiding any physical contact. If Nick felt any embarrassment about the situation, Eleanor was relieved that he didn't show it. He grabbed the remote control and began surfing the channels, stopping every now and then to take in a football result or snatch of music.

'Typical man,' moaned Eleanor. 'Hurry up.' She checked her watch. 'It's nearly the top of the hour.'

UK24 burst onto the screen in a cacophony of noise and colour.

'Levels are all wrong,' Nick said knowledgeably. 'Doesn't anyone ever check that?'

'Oooh, get you,' Eleanor laughed. 'So professional already.' She took a gulp of wine. 'Actually, I've no idea. Listen. Here come the headlines.'

They watched as the presenter read through the list of top stories, but there was no mention of Eric and Dora. Nick looked dejected. 'The Doric Imperative has fallen off the radar already,' he grumbled.

'I told you: be patient,' said Eleanor. 'We've only put out one report. It'll pick up. I promise you.'

Nick frowned at her. 'I hope so. Otherwise all this is a complete waste of time.'

'Oh, I don't know,' she said. 'I can think of worse ways of spending a Friday night.'

Nick arched an eyebrow. 'Whatever do you mean?' he asked mischievously.

'I mean,' said Eleanor, wriggling off the bed and heading for the door, 'I've got a travel Scrabble in my room. I won't be a tick.'

Chapter Fifteen

'Best of three?' Eleanor asked after they'd won one game each. She cleared the board and began setting up again.

'Enough,' said Nick, holding his hands up. 'I surrender. I'm knackered.' He collapsed backwards onto the bed and stared at the ceiling. 'Let's talk some more. Tell me more about this Daniel bloke.'

Eleanor was surprised. 'What about him?' she asked. 'He was ages ago. I told you at the restaurant, there've been others since then.'

'But none that meant as much,' Nick observed. 'You glossed over him. So now I know all about Toby and his indiscretions. But I don't know anything about Daniel.'

'Why would you want to?'

'Because he obviously meant – still means – an awful lot to you. You hide it well, Eleanor, but not well enough.'

Perhaps she wasn't being as blasé as she thought. 'You're very perceptive but I wouldn't say that, exactly.'

'What would you say, then?'

She sighed. 'OK, I'd say that I made an error of judgement, a miscalculation, I suppose. It hurt a lot. But I'm over it.' She pulled her feet underneath her and sat cross-legged, facing away from Nick. 'I didn't think –' She paused and took a breath. 'We were very much an item,' she recited. 'Now we aren't. That was then, this is now. We've moved on.'

'Have you?'

'I told you,' she waved her hand in a dismissive gesture, 'he's getting married.'

'That's not what I asked.'

Eleanor swung round to look at him. 'Of course I've

moved on,' she repeated. 'Anyway, what's with the third degree? Why do you want to know?' she carried on, her voice rising like a heroine in a Victorian melodrama. 'We hardly know each other.'

Nick sat up and took her hand. 'I know we don't,' he acknowledged seriously. 'But I'd like to rectify that.'

He reached out and touched her hair. For the second time that day, Eleanor felt as if she'd been struck by a lightning bolt; she imagined her hair sticking out from her head as if she'd been plugged into the mains. She giggled. Nick smiled quizzically and she noticed that one side of his mouth turned up more than the other when he did so, giving him a rather lop-sided grin. She couldn't take her eyes off it.

In the back of her mind a neon sign emblazoned 'Tricky Situation' was flashing on and off. She knew she should leave; she had arranged the advantage; but she was mesmerised.

With his left hand, Nick cupped the back of her skull and drew her gently towards him. He kissed the corners of her mouth and stroked the side of her face with slow, insistent caresses. He drew his lips across her throat, tracing the beating of her pulse with his tongue. She gasped. The notion that this was a most unwise course of action registered just as his mouth came down on hers and the small dissenting voice was silenced.

The raucous cries of dive-bombing seagulls competed with the clamour inside Eleanor's head as she strolled along the dramatic cliff top ramparts early the next morning. She felt as if she were unravelling like a piece of knitting; she needed to gather the dropped stitches and rework her life, incorporating the new pattern. Alongside her, Nick seemed oblivious to her disquiet. Thank goodness for the self-absorption of youth.

They turned towards the Tweed estuary and stood

watching the resident colony of mute swans waddle in comical single file through the mud at the bottom of the harbour wall. She knew how they felt, being sucked under by a quagmire of conflicting emotions, struggling to break the surface.

She shivered. The memory of the previous night was still crystal clear; her willing, even eager, participation had belied her initial uncertainty and Nick's evident enjoyment and wholehearted dedication to her pleasure had been a revelation. She hadn't had such a good time in ages.

'Are you cold?' Nick asked, putting his arm around her shoulders and pulling her close.

She smiled up at him. 'I'm fine,' she said. 'Just thinking about last night.'

'Hmm,' he said. He bent his head and kissed her. 'And this morning?'

'Sorry about …' she murmured.

He hugged her closer. 'Don't worry about it. I told you, it's not a problem. You were upset. I'm a big boy, I can cope.'

A failed relationship, Eleanor reflected, was toxic, polluting everything that came afterwards like a noxious gas. The combined effect of *two* failed relationships just didn't bear thinking about. She'd felt exposed; she hadn't wanted Nick see the hurt she thought she'd buried so successfully. She squirmed with embarrassment, reliving the humiliation of the tears she'd ultimately been unable to prevent.

She was supposed to be the one offering support and guidance, and not of the keep-doing-that-because-it-feels-so-good variety, either, but she couldn't even hold herself together. She felt like two separate people. One wanted to wind the clock back to last night and use the advantage she'd insisted on; the other half wanted to carry on feeling the way she did now: utterly exhilarated.

Oh, get over yourself, she thought irritably; it was only

a shag, for Pete's sake. Live in the moment for a change. She looked up at Nick and smiled. 'OK,' she said. 'It won't happen again.'

'What won't happen again?' he asked cagily.

'The wailing and gnashing of teeth.'

'Thank fuck for that,' he said. 'I thought you meant, you know, the other bit.'

'Oh, more of the other bit,' she pleaded. 'Much more of that.'

'Talking of which, we need to book a room for tonight.'

'Better make that two rooms,' advised Eleanor. 'We don't want tongues to start wagging back at base when our expenses get processed.'

'We'd be saving money,' Nick commented.

'Yes, but not my reputation.'

In the larger of two anonymous rooms in a Travelodge in downtown Edinburgh they watched UK24's 5 o'clock bulletin. There was no news.

'I'm beginning to have my doubts about this,' said Nick.

Eleanor had her doubts too. If the general public weren't spurred into action pretty soon, Julian would be calling a rapid halt to her mini adventure, and she didn't want it to end just yet.

'Chin up,' she encouraged. 'It's the weekend. There might have been sightings but people need to get back home to upload the photos,' she said.

'You're clutching at straws,' Nick said glumly, reading her thoughts. He moved towards the door. 'Let's go and do a recce, then we can grab something to eat.'

'It's always food with you, isn't it?' Eleanor teased.

'Not quite.'

The cathedral was in York Street, in the centre of Edinburgh. There were several approaches but only one main door; it would be easy for them to stake it out from a discreet vantage point.

'If we get there in time for the end of the early service, we can check the departures and stick around for the arrivals for the later one.' Nick advised. 'That way we won't be hanging around for too long trying to look inconspicuous, if anyone spots us.'

'Good idea,' agreed Eleanor, hoping it would be a wasted journey. 'We'll need a cover story, in case we're discovered by the vicar.'

'Priest,' Nick corrected. 'Maybe even a bishop, in this place, but never a vicar.'

'Whatever,' said Eleanor. She was cold and beginning to lose her patience.

'We could tell the truth, I suppose,' said Nick. 'We might even get a lead.'

They didn't have to wait to get any enlightenment from the priest; the UK24 midnight bulletin was very illuminating.

'It's them, I'm sure it is!' Nick exclaimed. He leaned nearer to the television and pointed at the fuzzy image of an elderly couple on the screen. 'Look, you can even see Prince,' he carried on, 'and Eric's got that daft hat on that he always wears when he's on holiday. Looks like a handkerchief knotted at the corners.'

'Are you sure?' Eleanor asked, 'because …'

'I'm positive. Because what?'

'Because if you're right, it's a long way away.'

'I'll get the map, see how far it is.'

Nick's excitement was infectious. Eleanor joined him on the bed as he produced a map from his holdall and turned to the right page. 'Here,' he said emphatically, pointing at the area around Oban. 'They're here at the moment. I bet they're heading for Skye.'

'Or maybe they've already been to Skye,' Eleanor suggested.

'Possibly,' agreed Nick. 'But I've got to make a decision one way or the other, haven't I? At least we know we're in the right country.' He looked at his watch. 'I should get on the road as soon as possible, shouldn't I?'

'You've got to sleep,' Eleanor advised. 'You can't drive through the night.'

Nick looked at her carefully. 'Do I take it that you're not coming with me?'

Eleanor sighed. 'I'd love to, Nick, but it's too far. I've got to get back. I can't be with you all the time, much as I'd like to be.'

'Typical. God never closes a door, but that he shuts a window,' he moaned. He pulled her towards him. 'In that case, get your arse over here. There's something you need to know.' He kissed her deeply. 'I'm missing you already,' he murmured. 'Will you come back soon?'

'As soon as humanly possible,' Eleanor replied. 'I promise.'

He began to undress her. 'I've got a long drive tomorrow,' he said, 'so I'd better get a good night's sleep. I only know one way to make sure of that.'

'What's that?' she asked as she pulled urgently at his belt and tugged his jeans over his hips. 'Anything I can help with?'

'Oh yes,' Nick breathed. 'Plenty.'

He wrestled her out of several layers of outer clothing until she lay beneath him in her underwear. Thank God she'd had the presence of mind to put on some nice lingerie, she thought. Those comfortable big pants would never have done.

Chapter Sixteen

A dense fog had descended over northern England by the time Eleanor crossed the border on her way back to London. It mirrored her mood. As she drove she was beset by doubts. Common sense swooped in, exposing myriad misgivings and insecurities that refused to be calmed.

That's the end of that, she told herself. He won't want me hanging around; I'm far too old for him. It won't go any further. By the time the Angel of the North loomed eerily out of the mist she was convinced that she'd get back to London and never hear from Nick again, that he would ask the newsdesk to send someone else when he finally tracked his grandparents down.

However, she reflected, she hadn't thought about Daniel once in the past two days.

She pulled into the next service area for a much-needed coffee and sticky bun. Rather than take them back to the car and continue driving she found a table near a window and opened her mobile.

'How're you doing?' she asked when Sam answered.

'Bored,' replied Sam. 'Are you doing anything tonight? Shall I come round?'

'I'm still up north,' said Eleanor. 'I've got a long way to go, but I should be back by eight-ish. You'll have to cook, or we can get a takeaway.'

'Takeaway it is then. You're not at work tomorrow, are you?'

'No. Not until Thursday. I can have a lie in tomorrow.'

'Are you OK? You sound a bit iffy.'

'I'm fine,' Eleanor assured her. 'Look, I'd better get back on the road now. See you later.'

Sam was sitting on the doorstep examining the takeaway menu from the local Indian restaurant when Eleanor pulled up, miraculously, into a parking space that wasn't three streets away.

'Why didn't you let yourself in?' Eleanor asked.

'Wrong handbag.' Sam always kept Eleanor's key separate from her own, so that, if she were to lose the key to her own front door, she'd always have somewhere else to crash.

As Eleanor unlocked the door, Mabel came hurtling down the stairs and wrapped herself around her legs in an ecstatic welcome.

'You'd think I'd been gone three weeks, not three days,' Eleanor said as she bent to stroke the purring cat. 'Let's go and get you a treat.' She led the way into the kitchen and made for the fridge. 'What're we going to have?' she asked Sam, gesturing at the menu. 'I haven't had anything to eat since ten o'clock this morning.' She pulled out a bottle. 'White wine?' she asked. 'Or beer, as it's a curry?'

'Wine,' said Sam. 'I'll pour, you choose.'

By the time the food arrived Eleanor was well into a blow-by-blow account of the previous two nights' events.

'I'm impressed,' Sam said. 'You made your move pretty quickly, for an old-timer.'

'Thanks for that,' said Eleanor dryly. 'But you're nearer the truth than you realise.'

'What's wrong?' Sam had a way of seeing right to the heart of Eleanor's problems. 'What aren't you telling me?'

'Well,' Eleanor paused. Sam would think she was being stupid. 'He's too young, I know he is.'

'And?' Sam shook her head in derision. 'He's young. So what? He's not too young. Too young would be seventeen or thereabouts. Didn't you say Nick was twenty-two, twenty-three?'

'Yes, twenty-three but …' There was no escaping

Sam's gimlet stare. 'Look, I'll give you a for instance. We watched a bit of television, in the hotel.'

'That's exciting,' said Sam. 'Shit. You are getting old.'

'We were choosing what to watch,' Eleanor continued. 'He said *Friends* and I said *Frasier*. Simultaneously. It was quite funny, actually.'

'Sounds it,' Sam said sarcastically. 'So, what's the problem?'

'Don't you see? It shows the gulf between us. I'm just not right for him. He wants comedy, I want something a bit more cerebral.'

Sam took an exasperated bite of naan bread. 'Oh, for fuck's sake, have you swallowed a psychology manual or something? There is a bit of middle ground here. Why can't you just enjoy the moment?'

'That's what I thought this morning,' Eleanor said. 'I hadn't thought about Daniel all the time I was with Nick, but I've had a lot of time to think, driving back.'

'That's always been your trouble,' Sam lectured. 'Too much thinking and thoughting. You know, El, it can get in the way of an awful lot of fun.'

'I know, I know.'

Sam was relentless. 'You went through all this psychobabble nonsense with Daniel, remember, and look where that got you. You have got to loosen up.'

'There was Toby in between,' Eleanor protested weakly.

'Ha! Wanker,' Sam retorted. 'What a waste of space he turned out to be, but you wouldn't listen would you? Oh no, Eleanor knows best.' She shook her head. 'You should be binding Nick to your breast with hoops of steel, just for the change of pace!'

'You're right!' Eleanor cried, as if a great weight had been lifted from her shoulders. 'I just need to relax. Stop all this bloody analysing. Just *enjoy*.'

She picked up her glass.

'To Nick,' she toasted. 'To being just what I need!'

'At last,' said Sam dryly. 'Pour me another glass of that delicious plonk.' She gestured at the uneaten food. 'D'you want another pakora?'

When her mobile rang, Eleanor snatched it up and looked at the number.

'Hello? *It's Nick*,' she mouthed at Sam. She took a gulp of wine and pointed to the kitchen. '*Better reception.*'

She was glowing when she came back.

'He's at the Skye bridge,' she reported. 'Asking round and showing photographs. No one's admitting to having seen the Pagets yet, though.'

'Is he going across?'

'Tomorrow.' Eleanor nodded. 'He'll stay on the mainland tonight and nip over in the morning. He sounds quite excited.'

'Did he whisper any little endearments?' Sam teased. 'Protest undying love?'

'Almost,' countered Eleanor. 'He's rather serious, which is a bit of a worry.'

'Now what did I just say, Eleanor?'

Eleanor pulled a face. 'Yes, Miss. Live for the moment. More curry?'

In his small, glass-fronted office at the back of the newsroom, Julian was pacing back and forth, gesticulating like a demented puppet. The door was firmly closed, unusually, and for a moment Eleanor hovered outside trying to catch his eye. The muffled curses and thunderous expression made her think again; better to make a tactical withdrawal and live to fight another day. She moved back to her desk, pitying the poor sod getting the benefit of Julian's speakerphone invective.

'What's going on in there?' She nodded towards Julian's office.

Ashok shook his head. 'He's been like that all week.

Came in like it on Monday morning, yelling at everyone.'

'He's not usually quite so bad-tempered. What's the matter with him?'

'Who knows? We've all got our opinions,' he added darkly. 'Anyway, best not bother him until he's calmed down, would be my advice.'

'Thanks for the tip,' said Eleanor. 'Honestly, you go away for a couple of days ...'

'How'd it go, by the way?' Ashok asked. 'On the road? Has Nick caught up with the oldies yet?'

'Well,' Eleanor started, 'he's had some sightings and now he's on the west coast of –'

'Eleanor!' Julian's voice boomed across the newsroom.

She jumped. 'Such lovely manners,' she whispered to Ashok. 'I wouldn't be surprised if they heard that on-air.' She picked up a pad and pen. 'Into the valley of death ...'

'Close the door,' Julian snapped as Eleanor approached his desk. 'Sit.'

She perched obediently on the only chair not covered with piles of papers, files, and magazines and waited as Julian turned his attention back to his screen and continued typing. She noticed that his hands were shaking as he pecked clumsily at his keyboard.

He punched *Enter* with an impatient flourish and swivelled round. For a moment he looked at her as if he was seeing her for the first time. 'What're you doing here?' he asked eventually. 'Why aren't you in bonny Scotland minding your protégé?'

'But you –' Eleanor was startled. 'I ... I rang the newsdesk ... Everyone knew I was coming back.'

Julian glared at her, eyebrows raised, with his I've-got-all-day-it's-your-time-we're-wasting expression, and Eleanor jumped in to fill the silence.

'I just thought it was too far,' she mumbled.

'Too far from where?'

'We were in Edinburgh. I thought ...'

'God preserve us from people who think,' Julian mocked. 'I ask you to do a simple job and you fuck it up.'

She stared at him. 'I haven't fucked it up,' she protested. 'Before I went you told me I could only be away for a couple of days. When the Pagets were sighted on the west coast, I thought it was too far; I'd be away too long.' She paused, her stomach clenching. 'Has something happened?'

'How would we know?' Julian sneered. 'There's been no contact.'

Eleanor was getting exasperated. Everyone knew that Nick was touring the Western Isles, most probably outside the reach of modern technology. She glanced across the newsroom uncertainly.

'Nick told the newsdesk where he was going before he set off. I'm sure he did. He knew there'd be no mobile reception or internet connection out there in the boonies.' She remembered the last phone call they'd shared before Nick had put himself beyond communication. 'He said –'

'Has he never heard of landlines?' Julian interrupted. 'Couldn't he find a telephone kiosk? He's not camping out in a sodding tent – doesn't the hotel have a bloody phone, or didn't he think to ask?' He blew out a long exasperated breath. 'Kids today. Jesus Christ.' He moved to the door and bellowed across the newsroom. 'Let's see what the newsdesk has to say, shall we?'

At the sound of his name, Ashok leapt from his seat like a greyhound from a starting trap.

'Yes, boss?' he asked as he bounded into Julian's office.

'What's all this about Nick phoning you guys with his whereabouts?' Julian asked in the scornful tone of one who already knew the answer.

'Yes.' Ashok nodded with short-lived relief. 'He rang on Sunday evening and again on Monday morning, telling us he'd be out of range for a couple of days. He planned to sleep in the van and keep moving as much as possible.' He looked from Julian to Eleanor. 'Why, is something wrong?'

Julian's eyed bulged comically. 'And why did no one think to tell me?'

Ashok seemed to be debating the best response. 'Er, I'm pretty sure you were told, Julian,' he ventured. 'But it's in the diary. I put it there myself …' he tailed off.

Julian shuffled some papers around his desk and uncovered his mouse. He began scrolling through the electronic diary on his screen. 'Right. Well, that's all as it should be.' He looked up. 'You still here?' he grunted, waving them out of his office. 'Get out, get out. There must be something you should be doing.'

As they turned to leave Julian called Eleanor back. 'Hang on a minute. There's something I forgot to tell you. About your screen test. We've decided to change the whole look of our presentation, go for a bit more gravitas, you know? So we won't be needing you after all. Thanks anyway.' He dismissed her with a perfunctory nod.

Dodged a bullet there, she thought as she backed out of the office and joined Ashok safely outside projectile distance.

'What was that all about?' she asked. 'He's acting like a lunatic. I thought he was going to throw something at us.'

'Belle reckons he's got early-onset Alzheimer's,' Ashok sniggered. 'But I'd say he was suffering withdrawal symptoms.'

This was interesting. 'What from, though?' Eleanor wondered.

'Usual suspects – girlfriend, drink, drugs. I'd say it was drink.'

Eleanor stared at him. 'Really?'

Ashok nodded. 'Oh yeah,' he said knowledgeably. 'Classic symptoms of man's inner struggle: mood swings, explosive temper, forgetting stuff, feeling like he's being excluded, general paranoia … I could go on.'

'It would explain that little outburst,' Eleanor agreed.

'He hasn't been down the pub with us this week,' Ashok added. 'And that's raised a couple of eyebrows. Foreign Desk's running a book on how long he'll last.'

'That's a horrible thing to do. Poor man.' She grinned. 'I'll have a fiver on two weeks.'

Chapter Seventeen

Belle wasn't in character today. Eleanor didn't know how she kept it up so regularly, and a day off was only to be expected. Belle was wearing a perfectly ordinary pair of jeans, a linen jacket the colour of dried apricots, and pink Converse trainers. She was busy rattling her keyboard when Eleanor approached the Forward Planning desk. 'So, how's our friend in the north?' Belle asked.

'Nothing doing at the moment,' Eleanor replied. 'After that first sighting, Nick's on a tour of the islands off the west coast. He should be back within shouting distance sometime today. Nothing else come in?'

Ashok nodded towards Belle. 'Meg Ryan's on the case. She's got all the info.'

Eleanor frowned. 'Meg Ryan? Can't see it myself.'

'Come and look at this, Eleanor!' Meg's alter ego was beckoning her over to her computer. 'See?' She was poking the screen with a long fingernail. 'It looks like them, doesn't it?'

Eleanor leaned closer. 'Bloody hell. It *is* them,' she whispered. 'And Prince as well. Where are they?'

Belle peered at the caption. 'Kilmarnock.' She squealed with excitement. 'Oh, here's another one. This one's in Dumfries.'

'Get Nick on the phone,' Eleanor instructed. 'They're heading south. Is there anything in the emails, Belle? Has anyone approached them yet, told them about the search?'

Belle tapped a few keys and quickly scanned the accumulated emails. 'Everyone's keeping their distance at the moment,' she said. 'But that will only last so long. Eventually someone will just have to say something.'

'That's what I'm afraid of,' said Eleanor. 'I need to talk this through with Julian again.' She glanced towards his office; the door was firmly closed again. 'But maybe later.'

'They're coming in thick and fast now,' cried Belle. 'Is there some sort of oldies convention going on in Cumbria? They're all snapping away in Carlisle. I'll organise them properly so Nick can see them when he logs on again.' She started rapidly manipulating the images. 'Are you going to meet him somewhere?'

Eleanor looked across at Julian, who was talking to a pretty young woman in a corner of the newsroom. Actually he was talking *at* her, in that aggressive manner some people adopt when they're trying to intimidate. He was succeeding, Eleanor thought, as she watched the woman back towards the wall, effectively trapping herself. She wasn't looking forward to having to speak to him. 'I'll have to see what Julian has to say,' she said. 'Maybe later this week, when we see if Nick's catching them up.'

Ashok handed her the telephone. 'Nick for you.'

Having left the Western Isles, Nick was speeding through Scotland. 'It was a waste of time doing all those islands,' he moaned. 'All that coastline. I've lost so much time.'

'It's not your fault,' Eleanor reassured him. 'You were following your instincts. Where are you now?'

'Midway between Kilmarnock and Dumfries, on the A76. It's very slow. Lots of farm traffic. I'm going as fast as I can, but I won't catch them today.'

'Of course not. And you've got to rest.'

'No time. I'll grab something to eat, then I'll be on my way again.'

'Nick,' Eleanor lectured. 'You have to rest. Your grandparents aren't chasing around, they're taking a leisurely trip. You'll catch up.'

'Yes, I know, but time's running out, don't forget.'

Eleanor felt ashamed. It was easy to forget how important this pursuit was to Nick. 'Yes, of course,' she said. 'I'm sorry for being so insensitive.'

'And I've got to shoot another report,' Nick added. He sounded harassed. 'When are you coming up again? I miss you.'

She laughed. 'It's only been two days. I'll speak to Julian and get up as soon as I can, hopefully by the weekend.'

'I could just lie, of course,' Nick said. 'Tell you I've spotted them. You'd have to come then, wouldn't you?'

'I would,' Eleanor agreed. 'But I'd never trust you again, so it wouldn't be worth it.'

'Suppose not. Come soon though, won't you? It gets very cold up here at night. I need you to keep me warm.'

Eleanor had a vision of the two of them wrapped round each other, bathed in sweat, panting. She looked round, hoping no one had seen the blush creep up her neck and colour her cheeks. She giggled nervously. 'I'll see what I can do.'

Julian was surprisingly approachable when Eleanor finally plucked up the courage to ask permission to go after Nick. It was nearing the end of the shift and he seemed to have regained control of his volatile temper as the day had gone on.

'Just watch this,' he said, waving her into his office and gesturing towards the TV screen mounted on the wall. 'An object lesson in how not to conduct an interview. We should use it in one of our training sessions.'

He was talking about Heather Bailey, the young new recruit he'd been talking to in the newsroom that morning. 'This is her first attempt at a two-way. She's covering that fraud case. But Susan is a grade A bitch,' said Julian. 'Never gives anyone a break, particularly if she's female.'

'She's just jealous,' said Eleanor, listening closely to

the two-way. 'Did you hear that ridiculous question? Susan's covered every point. She's not leaving Heather anything to say.'

The reporter was staring blankly out of the screen. Her mouth opened and closed silently, goldfishing, until eventually she shook her head and put her hand to her ear.

'Good thinking,' said Julian. 'Blame the equipment.'

'I'm sorry,' Heather was saying, 'I can't hear you. The link must have gone down.' Heather disappeared from the screen and Susan went smoothly on to other news.

'Well, she won't be on-air again for a while,' predicted Julian. 'She needs a bit more training. That's if we let her carry on. She might get the DCM.'

'DCM?'

'The Don't Come Monday,' Julian explained. 'The *I don't know how we'll manage without you, but come Monday, we're going to give it a try* award.'

Eleanor thought back to her screen test and how difficult it had been just reading some lines from the autocue, never mind having to answer questions that had been deliberately designed to confuse. She was glad that Julian had decided she wasn't fit for the job, after all.

'It was a bit of a baptism of fire,' she said.

'Give over,' Julian laughed nastily. 'If you can't stand the heat ...' He pressed the mute button on the remote control. 'Anyway, what can I do for you?'

Eleanor gathered her nerve, reassured by Julian's chatty demeanour. 'I think Nick is closing in on the Pagets,' she said. 'I'd like to join him in Cumbria, if that's OK.'

'Cumbria? I thought he was in Scotland.'

Eleanor neatly side-stepped a re-run of their previous conversation about Nick's whereabouts. 'He was, this morning,' she said diplomatically, 'but there've been lots of sightings further south, just today. He's on his way there now. I'm sure he'll catch up soon.'

'Hmm,' muttered Julian. 'I'm not happy about the

timescales here. I thought Nick would've found them by now. What's he dragging his feet for?'

'He's only going where there've been sightings,' Eleanor protested. 'And there've been lots,' she repeated. 'Which is why I'd like to go and join him. I think we're getting to the end game, Julian,' she added.

Julian seemed to cave in suddenly. 'OK. I suppose you should, then. What's today?'

'Thursday.'

'I suppose we could do without you from tomorrow evening,' Julian continued. 'It's usually quieter at the weekend. And we need to keep on top of this. It's a long way,' he added. 'Spend the weekend. Hopefully you'll have something positive to tell me by Monday.'

Gee thanks, Eleanor thought. He made it sound like he was doing her a favour, but it was hardly a grand gesture; it would take most of Saturday getting up there and most of Sunday getting back. Never mind, at least she'd get to see Nick again. She could set off early, save some time. She skipped smartly out of the office before Julian could change his mind.

Mabel was perched on the top of a chest of drawers, looking like an enormous porcelain ornament and emitting disdain in waves. She watched as Eleanor gathered clothes and toiletries and threw them into an overnight bag on the bed. Eleanor paused only long enough to consider her choice of underwear. 'What d'you think, Mabes?' she asked the cat, holding up various sets of bras and knickers in an array of colours. 'This is very important. The pink, or the purple? Or the blue?' She held up a set the colour of sunshine. 'What about yellow? They're quite nice.'

If Mabel had an opinion, she was keeping her own counsel.

Eleanor had been tingling with anticipation ever since Julian had given her the go-ahead. She couldn't wait to see

Nick again and she was setting off at stupid o'clock on Saturday morning to make the most of the empty roads. 'Sorry, Puss,' she said as she zipped up the bag and pulled it off the bed. 'I'm off again.' She was almost hugging herself with delight. 'Back Sunday night. I'll bring you a treat. Promise.'

By the time she joined it at Spaghetti Junction, the M6 was clogged with traffic and Eleanor opted to pay the toll and skirt round the worst that a Birmingham weekend could offer. She'd arranged to meet Nick in Kendal, where they'd shoot another instalment of the pursuit.

The Doric Imperative seemed to be finally engaging with the public. Belle had told her that morning that Nick's last report had attracted a lot of attention and there'd been multiple sightings of the couple sent in overnight. Mobile phone footage and photographs had featured in all the UK24 news bulletins since yesterday and a couple of the red-tops and a glossy magazine had been making enquiries, giving Julian much to crow about. Money had started to flow in and a charitable fund had been set up in the Pagets' name.

So why hadn't they been intercepted yet? The English at large weren't usually so reticent. How did Nick keep missing them? The question was still puzzling Eleanor when she arrived at the designated meeting spot.

She eventually caught up with Nick, wandering round the ruins of Kendal Castle. He was munching a block of Mint Cake. He grimaced as she approached.

'Never had this before. It's making my teeth hurt, it's so sweet.'

'It's supposed to be. Lots of sucrose to sustain you through the rigours of one of those walks in that book by ... by ... can't remember.'

'Wainwright,' Nick supplied. He took her in his arms and kissed her. 'I'm so glad you're here,' he whispered. 'I've missed you so much.'

'Where are we staying?' Eleanor asked eagerly.

'Get straight to the point, why don't you?' he laughed. 'I remembered the rules and I've booked a couple of rooms at a B&B in Crook. It's a few miles up the road, near Windermere.'

'I know,' she said. 'I grew up not far from here.'

'Really? Where?'

'Skipton. A bit further south and east.'

'Oh. You never told me. Does your family still live there?'

'Mum and Dad, yes.'

'Maybe I can meet them sometime?' Nick suggested.

'Yes, well, I'll have to think about that,' Eleanor prevaricated. I don't think I'm ready for that just yet, she thought. 'Anyway, have you seen enough ruins? Shall we get back to the digs and sort out some food?'

'Mrs Johnson says she'll make us an evening meal,' said Nick. 'Save us having to go anywhere tonight. We've both driven miles today.'

'Excellent.' Eleanor was relieved. 'And we can look over all the new info later.'

'There's other stuff I want to look over too,' said Nick, hugging her close.

Again she thanked God she'd remembered to bring some decent underwear.

Chapter Eighteen

'I think we deserve a day off,' Nick suggested over a huge dinner of roast beef and all the trimmings.

'Why would we want to do that?' Eleanor asked, puzzled. 'Don't you feel the thrill of the chase? We're closing in. I thought you were worried about them. There'll be plenty of time for a day off when we've caught up with your grandparents.'

'Well, I, er ...' Nick prevaricated. 'You were the one who suggested some time out.'

'Only because –'

'Never mind,' he snapped, shaking his head. 'I just thought it'd be nice to spend some time together. You know, rather than haring about the countryside like crusaders after the Holy Grail.'

Mrs Johnson bustled in at that moment and stared clearing the table. 'Everything all right, dears?' she asked. 'Would you like some pudding? I've got some lovely –'

'No, thank you,' Eleanor interrupted. 'We're absolutely stuffed.' She smiled at Mrs Johnson. 'It was delicious.' She waited until the woman had left the room. 'I don't understand you,' she said. 'This *is* the Holy Grail. Well, yours, anyway. This could make your name, Nick. You know some of the dailies have been asking questions, don't you? After this, you'll be set up.'

'Only if we get the right outcome.'

'Which is why we can't relax yet.'

'It might be all for nothing,' he carried on. 'What if we're too late?'

'You're contradicting yourself, Nick.'

'I know, I know. Sorry.' Nick looked shamefaced. 'I'm

just tired. Forget I said anything.' He took her hand across the table and stroked her fingers. 'I just want to spend as much time with you as possible.'

Despite her irritation, Eleanor glowed. 'I know,' she said, looking at him, wide-eyed, and putting an ironic hand to her forehead. 'I've always had that effect on men. It's been the bane of my life.' She got up from the table. No point beating about the bush. 'Shall we retire?'

The plan was to check out any overnight sightings in the morning and head off in whatever direction they suggested.

'Actually, Gran and Pops might want to hang around here a bit,' Nick said as they climbed the stairs. 'Plenty of scenery to take in. I don't think they'll be in much of a hurry to leave, do you?'

'You might be right,' Eleanor agreed. 'No point in just whizzing through such dramatic countryside. They're not actually on their way anywhere, are they?'

'Er, no ...' Nick chewed his lip thoughtfully. 'We'll probably have to head back the way I came. I wonder why they've come so far south. The Lakes are all north of here.'

'I didn't know they had,' said Eleanor. 'I thought the last video of them was in Carlisle.'

'No, it wasn't, it was ...' Nick stopped. He frowned at Eleanor. 'I thought ... Well, never mind. Neither of them has a very good sense of direction,' he added dryly. 'Unlike me.' He stopped outside his room. 'You're upstairs, in the eaves. I'll give you five minutes to make yourself indecent, then I'm coming up.'

'Make it ten,' she pleaded. 'And don't make a noise.'

The room was small and beautifully decorated to make the most of the stunning view but the bed was wedged between the rafters in the only available space. It was slightly claustrophobic and Eleanor thought Nick would be bound to bang his head.

She spent a few minutes freshening up in the tiny en-suite bathroom then sat down on the bed with the laptop. She wanted to check Eric and Dora's latest whereabouts; something about Nick's itinerary didn't quite chime, but she couldn't put her finger on what was wrong. But she didn't have time to log on before there was a faint knock on the door and Nick blundered in, almost knocking himself out on a beam.

'Fuck's sake –' He clapped a hand over his mouth. 'Sorry.' He rubbed his head. 'That really hurt.'

'Where there's no sense, there's no feeling,' said Eleanor, laughing. 'Come over here and I'll kiss it better. And be quiet. You'll have Mrs Johnson running up those stairs, wondering what's going on. She looks the sort to be totally against any impropriety.'

'Oh, that's what we're calling it tonight, is it? Impropriety?' Nick grinned at her as he settled on the bed beside her. 'Well, I'm happy to be as improper as you like.'

Eleanor muffled a shriek as he pulled her toward him. He tugged impatiently at her clothes until a small heap the colour of sunshine lay discarded on the floor.

He hadn't even noticed.

When they checked the laptop in the morning they discovered that Eric and Dora had indeed gone to ground. There had been no more sightings since the previous day.

'I'm starting to get worried,' Nick said, 'Anything could have happened. You don't think –?'

'No, I don't,' Eleanor reassured him. 'They looked perfectly fit and healthy in all the videos we've had.'

Nick had a sudden flash of inspiration. 'We should check out the church,' he said. 'The Catholic one's Holy Trinity and St George. You never know, it is Sunday.'

'Of course!' exclaimed Eleanor, feeling stupid. 'Why didn't I think of that?'

'Not the religious sort, are you?' Nick declared. 'Doesn't come naturally to heathens like you.'

'What times are the services?'

Nick checked the time on his mobile phone. 'We might catch the tail end of the early Mass if go now.' He pulled a mournful face. 'We'd miss breakfast, though.'

'Never mind that,' said Eleanor, picking up the camera. 'Duty calls. Come on.'

It was a disappointing turnout. Only a small trickle of worshippers filed out of the church at nine o'clock.

'Next one's at 11 a.m.,' said Nick. 'We could go back to Mrs Johnson's and have that breakfast,' he added hopefully.

But the later service yielded no better results.

'I can't believe it,' said Nick as they sat under a huge oak in the churchyard and counted everyone out. 'I was so sure they'd be around here.'

'They probably are,' said Eleanor. She glanced at Nick's frustrated expression. 'We just chose the wrong town, or the wrong church. Don't forget the Lakes cover a huge area, and we've got the old reception problem, too. That might be why the sightings have dried up.' A thought struck her. 'Are Eric and Dora walkers?'

Nick shook his head. 'Not that I know of, but you never know. Some of the fells are quite gentle, aren't they? They might have taken it up.'

'And the weather's very good.' Eleanor made a decision. 'There's nothing else for it, Nick, you'll just have to stay here until they resurface. There's no point in you setting off when we don't know where they're headed.'

'No, I suppose not.'

'So, I think you should stay another night at least with Mrs Johnson.'

Nick's eyes lit up. 'Will you stay with me?' he asked, encircling her waist and pulling her in for a kiss.

'No, I can't,' she said, kissing him back. 'Julian wants me back in London tomorrow to give him my report.' She shrugged. 'He's acting a bit strange lately and I don't want to antagonise him too much. There's no telling what he might do.'

'I didn't think he was that bad,' said Nick. 'He's always seemed quite reasonable when I've met him.'

'Yes, but that was then,' Eleanor said. 'This is now.'

'So you can't spare another night for some more impropriety, then?'

Eleanor was torn. She briefly considered staying the night and leaving ridiculously early. She dismissed that stupid idea out of hand; she'd rather not stay at all than have to get up before the sun again.

'Sorry,' she said. 'You don't know how much I'd love to, but … you know how it is. I can make myself useful before I go, though,' she added. 'Have you written your piece yet?'

'No, not yet. I wanted to wait until we had a sighting. Why? Are you going to write it for me?'

'No, you make a good job of it yourself, and besides, if I wrote it, it would change the tone. The viewers like what you've done so far, so why change?'

'So how're you going to help?'

Eleanor got up and brushed leaves from her jacket. 'This way,' she beckoned. 'Your public needs you. I know the perfect spot.'

They walked back to the castle ruins and, with Eleanor holding the camera and a distant view of Lake Windermere behind him, Nick recorded his piece to camera.

Eleanor decided to make a slight detour on the way home. If she stopped off in the Dales, she could catch up with her parents and avoid the worst of the Sunday evening mass exodus back to London. She wouldn't get home until very late, but that would be less tiring than sitting in a traffic jam for several hours. She picked up her mobile and found her mother's number.

'Hi Mum,' she said. 'I'm in the area, briefly. Fancy meeting up?'

For a Sunday afternoon, the high street in Skipton was unexpectedly crowded as mother and daughter pushed their way to the edge of the pavement and waited impatiently for the little man to turn green.

'Can we grab a drink now, please?' asked Eleanor, as they crossed the road. 'My feet are killing me.'

'There's that nice little café just down there.' Sylvia gestured with her head. 'We could go there if you like.'

'Anywhere. I just need to take the weight off.'

They settled at a table in the window of the quaint little tearoom.

'Should never have worn these today,' Eleanor moaned, stretching a foot out in front of her and twisting it back and forth admiringly. 'Lovely shoes though, aren't they?'

'Lovely indeed, darling,' agreed Sylvia, looking up from the menu. 'What would you like? A selection of cakes and a pot of tea?'

'Fine,' said Eleanor, kicking the lovely shoes to the floor. 'I never eat cake at home,' she observed as a bored waitress wandered over and took their orders.

'Neither do I,' said Sylvia mournfully. 'I bake lots for your dad, though. He loves it, but he won't let me eat any of it. Says it's for my own good. I put weight on so easily now.'

'How do you live with such a tyrant?'

'Only joking, darling,' said Sylvia, smiling thinly.

Eleanor glanced idly out of the window as her mother applied herself to an enormous slice of Victoria sponge. The traffic had ground to a halt and she looked into the window of the nearest car. She blinked. Can't be, she thought. Must be his doppelganger. As she watched, the driver leaned across to his passenger and pulled her into a passionate embrace. Eleanor stared after the car as it began to move away. The passenger was almost as familiar as the driver.

'What's up, darling?' asked Sylvia, a forkful of cake half way to her mouth. 'You look like you've seen a ghost.'

'I, er, I... nothing. Just someone I thought I recognised.' She shook her head. 'Couldn't be, though.' She lapsed into a thoughtful silence as she watched Sylvia run a damp finger round her plate, picking up the dusting of icing sugar.

Chapter Nineteen

There was a mild panic in progress when Eleanor arrived at work the next morning. The news output was showing a live shot of a tower block that was destined to be demolished within a few minutes but the director in the gallery was getting twitchy; there was a distinct lack of interesting action.

'What's going on?' Eleanor asked as she logged on.

'This building is going to be blown up soon,' supplied Ashok, nodding towards a monitor. 'We're debating whether to ask the viewers to phone in to say whether they would prefer us to wait for the explosion, or go on to something else.'

'What, television by democracy?'

'Yes, that sort of thing.'

'That would never work,' Eleanor snorted. 'We work in a dictatorship. Ask Julian. Anyway, look.' She pointed towards the screen as the building in question disintegrated in spectacular fashion. 'Worth a few boring minutes, wasn't it?'

'I've been looking for you.'

Eleanor spun round as Paul Fitzgerald, senior reporter from the Foreign Desk put a comradely arm round her shoulder. Paul wasn't around the newsroom very much; he was always out of the country on some jaunt or another and Eleanor didn't know him very well – certainly not well enough for this level of familiarity.

'I've just got back from Frankfurt,' he said. 'I met a friend of yours,' he added knowingly.

For a moment Eleanor was nonplussed. She didn't know anyone in Frankfurt.

'Dan,' Paul carried on. 'Dan Hardwick? Works for *The Post*?'

Eleanor's stomach flipped at the mention of Daniel's name. 'Oh yes, I know Dan. Sorry, I didn't twig straight away – couldn't think who you were talking about.'

'Yes, well, he speaks very highly of you, too,' Paul added sarcastically. He raised an eyebrow. 'Very highly. I got the impression that there was a bit of a shared past …?'

Eleanor had no intention of discussing any shared pasts she might have with Paul. 'No, no shared anything,' she said dismissively. 'You must have got your wires crossed.'

Paul shrugged. 'Doesn't matter. None of my business, anyway. Just thought I'd mention it.' He turned to go. 'Dan seemed rather impatient to be getting back. Can't think why.'

Eleanor had no time to reflect on the comment; Julian had appeared at his window and was beckoning at her, telephone clamped to his ear. He ended the call when she came in.

'Britney,' he explained. 'She gives great phone. Anyway, what news?'

'Not much, I'm afraid,' Eleanor admitted. 'Everything was pointing towards them being in the Lake District, but wherever we went, they weren't there. I don't understand it, really.'

'Well, if they're not found soon, I'll have to call it all off,' Julian warned.

'But –'

He held up a hand to stem her protests. 'We can't carry on like this, Eleanor,' he said. 'End of the week, then that's it.'

She knew it was useless to argue but she had to try. 'Monday?' she pleaded. 'Just give me the weekend to sort things out, please.'

'Monday. 10 a.m. And not an hour longer.'

'Hello? Eleanor?'

She felt a twang of girlish excitement. 'Daniel?'

'Sorry to call you at work, but the landline's the only number I could find,' Daniel said, 'and I couldn't get hold of Grace. Anyway, I couldn't let ... I wanted to ...' He ground to a halt. 'You see, I –'

She swallowed her initial shock at hearing Daniel's voice. 'What's the matter? Has something happened?'

'I wanted to apologise,' he said bluntly. 'For Angie, mainly, but also for me. I should have been firmer.'

Disappointment deflated her. 'What are you talking about?'

'Angie has a habit of speaking before engaging her brain. She gets carried away with an idea and doesn't stop to think about the effects.'

'I'd noticed.'

Daniel hurried on. 'She didn't mean to blurt it out quite so baldly. She was so excited after she heard you sing, but she realises now how bad it must've sounded. She's very sorry.'

Not sorry enough to pick up the phone herself, Eleanor thought. She was silent.

'Hello? Are you still there? El?'

'Yes, I'm still here,' she muttered. 'It's not a problem,'

'It sounds like it is.'

'Look, it's good of you to call. I'll admit I was a bit taken aback at the time, but don't worry about it.'

'I don't want to hassle you into making a rash decision. Take your time and think about it. And I'll completely understand if you don't want to do it; I appreciate how insensitive it is to even ask, but never mind Angie. After hearing you sing again at Grace's party, *I* would really like you to do it,' he added softly.

Her heart felt as if it was being squeezed. 'I'll think about it. I'll let you know when you get back. I hear you're pretty keen.'

'Who told you that?'

'A colleague on the Foreign Desk, Paul Fit –'

'Oh yes, Fitz. I remember; good man. Bit of a stirrer, though.' He hurried on, 'Angie wasn't terribly happy about me coming over here, but I couldn't turn it down. I asked her to come and visit, but she says she's got too much to do with the new flat.'

'I expect she has. There's a lot to organise.' Strange to find herself on this side of the argument. 'Choosing curtains, carpets, all that sort of stuff.'

'Promise me you'll think about the wedding?' There were obviously no limits to an ex-lover's expectations.

She laughed despite herself. 'Give me your mobile number and I'll call you next week. But I warn you, I've got a lot on at the moment – it might not ... I'll think about it, OK? I promise.'

'There's plenty of time. No pressure.'

As Eleanor ended the call she couldn't shift the impression that Daniel didn't want to be the first to hang up.

'Is the hokey cokey *really* what it's all about?' Sam asked. She moved away from the table where she was working and swung her left leg back and forth rhythmically, as if practising at the barre, tapping her foot on the floor in front and behind her. 'I'm serious.'

Sam lived in a small maisonette in Soho, where she designed CD and DVD covers for up and coming musicians as a sideline to her real graphic design job. Her studio, where they were now, was on the upper floor – a chilly room filled with light and colour.

'It's certainly the question uppermost in the nation's mind,' Eleanor agreed.

Sam returned to the table and unscrewed the cap of a tube of acrylic paint. 'I've got nothing in, *quelle surprise*, so we'll have to go out to eat,' she said.

'No problem.'

'I'll just finish this section, so it can dry overnight.'

She bent to the intricate task as Eleanor wandered around. She loved it here, the walls hung with vibrant swatches of colours and patterns in combinations that she wouldn't have considered but which worked so well together.

Sam had a taste for the dramatic, the striking, and the theatrical. No cosy, complementary palettes for her. The clash of the neon citrus colours was almost audible, the union of geometric stripes, spots, and florals a mugging of the senses.

'You're so talented, you know?' Eleanor commented. Sam had passed the occasional reject on to her and the artworks now adorned her own walls, accruing value, or so she liked to think.

'S'pose so,' agreed Sam artlessly. 'Just comes naturally.'

'Bitch,' said Eleanor mildly.

They chose a wine bar just up the street, a favourite of Sam's, where the bar staff were friendly and protective of their regulars. They ordered a bottle of red and claimed a table in the window.

When they were seated Sam leaned forward and said, 'Well, I'm all ears. How's it going with the boy? Tell me all about it.'

Eleanor frowned. 'He's absolutely lovely, but …'

'But what?' asked Sam. 'I thought you were all loved-up.'

'Don't be daft. Nick's great company, and he's very good in bed. But I've got a funny feeling. I think there's something iffy going on, I'm just not sure what.'

Sam took a gulp of wine. 'What? With Nick? Has an old flame come out of the woodwork or something?' She took in Eleanor's serious expression. 'What makes you think something's going on?'

'Nick's been a bit, well, strange lately. At the weekend, he wanted to have a day off and go sightseeing.'

'Nothing wrong with that, is there? I thought you were in the Lakes. Very pretty up there, isn't it?'

'We've nearly caught up with his grandparents, Sam,' Eleanor hissed in exasperation. 'This isn't a good time to be taking a day off.'

'Oh, I see.' Sam nodded. 'You're right. That is odd.'

'I know,' said Eleanor. 'It's very odd. We seem to be closing in on his grandparents, but whenever we get a really good sighting, they either disappear or Nick goes in a completely different direction. The whole thing isn't gathering momentum like it should. I know how these things work, Sam. It should be like a snowball, you know, rolling along, getting bigger all the time. But it isn't. Something's wrong but I just can't put my finger on it.'

'Sounds like they're in this together,' Sam laughed. 'You'd better be careful they're not ...' The words died on her lips.

'Oh. My. God.' Eleanor stared at her friend in horror. 'Tell me I'm imagining this, Sam. Tell me he's not tipping them off.'

Chapter Twenty

'He wouldn't do a thing like that, would he?' Sam asked.

Eleanor stared at her miserably 'I've got absolutely no idea,' she said. The realisation that she didn't know Nick very well at all sent shivers of apprehension tingling up and down her spine. 'It's not something I've ever considered,' she added. 'His credibility never came up before. Everyone was so taken with him; he's so ... so ...'

'Stop right there,' Sam interrupted. 'Let's get this in perspective.' She refilled their glasses and sat back. 'Has something specific happened to make you suspicious?'

'Not really,' Eleanor admitted. 'But the day off thing was a bit strange. Why, when he's closing in on the target, would he want to ease off the chase?'

Sam nodded. 'The only reason for doing that would be ...'

'To give them a chance to get away, I suppose. It's obvious, when you think about it,' Eleanor said finally. 'They're in this together. They must be.'

Sam, the voice of reason, argued the point. 'Hang on,' she said. 'I still don't get the *why* part. We're talking about trying to prevent a pointless suicide here, aren't we?'

'We are,' agreed Eleanor. She laughed bleakly and shook her head. 'I'm so wound up I'd forgotten all about that.'

'Never mind.' Sam dismissed the scruples with a wave of her hand. 'So it's unlikely that Nick would knowingly jeopardise his gran's wellbeing.'

'Well, yes ...'

'Unless,' Sam thought for a moment. 'Nick knows that suicide isn't on the cards because Dora and Eric have known all along about the hospital mix-up.'

Eleanor shook her head. 'But they don't. What do you mean?'

Sam rolled her eyes. 'What if Dora and Eric *do* know?' She folded her arms. 'What if this is all an elaborate set-up?'

'Bloody hell. Do you really think so?'

'Looks that way to me.'

'And they've been in it together, right from the start?'

'Come on, El,' Sam said. 'You're not usually so slow. All this sex must be skewing your judgement.' She snagged a passing waitress and asked for a bowl of olives and some focaccia. 'It's the only explanation.'

'But we could be jumping to the wrong conclusion,' Eleanor argued. 'How, for instance, does Nick make sure that Eric and Dora aren't seen by anyone?'

'That's easy,' snorted Sam. 'Think where they're been – Scotland; the Western Isles; the Lakes. Hardly overcrowded locations, are they? Easy to avoid publicity, I'd have thought. Except when they want it. Then they just come out of hiding long enough to be snapped, to keep the public's interest alive. They probably pose for photos,' she added.

Eleanor rewound the initial appeal in her head. 'And we specifically asked the public not to approach the Pagets when we launched this ... this farce,' she said miserably. 'Nick must be orchestrating their every move. Fuck. What am I going to do?'

'I'd cut his balls off,' Sam replied succinctly. 'But that's up to you. I think you'll have to confront him.' Her eyes lit up playfully. 'Can I come? You'll need some moral support.'

'I can't believe Nick would do something like this,' Eleanor persisted. 'It's all so out of character.'

Sam shrugged. 'I don't know the boy,' she said. 'And actually, neither do you. Not really. How do you know what he's capable of?'

She patted Eleanor's arm. 'You've never been a great judge of character, El, let's face it.'

Eleanor leaned forward. The wine bar was filling up and the general hubbub was making it difficult to hear what Sam was saying. 'But this is could be fraud,' she hissed, ignoring Sam's remark. 'All three of them are involved.'

She thought back to her first conversation with Nick, when he'd been so angry about the family feeling against Eric and Dora; how sad he'd been about his gran's illness and his elation when he'd found the letter from the hospital.

'I feel used,' she said. 'Even all that nonsense about them not having mobile phones; they must have made it all up.'

Sam burst out laughing. 'Sorry ...' she spluttered. 'But you've got to hand it to him El; it's quite clever. The guy's got some nerve ...'

'But for what?' Eleanor demanded. 'A free holiday and some work experience? He'd be mad. No one would touch him with a bargepole if it got out.'

'Personally, I don't think it would matter at all, but anyway, how will it get out?' Sam asked. 'Nick knows that you won't say anything because it could wreck your career. It's your reputation at stake, not his. He's just in it for the crack. And, even if he was exposed, there's no such thing as bad publicity. He'll have his own reality TV programme before you know it.'

Eleanor scowled at her.

'Well, I'm just thinking,' Sam carried on. 'It'd be a rather imaginative thing to put on your CV.'

'What? That you spent the summer filming a pursuit story that wasn't actually a pursuit at all, for a news channel you were conning, and how you managed to stay one step ahead? Get a grip, Sam. Who would believe it?'

Sam sniggered. 'Sounds pretty good to me. A bit of notoriety never hurt anyone, especially if he wants a career in the media. I'd employ him. It shows initiative. And anyway, he's young enough to think it's just a bit of fun. No one's going to get hurt.'

'Except me.'

'Oh yes, sorry, El. I forgot you were ... involved.'

'Never mind the relationship,' Eleanor snapped. 'That was never going to be a lifelong commitment. It's over, anyway, unless he can convince me he's on the level. But what about my sodding career?'

'Hmm,' Sam mused, chewing a piece of bread. 'Is he telling the truth or is this an almighty wind-up?'

'And what about the Pagets in all this?' Eleanor wondered. 'They obviously know what's going on. They must have agreed in the first place.'

'Taken in by their golden grandchild,' supplied Sam. 'From what you've told me, they practically brought him up –'

'To tell right from wrong, hopefully,' interrupted Eleanor.

'They probably think the sun shines out of his –'

'Very possibly,' said Eleanor quickly. 'But it's still fraud. He must have convinced them that there wasn't any risk.'

'He's probably right,' said Sam. 'On the face of it. Who's going to tell?'

'I'll have to talk to Jim. See if he knows what's going on.' Eleanor took an enormous gulp of wine. 'I got to know him quite well during that obesity piece we did. I would've thought he was trustworthy. He's probably completely in the dark ...' She frowned as another unpalatable thought registered. 'And what if another channel started investigating? It's not unheard of, you know. They might speak to the family or friends. We couldn't stop them. I'll have to get to him first. Be discreet ...'

The waitress brought over the tray of bread and olives. Sam exchanged a few pleasantries but waited until she'd moved away before asking Eleanor, 'Is it a big enough story to interest anyone else?'

'I don't know! Oh Christ, Julian's going to kill me,' Eleanor bleated.

'Seriously, what will happen at work? If you turn out to be right, I mean?'

Eleanor shuddered. 'Let's not even think about that before I speak to Nick,' she said miserably. 'There still might be some perfectly logical explanation.'

'You don't really think there is, do you?'

'To be honest, I don't know what I think at this precise moment.'

'Maybe you should talk to someone, someone who isn't connected,' Sam suggested. 'Get some advice.'

'Like who?'

'I was thinking about Daniel,' Sam said. 'He's in the same business. Maybe he'll know what to do.'

'No, no,' said Eleanor shaking her head. 'I can't ask him; he'll say I've been a complete fool to be taken in.'

'You and the rest of UK24.' Sam shrugged. 'Well, it was just a thought,' she added in a placatory voice.

'Anyway, he's in Frankfurt. It's hardly round the corner. I can't just pop round tonight.'

'No. But he won't be there forever, will he?' Sam speared an olive with a toothpick, pointing it at Eleanor. 'Maybe you're right. You need to speak to Nick first, get the whole story.'

'The more we talk about it, the more I think I know the whole story,' said Eleanor resignedly. 'And I'm not going to come out of this very well at all. This will probably be the end of my brilliant career.' She swirled the wine around in her glass. 'What with Julian making sure I'm never going to be a presenter, and now this, I should be looking into an alternative occupation.' She smiled brightly at Sam. 'Anyway, let's talk about something else,' she said. 'I don't want to ruin the rest of the evening moaning about things that might never happen.' She took a sip of wine. 'How's Rob?'

'Rob is ... Rob,' said Sam wistfully. 'Same as ever. Working hard, playing harder.'

'Is that bothering you? He's always been a bit like that, hasn't he?'

'I don't know. He seems to be drawing away from me. Do you know what I mean? It's like he's only giving me half his attention.'

Eleanor raised an eyebrow. She recalled seeing Rob outside the shop in the rain. 'You don't think ...?'

Sam shook her head, 'I honestly don't know. Anyway, I don't want to talk about it. It'll resolve itself soon enough, I'm sure.'

Eleanor knew better then to go on about a subject her friend did not want to pursue. 'No problem.' She paused to eat a couple of olives. 'I've got another shocker to tell you about,' she said eventually.

Sam looked at her in surprise. 'More revelations?'

Eleanor nodded before saying, 'I'm sure I saw my dad out with an old friend on Sunday.'

'What's wrong with that?'

'Remember Tamsin Schofield?'

'What? Tarty Tamsin, that posh piece from school? The one who got that nice Mr Docherty into trouble with her accusations?'

'The very same,' said Eleanor.

'With your dad?' Sam was incredulous. 'Wouldn't have thought she was his type. Or vice versa, come to think about it.'

'Me neither.' Eleanor shook her head. 'They were in a car. Stopped outside the café where Mum and me were having tea and cake. Snogged her right there in front of me.'

'In the town where he lives?' Sam was aghast. 'Jesus, what a daft thing to do. Anybody could have seen him.'

'They did,' Eleanor reminded her.

'Maybe he wants to get caught. That's what they say, isn't it? Did he realise he was being watched?'

'No, thank God.' Eleanor cringed. 'How embarrassing would that have been? Luckily Mum had her back to the window, so she didn't see. It'll kill her if she ever finds out,' she added miserably.

Sam eyed her suspiciously. 'What d'you mean *if*?' she asked. 'Surely you're going to tell her?'

'I don't know what to do for the best,' said Eleanor. 'Mum seems to have turned a corner lately. She's on the HRT, she looked fabulous yesterday. I don't know what it'll do to her. Dad's convinced her that he's changed.'

'Well, that never happens,' Sam said cynically. 'But look at it from her point of view. How do you think she'll feel when she eventually finds out, and discovers that you knew all along? She'll feel doubly betrayed, and humiliated. She'll hate you.'

'What is this, Devil's Advocate evening?' Eleanor asked. 'She'll hate me if I tell her, as well,' she echoed. 'Oh shit, what shall I do?'

'Tell her,' said Sam. 'You'll probably be surprised at her reaction. If I know your mum, she'll have a good inkling anyway. She always has done. And besides, what doesn't kill her will make her strong.'

'I suppose you're right.'

'I am,' Sam said, in a let's-close-the-subject tone of voice. She leaned across the table to pick up the empty bottle. 'Shall I get another?' As she turned to signal to the bar staff her hand froze in mid-air. 'Hey,' she whispered, nodding towards the street outside. 'Is that who I think it is?'

Eleanor followed her gaze. It was all a blur until the

throng parted for a moment, revealing two figures walking arm in arm on the opposite pavement, oblivious to the passing multitude. She stared, open-mouthed. It couldn't be, surely?

Chapter Twenty-one

On the opposite side of the street, Angie Gold and a tall, good-looking stranger stopped and gazed at each other as if there was no one else in the entire world.

'Who's he, I wonder?' Sam asked. 'He looks old enough to be her father.' She caught Eleanor's scowl. 'Oooh, sorry.'

'Probably someone from work,' Eleanor suggested, her mind already working overtime. 'Angie does the occasional bit of temping round here, I think.'

'When she can be bothered to get out of bed, you mean, but …' Sam paused. 'Look at that.' Eleanor looked. Angie and her colleague were rooted to the spot, engaged in the sort of embrace usually reserved for post-watershed TV dramas starring Trevor Eve. 'Doesn't look terribly work-related to me.'

'D'you think she's found herself a sugar daddy?'

Sam choked on her wine. 'I thought Daniel was her passage to riches.'

'He won't be properly rich until his dad dies,' Eleanor said. 'And Peter will be around for a long time yet. I don't believe this,' she moaned. 'Have I really got to tell two people that they're being cheated on, both in the same week?'

Sam pursed her lips. 'Ooh, I'm not sure I'd tell Daniel just yet,' she advised quickly.

'Why, what's the difference?'

She waved her hand at Eleanor. 'Just don't interfere. Ever heard of shooting-the-messenger syndrome?'

'You've just made that up.'

'He'll blame you,' Sam explained, nibbling on an olive.

'In his mind, you'll be inextricably linked with all the bad feeling. He'll never be able to look at you without remembering how you scuppered the relationship. It'll be All Your Fault,' she emphasised. 'It's just not worth it, El.'

Eleanor thought about this. 'OK. I get that. But what's she playing at?'

'Anyway,' Sam carried on, 'it's actually none of your business. You don't want to wade in and accuse Angie when it might be something quite innocent ...'

'Innocent?' snorted Eleanor. 'He had his tongue so far down her throat he was practically giving her a heart massage!'

'It did look rather surgical, didn't it?' She looked at her friend suspiciously. 'Don't go getting any daft ideas. It won't get him back.'

'But –'

'Your feelings are clouding the issue. Telling tales about Angie's indiscretions will not bring Daniel crawling to your door asking for a second chance.'

'But I've got to tell him,' Eleanor persisted. 'Think how he'd feel if it came out that I'd known all along? He'd be so humiliated, just like Mum ...'

'He's a big boy, he'd understand.'

'You've changed your tune,' Eleanor challenged. 'That's the complete opposite of what you said about my mother!'

'This is different. Your dad's got a history and your mum needs to know.'

'You're not making any sense,' Eleanor said. 'He'd never speak to me again.'

'He'd never speak to you again if you told him!' Sam shouted. 'Think, woman! This might just be a flash in the pan. Not worth getting upset about.'

'It didn't look that way to me.'

'It never does!' Sam exclaimed. 'That's what flings are

all about, for God's sake; getting caught up in the heat of the moment. Doesn't mean it's serious. I mean, look at you and Nick.' She frowned at Eleanor. 'Seriously, El, it would be a big mistake, and it wouldn't have the desired effect.'

'We-ll,' Eleanor said eventually. 'But I still think –'

'On second thoughts,' Sam interrupted, 'maybe you should call Daniel after all. You could ask his advice about the Nick problem and while you're at it,' her eyes glinted with mischief, 'see how the land lies with him and Angie.'

She grasped the empty bottle. 'Where's our wine got to?' As she struggled to her feet she turned back to Eleanor. 'Who was it that said bad things always come in threes?'

There had been some very obvious sightings since Monday; Eric and Dora seemed to be moving from the Lakes towards the Peak District, with Nick in hot pursuit. Belle showed Eleanor some convincing photographs.

'He's been very unlucky,' Belle said, as they scrolled through files of stored images the next day. 'He just misses them every time. It's almost like he's doing it on purpose,' she added innocently.

'Hardly,' Eleanor retorted quickly. 'Why would he do a thing like that? He's trying his best to avert a disaster, remember?'

'I only meant that –'

'I know,' Eleanor said. 'Sorry. Look, I'm sure there's nothing untoward going on, but I see how it could look that way.' She glanced across the newsroom. 'Has Julian said anything?'

'No. Well, not to me anyway. Why?'

'Nothing, I just wondered if he was getting impatient.'

Belle smirked. 'I wouldn't worry. He's away with the fairies at the moment. I don't think he knows what's going on.'

'What makes you say that?'

Belle leaned closer. 'Yesterday,' she confided, 'he ordered two camera crews to doorstep that MP who was involved in that rental scam. He had a fit when he realised that they both arrived at the same time and made us look pretty stupid. And the MP complained, so Britney wasn't very happy. It was all Julian's fault but he wouldn't admit it. Then, he left instructions for the overnight crew to follow some mysterious tip-off that he'd been given, when they should've been outside Tory Central Office waiting for the outcome of the Cavendish enquiry, so they missed that.' She paused. 'If you ask me, he's losing it, big time.'

'I had no idea,' said Eleanor. 'Although I did think he was acting a bit strange the last time I saw him.'

Belle nodded. 'If you want to go and see Nick again, now would be a good time,' she advised. 'Julian will hardly notice, he's got other stuff to think about.' She peered at Eleanor. 'But don't look so bloody miserable about it. A day out in the Peaks with a handsome young man in tow would be my idea of heaven right now.'

Eleanor smiled brightly. She shouldn't let anyone see her disquiet. 'Yes,' she said. 'You're right. What's not to like? I'm supposed to be off shift after today, anyway.' She picked up the phone and dialled Nick's mobile. Hopefully he'd be so pleased to see her he wouldn't suspect her motives.

They arranged to meet in the middle of Buxton. Nick tried to persuade her to stay overnight, but she made an excuse.

'I'm sorry but I can't. It's only a flying visit. I'd really love to, but I'm on the early shift the morning after,' she lied. 'But we could go and grab something to eat before I have to come back.'

'I'd rather stay in the room with a takeaway,' he said. 'And a bottle of wine.'

She was torn. 'Well, OK then,' she agreed reluctantly. 'That sounds good.'

Something in her tone must have alerted him. 'Are you OK, Eleanor?' he asked. There was silence on the line for a few beats. 'You're not checking up on me, are you?'

The M1 wasn't as crowded as Eleanor had expected. All the early morning traffic was heading the other way once she got past Staples Corner. The sky held the promise of rain but for the moment it was dry and relatively bright and she was thankful for the calm conditions; she intended to use the next few hours to examine her position from every angle.

She could hardly credit how stupid she'd been. A detached observer would assume she'd been so grateful for the attentions of a much younger man that her usual scepticism had languished. The only comfort she could take from the situation was that Julian had been taken in too.

This period of relative calm wouldn't last; the whole debacle threatened to blow wide open and she would soon be exposed. She shuddered at the prospect and gripped the steering wheel, staring across the central reservation but seeing nothing. She didn't notice the line of stationary traffic in front of her until she was almost upon it. She stamped on the brakes, causing the car to judder to a halt just in time to avoid a collision. Her heart was hammering and her hands were slippery with perspiration when the traffic started to move again.

She tuned the radio to a classical station and let the strains of a violin concerto soothe her as concentrated on the road.

By the time she turned off the M1 the sky was the colour of old school socks and the scenery was as damp and brooding as her mood. Sheep dotted the sodden landscape and birds huddled together on the overhead wires, crowding the pylons in their search for warmth. She was still struggling with the notion that Nick was a duplicitous liar and as she drove through the bleak countryside towards Buxton, her frame of mind dithered between desolation and disbelief. If her suspicions were correct, she had no idea where they would lead.

She prayed that she was wrong

Chapter Twenty-two

'What do you mean, suspicious?' Nick demanded.

They were in a scruffy little room in a side-street B&B in Buxton, the remains of a Chinese takeaway and bottle of wine still evident on the table. As the summer wore on, it was getting more difficult to find decent rooms at short notice. Nick didn't seem to mind; he'd just left university, and clean sheets were probably a bonus. He'd told Eleanor that he'd rather stay locally, in squalor, than miles away in more luxurious surroundings. Now, he was leaning against the windowsill, glass in hand, staring at her.

She'd intended to keep the conversation light and instantly regretted using such a loaded expression. 'What I mean is ...'

He was immediately on the defensive. 'Hang on a minute. Are you telling me, at this stage in the proceedings, that you don't believe me?'

'Not exactly.' Eleanor tried to qualify her statement. 'I mean, well, you've got to admit it looks a bit odd that every time we seem to be closing in on Eric and Dora, they suddenly disappear for a few days.'

'That's not odd, that's –'

'Well, a coincidence, then.'

'I'm only following the leads,' he said petulantly. 'I don't set them up.'

'Don't you?'

'In fact,' he carried on, ignoring her protestations, 'it's your bloody newsroom that's been sending me all over the country. How can you possibly think that I set everything up?' He began to pace around the small room. 'Have you forgotten what we're doing here? We're trying to save my gran's life!'

'I know that!' she shouted back. 'And bloody good telly it is too. The viewing figures are going up all the time. We couldn't have asked for a better story.'

'So, what's your problem?' Nick asked. 'I don't understand. If this was a set-up, why would I be staying in this mouldy little room?' He swept his arms out widely to encompass the tiny space. 'Surely I'd be using the expense account to stay in a much nicer place? I'm sure there'd be something available at the 4-star establishment down the street.'

Eleanor threw her hands up in irritation. 'There is no problem, Nick, as long as you're telling me the truth,' she said with an exasperated sigh. 'We have to maintain our integrity or they'll tear us apart.'

'That's a bit melodramatic, isn't it?'

'No, it isn't!' she cried. 'You don't know this world like I do.' She sat heavily on the bed and pulled him down beside her. 'Just don't lie to me about this, Nick,' she warned. 'I need to be able to trust you. If you're not telling me the truth I can't protect you. You'll lose everyone's confidence. And I'll lose my job,' she added bleakly. 'If you have any feelings for me at all, you've got to tell me the truth.'

The bravado suddenly melted away. He seemed to shrink, his shoulders sagging, and he looked so stricken that Eleanor was overwhelmed with remorse.

'I'm sorry,' she murmured. 'I'm really sorry about your gran and I haven't forgotten why we're here.' All her instincts told her to her to tread carefully. She searched his face for clues but his brow was clear and she couldn't see a hint of deception. 'But look at it from my point of view,' she carried on. 'I'm the one having to explain everything back in London. They've been asking questions, Nick, and I've had to defend you.'

'Let me speak to them.'

'No, no, that's not the issue. I can deal with them. But only if you're straight with me. I've got to be absolutely sure you're telling the truth.'

'What's the point?' he muttered. 'You don't believe me. I can tell.'

She put a hand on his arm. 'Nick, I want to believe you. You have no idea how much. Just convince me. There's a lot at stake.'

'Come here,' he said. He pulled her into his arms and stroked his fingers through her hair. 'I wouldn't do anything to hurt you,' he whispered. 'You should know that by now.'

'I wish Eric and Dora had gone to bloody Madagascar or Tibet,' she complained. 'Or somewhere else where we couldn't follow them.' She relaxed slightly, trying to dislodge the conversation with Sam.

He laughed. 'If they were, we wouldn't be here, in this beautiful room, eating this delightful Chinese food, would we?' He put his hands on her shoulders and held her at arm's length. 'Look,' he said softly, brushing a strand of hair from her cheek. 'I know what you're thinking, but it's not true. We've just had a bit of bad luck, that's all. I've no more idea where Gran and Pops are than the rest of the general public. I'll catch them eventually, Eleanor. It's only been, what? A week and a half?Cut me some slack, OK?'

He sounded so plausible. And he was right; maybe she hadn't given him enough of a chance. She'd allowed Sam to spook her.

'I reckon we'll have a result on the Doric Imperative by next week,' he pronounced.

She was on the alert again. 'How can you be so sure?'

'I'm not certain,' he retorted. 'I just have a feeling, that's all. I know them, Eleanor. Trust me.'

She was torn: one minute Nick seemed completely genuine, his confidence rubbing off on her, making her feel very positive; the next, he planted more suspicions, pushing her back into a chaos of uncertainty and doubt. She tried to pull away as he began to kiss her. 'Nick,' she protested, 'this isn't a very good idea. I'm ... I'm too wound up.'

'In that case,' he said, starting to unbutton her shirt, 'this is very much to be recommended.' He nuzzled her neck, making her gasp with pleasure. 'It's a very good idea. Just what you need to make you relax.'

His touch made the tiny hairs on her arms bristle in anticipation. His fingers traced shivery lines of goose pimples down her back as his hands crept under her tee-shirt.

Her last coherent thought before he'd undressed her completely was that she could always busk in the Underground, or stack shelves in Tesco.

Six hours later she was driving through the dark streets on her way back to the motorway. She'd been very tempted to stay the night but in the end she'd decided that a little distance would be a good thing. She'd crept out of the dingy room leaving Nick in a post-coital stupor she didn't share.

She was feeling mildly exhilarated; their lovemaking had relieved the tension between them, allowing Nick to allay her anxiety and she was more confident than she'd felt in a while. She believed him. She said it out loud, as if to confirm the thought. Never mind what Sam had said, she was the one who had to be persuaded, and she was convinced he was being truthful; she just didn't believe that he'd lie to her on such a grand scale. Now she could look forward to a free weekend and lunch with Daniel on Sunday.

She relaxed her shoulders and switched on the radio, scanning the stations until she caught the tail end of a local news bulletin.

'And finally ...' the newscaster was saying, *'we are receiving information that the pursuit being mounted by UK24's news channel in a bid to avert an assisted suicide, and now reported to be based in our region, could be a hoax. The fund now stands at over a hundred thousand pounds. Sources close to the couple are saying that Mrs Paget, a devout Catholic, would never consider such an avenue. In an interview with the Reverend Michael ...'*

Eleanor tuned out. The heavy stone of suspicion settled once more into the pit of her stomach and she squirmed as she flashed forward to the inevitable meeting with Julian on Monday. If it was all over Derbyshire, it wouldn't take long for word to reach the London newsroom.

Eleanor swallowed her anxiety and called Daniel at the newspaper in Frankfurt the next morning.

'How's Frankfurt?' she asked.

'Wunderbar!' He hesitated. 'Should I get ready for bad news? You've decided not to do it, haven't you?'

'What? Sorry, what are you talking about?'

'Singing at the wedding. You haven't had long to think about it; I presume you've decided against it.'

'Oh, I see! No, no, I'm not calling about that. I haven't had chance to even think about that yet. Sorry.'

'That's a relief.' He hesitated. 'So, how are things otherwise?'

She resisted the urge to bring him up to speed with every aspect of her life in one huge sentence. 'Fine,' she lied. 'Everything's fine. How're Gwen and Peter?'

'Funny you should ask,' Daniel replied. 'I'm being a bit cautious here because I don't know all the ins and outs, but Dad's been having a hard time of it lately.'

'What's happened?'

'Oh, financial stuff mostly, run of bad luck, you know? But it's been getting him down.'

'Has he ...' Eleanor didn't like to ask the question.

'Has he lost much?'

'Difficult to say,' said Daniel. 'He doesn't confide in me. If I asked he'd say everything was fine. But I know a bit about his investments and they aren't performing terribly well at the moment.'

'How's your mum taking all this?'

'Stoically, as usual. You know Gwen; if she has to sell the family silver, she will. I'm sure they'll turn a corner soon. Though I think Grace's party was a bit of a burden. Shouldn't have let Angie talk them into the outside caterers. Cost a fortune, apparently. Never mind, I'm sure everything will be fine.' She could hear the smile in his voice.

'When are you coming back to London?' Eleanor asked. 'Only, I want to pick your brains, in person. It's too complicated to explain on the phone.'

'It's not to do with this mercy dash that you guys are running, is it?' he asked. 'The suicide? It's creating a bit of a stir in medialand.'

Her heart sank. 'Could be,' she prevaricated.

Jim Paget was as amiable as ever and Eleanor was at a loss as to how to bring up the subject of his son, the possible fraudster.

'I haven't seen you in here for a while,' he said. 'Having a few days off?'

She decided on the direct approach. 'You know how it is, Jim,' she said. 'I've been all over the place since last week. No time for exercising. How's Nick?'

Jim stared into the swimming pool, which was empty except for two elderly women swimming sedately up and down. 'No idea,' he said. 'He took off over a week ago for a hard-earned holiday with some uni friends. Not so much as a postcard so far.' He shrugged. 'Kids, eh?'

She searched his face for clues but Jim's expression remained placid. 'Where's he gone?' she asked innocently.

'I've absolutely no idea. He doesn't tell me details like that. Though I daresay he'll be back soon, when he runs out of cash. Which I gave him, by the way.'

Eleanor opened her mouth to speak but she couldn't think of a way of asking about Eric and Dora without arousing Jim's suspicions. 'I'm sure he'll be in touch soon,' she said instead.

Chapter Twenty-three

Eleanor pressed the entry button and waited to be admitted into the smart foyer of the modern apartment block. Despite the awkwardness of the invitation, she was curious about the flat. And she was nervous at seeing Daniel again; she felt like a schoolgirl on a date, not a grown woman visiting an old friend. And the last time she'd seen him she hadn't been in possession of the explosive information she was now wondering if she should keep to herself.

The door buzzed and she pulled it open. Buying herself more time, she decided against the lift and climbed the carpeted stairs to the third floor and rang the bell of Flat 17.

Daniel answered the door almost immediately, as if he'd been standing on the other side, waiting. He was wearing jeans and a blue chambray shirt with a button-down collar, open at the neck.

'Hello,' he said, and stepped forward awkwardly to hug her. His familiar scent almost overwhelmed her and she realised why she'd recognised Julian's cologne. She stood in his arms and let him hold her, not daring to reciprocate, feeling the anxieties of the past two days slowly retreat. Regret gathered in her chest like heartburn. She didn't want to leave the safety of his arms. Ever.

She quivered.

'You're shaking,' he murmured into her hair.

'It's a bit chilly outside,' she replied, reluctantly pulling away, presenting him with the bottle of wine and bunch of flowers she was clutching. She searched his face for some sign of recognition of a shared, unfinished past, but his smile was open, warm and utterly guileless.

He showed her into a large room where sparse, well-chosen furnishings revealed an expanse of deep, strawberry pink carpet. The far wall was taken up entirely by windows and moody black and white photographs were dotted about the cream coloured walls in a carefully considered jumble.

'I'll get us a drink,' Daniel said. 'Lunch won't take long to rustle up.'

He came back into the room carrying a bottle of champagne and two flutes white with frost. A smile lit up his face as he came towards her and a warm feeling suffused her entire being.

'I thought we should push the boat out,' he said. He handed her a glass and poured the wine. 'To all of us. May we live long and prosper.'

'Amen to that,' she said, chinking her glass against his. 'Is Angie in the kitchen?'

'No, she's not here at the moment,' he said. 'Her mother's ill, so she's gone to check on her. She'll be back in about half an hour, so she'll eat with us,' he added. 'It'll give us a chance to catch up; Angie's already bored to death with me talking about my Eurozone assignment.'

For a moment, Eleanor wondered if Angie knew she'd been spotted in Soho and had deliberately decided not to be at home. 'Oh, that's a shame,' she said. 'I hope her mum's OK.'

'I don't think it's anything too serious.'

They moved across to the window and Daniel stood beside her, taking in the spectacular view across the Thames. The flat was in a new block on the south side of Putney Bridge and they watched the flow of pedestrians part round the lampposts, like a river round rocks.

She was acutely aware of his proximity. When she stood within his orbit she could feel the pull; she was drawn to him like the tide to the moon. She turned back into the room, hoping that he hadn't noticed her flushed cheeks. 'It's a lovely flat,' she said. 'You made a good choice.' I would have made the same one, she thought. This is where I should be living. This is my life, not Angie's.

'Angie loves it,' Daniel said. 'This area suits her much better – it's a bit trendier than Kensington. She hated being surrounded by the crusty old fogies at the other place.'

'You were just round the corner from Harrods and Harvey Nicks! Shopping heaven!'

He laughed. 'I know, but this is much better. Angie picked out all the furnishings.' His voice was filled with pride. 'She's launching an interior design business. She spends a lot of time in town at the moment, schmoozing potential clients.'

She had to say something. 'Daniel,' she began. 'Are you absolutely sure about this?'

'About what? This flat? I though you liked it.'

'I do. I mean about Angie, and your … your future.'

He put his glass down on a small end table and turned to look at her. 'I think I need to explain something. I … I mean … God, this is a bit difficult.'

She waited.

'I never told you any of this,' he said in a rush. 'Everything was so sudden. But …' He lifted his eyes. 'When I … we … At the time, I was in a lot of trouble at work.'

'I know. You said. Though you never explained,' Eleanor added pointedly. 'You just said something about being under pressure.'

'Well yes, I was. I couldn't tell you, Eleanor. I was too ashamed.' He swallowed. 'I lost the firm a shedload of money with a stupid speculation.'

She stared at him. 'I thought you just didn't like the work. I had no idea.'

He brushed her words aside. 'I told you the bank had sworn me to secrecy, they didn't want any whiff of scandal. But I didn't tell you how big a secret it was, and that day when I planned to propose, I realised that I couldn't do it to you. I went straight back down to London and resigned the same day. Needless to say, they weren't bothered about me serving my notice.' He shrugged. 'But they made me get it all back first, though.'

'Was it a lot?'

'Enormous. Millions. Tens of millions. You'll think I was a complete incompetent. I had to work really hard to get it all back. I was in the office all hours. I started taking stuff to keep me awake, then stuff to help me sleep. Before I knew it I had a full-scale habit. I did it, though,' he carried on. 'I got it all back. Or most of it.

'That's brilliant. But what's all this got to do with Angie?'

He waved his hand. 'I'm coming to that.' He took a deep breath. 'I got clean when I was travelling. Life was good, it wasn't too difficult. But when I was got to Paris I really entered into the lifestyle. I started burning the candle at both ends and soon I was using again. Angie came along just at the right time. I was at rock bottom – she was such a support. I don't think I could've done it without her.'

'I see.'

'It's all in the past now,' he said. 'But I owe Angie an enormous debt of gratitude. And she keeps me on the straight and narrow.'

'I wouldn't have thought she was so altruistic,' Eleanor said. 'Even so, it's no basis for marriage, is it?' She tried another tack. 'Don't you think that what she did then might be colouring your view of the present?'

He wiggled his hand. 'Possibly. But I don't think it matters. I won't change my mind.'

The words were like a dagger in her heart. She waited for him to explain further but he was silent. 'Just be careful, Daniel. These are big decisions.'

He walked to the door. 'Come into the kitchen and we

can talk some more while I chop.' Eleanor raised an eyebrow. 'I can just about manage a stir-fry. Is that OK?'

'Anything that I don't have to cook is OK with me,' she said, following him out of the door.

'Can you believe, not a single carbohydrate passes our lips when we're at home?' Daniel grumbled. 'It's forbidden under Angie's pre-wedding regime. Could you open this, please? It needs to breathe.' He handed her a bottle of red wine from a rack. 'We don't count alcohol, obviously.'

The kitchen was almost as large as the living room, fitted out with top-of-the-range stainless steel appliances, the starkness relieved by long stretches of translucent scarlet worktop that seemed to be lit from beneath. Eleanor sat on a stool and watched Daniel pull a lethal-looking knife from a block and start preparing a mountain of vegetables.

As he worked he regaled her with anecdotes from the political circuit in The Hague. She listened with half an ear, preoccupied with her own dilemmas and impatient to tell Daniel about them before Angie got home.

'And by the time I realised ...' Daniel was saying. He stopped, waited for a response. 'Hello? You're not listening, are you?'

Eleanor looked up sharply from the watery ring her glass had created on the counter and which she was absent-mindedly expanding with her finger. 'Sorry. Yes, no, sorry, I'm ...'

'It obviously bores you too,' he moaned theatrically.

'No, no it doesn't,' Eleanor spluttered. 'I'm sorry, Daniel, I wasn't concentrating. I ... I've got something on my mind.'

'I know,' he said. 'I can see you're preoccupied. You always were completely transparent.' He refilled her glass. 'Sorry, I should have given you chance to get a word in edgeways. I guess it's to do with the story your newsroom's been running about the Pagets? What did you call it, The Doric Imperative? Clever title, pity it seems to have been dropped. I haven't heard it for a while. It hasn't resolved itself yet, then?' She shook her head. 'Come on, then,' he encouraged. 'Tell me all about it.'

She took a fortifying swig of champagne and opened her mouth to speak, but before she'd said a word the front door banged shut and Angie swept into the kitchen.

Chapter Twenty-four

Angie wafted across the room carrying an enormous bouquet of flowers, completely dwarfing Eleanor's bunch which were still lying limply on the worktop.

She was wearing jeans and a skimpy top; if anything, she was slimmer than she'd been at Grace's party, her bare shoulders and arms lightly tanned and bearing the telltale signs of a life divided between the spa and the gym. Eleanor felt like a pudding by comparison.

'Hi!' Angie cried. 'How are we all?'

'Hello, darling,' said Daniel, setting his knife down and walking towards her. 'What lovely flowers.' He put his arms round her and kissed her cheek so tenderly it pinched Eleanor's heart. 'How's your mum?'

'On the mend.' She frowned at Eleanor's flowers and gathered them up with her own without comment. 'I'd better put these in some water.' She turned to Eleanor and kissed her warmly on the cheek. 'And how are you?' she asked, smiling broadly. 'Been up to much since we last saw you?'

When she was in the mood, Angie could make you feel like there was no one else in the room. She could be charming and thoughtful to those who piqued her curiosity but the spotlight of her attention would linger only briefly before moving on, withdrawn as abruptly as it had been bestowed, leaving the recipient wanting more. Eleanor could see how she would be a runaway success in her new business.

She looked for a chink, a well-disguised crack in an otherwise unblemished shell. But Angie's demeanour was faultless; she seemed so obviously in love with Daniel there was no room for doubt. If Eleanor hadn't seen it with her own eyes, she wouldn't have believed Angie capable of any disloyalty. 'I'm well, thanks,' she said. 'Been very busy. How about you? Daniel was just telling me –'

'About my brilliant new idea? Exciting, isn't it? I'm in town all the time, these days, drumming up business.'

Eleanor smiled. 'So I hear. I hope it'll be a great success.'

'It will be,' Angie assured her. 'I'll be expanding into the provinces soon.'

Eleanor didn't doubt it for a second.

'Have you had any more thoughts about what you'll be singing at our wedding?' Angie asked suddenly. 'Only –'

'Eleanor's got a bit of a problem, darling,' Daniel interrupted. 'She wants to talk it over.'

'What?' Angie put the flowers down and turned, concerned, to Eleanor. 'Don't tell me your voice has broken, or something. That would be a disaster.'

'God, no,' Eleanor laughed. 'It's nothing like that. Nothing to do with the wedding.' She couldn't remember actually agreeing to sing.

'Thank goodness. We're counting on you, aren't we, darling?' She turned to Daniel. 'But we need to find something even better than what you sang for Grace, don't we?'

'I'm sure we will,' Daniel reassured her. 'But not today. El's got something more important to discuss.'

Angie pursed her lips in annoyance. 'Oh. OK. So, tell me about your little crisis, Eleanor,' she said. 'What's it about? I've just done a course in life coaching. I could –'

'It's not that sort of problem,' said Eleanor, glancing at Daniel who seemed oblivious to her disquiet. 'Anyway, I thought you were doing interior design these days.'

'I am,' Angie agreed. 'But that doesn't mean I can't practise my other skills, does it?'

'No, I suppose not,' Eleanor said. 'It's just that ...' She

hesitated.

Daniel dumped marinated chicken into a smoking wok and fragrant spices filled the air. 'Let's wait until we sit down. Won't be long now,' he said. 'Angie, can you get some knives and forks, please?'

He put fresh flatbread on a board and brought the wok to the table.

'This looks lovely, darling,' said Angie, tasting a morsel. 'But I can't wait any longer.' She tapped Eleanor's hand. 'Come on then,' she urged. 'Tell us all about it.'

Eleanor glanced at Daniel. 'Well, it's a bit sensitive. I'm not sure how much ...'

Daniel looked pointedly at Angie and putting his hand over hers for emphasis, said, 'I think Eleanor's going to tell us something that must not, under any circumstances, leave this room. You understand about privileged information, don't you?'

'Of course I do, darling,' Angie drawled. 'But it can't be that earth-shattering can it?' Her eyes widened. 'You haven't murdered someone, have you?'

'Don't joke about it, please,' Daniel said. 'This is serious.'

'Sorry.' Angie looked crestfallen and took a desultory bite of chicken.

'Go on.' Daniel nodded at Eleanor. 'We're listening.'

Eleanor took a gulp of wine. 'You're going to think I'm an absolute idiot.' She launched into the tale.

'You're right,' Angie pronounced when she'd finished. 'You are an idiot. I can't believe you've been so naïve, Eleanor.'

'Thanks for the vote of confidence,' Eleanor said ruefully. 'And there's something I haven't told you. We set up a fund for donations to a cancer charity in Dora's name. It's adding up to quite a lot. How the hell are we going to deal with that? If it got out that we've been taking money under false pretences ...' she trailed off.

Daniel looked thoughtful. 'That's a bit of a problem, I admit,' he said. 'But are you absolutely certain it's a set-up? You said you were sure Nick was telling the truth by the time you left him on Thursday night. Why have you changed your mind so suddenly? Was it the local news report that made you wobble?'

Eleanor nodded. 'It threw me, that's for sure.' She shrugged. 'I don't know,' she added. 'It's just a niggle that won't go away.' She didn't particularly want to reveal how far things had gone with Nick. She knew now that the relationship wasn't going to last much longer; in the scheme of things it would be best to disregard it altogether.

'I know you, El,' said Daniel, ever the investigative journalist. 'There's something you're not telling us.'

Eleanor's heart sank. She squirmed with embarrassment, biting her lip. 'Well ...'

Angie pounced. 'You've been sleeping with him, haven't you?' she cackled. She raised her eyebrows comically. 'Miss Wragby, I'm shocked.'

'Ah ...'

Angie burst out laughing. 'There's no need to look like that,' she joked. 'Who you sleep with is your affair. We don't care, do we, darling?' She looked across at Daniel, who was staring at Eleanor as if she'd just revealed that she'd slept with the entire Arsenal football team.

'Er, no,' he blustered. 'It's nothing to do with us. But ...'

Eleanor examined the strip of red pepper on the end of her fork, thinking that her face was probably the same colour. She didn't bother trying to defend herself.

'Your relationship's irrelevant,' Daniel said, taking a sip of wine. He put the glass down carefully on the table.

'But darling,' Angie interjected. 'Don't you think Eleanor's –?'

Daniel held his hand up in a stop-right-there gesture.

'Hang on,' he said. 'Let's say you're right, El, and the secret is out. With any luck the Pagets will have moved out of the area and the story will have been overtaken by some other non-event. You know what local news is like: another cat stuck up a tree and the Pagets will be at the bottom of the rundown.' He pulled a hunk of bread off the loaf, tearing it into crumbs as he spoke. 'Actually, if it's been taken up by one of the nationals, someone would've contacted UK24 by now.'

'You said you'd heard some rumours, didn't you?' Eleanor asked.

He nodded. 'It's being talked about. No mention of any set-up, though.'

'So, it might all be forgotten about?' asked Angie helpfully.

'Unlikely,' said Daniel. 'But we can hope. Have you heard anything from work?' he asked Eleanor.

'Not that I know of,' Eleanor admitted. 'I've kept my mobile turned off, and the voicemail on. No messages, which is distinctly odd in itself. Julian usually gets in touch over the weekend when I'm off.'

'I haven't seen it reported anywhere else, have you?'

'No, thank God,' said Eleanor.

'So it'll all kick off tomorrow, will it? When you go into work?'

She nodded. 'If I still have a job.'

'OK,' he said, refilling their glasses. 'Let's play devil's advocate.'

'Oh, I'm getting used to that,' Eleanor laughed wryly.

Daniel carried on, 'What if the Pagets come in next week, after three weeks at large, when they've effectively been "found" by their grandson and the great British public, disaster averted and all that, who's to know any different?'

'I'm surprised at you, Daniel,' Eleanor scolded. '*I'd* know. We're syndicating this fairy tale round the world, for God's sake! How could I look at my colleagues, day after day, knowing that I'd spun them a yarn? How would you feel?'

Daniel put down his fork. 'But you haven't spun them a yarn, Eleanor. You were acting in good faith. This isn't your fault –'

'It'd look a bit better if she hadn't been sleeping with the enemy,' Angie interjected.

Eleanor ignored her. 'But what if the truth came out eventually? Which is a distinct possibility. Then what would happen? What could I possibly say in my defence? *"Oh I'm so sorry, of course I knew all along, but I made an executive decision not to let anyone in on the secret because I know best!"* I'd be sacked for gross incompetence.' She paused to take a swig of wine. 'Either way, I'll be out of a job pretty soon. What on earth am I going to do?'

'You can't take all the blame yourself,' Daniel said. 'You were always very good at that. There are others involved here. Julian, for instance.'

'He's going to go up in a blue light,' Eleanor predicted.

Chapter Twenty-five

The newsroom was just gearing up for the day shift when Eleanor slipped into her chair on Monday morning and logged on, relieved that no one seemed to have noticed her bleary-eyed arrival.

Almost immediately Belle sat down beside her. 'I was watching the car park,' she explained. 'Wanted to show you this before anyone else had a chance.' She pushed a sheet of paper towards Eleanor. 'Looks like the wolves are circling.'

It was just what Eleanor had been dreading. The article, a scant column inch from that week's edition of a satirical magazine, advanced the theory that UK24 was stringing the public along with its 'fabricated' story about the prevention of a possible suicide.

Sam and Daniel had both been wrong about that, then, thought Eleanor. She felt her career draining away as surely as if she was pouring it down the plughole herself.

'There's not any truth in it, is there?' asked Belle.

Eleanor shrugged. 'I don't know, is the honest answer,' she replied, indicating the masthead. 'But they don't like us much, though, do they?'

'No, they'd love to see us fall flat on our faces. But they have a smallish circulation and almost no internet presence, so hopefully the powers that be won't take it too seriously.' Belle looked at Eleanor quizzically. 'Why? What have you heard?'

'There was something on local radio the other night,' Eleanor said. She groaned. 'I suppose I'll have to go and confess to Julian and Britney.'

'Oh, some good news, though,' Belle continued.

'Julian's been off sick. He won't have heard anything yet.'

'Where's he been? Under a stone?' She couldn't believe that Julian, a man with the word 'journalist' running through him like a stick of Blackpool rock, wouldn't have heard this news, wherever he was. The newsroom grapevine didn't work like that; some jobsworth could always be relied upon to pass on juicy gossip, wherever you happened to be and in whatever state of consciousness.

'Man flu, apparently. He's been completely incommunicado since Friday. No one's been able to speak to him.' She nodded across the newsroom. 'Seems like he's recovered, though. He's here today.'

'I think I'll wait until he shouts,' Eleanor said. 'No point in pre-empting a bollocking, is there? Somebody will bring him up to speed soon enough, I'm sure.'

She had her doubts about Daniel's advice, but it seemed she had little to lose. She was scrolling idly through her emails when she received a text from Sam. *Just had horrid thought*, it read. *What if there are no Pagets out there?*

She speed-dialled Sam's number. 'Did you mean to send that? Your predictive text said something about no Pagets.'

'That's right. What if there aren't any Pagets to find, because they're not in this country? I saw a film at the weekend,' Sam explained. 'Similar proposition. A group of students try to fool the public. I know it's a bit far-fetched, but what if Nick isn't having any success finding the Pagets because they can't be found, because they're not in this country?'

'Sorry, I'm not following.'

'What if the Pagets are actually out of the country, having the holiday of a lifetime somewhere exotic, after getting the news that Dora isn't terminally ill after all? They're completely oblivious to what's happening back home. And Nick –'

'Is on a wild goose chase? But –'

'He could be,' Sam agreed, 'but I don't think he is. No, my theory is that Nick is chasing two *other* people. And a dog. Two people who've been in on this from the start.'

'Which people?'

'Friends of Nick, probably. All in it together.'

'But Nick said he found the Paget's passports at the house. They can't be abroad.'

'And you took him at his word?'

'Well ... yes.'

'Whatever happened to your famous journalistic acumen?' Sam asked. 'Isn't that one of the first things you're taught, to double-check your sources?' She sniggered down the phone. 'He must be even better in the sack than you've told me.'

'I know I asked him to bring the passports in,' Eleanor insisted. 'But now you mention it, I can't remember actually seeing them. But I must have done. Or it got forgotten about in the general excitement. I'll ask Belle.'

'I wouldn't bother,' Sam snorted. She hurried on. 'How do you know what the Pagets look like?'

'I've seen photographs. Nick showed me some.'

Eleanor suddenly realised what Sam was getting at. 'But –'

'Which could have been photographs of anyone, let's face it. Particularly as you can't remember seeing the passports.'

'No, no,' Eleanor protested. 'I don't buy this. It's ridiculous.'

'El, you've only got Nick's word for it that you're chasing the right people,' Sam persisted. 'The photographs and video that have been sent in by the public have hardly been magnificent quality, have they?' she asked. 'They're usually all jerky and fuzzy and the couple have been in the distance. If you ask me, they could be anybody. They just needed to have a passing resemblance.'

'But what about the rest of the family? They'd know, surely?'

'People believe what they want to believe, especially if they've seen it on the telly. You of all people should know that,' Sam replied. 'But maybe they're all in on it together.'

'That would mean that Jim knows, too. I can't believe it.' Eleanor suddenly remembered the radio report. 'Hang on, though. When I was up in Buxton, I heard a piece on the local news; there was an interview with a family friend who said Dora wouldn't commit suicide.'

'I rest my case,' said Sam smugly.

'But there was no mention that the person in the video didn't even look like Dora. It's just too convenient, Sam, even for you.'

'It's just a theory, El. But it could explain everything.'

'But who would these other people be?'

'Nick's just finished university, hasn't he?'

'Yes,' Eleanor said. 'He graduated in June.'

'So, presumably he's still in touch with all his uni friends. And they'll all be looking for jobs. This exposure would be just what they need to springboard their careers. And let's not forget the money that's been coming in. That must be mounting up by now. Probably enough to pay off the student loans ...'

'More than enough, ' said Eleanor. 'But I get the idea.' And the idea had the terrible ring of truth about it. 'And if you turn out to be right, how do I play it here?'

If they were aware of any developments, none of Eleanor's colleagues were letting on, so she continued acting as if nothing had happened. Only Belle knew what she'd heard on the radio during her trip to Buxton the previous week. She tried to be positive but she couldn't shake off the sense of foreboding.

By mid-morning she couldn't bear the tension any longer; she had to find out about the passports. She walked across to the assistant's desk. 'Hi Belle.'

'Oh, hi Eleanor,' Belle smiled. She seemed rather agitated.

Today, Belle was reprising Liza Minnelli in her *Cabaret* role. She'd stopped short of the stockings, but she was wearing black leather hot pants, killer heels and fishnet tights, and a bowler hat. Occasionally, she fell into a faux-German accent in the manner of Joel Grey playing the MC of the Kit Kat Klub. Just to add a touch of authenticity, she explained.

Eleanor watched as Belle sorted through various files on her computer. Her usually accurate finger strokes had been replaced with a more fundamental hunt and peck approach. 'Are you OK?' she asked. 'You seem a bit distracted. Is Julian on your back again?'

'What?' asked Belle vacantly. 'No, no, I'm absolutely fine. Just a bit nervous, that's all. Remember that theatre workshop we showcased last week?'

'Ye-es,' said Eleanor, wondering where this could possibly be leading.

'The director's coming in today, to be interviewed.'

'Tommy Trivia, or whatever his name is? Yes, I know. I set it up.'

'It's so exciting!' Belle gasped. 'I've got to try to speak to him. Marcus Nicholson. You know, about getting a place in one of his workshops. He does a lot of Lee Strasberg stuff.'

'Really?' Eleanor didn't have a clue what Belle was talking about.

'Method acting,' Belle explained. 'Acting's all I've always wanted to do. That's why I've made an effort today.' She gestured to her outfit.

Let's hope he's a leg man, thought Eleanor. 'I'll be greeting him when he gets here,' she said. 'I'll put in a good word for you, if you like. Maybe even introduce you.'

'Would you?' Belle gripped her hand. 'That would be so cool!'

'On one condition,' Eleanor said. 'I can't remember where we put the scans of the Pagets' passports. I just wanted to refresh my memory about what they look like. Do you know where they are?'

'Sure,' Belle replied, revitalised fingers rapidly tapping keys, opening files. 'They should be ... no, they're not here. Let's try in here.' She glanced nervously at Eleanor. 'That's strange. I can't find them at the moment. Someone must have stored them somewhere obscure.' She opened a couple of drawers in her desk and scrabbled around. 'I don't think we've got the originals any more, either. Shit, I'm sorry Eleanor. I don't know what's happened to them.'

'Don't worry about it,' said Eleanor. 'I'm sure they'll turn up.' But I won't hold my breath, she thought to herself. 'Any more sightings?'

'They're still in the Peaks, from what I can gather from all the photos.'

'Have there been many?'

'Yeah, some. Must say, they're all starting to look the same, you know? Up hill and down dale, it's a bit monotonous, isn't it? Would it be too much to ask them to pose in front of a road sign from time to time?'

'Ha ha,' Eleanor laughed emptily.

'Where d'you think they'll go next?' Belle asked.

'I don't know,' said Eleanor. 'But I wouldn't be surprised if they're on the move pretty soon. I bet they'll head for somewhere like Shropshire or Gloucestershire.'

'Urgh,' moaned Belle. 'More bloody hills.'

Eleanor started to walk away when Belle called after her. 'Don't forget you know what, will you? Oh, and are you free a week on Friday night?' she asked. 'Only it's my thirtieth and I'm having a karaoke party.'

'Well, I, er ...'

'Oh, go on,' Belle urged. 'After what you told me about your performance last weekend, you'll be the star of the show.'

Eleanor's heart sank when Julian eventually beckoned her across the newsroom. She'd decided not to tell him about Sam's preposterous suggestion just yet. That needed time to percolate. She steeled herself and walked into his office, leaving the door ajar.

Julian seemed suspiciously well for a recovering flu victim. He smiled at Eleanor and invited her to sit down. The door remained open. Penitents and patent wrongdoers in receipt of a dressing-down got the closed-door treatment, so this was a good sign.

'So,' he began, 'how's it all going? I've been out of the loop for a few days, had the flu, so I'm not quite up to speed. Are we closing in?'

'I think so,' Eleanor started. 'I, er, that is, we, Nick and I think we may see the end of this little adventure later this week.'

'Excellent news!' He scribbled something on a sheet of paper then looked up. 'Still here? Report back when you've got something concrete.' He made a shooing gesture. 'Off you go, then. Work to do.'

Eleanor walked back to her desk in a daze. There'd been no mention of last week's deadline. Either Julian was losing it, or she was. Whichever, she was mightily relieved. She felt the burden shift slightly. She decided to call Daniel and run Sam's idea past him.

'You don't really think she's right, do you?' Daniel's voice was sceptical. 'About it all being a con?'

'I don't know,' she said. 'It all fits, though, doesn't it?'

'You'll just have to go and confront him, El,' Daniel advised. 'And hope he doesn't make a scene.'

'What if he threatens to expose us?'

'Would he do that to you?' he asked. 'I ... I thought you were very close.'

Eleanor cringed. 'Not that close, apparently,' she admitted. 'I can't believe I've been so stupid.'

'Don't beat yourself up,' he said kindly. 'We all make errors of judgement sometimes.'

Quite, thought Eleanor. 'I know,' she said. 'But I feel such a failure.'

'You don't know if you're right yet.'

'It's looking more and more that way, though.'

'When will you go?'

'As soon as possible. Sometime tomorrow.'

Chapter Twenty-six

Another anonymous street, another dingy room. At least that was one thing she wouldn't have to make excuses about: Nick had been true to his word; he hadn't filed excessive expenses claims for pricey meals and smart hotels.

Eleanor was reminded of a colleague who had claimed a mysterious 'LOA' for years. No one challenged this regular expense and he earned everyone's grudging respect when he eventually revealed his Leg-Over Allowance.

The memory brought an involuntary smile to her lips, which Nick noticed. 'Would you like to get a takeaway?' he asked, his eyes twinkling wickedly. 'I've already got some wine in. Or would you rather go out?'

'I'm not hungry, actually,' Eleanor said stiffly. 'I want to talk to you.'

'Can't we do that over some food?' he asked. 'I'm starving.'

'You'll just have to wait,' she snapped.

A puzzled expression clouded his features. 'What's the matter?' he asked.

'We aren't going to find them, are we, Nick?'

There, she'd said it.

He stared at her for a long moment and Eleanor felt an icy prickle of dismay stroke her spine.

'How long have you known?' he asked bluntly.

'I've just figured it out. Well, Sam did, actually.' She waited. 'So you're not going to deny it?'

'I, I …' He exhaled suddenly, as if someone had let the air out of him. 'No. There's no point now, is there? I knew it was just a matter of time.'

Eleanor struggled to find her voice. 'Is that all you've got to say?' she finally managed.

'Well, it was such a good story, Eleanor. I didn't start out to deliberately deceive you, honest. It was just so easy. After I had the idea it seemed to take on a life of its own.' He grinned mischievously. 'I've had the best time.'

Anger sizzled through her. 'Yes, I bet you have,' she snapped. 'An all-expenses-paid working holiday. Very nice.' She made herself calm down. 'Have you any idea what you've done to me, Nick?' she asked.

'What d'you mean?' he asked disingenuously. 'We've had a laugh, haven't we? And you said yourself that the summer ratings have gone up. Job done, as far as I can see.' He caught her expression. 'And it was never going to last for ever, was it? I mean, get serious. You and me? That was just a bit of fun. We knew that from the start, so don't try and lay that guilt trip on me.'

She gasped at his callousness. He sounded like a spoilt teenager; she couldn't believe she'd been taken in by someone so immature.

'Don't be so juvenile!' she spat. 'Regardless of anything between us, my reputation, the channel's reputation, is shot to pieces if any of this gets out. If anyone finds out that we've been wilfully deceiving the public, collecting money ...'

'Don't worry, it won't get out.'

'How can you be so sure? It only takes –'

'I said, don't worry. No one will find out. I've made sure. And anyway,' he carried on, 'you haven't been deceiving the public. It's only me and the guys, and we won't tell!'

'Yeah, right,' said Eleanor sarcastically. 'Never mind *the guys* for the minute,' she added. 'What about Eric and Dora and your dad and the rest of the family? They must have been in on it, or I'm sure they would have been in touch.'

'Er, erm ... well, no, actually,' Nick said finally. 'Gran and Pops were safely out of the way.' He laughed hollowly. 'They're in Bhutan, by the way. You were bang on when you said you wished they'd gone somewhere we couldn't follow. I almost gave myself away –'

She stared at him, aghast. 'So, you never did give me their passports, did you?' she interrupted.

Nick frowned. 'Did I say I was going to?'

'Yes. They were supposed to be proof that they hadn't left the country.'

'Oh yes. I remember now. Sorry.' He smiled sheepishly. 'I thought I'd sorted that out with Julian. It must have slipped my mind.'

'Obviously. Did your grandparents know what you were going to do in their absence?'

'Er, just the basics. I told them not to pay any attention to the press, if they happened to come across anything on their travels. They didn't know about the money or anything,' he added hastily.

'It must have been tricky, thinking up an excuse to get round Dora's beliefs,' Eleanor persisted.

'Beliefs?' Nick asked. 'What do you mean?'

'Her Catholicism,' she supplied. 'Or had you forgotten?'

'No ... I ... er ...'

'Come on,' she cajoled. 'You must remember. You told me yourself that she'd come to an *arrangement*,' she emphasised the word, 'with God. About her possible suicide.'

'Oh, that.' He shrugged. 'I didn't think it'd make much difference, to be honest.'

Eleanor laughed. 'Shame you didn't do some more research. That was the start of your undoing. Real Catholics wouldn't countenance suicide. It's against their religion, funnily enough.'

'Yeah, well, I knew that, obviously,' he blustered. 'I

just made the rest up as I went along.'

'One thing you'll have to learn, Nick,' she lectured, 'if you're going to stay in this business – and I sincerely doubt that you will, actually – is that the public will always point out your mistakes.'

'I wasn't –'

'Someone spoke to a local radio station,' Eleanor carried on. 'She said a committed Catholic just wouldn't do such a thing. Rules is rules, apparently.'

Nick waved his hand impatiently. 'Interfering old busybody. What does she know?'

'Doesn't matter,' Eleanor said. 'The result was that other parties became interested. They started to ask questions. And once that happened ...' She shook her head. 'Why I ever let myself be taken in, I really don't know.'

He took a step towards her. 'Don't take it so hard, Eleanor,' he joked. 'You weren't the only one. I was so good I convinced a lot of other people too!'

'What about Jim?' asked Eleanor. Another person she'd trusted. 'Was your dad in on it, too?'

Nick shook his head. 'He doesn't know. Or the rest of the family.'

'I don't believe you.'

'Please yourself.' Nick shrugged. 'It's the truth. They didn't know about the mix up or the letter from the hospital.'

'But –'

'Seriously, they know Eric and Dora are on holiday. End of.' He tried to take her hands but she pulled away. 'Look, none of them watch UK24. Auntie Julie never watches anything but the BBC News, says she doesn't trust anything else. I figured it wouldn't be a problem as long as the mainstreams ignored us.'

Eleanor's head was spinning. She had to get away, to be alone to work this out. The ramifications were enormous. So much goodwill was riding on this search. UK24 had people tuning in night after night to hear the latest. What was she going to say? Who was she going to tell?

She gathered up her coat and bag. 'I've got to get back,' she said. 'I'll be in touch.'

'You can't just leave, Eleanor.' Nick blocked her way to the door. 'We haven't finished yet.'

Panic shot through her. 'What do you mean?'

'I mean, we need to talk about what happens next.'

'I don't understand.'

'Sit down and relax,' Nick invited. 'Would you like a glass of wine?'

Driving back home later that night she tried to decide if she could, in fact, tell anyone. She considered Daniel; he was a huge risk. He could use the information for his own scoop. If his superiors found out, they might insist he did, or he might lose his job if he didn't. The dilemma was giving her indigestion.

She pulled into a motorway services and took out her mobile.

'How did it go?' Daniel asked immediately.

'Not brilliant. Sam was right, though, he had it all worked out.'

'Fucking hell. What a devious bastard.' He was silent for a moment. 'So, what's next? Have you got to confess all to Julian?'

'I will, eventually, but there's another slight problem to sort out first.'

'Which is?'

'Nick wants the money. It's exactly like Sam said, he's doing it to pay off his and his pals' student loans. If we don't pay up, he'll go to the papers and expose us for the complete fools we are. I don't know what to do. How do we get out of this?' She sighed wearily. 'I'll just have to resign before they sack me.'

'Hang on. Not so fast. Let me have a think. Where are you?'

'God knows. Somewhere on the M1. And it's dark.'

'Ring me when you get home. I'll have thought of something by then.'

'But –'

'Trust me.'

Chapter Twenty-seven

In place of the monster that usually inhabited Julian's office, a pussycat had taken up residence. Eleanor let out an unconscious sigh of relief when her head wasn't bitten off. She would wonder why later. At the moment she needed his undivided attention.

'Could we go somewhere a little more private?' she asked. 'I've got a lot to tell you and I'd rather we weren't interrupted.' She led the way through the newsroom and out into the car park, away from prying eyes.

'Let's walk a bit, we can get a coffee at the stand at that DIY store up the street,' said Julian, steering her towards the road. 'Let's get away from here. Walls have ears and all that. We won't be missed. It's the Business half hour.'

As they walked Eleanor explained the situation.

When she'd finished Julian frowned at her, slowly rubbing his forehead as if encouraging her words to penetrate his skull. 'Run that past me again,' he said, I think I must have …'

'No, you haven't misunderstood anything. You heard correctly. Nick intends to go public with the story of how he duped us, if we don't pay all the money over to him. I think he wants me to suffer,' she added miserably.

'Just you? Sounds like he wants the rest of us to have a taste, too.'

He stopped and looked at Eleanor. 'So he wants money in return for his silence,' he mused. 'And why does he think we'll be willing to pay up?'

'Because it's not a fortune and –'

'Depends on your idea of a fortune,' interjected Julian. 'It's over £150,000 now.'

'That much?' Eleanor marvelled. 'Anyway, he thinks the publicity would be too damaging for us to risk.'

'Maybe he's right,' Julian said philosophically. 'Or it could be just a nine-day wonder. Doesn't he know that there's no such thing as bad publicity?' He stood still for a moment and stared into the middle distance, as if expecting a solution to descend from the sky. 'However,' he continued, 'I never did like blackmail. Nasty business. But we don't want to involve the police,' he added hastily.

'Of course not. I've had a thought, though, but we need to move fast.' They had arrived at the stall and Julian ordered two coffees. He gestured towards a couple of garden chairs arranged by an aluminium table, taking up two parking spaces. 'Do tell.'

Eleanor explained about her conversation with Daniel the previous evening. 'We make the discovery into a whole new story,' she said finally. 'You know, get in there first. Turn it on its head.'

Julian stroked his chin thoughtfully. 'Sorry, this flu seems to have rendered my brain completely useless,' he complained. 'Say again.'

Eleanor went through it again slowly.

'So this Daniel approaches Nick, because he's heard a rumour?' Julian still seemed confused. 'That's stretching it a bit. Even I wouldn't believe that, Eleanor.'

'No, not quite. There've been some small items on local news and there was that piece in the magazine, so it wouldn't be completely outside the realms of possibility if Daniel, being a journalist, picks up on it and gets in touch.'

'How will he do that?'

'We'll tell him where Nick is. Nick will just assume that a journalist has his sources,' Eleanor added. 'It's a lever to get Daniel into the situation. When he meets Nick, Daniel will tell him it's such a good story it's bound to make the front page. And he'll mention a ridiculous fee. Nick won't be able to resist.'

'That's too risky,' Julian said. 'We'll lose public sympathy.'

Julian didn't seem terribly quick on the uptake today. 'No, we won't. Daniel will be telling the story from our point of view, not Nick's. We'll be the wronged party.'

Julian brightened visibly. 'Don't let the truth get in the way of a good story, you mean?' he said.

Eleanor grinned. 'That's just what Daniel said.'

'A double-cross,' said Julian. 'Hmm. I'm still not sure. What if –?' He broke off to taste his coffee and grimaced. 'Yeuch, this is worse than the stuff we get at work.'

Eleanor put her cup down. She needed to take the initiative while Julian was still undecided. 'Anyway, what we thought …'

'Which rag does Daniel work for?' Julian interrupted. 'Why would they want to support us?'

'He works for *The Post*, which isn't too bad. At least they're independent. But they'll have to be persuaded.'

Julian narrowed his eyes in concentration. Then his face cleared, as if he'd reached a decision. 'Might work,' he conceded. 'I happen to know the editor quite well. Very well, actually. We'd have to be very careful about the wording though, get it properly legalled and all that. And of course, Britney will have to OK it all,' he said, tipping the remains of his coffee into the waste bin and nodding at the guy wiping the counter with a filthy cloth. 'Thanks, mate, that was really lovely.' He turned to Eleanor. 'I think you might have something. It's a bit of a no-win situation, I grant you, but we might be able to salvage a smidgen of self-respect out of it. How long have we got?'

'Nick's giving us a week to sort it all out.'

'That long?' said Julian sarcastically. 'Better get onto it, then. Actually,' he added, 'do you want me to get Sara Cassidy involved? She'd be great at pulling all the loose ends together. It'll make a great programme for the back half hour.'

Eleanor stared at him. 'Sara? But she doesn't know anything about it. She hasn't been involved. I thought we were doing this on our own. And besides, we don't want to attract too much attention, do we?

Julian nodded. 'Yes, of course. You're absolutely right. I'll speak to him, let him know how things stand.'

She looked at him in surprise. 'No, Julian, you can't do that yet. Not until Daniel has seen him and the piece has appeared in the paper.'

'No, of course not. Sorry, that's what I meant. Are you going to call him and bring him in?'

'No. I don't want him around; he's a loose cannon. God knows what he's capable of. Or his friends. I think it's better if they all stay out of the way.'

'You're probably right.'

'D'you think Daphne will blame me?' asked Eleanor.

'Undoubtedly,' Julian laughed. He patted her on the shoulder. 'But I don't think it'll be terminal. She's not that vindictive.'

'How do you know?' she muttered. 'Don't you think it would be better coming from you?'

He shook his head. 'Sorry, Eleanor, this is your problem. You created the monster. Go and get it over with,' he advised. 'The sooner the better. Before someone else does it for you. You know what this business is like for gossip.'

'Indeed I do,' said Eleanor mournfully. 'I'll do it as soon as we get back.'

'She can't eat you,' said Julian reassuringly. 'The worst she can do is …'

'I know what she can do,' said Eleanor. 'I know exactly what she can do.'

Daphne was also remarkably calm about the whole thing, as it turned out. After she came down from the ceiling.

'You did *what*?!' The exclamation reverberated round

the goldfish bowl office, causing everyone in the immediate vicinity to raise their heads in unison and peer over their computer screens like a family of bemused meerkats. Daphne had no qualms about being overheard. 'On whose authority, may I ask?' she demanded. 'Certainly not mine.' She moved across to the window, her thousand-yard stare raking the newsroom beyond like the beam from a lighthouse. 'Where the hell is Julian when I want him? He must be implicated in this somewhere.' She tapped her fingers on her chin. 'That boy is becoming a liability.'

Eleanor took a deep breath. She'd never seen Daphne so agitated. 'It wasn't Julian's fault,' she mumbled. 'If you'll let me explain, I think we might be able to save the situation.'

'Really?' Daphne asked caustically. 'I sincerely hope so.' She folded her arms and nodded to Eleanor. 'Off you go then, convince me. But I'll tell you now, it'll take a lot.'

Daphne paced round the cramped office, sometimes glaring out into the newsroom, sometimes lifting her eyebrows in amazed incredulity as she listened to Eleanor. She shook her head and tut-tutted at Eleanor's unfortunate choice of boyfriend and regrettable lapse of judgement and then put her formidable mind behind the problem.

'So, let me get this straight,' she said when Eleanor had finished. She perched on the edge of her desk, displaying a quantity of shapely, tanned legs. 'Little Lord butter-wouldn't-melt, the housewives' choice, thinks he can stab us in the back, does he?'

Eleanor nodded miserably.

'Little prick. After all we've done for him, too.'

Eleanor sensed a puzzling softening in Daphne's tone. Britney had never been known to offer any comfort to members of her own sex; in the past she'd left them to struggle up the greasy pole unaided. 'I know,' she agreed. 'I told him he wouldn't get another job anywhere, after we'd finished with him.'

'Too right. He might think he'll be the next big thing, but no one would touch him if they found out what he'd done. And they'd find out all right.' She smiled wickedly. 'He's forgetting one vital thing, you see. This business isn't just about what you know. It's about *who* you know. And I know plenty of people,' she added with a satisfied nod. 'I'll make bloody sure they all know. Nobody will trust him after this.'

'At the moment, he believes he's fireproof,' said Eleanor.

'Does he indeed?' sneered Daphne. 'Burgeoning with the arrogance of youth. Well, we'll see how he reacts when we light a fire under his arse.' She reached for the telephone, thought better of it, and replaced the receiver. 'Obviously, we can kiss goodbye to the RTS News Channel of the Year award if this doesn't go our way,' she said. 'But we might be able to salvage something and keep our reputation intact into the bargain. Bring me some cuttings from this Daniel person,' she instructed, sitting down at her desk and scribbling notes. 'I want to see what his writing's like before I give the final go ahead. Not that I don't trust you, Eleanor, but …'

The words hung in the air between them, leaving Eleanor in no doubt about Daphne's true feelings. She shuffled loose papers in a gesture of dismissal. Her brittle smile turned Eleanor's insides to ice. 'If he's as good as you say, there won't be a problem, will there?'

'Maybe she's on a promise tonight,' Eleanor said to Julian. 'She wasn't anywhere near as bad as I thought she was going to be. Though she was pretty bad,' she added.

'I could hear her from here!' he snorted. Julian's office was diagonally opposite Daphne's, on the other side of the newsroom. 'Everyone thought you were getting your P45. We were laying odds.'

'Thanks for that vote of confidence,' said Eleanor. 'But

actually, she was quite understanding, when she'd calmed down and heard the whole sorry story.'

'Probably remembering when she'd been in a similar situation,' Julian offered.

'What? Got herself into no end of trouble over a boy?'

'Indeed,' he said mysteriously. 'You'd never guess, would you? With her always overflowing with the milk of human kindness.'

'What happened?'

'Apparently,' said Julian, tapping his nose with a finger, 'in the early days – I'm talking prehistoric now, pre-rolling news anyhow – when she was mere Home News editor, she got herself involved with an intern. A bit like you did, I suppose.' He grinned. 'Ancient history now, no one gives a stuff, but in those days it was dynamite.'

'How do you know all this?'

Julian assumed an expression of angelic innocence and Eleanor looked at him nonplussed for a moment.

'What? Oh my God, it wasn't you, was it?'

He rested his chin on his hands and grinned like a cherub. 'Difficult to credit, isn't it?'

'Sorry,' spluttered Eleanor. 'I assumed you were … So what happened?'

'Ah,' he said, putting the back of his hand to his forehead theatrically. 'It was in those heady days of youthful angst. I wasn't completely sure, I was curious, so I experimented a little. Daphne was instrumental in persuading me down the right path.'

'Fucking hell,' said Eleanor.

'It was, lovey, it absolutely was. But don't tell anyone.'

Chapter Twenty-eight

Eleanor walked back to her desk hugging this little secret to herself. She had to tell someone, but who? Her mobile rang as she reached for it. She squinted at the screen. Daniel. Her heart did a little flip. 'I was just going to call you,' she said. 'How's it going?'

'Just wanted to let you know that Julian was true to his word,' Daniel said. 'Turning the tables on Nick has all been OK'd by my editor. Ed's very keen, actually; it's a very slow news week.'

'Good old silly season,' Eleanor observed. 'Daphne wants the story wound up as quickly as possible,' she carried on. 'But no on-air revelations just yet. As far as Nick is concerned, UK24 will appear to be going along with his demands. But in return Daphne has insisted that Nick makes one final appeal to keep public sympathy riding high.'

'Sounds reasonable to me,' Daniel said.

'When will you set off?'

'Hopefully this afternoon. I'll call you when I've made contact. He shouldn't be too difficult to find,' he added, 'but keep me posted if he moves further afield.'

'Will do. He was still hiding in the wilds of South Yorkshire when Belle spoke to him this morning. He needs to stay fairly static, I suppose, to do this evening's piece. But I'll let you know if he heads off in another imaginary pursuit. As if,' she snorted.

'Can't wait to get on the road again,' said Daniel. 'Just like old times,' he added wistfully.

As she put the phone down, Eleanor noticed Belle

approaching from the other side of the newsroom. She was wearing a very determined expression and, Eleanor couldn't help noticing, the same outfit as yesterday. 'You obviously didn't get home last night,' she observed dryly. 'That's the trouble with always dressing up, Belle. You never blend into the background.'

'And I never want to, either,' Belle retorted. 'You're right, though. I didn't.'

'Good night?' Eleanor asked.

'Brilliant. Absolutely brilliant. I went out with Marcus,' she added.

'Oh good.' Eleanor shook her head blankly. 'Anyone I know?'

'You can't have forgotten, Eleanor. That lovely man we interviewed yesterday. Tommy Trivia, you called him, remember?'

'Oh, *him*,' said Eleanor. 'Yes, of course. Sorry, Belle, too much going on. Quite good looking, wasn't he?'

'He is,' Belle murmured dreamily. She stared off into the middle distance, obviously reliving some part of her evening with Marcus. 'And ...'

'Hey, love's young dream.' Julian leaned across the pod of desks and spoke pointedly to Belle. 'I thought I asked you for an update on that flood story.' He rapped the desk impatiently. 'Where is it? I need the printouts, like, now.'

'Oh, sorry, Julian,' Belle blustered. She nudged Eleanor to one side and pressed a couple of keys. 'Printing it now.' She handed him a sheaf of papers. 'There you are. Anything else?' Julian grunted and strode away wordlessly. Belle turned back to Eleanor, unconcerned. 'What the hell's the matter with him? I thought he'd turned a corner. Anyway, where was I?'

'Marcus,' Eleanor prompted.

'Oh yes, Marcus.' Her eyes lit up with excitement. 'Well. He's offered me an audition. He was very impressed when he saw me in character yesterday. Only,' Belle looked round furtively, 'don't tell anybody yet. I'll have to see how it pans out first.'

'Is it serious, then?' asked Eleanor. 'I mean, would you leave if you got a chance at acting?'

'Are you mad?' Belle demanded, astounded. 'I'd be out of here like a shot. It's all I've ever wanted to do. I'm so grateful to you for sorting it out, Eleanor. I could never have engineered a meeting with someone so powerful.' She grimaced. 'Especially after I ... you know, lost those passports, too.'

'You didn't lo –' Eleanor began. 'Don't worry about it, Belle. It wasn't your fault,' she finished. She would have to tell Belle the truth at some stage, but not yet.

Belle seemed oblivious. 'By the way,' she carried on, 'I've changed the venue for my thirtieth. So many people have promised to come they won't all fit in my flat, so we're having it at The Swan. They've got a karaoke machine in a small bar at the side and we can have it to ourselves. You're still coming, aren't you?' she urged. 'Only I've arranged for Johnny the cameraman to film us all.'

'Whatever for?' Eleanor smiled thinly. She was already hoping for an emergency that would mean a last minute change of shift. She really didn't want to be filmed.

'Well, you never know, do you?' said Belle.

Daniel rang in the late afternoon.

'Where are you?' Eleanor asked eagerly.

'In a part of the country where fried bread constitutes one of your five-a-day,' he replied. 'Somewhere in God's country. You'd feel right at home.'

'Great. Have you found Nick yet?'

'I know where he is, but I haven't contacted him yet. Daphne wanted me to let him deliver tonight's piece before we sprang the trap. He's got a reservation at a place near the racecourse, so I'll go and wait for him there.'

'You will be careful, won't you?' Eleanor begged.

'Why? Is he dangerous?' Daniel groaned theatrically. 'He's not going to come at me with a sock full of sand, is he? Now you tell me.'

'No, but ... well, these things can be a bit unpredictable, can't they?'

'I'm a grown-up now, El. I can handle myself. Nick will just roll over, you'll see.'

'I hope so. When will you be back?'

'I don't intend to hang around afterwards. I'll be on my way back as soon as I finish the interview. I'll call you.'

'OK. Don't worry if it's late. Call me anyway. I won't sleep until you do.'

'Will do,' he said. 'Anyway, gotta go. I've got an assignment to finish.'

Nick's evening report was a tour de force and Daphne was very happy.

'He's played right into our hands,' she said gleefully. 'Listen to him, he's contradicted that radio report of our supposed misconduct, but it's like he's got a death wish. He's taunting us, as if we haven't seen through him yet. Pompous little git. I can't wait for this to be over and see him get his comeuppance.'

Eleanor was sitting nervously between Daphne and Julian, her mouth too dry for speech, as they watched his final offering.

As instructed, Nick didn't mention that his odyssey was about to come to an unceremonious end. Instead he concentrated on how close he was to finding his grandparents and how relieved he'd be when he could finally deliver the good news.

'Good God,' said Daphne as Nick prattled on about loyalty and sentiment. 'He'd bring tears to a glass eye, wouldn't he? We wouldn't normally let that kind of stuff go out; it's too twee for us, isn't it? Still, you've got to admire him in a way,' she continued, ignoring Julian's and Eleanor's incredulous stares. 'I mean, it takes a special kind of talent to concoct such a pile of complete shit, and string people along for so long, hanging on his every bloody word.'

'Quite.' Julian coughed embarrassedly. 'Anyway, have we heard from Daniel?'

'Not yet.'

'When's he going to report in?'

'After he's done the deed,' said Eleanor. 'He'll let me know tonight, when it's all sorted.'

'And when he's going to print?'

'Day after tomorrow.' She looked at Daphne. 'That's the arrangement, isn't it?'

Daphne nodded. 'That's right. Saturday.' She stood up and beckoned to Julian. 'We've got to decide how we're going to play it on Saturday. Do we start the day with a confession, or let the paper reveal all first?'

Julian looked at her quizzically. 'Didn't *The Post* stipulate? I would have thought that –'

'No. Well, you know Ed. He said he'd leave it to us. Works for him either way. Though I suppose there's a marginal gain for him if he gets in first. But we should tease it up in the six o'clock, then we'll have the rest of the day to make hay.'

'Whatever you say,' agreed Julian, leaving the room behind Daphne. 'I'll get someone onto it straightaway.'

'I'm going to the gym,' Eleanor said. 'Try to relieve some stress.'

There was no word from Daniel by the time she got home. The gym workout had done the trick and she snuggled into bed with mobile and landline within easy reach and picked up her novel. Half an hour later, realising she hadn't taken in a single word, she abandoned the book and switched on the television. She was channel surfing, holding her mobile in the other hand and willing it to ring, when the landline on the bedside table jangled into life. She dropped the remote and grabbed the handset. 'Hello?'

'Hi, it's me,' said Daniel unnecessarily. 'It's done.'

'What did he say?' Eleanor asked eagerly.

'Actually, he was a very amenable interviewee.'

'Was he suspicious?'

'He was, at first. He wanted to know how I'd found out.'

'What did you say?'

'I said a friend who lives in Derbyshire called me after the local news report that you'd heard. I acted innocent and said I was just on a fishing expedition.'

'So he fell for it ...?'

'You should have seen his face when I mentioned the fee!' Daniel interrupted. 'His eyes were like saucers.'

'I can't believe he was so easily taken in,' Eleanor said. 'He always seemed so switched on, you know?'

'I think you'll find that's called greed, El. I did string him along a bit. Exaggerated things. I told him that the big networks were contributing to the fee, to make it look as if they were keen to see UK24 in the shit.'

'Not difficult to imagine.'

'No, I suppose not,' Daniel laughed. 'Anyway, it always comes down to money, Eleanor. You were right,' he carried on. 'He said it'd pay off a big chunk of student loan.'

'What about his friends? Has he left them high and dry? I wouldn't be surprised.'

'No, he was very honourable. He said they'd divvy it up between them.' He chuckled. 'He was quite interested in the notoriety angle too. Said it would make his career. But I didn't want to get involved with all that. I just concentrated in getting him to believe me.'

'That's brilliant,' Eleanor cooed. 'I knew you could do

it. So, what now?'

'Head down and write the thing. Actually, Nick was very forthcoming, once I'd bought him a couple of drinks and established some trust. He even played me his final report. It was quite clever, wasn't it? You'd never have known that he'd been rumbled.'

'That was part of the deal. But even then Daphne nearly pulled it because it was a bit nauseating. Twee, she called it. Not up to our usual standard.'

'I don't agree. It pulled at the old heartstrings; usual UK24 fodder, I'd have thought.'

'Did he say anything else?' Eleanor asked tentatively.

'Oh yes, he told me everything.'

'Everything?' Eleanor echoed. 'Well, that's ... that's good, isn't it? I mean ...'

Daniel laughed. 'He didn't say anything about you, if that's what you're getting at. Except, you know, in passing.'

Eleanor was horrified. 'What do you mean, *in passing*?'

'Just that he'd spun you this yarn and you'd swallowed it, hook, line and ...'

'The bastard!' she shouted.

'I'm joking. Actually, he didn't mention any names, even when I pressed him. He said he wanted to preserve your anonymity. For the sake of your career, he said.'

'Big of him,' she conceded. 'Not that I'll have a career left after this.' She sighed. 'No matter how you write this, Daniel, I'm not going to come out of it smelling of roses, am I?'

'You just leave that to me,' Daniel assured her.

'Did he mention –?'

'What? Oh, you and him, you mean? Well, actually, he went into graphic detail ... I didn't realise you were quite such a goer ...'

'He didn't!'

There was a definite pause. 'No, he never said a word.'

Eleanor let out her breath. 'I should bloody well hope not!' she snapped indignantly. She settled back comfortably into the pillows. 'Thank God for that. Now, tell me what you're going to write.'

'You'll have to wait. I tell you what, I'll meet you in the Kings Arms on Saturday lunchtime. It's just round the corner from the flat. We can go over it together then.'

Chapter Twenty-nine

Eleanor was enjoying a cup of tea in bed very early on Saturday morning when the telephone rang. Her thoughts turned immediately to Nick and today's newspaper exposé. She grabbed the phone, expecting it to be the newsdesk calling with an update. It was her mother.

'Hello, darling. Hope I didn't wake you.' Sylvia seemed very upbeat for this ungodly hour. 'I just thought I'd better let you know. Your father's left. Actually, I asked him to leave last night.'

Eleanor stared at the phone, remembering the scene through the café window in Skipton high street in all its stark detail. 'Blimey. Why?' she asked tentatively.

'He's been at it again. With Tamsin Schofield, of all people. You were at school with her, weren't you? Anyway, I've had enough this time, Eleanor. I told him to pack his bags.'

'Oh,' Eleanor repeated.

'You don't seem very surprised. Did you know something?'

'No, of course not!' Eleanor blustered. 'How would I?'

'No reason. Sorry, I feel as if the whole world knew what was going on before I did, that's all. Even Gladys from next door gave me a very knowing look yesterday, and she's usually very slow on the uptake. So humiliating.'

'Don't be silly. You're imagining it.'

'Maybe,' Sylvia conceded.

'Would you like me to come up? Do you need a bit of hand-holding?'

'No, no, darling. Thanks for offering, but I'm very well, considering. I should have done it years ago. I know he's your father and all that, but ...'

Eleanor was actually deeply impressed. She hadn't wanted to completely reject her father despite being painfully aware of his extra-curricular activities. Rather than confront him and hurt her mother immeasurably in the process, she'd pushed the feelings of betrayal to the back of her mind and father and daughter had managed to build an affectionate relationship. She'd long given up hope that her mother would finally see the light.

'No, actually I think you've done the right thing ...' she reassured her. 'Is this a permanent arrangement?'

'Not sure yet. I'm still thinking about it. Too soon to tell.'

'You're probably right,' Eleanor agreed. 'Let him stew for a while,' she added, feeling strangely disloyal to her father.

'I told him I knew about all the other ones, too,' Sylvia carried on. 'Of course he tried to deny them all.' She laughed shortly. 'His face was a picture.'

'You sound like you've lost a pound and found a tenner,' Eleanor joked.

'I know!' Her mother was suddenly serious. 'But this whole affair, pardon the pun, has taught me a very important lesson.'

Eleanor couldn't think what this could possibly be, but it sounded as if a parental lecture was looming. She pulled the duvet up to her chin and prepared to listen. 'What's that?' she asked.

'Well, it's quite difficult to put it into words, but I've had all night to think about it.' Eleanor heard Sylvia draw a deep breath. 'Whilst he was protesting his innocence, your father informed me that I was partly to blame for what had happened.'

'What?' Eleanor was appalled. 'Sounds like a typical guilty man response,' she snorted. 'Why was it your fault?'

'That was my question. Apparently,' Sylvia continued, the word loaded with irony, 'it was partly my fault because I hadn't told him how I felt about anything for years.' She sniffed ruefully. 'Funny that the longest conversation I've had with your father in years was about where it all went wrong. There was I, suffering in silence, thinking that turning a blind eye was holding the marriage together. Unfortunately, he was taking my silence as a sign of approval. Like I was giving him permission to carry on. Stupid man assumed I didn't care.'

'But he would say that, wouldn't he, Mum?' said Eleanor. 'That's just him trying to shift the blame.'

'Partly,' Sylvia agreed. 'But he does have a point.' She paused for a moment. 'And it's made me reassess everything.'

Eleanor held her breath. Her mother hadn't been so frank and forthcoming for a long time.

'I should have got it out into the open,' Sylvia said. 'I shouldn't have been a martyr. All this looking inwards, keeping things to yourself, it just doesn't work.' Sylvia sounded like she'd swallowed a self-help manual. 'It's like a weight's been lifted. Now that I've finally told him how he's made me feel all these years, it's liberated me.'

'What did Dad say?'

'Just what you'd expect. Full of remorse. "I'll never do it again, if you'll only forgive me."' she mimicked nastily. Sylvia slurped something, hopefully not gin at this time in the morning. 'Then he tried to blame me again.'

'Oh, Mum,' Eleanor sympathised. 'It's not your fault.'

Several years ago, when she'd been feeling particularly miserable about gaining a few pounds, Sylvia had confessed to Eleanor that she'd never felt worthy of Doug. In what she called her 'beige years', the shy and mousy Sylvia had been so flattered that Doug had even noticed her that she'd been happy to bask in his reflected glory, not realising until after they were married and it was far too late, that Doug needed just such a companion by his side so that he would shine.

'I know,' Sylvia carried on, 'but now I think things would've been different if I'd stood up for myself and given him hell from the beginning.'

'Do you think they would have been?'

'I don't know.' Sylvia took another swig. 'It's not important now. But the thing is, darling, I wanted to warn you.'

'What about? I'm not having an affair with a married man or anything.'

'Of course you're not. But Eleanor, I've noticed that you've not been the same since you found out about Daniel being engaged to that Angie person. I'm worried that you're still hankering after him.'

Eleanor said nothing.

'Hmm,' Sylvia declared. 'Your silence speaks volumes. I'm right, aren't I? A mother can tell, you know. Sweetheart, you're worth so much more than this, and you have the right to let him know how you feel. You know, you only regret the things you don't do,' Sylvia carried on, sounding even more evangelical, 'not the things you do. Anyway,' she added, 'I won't pursue it. I'll leave it with you. It's your life, and I'll get out of it now. I'll ring you next week, let you know how things are going. Bye.'

Eleanor put the phone down and stared thoughtfully at the wall for a long time. She sat up and rearranged the pillows, crossing her legs yoga fashion to make a hollow space which Mabel settled into immediately, purring loudly.

'What do you think, Mabes?' she asked. 'I can't say anything, can I? He left me. I obviously wasn't worth worrying about then, so what's changed? I know he's apologised, but that doesn't mean we can go back to the way we were. It's ridiculous. Still, we can dream, can't we?'

Eventually she scrabbled about under the bed for her handbag and pulled out the Mont Blanc ballpoint that Daniel had given her on her twenty-first birthday. She found a pad of writing paper in the bottom drawer of her bedside table and was just beginning to scribble when the phone rang again.

'You fucking bitch!' Nick shouted furiously down the phone. 'You're all in it together, aren't you?'

Nick had obviously seen that morning's newspaper. Eleanor had been anticipating a reaction, but he was even angrier than she'd expected. 'I don't –'

'Spare me the excuses,' he snarled. 'You've stitched me up.'

Eleanor finally found her voice. 'Don't be so melodramatic,' she snapped. 'What the hell did you expect? Anyway, *you* stitched *me* up first.'

'You didn't honour the spirit of the agreement. And Julian said –'

She almost laughed at his petulance. 'Honour?' she scoffed. 'You don't know the meaning of the word. Get real, Nick, it was always going to end in tears. We just turned the tables, that's all. Admit it; you're mad because you didn't see it coming.'

'I'll get even, you know,' he warned. 'You can depend on it.'

'Don't threaten me, Nick,' Eleanor said, gaining confidence. 'I've got a whole legal team behind me.'

He grunted. 'I've not finished with you yet, Eleanor, or Julian. Just you wait.' He hung up before Eleanor could say another word.

Her hands were shaking so badly she fumbled the keys on the next call.

'Don't let him worry you,' Daniel reassured her. 'He can't do anything. He hasn't got a leg to stand on and he knows it. It's just empty threats.'

'But –'

'I said don't worry. I'll see you at the pub later like we arranged. We can look at the paper together.'

Eleanor couldn't wait that long. She pulled on a T-shirt and jeans and went downstairs. Grabbing an assortment of coins from the kitchen counter, she picked up her keys and slammed the front door behind her.

Chapter Thirty

Daniel was already sitting by the window when Eleanor walked into the pub. His jacket was hung over the back of the chair and he had the newspaper spread out on the table. He put down his pint of bitter when he saw her and moved across to the bar. 'Half of lager?'

'Yes, please. And some crisps. I haven't had anything to eat yet.'

'Me neither.' He picked up a menu. 'We could get a meal, if you'd like.'

'No thanks,' said Eleanor. 'I haven't got much of an appetite, actually. Crisps will be fine.' She scooted her chair closer to his and basked in his proximity as they pored over the newspaper. 'It's no wonder Nick was annoyed,' she said. 'He had a right go this morning. He was very shouty. Said we'd double-crossed him.'

'Well, strictly speaking, we have.'

'Will you pay him the money?' Eleanor asked. 'The fee you mentioned?'

'Not a hope. Will you?'

'"The appeal has been closed and all donations will be refunded."' Eleanor quoted. 'That's the official line. So, no, he won't get a penny.' She giggled. 'Serves him right.'

'Couldn't have happened to a nicer person,' Daniel joined in. 'My editor likes it too. Have you heard from Julian or Daphne?'

'Yes, Daphne's sent a text. She seemed to like what you had to say.'

'What about you?'

Eleanor thought for a while. 'Well,' she began, 'I liked that you didn't make me out to be a complete idiot.' She swivelled the page round to face her, scanning the paragraphs. 'What did you say? Oh, here it is. "*The experienced news researcher had no reason to doubt his word. All angles had been checked thoroughly ...*"' She grimaced. 'The truth suffered a bit there, didn't it?'

'Well, what's a little white lie between friends?' Daniel asked. He put his hand over hers. 'It was a good story, El, and like all the best fairy stories, the baddy got his comeuppance.'

'A modern day morality tale.'

'If you like. Nick got what was coming to him because he crossed the line. In his last report he went too far, talking down to the public like they were a bunch of fools. Patronising twat. He was easy meat. Anyway, enough about that,' he said, folding the newspaper and moving it aside. 'I've got something to tell you.'

Eleanor was surprised. She smiled nervously. 'I've got something to tell you, too.'

'Oh? I ... I –' He frowned at her. 'Go on, then. Ladies first. Mine can wait a while.'

'No, it's OK. You –'

'Just tell me, Eleanor! I insist. The floor's yours.'

Eleanor checked the door. The last thing she needed was Angie coming in unexpectedly. 'Well,' she began. 'I just wanted to say ...' This was even more difficult than she'd anticipated. 'You know when ... well, what happened four years ago?'

'As if I could forget.' He wriggled uncomfortably. 'El, if this is about –'

She put up a hand to silence him. 'Let me finish, please. It's important that I say this.'

'I don't think you need –' He sat back suddenly, raising his hands palms up in surrender. 'OK, go on.'

As Eleanor opened her mouth to continue Daniel's mobile burst into the theme from *Thunderbirds*.

'Bugger,' he said, twisting the phone away from the

sunlight reflected on the screen. 'I can't see the number. Sorry, I should take it. It might –'

Eleanor pantomimed another drink, but Daniel shook his head as he listened. He put the mobile down. 'I've got to go. I'm really sorry.' He passed a hand over his face and rubbed his chin. 'Sorry,' he repeated.

'Whatever's the matter?' Eleanor asked. 'You look like you've seen a ghost.'

He laughed bleakly. 'Almost.' He took her hand across the table. 'Sorry,' he said again. 'I'll tell you all about it another day. But I really must go now. Honestly. Let's talk tomorrow.'

'Thank you, by the way,' she gestured at the newspaper, 'for all this. I really appreciate it.' He nodded distractedly then he went, leaving Eleanor wondering what the hell was going on. This behaviour was completely unlike the Daniel she'd known so well. But she had no choice but to take him at his word and wait until the next day for an explanation.

Being Saturday, there wasn't a parking space anywhere near her house. She parked two streets away and walked leisurely back, wondering how to fill the afternoon after Daniel's mysterious phone call had curtailed their arrangements. She might give Sam a call, see if she was free. They could dissect the conundrum and celebrate the end of the Pagets' story over a bottle of wine that evening.

She took out her phone, but dropped it back into her bag as she turned the corner. There was a familiar figure on the pavement in front of her gate.

Nick was leaning on the garden wall, watching her approach. After the way their conversation had gone that morning, Eleanor would have liked some support but there was no time to text Sam. She looked around surreptitiously; the street was deserted.

'What do you want?' she asked nervously as she

reached the garden gate.

'I would've thought that was obvious,' Nick sneered. 'I told you we hadn't finished, Eleanor.'

'Well, I've got nothing to say to you,' she said, with more bravado than she felt. She put her hand in her pocket but deliberately didn't pull out her keys; instead she manoeuvred them between her fingers like she'd learned in a self-defence class years ago. 'And you're not coming in.'

'Why so hostile, Ellie?' he asked. His casual use of the hated diminutive jarred. 'I've had a long drive. Surely you don't begrudge me a cup of tea and a slice of toast?'

'I haven't got any bread.'

He shrugged. 'A chocolate biscuit will do. And I know you've always got lots of those in the cupboard.'

She dithered, looking up and down the empty street. Why was there never anyone around when she needed them?

'Come on,' Nick urged as she hung back. 'What do you think I'm going to do?' He walked up the short path. 'I only want to talk.'

'I don't want to talk to you,' Eleanor said. 'In fact, I have nothing whatever to say to you.'

Nick pointed down the street. Eleanor recognised the navy blue camera car, parked a few yards away. 'I sort of assumed you'd want the kit back.'

'Of course we do,' she snorted. 'Why didn't you take it straight to work and leave it there?'

'What do you take me for, Eleanor? I wanted to hand it over personally. Show there's no hard feelings. And anyway, if I'd left it there, how was I going to get to the station?'

Eleanor's heart slowed marginally. Maybe she was over-reacting and he just wanted to tidy things up after all. She took out her keys and opened the front door. 'One cup, all right?'

'And a biscuit. Don't forget the biscuit.' He crowded

behind her into the narrow hallway, bending to stroke Mabel in a gesture of propriety that had the cat streaking upstairs immediately.

'You've frightened her,' Eleanor said.

'She's just timid,' Nick retorted. 'Like her owner.' He started up the stairs to where Mabel occupied the top step tentatively, poised for flight and watching his progress with her inscrutable topaz gaze. 'I don't think she likes me,' he said.

'I don't blame her,' Eleanor scoffed. 'Cats are very good at reading a person's character, you know.'

'You don't say,' he drawled. 'Well, as I don't want to get scratched, I'll leave her to it.' He made a tactical retreat and took off his jacket, hanging it over the back of a chair. He walked into the kitchen and filled the kettle as if he owned the place, then began opening and closing cupboard doors, hunting for biscuits. 'Where do you keep them?' he asked, peering into an empty tin. 'I forget.'

'I never said I had any,' Eleanor said with some satisfaction. 'Just have your tea and go. You can find your own way to the station.'

'Not so fast. It's too hot, anyway.' He carried the two mugs into the sitting room and sat down on the sofa, patting the space next to him. 'Come and sit down.'

Eleanor perched on the arm of the chair opposite. 'I'm OK here, thanks. What did you want to say?'

Nick took a sip of tea. 'Ugh, no sugar,' he moaned.

Eleanor waited, grasping her mug tightly and hoping Nick wouldn't notice that her knuckles were white but being utterly unable to relax her grip. He put his mug down on the small table beside the settee and picked up the TV remote control. She leaned over and snatched it out of his hand. 'There's no time for that,' she snapped. 'Just say what you have to say and go, please.'

She stood up and moved towards the door. Nick did the same. He put out a hand and stroked the side of her face.

She willed herself not to panic. She had no idea what he was going to do; she just had to keep calm and get him out of the house. He pinned her against the wall, pressing himself against her. 'You're so lovely,' he said, his voice almost a caress. 'How about one for the road?'

Eleanor froze. 'I told you, I haven't got any biscuits,' she managed.

'You know what I mean,' Nick said, his mouth grazing her neck. 'Let's go upstairs, for old times' sake.'

She struggled to free herself from his grasp, but he was very strong. She could hear the self-defence instructor – *Fight. Don't fight. Go limp. Stamp on his instep. Do whatever he says. Gouge his eyes out.* The contradictions made her head spin as Nick pulled her into the hallway and towards the stairs.

She bought herself a little time by stumbling deliberately on the first step. 'Leave me alone,' she grunted, seizing the moment to turn awkwardly and plant a knee firmly between his legs.

He leapt back, clutching his groin. 'You bitch,' he shouted again. He lunged towards her and grabbed her shoulders. She managed a small, muffled scream just as the doorbell shrilled, followed by a loud rap on the front door.

'Eleanor, sweetheart,' a voice shouted through the letterbox. 'Are you all right? What's happening?'

Chapter Thirty-one

Eleanor wrenched the door open and sagged with relief against her father. 'Nick's just going,' she explained brightly, unwilling, for the moment, to tell Doug the whole truth.

'He just popped in to drop the kit off, didn't you, Nick?'

Nick muttered something about catching a train and pushed past Doug, dragging his jacket on as he went. 'The keys are in the kitchen. See you later,' he said, avoiding Eleanor's eye and pulling the door shut behind him.

Doug looked at her suspiciously. 'What did I interrupt?' he asked. 'Wasn't he the boy who was trailing his grandparents?'

Eleanor nodded, close to tears.

'What was he doing here? He didn't hurt you, did he?'

'It's all finished now,' she said wearily. 'It's in today's paper.' She fished about for the newspaper on the table, folded it at the right page, and handed it to Doug. 'He's a fraud, Dad. Daniel wrote it all up. Look.'

Doug was silent for a while as he skimmed the article. 'And he came round here to exact his revenge, did he?' he asked eventually.

'Sort of.' Eleanor was impressed with her father's acuity.

Doug gathered her in his arms as tears welled in her eyes. 'Looks like I got here just in time.' He waited until her sobs had subsided before asking, 'Shall I put the kettle on or call the police?'

Eleanor laughed weakly and dabbed at her cheeks, shaking her head. 'The kettle. We don't need the police.

Nothing actually happened.'

'But ...'

'No, Dad, it's OK. He's not normally like that. He's just annoyed that things didn't work out and he won't get any money, that's all.' She smiled at him. 'Let's leave it, eh?'

'If you say so, El, I won't push it. But if he ever ...'

'He won't.' She giggled suddenly. 'Anyway, if he did, Daniel would just write another article.'

'Are you going to tell Daniel about this?'

Eleanor shrugged. 'Probably not. There's no point. It would only get him all worked up for no good reason. She turned her attention to her father and folded her arms. 'Thanks for being my knight in shining armour,' she said. 'But what's going on? Mum said ...'

'Before we get into that,' Doug interrupted, 'have you got any food in?' He picked up a cork place mat from the table. 'Sorry, sweetheart, I haven't eaten anything since yesterday lunchtime. I'm so hungry I could eat this mat.'

Eleanor looked at him properly for the first time since he'd arrived. He looked unkempt, dishevelled. His hair was longer than usual and he needed a shave.

'You look like you slept under a hedge,' she said. 'Where've you been staying?'

'A shabby little B&B in Brentford,' he snorted. 'The hedgerow would have been preferable.'

'Come into the kitchen,' Eleanor said, leading the way. 'Let's see what we've got.' Her evening with Sam a distant memory before it had even been arranged, she opened the fridge door and started pulling out the ingredients for a very large sandwich.

'Look at this, poppet.'

Overnight, Doug had settled happily into life as a temporary lodger and Eleanor was already hoping it wouldn't become permanent. It was almost as if he was recreating her childhood, except that Eleanor had taken on Sylvia's role, waiting on her father hand and foot. She'd let him stay a couple of nights, she thought, until he'd sorted himself out, but any longer and they'd both be climbing the walls. She shuddered at the thought of Doug hogging the sofa and the TV remote, eyeing up all her female friends when they came to visit.

She looked over his shoulder at the business section of the Sunday newspaper. He was tapping an article with his finger. 'Isn't this Daniel's family?'

'The Hardwicks? Yes, that's them. Why, has something happened? Read it to me, I can't read the small print without my glasses.'

'Looks like they've lost all their money.'

'What, all of it?' Her heart landed in the pit of her stomach like a small rock. 'You're joking.'

'Apart from a small apartment in London where they're holed up at the moment, doesn't say where, they've lost the lot. The official receivers are already at Mensum Hall ...'

Eleanor was horrified. 'That's what Daniel's phone call must have been about yesterday, when we were in the pub. Poor Gwen and Peter. How did it happen?'

'Says here that Peter gambled on a few investments that went bad.'

'That can't be right!' Eleanor exclaimed. 'Peter's always been so sensible. He must have had some duff advice.'

Doug waved his slice of toast, dripping strawberry jam down the front of his pyjamas. 'Oops, sorry.' He caught the dollop with his little finger and transported it to his mouth sheepishly, then swiped ineffectually at the stain. 'Hardwick's not blaming anyone else. He's saying it was market forces and his own reckless behaviour that caused it.' Doug swallowed another bite of toast before continuing the commentary. 'Apparently the business had been on the skids for a while and Hardwick didn't do enough to shore it up.'

Eleanor remembered the recent visit to Mensum Hall for Grace's birthday, when there had been no staff in evidence, where broken fences went untended, and where the stables were empty.

'The expense of the party must have been the final nail in the coffin,' she observed.

Doug nodded. 'Just as well you didn't marry into the family,' he teased. 'You'd be on your uppers, too.' He grinned widely. 'Hey, now's your chance! I don't suppose that gold-digger Angela will want anything to do with Daniel now. He's practically a pauper!'

'Dad!' She laughed. 'But who knows?' She didn't mention seeing Angie in Soho.

'Appearances can be deceptive,' Doug said blandly. 'I know her type.'

'I'd better give him a ring.' Eleanor said, picking up her mobile. 'On second thoughts, maybe a text would be better. I don't really want to speak to Angie.'

Almost as soon as the text was sent, a message bounced back.

'I'm going out,' she said as she responded. 'Daniel is by himself. He's asked me to go round. He's just been reading the papers too.' She stopped. 'Oh my God. What if he's just found out? What if Peter didn't tell him anything?'

'He must have done,' Doug reassured her.

'You'll be OK by yourself, will you?' she asked. 'I don't know what time I'll be back, but help yourself to whatever's in the fridge.' She plucked a sheaf of takeaway menus off a shelf and thrust them into his hand. 'They all deliver. We'll talk a bit more about what you and Mum are going to do when I get home.'

'Sure, sweetheart. You have a good time.' He pointed to the flat screen television. 'Leeds are playing today, anyway, so I can put my feet up in front of this magnificent contraption and watch a bit of footie, without feeling guilty.'

Eleanor was continually surprised at her father's capacity to ignore the finer details of life. 'You do that,' she laughed as she went out of the door.

Daniel answered the door as soon as Eleanor knocked. 'Come in, come in,' he said as he ushered her into the hallway. 'Let me take your coat. Are you sure I'm not mucking up your Sunday afternoon? I know how precious your days off are.'

She shrugged her jacket off and turned to face him. 'No more precious than yours,' she said reasonably. 'Anyway, I'm glad to be out of the house, to be honest. My dad turned up yesterday, completely out of the blue.'

'Flying visit?'

'Not quite. Mum threw him out on Thursday night.'

'What?'

'She found out about his latest conquest and decided enough was enough.'

'Fuck. What's he doing now?'

'I left him watching the football. Leeds versus QRP or something.'

Daniel snorted with laughter. 'QPR,' he stuttered. 'Queen's Park Rangers.'

'Whatever.'

'No, I mean, what are his plans?'

'When he tells me you'll be the first to know. I just hope he doesn't hang around too long. He'll outstay his welcome pretty quickly. There's only so much sport and comedy I can stand.'

'Why didn't he go and stay with, er ... with the other woman?'

Eleanor raised an eyebrow. 'Tamsin's married, apparently. And not about to upset her happy home.' She shook her head. 'Serves him right, you know. I can't muster up much sympathy. But he is my dad.'

'You sound as if you've been expecting this. You didn't know anything about this recent philandering, did you?'

'Not until Mum told me the other night.' Eleanor chewed her lip. 'But actually, I did see him with her.'

'You didn't! When? And you didn't say anything to your mum?'

'It was only a couple of weeks ago! I was going to tell her, honestly. But I wanted to do it face to face, when Dad wasn't there. Not on the phone. Her going off on one like this is completely unexpected.'

'Is this permanent?'

'I'm not sure. The other night, Mum just said she was going to have some fun. She didn't say anything about the future.' She waved her hand impatiently. 'But never mind about that. Why didn't you tell me about this before?'

Daniel looked momentarily dumbfounded. 'How did – ?'

'All the stuff in the papers about your dad,' she carried on. 'Did you know what was happening?'

'Oh, sorry, I thought you meant –' He broke off. 'Of course I did. Come through.'

Eleanor walked into the kitchen and frowned. 'Angie not here?' she asked. 'Is her mum sick again?'

'No, nothing like that.' He pressed his lips together as if he was trying to make a difficult decision. 'I'll tell you about that later.'

Over a pot of tea, Daniel gave her a précised version of his father's financial disaster.

'Dad told me ages ago that things weren't going well, but he seemed confident that he could stem the flow.' He shook his head. 'The business was haemorrhaging money. If only he'd listened to the warnings. He's always been a bit pig-headed like that. "I know best", that sort of thing.

He's never taken advice gladly.' He shrugged. 'I just assumed he'd pull out of the downward spiral and everything would be fine, but he rang yesterday to warn me about the story in the papers.'

'Your poor mother,' said Eleanor. 'How's she taking it? She must be devastated.'

Daniel shook his head and took a gulp of tea. 'Actually, she's being pretty stoical about things at the moment. She came from more humble beginnings, as you know. She'll be happy living in a shoebox as long as Dad's with her. Between you and me, I think she's probably relieved that she doesn't have to run that enormous estate any more.'

'What's your father going to do?'

Daniel thought for a moment. 'He'll be fine, El. You know what he's like. He'll rise like a phoenix out of the ashes. He'll soon have his fingers in some more pies. His friends will rally round. Mum's pension will keep them in beer and fags for the time being, and the flat's in her name, so the receivers can't touch it. It's worth a small fortune.'

He poured her another cup of tea and offered the biscuit tin. She shuddered involuntarily and ducked her head to take a sip of tea, hoping Daniel hadn't noticed the unbidden tears that sprang into her eyes.

But he had. 'I know it's only a digestive,' he joked. 'But there's no need to cry.'

Eleanor pulled out a tissue and blew her nose. 'Sorry,' she said. 'I don't know –'

Daniel immediately put his arm round her shoulder. 'Whatever's the matter? Is there something up with your dad?'

She shook her head and tried to smile. 'No, nothing like that. It's ... it's ...' She gave up being brave. 'Nick came to the house yesterday and he was really unpleasant.' It all came out in a rush before she dissolved in tears again. Daniel held her tightly until her sobs calmed to a gentle hiccup. 'He said some nasty things and then he tried ... he was going to …' She sniffed heroically. 'But Dad chose that moment to arrive on the doorstep and Nick left without another word.'

'Every cloud … Thank God for that. Did he …?'

'No, like I said, my knight in shining armour came to the rescue just in time.'

'Bloody coward,' Daniel said. 'I didn't have Nick down as such a worm.'

'Me neither,' Eleanor agreed. 'He shook me up a bit, that's all. I'm all right now.' She stayed within the comforting circle of his arms. 'So, where did you say Angie was?'

Chapter Thirty-two

Daniel let her go and she knew immediately that something was wrong. 'That was your news, wasn't it?' she asked. 'Yesterday, at the pub?'

He nodded, busying himself sweeping biscuit crumbs off the scarlet worktop.

Eleanor looked round the kitchen. There were no flowers on the table, no abandoned magazines on the counter. 'She's gone, hasn't she?' she said cautiously. 'When she heard about your dad? I can't believe she'd be so callous. The –'

Daniel silenced her with a look. 'Don't jump to conclusions.' He started clattering cups and saucers, stacking them in the dishwasher. 'It's not like that. She's actually in Paris.'

'Very nice,' said Eleanor frostily.

'She's gone to see the ex-boyfriend,' Daniel continued. 'Jean Valjean or whatever is his name is.'

'What, him from *Les Misérables?*'

'Not him then,' Daniel joked feebly. 'I can't remember his last name.'

'When did she go?'

'Yesterday. Seems that love never dies, after all.'

No need to tell me, she thought. She was silent for a while, imagining Daniel alone, devastated, in the flat. Her heart went out to him

'It's probably for the best, El,' he added. 'You know what she was like. It just takes a bit of getting used to.'

'Is she coming back?'

'That's what she's gone to find out. Whether she still loves him enough. They had a long affair,' he explained, 'before I came on the scene. They'd only recently separated when we met up in Paris.'

'So what's changed?' She recalled the intimate scene on the street that she'd witnessed.

'He's been in touch. Wants to try again.' He sounded utterly defeated.

'So nothing to do with your dad losing all his money then?' Eleanor asked.

Daniel looked at her sharply. He shook his head. 'She didn't know about that when she went. I'd been putting off telling her. She does have a heart, Eleanor,' he said, 'regardless of what you might think.'

'Hmm.' She couldn't have agreed less.

'Actually, she rang this morning when she saw the papers. She said she'd come straight home, but I told her to stay where she was until she was ready. There's nothing she can do anyway.' He sat down and began toying noisily with a spoon until Eleanor gently removed it from his hand, as if she was taking a dangerous plaything from a child. 'Sorry.'

Eleanor waited patiently and he carried on. 'It was going wrong before all this business with Dad, you know. We both knew something wasn't right. She was out all the time, wouldn't explain her absences …'

I bet I could, Eleanor reflected indignantly, biting back the thought before she could voice it. 'Wasn't she building up her business?'

'That's what I assumed. Seems it was other contacts that she was cultivating.'

Eleanor now knew the identity of the mystery guy she'd seen kissing Angie in Soho. No need to say anything about that now. Thank God she hadn't opened her mouth when she was last here.

'Has he got any money, this Jean chap?'

Daniel nodded. 'This'll make you laugh. He's just come into a fortune.'

Eleanor snorted with laughter. 'Sorry. But you've got to admit that it looks suspiciously like she's been hedging her bets,' said Eleanor. 'She must have noticed that things weren't all they should have been down at Mensum.'

He ignored her. 'Angie says she prefers the French lifestyle.'

'What? The one to which she'd like to become accustomed? She probably knew this was a possibility all along. It's all a bit fortuitous, don't you think?'

'How would I know?' He looked at her so forlornly it almost broke her heart. 'She was very keen on the whole Lady Marchmain bit,' he mused. 'She saw herself overseeing Mensum Hall like it was a small scale Brideshead, with platoons of servants at her back and call. I tried to tell her, but she had no idea what it really entailed.' He looked at Eleanor closely. 'You would have taken it all in your stride though, wouldn't you?'

Eleanor blushed furiously. 'Daniel, I –'

'Sorry, that was cruel.' He shrugged. 'We'll never get the chance now, any of us. Funny that it turns out Dad was about as good a speculator as me! Like father, like son.'

'That's not very funny. And, for the record, I would probably have made a complete hash of it, too.' She felt extremely tired suddenly, as if she'd run a very long way. 'I'm very sorry about Angie, I really am. I hope it all works out.' She took her bag off the counter and fumbled for her car keys. 'I really should be off now. You know where I am if you need a shoulder to cry on.'

Daniel came towards her, arms outstretched. 'Where are you going?'

'Home. My dad's probably burnt the place down by now if he's tried to cook himself anything. And you need some space. To reflect about things. You obviously –'

'Eleanor,' Daniel said calmly, taking her hands in his. 'I don't need any time to reflect. I've known for ages. Ever since I came back from travelling and saw you at Mum and Dad's. I realised then that I should never have stayed away so long.'

They stared at each other. A warm glow suffused Eleanor. For the first time in weeks she felt calm; the confrontation with Nick receding rapidly into the distance. There was an air of expectation in the room. Maybe everything was going to be all right.

'Why didn't you say something then?' she asked hesitantly.

Daniel sighed and dropped her hands, pushed his fingers through his hair. 'I don't know. By then things with Angie had taken on a life of their own. I got caught up in flat buying, job hunting, and all the rest of it. I tried to put you out of my mind.'

'You gave her the ring,' Eleanor heard herself say. 'The one you wanted me to have.' She almost couldn't believe she'd said that out loud.

'I know, I know. I knew I'd lost you, and that was my fault. And there was Angie to consider. I –'

'You hadn't lost me.'

'As far as I knew, I had,' he said patiently. 'You gave me no signals, no reason to hope, so I just got on with it.'

'Hang on.' Anger bubbled up from nowhere. 'You left the country for four years. You came back engaged, for God's sake! What was I supposed to do? "Oh, just hang around for a couple of months, Eleanor, he'll come to his senses?"'

'Eleanor, please. Listen to me.'

But Eleanor was on a roll. 'Angie knew, didn't she? She shoved the ring in my face at every opportunity. She knew I'd missed my chance, again – she took great pleasure in reminding me.'

'What? Everyone knew what had happened. I don't think I told her about the ring, but I suppose she might have guessed. What does it matter?'

'It was a family heirloom, wasn't it? How many of

those do you have hanging about the place? She must have known you'd offered it to me.'

Daniel sighed. 'Angie knew that history was important to me. That ring would be hers, or more accurately, my future wife's, because I'd inherited it. There wasn't another one, and I couldn't afford to buy one anything like that quality. But, again, what does all this matter?'

Eleanor wasn't listening. 'I thought she was taunting me about losing you, but she actually thought I'd be more bothered about not getting the fucking diamond.' She sniffed. 'That just about says it all.'

'Eleanor, don't,' Daniel pleaded. 'You're getting all worked up about nothing. I won't listen to this.'

'I'm not getting worked up,' Eleanor protested. 'I just want you to see that you're well rid of her. Dad was right,' she added. 'He called her a gold digger.' Her words were making him flinch but she didn't stop. 'Did she give it back before she left?'

'No. And she hasn't officially left, remember?'

'Sorry. Will you ask for it back?'

'Of course not! How can I? It was a gift.'

'But a gift with strings,' she reminded him.

'Doesn't matter. I won't ask for it back.' He frowned at her. 'But Valjean is so loaded he'll probably present her with something even bigger, so she might feel honour-bound to return it.'

'Honour-bound? Do me a favour,' Eleanor snorted.

'This isn't like you, El,' Daniel said angrily. 'Are you trying to turn me against Angie? Because if you are, it won't work. It's far too soon. It'll take time, getting used to all this. Angie and I were together quite a while and obviously I still ... I ...' He stumbled over the words. 'There's more to it than you realise. There are some residual feelings I need to work through.'

Eleanor recoiled as if she'd been slapped.

This wasn't going the way it had in her dreams. This

was the moment she was finally supposed to get her heart's desire, not this declaration about another woman. She said nothing and the silence lengthened. Her brain seethed with years of hurt, betrayal, and regret. If she didn't leave now the torrent of accusations and remorse dammed up inside her might just burst forth.

'I'm sorry,' he said finally. 'That came out all wrong.'

'No, I'm sorry,' she interrupted. 'That was unforgivable. You must think I've lost it completely.' She grabbed her handbag. 'I really am going this time. I've just remembered; Dad's taking me out to dinner. Big treat!' Her smile, as brittle as ice on a midwinter birdbath, betrayed the lie. 'I'll speak to you later.'

She grazed her lips across his cheek and headed for the door, the expression of utter bewilderment on his face clenching her heart.

Chapter Thirty-three

Her father's bag had been in the living room when she got home, its contents scattered over the floor like the aftermath of an explosion in a teenager's bedroom. Eleanor had put her handbag down and bent automatically to start clearing up. Doug had stopped her, his daughter's evident distress unnerving him so much he'd turned the football off and made a pot of tea.

'You've always been like this, Eleanor,' said Doug. 'I don't know where you get it from. Must be your mother. Certainly not me. You manage to sabotage things for yourself time after time.'

'What're you talking about?' Eleanor demanded.

'Why can't you just let things take their natural course?' Doug carried on as if he hadn't heard her. 'I'm not a psychiatrist, but it's almost as if you think you don't deserve something so you make sure it won't happen.'

She raised an eyebrow over her mug. 'Tell me about it,' she said.

'I mean, that time you could have auditioned for the Choral Academy. You engineered it so you'd be ill and couldn't go to the auditions. Twice.'

'That's a bit harsh.'

'But true. You blamed Julian for not getting the presenter's job you had that screen test for, but I have my doubts. You probably sabotaged that too.'

'No I didn't! I feel like I'm being judged here. It's not all my fault, you know.'

'And now this business with Daniel,' he went on relentlessly. 'It just beggars belief. If he's free of this Angie person …'

'It's complicated,' she said wearily.

'Even when it's handed to you on a plate, you still manage to fumble it.'

'Thanks, Dad. I get the picture. Fancy another cup of tea?'

'No.' He pointed at his wristwatch. 'Surely the bar's open by now?'

Eleanor went into the kitchen and mixed Doug a whisky and soda and a gin and tonic for herself. She felt like drinking herself into oblivion. She sat down heavily next to him.

He took her hand and squeezed. 'It'll all come out in the wash,' he said gently. 'Give it a bit of time. Let the dust settle. It's survived all this time, it'll take more than this to kill it.'

'Are you talking about me or you and Mum?'

He looked at her in surprise. 'You, of course. Although, come to think of it ... d'you think she'll have me back?'

It was a relief to talk about someone else's problems. 'I don't know, Dad,' she said truthfully. 'But if you feel that strongly, you're going to have to prove to Mum that you're worthy of her. She trusted you and look what you did with that trust. You threw it back in her face.'

Doug looked at her sheepishly. 'I *am* worthy of her.' He was quiet for a moment. 'But I see what you mean. I hadn't thought about it like that before,' he admitted. 'I always assumed your mum would just be there. That I didn't need to make an effort.'

'You humiliated her, Dad. She made an effort for you all the time, and look how you repay her!'

'I still love her, you know,' he said mournfully. 'I never stopped.'

'God, you sound so maudlin. It's your own stupid fault, you idiot,' Eleanor snapped. 'So there's no point in feeling sorry for yourself. Never mind going on at me about who's to blame, just take a long look at yourself.'

He grinned sheepishly. 'We're a right pair, aren't we?'

'Have you spoken to Mum?'

'She's been screening her calls. She won't speak to me at the moment.'

'Quite right, too. But you have to keep trying, or she won't believe you're serious.'

They sipped their drinks in a companionable silence for a while and Eleanor contemplated switching the football on again.

'Will you speak to Daniel soon?' Doug asked suddenly.

'You've just told me to let the dust settle,' she protested. 'Anyway, don't change the subject. We were talking about you and Mum.' The ice had melted in her drink, so she swirled the slice of lime round the viscous liquid. 'But no. Yes. Oh, I don't know.'

'What made you react so strongly this afternoon? When you told me about the gold digger leaving, I thought it'd all be plain sailing. So what happened?'

Eleanor contemplated her reply. Her father might be a complete twat when it came to his relationship with her mother, but he was very astute otherwise. She swallowed. 'I didn't reckon on him feeling so strongly about her,' she finally admitted. She may as well tell the whole truth, being as she was urging her father to do the same. It might be cathartic. 'I'd made myself believe that he couldn't possibly love her,' she carried on. 'Not like he'd loved me.' She paused for a moment. 'But he must have done, and maybe I didn't want to acknowledge that. It was a bit of a shock when I actually heard him say it.'

If he was embarrassed by this confession, Doug had the grace not to show it. He put his arm round her shoulders and hugged her.

'The bounder,' he joked. 'He didn't actually mention the dreaded "L" word, did he?'

'No, not exactly. Just that he had feelings for her.'

'Well, that's all right then,' he said airily. '"Feelings"

can mean anything.'

Sam said much the same thing when Eleanor called her later, after she'd had a rather drunken dinner with Doug at the local Indian restaurant. 'I don't know how you do it,' she moaned down the phone. 'Only you could get so close to paradise and fuck it up at the last minute!'

'Thanks a bunch,' Eleanor said.

'Don't take it to heart,' Sam carried on. 'He'll come round. Poor sod, he's probably shell-shocked. Losing one woman could be construed as accidental; losing two is downright careless. I can just see him, sitting there, nursing a drink, wondering where the hell it all went wrong. Have you spoken to him since?'

'No. Dad advised waiting a while.'

'And Doug should know; he's had enough practice. Just leave Daniel to lick his wounds for a while. Everything'll be all right, I promise.'

'Maybe I misunderstood him,' Eleanor persisted. 'Maybe he was trying to tell me that it's too late for us now.'

'You're determined to talk yourself out of this, aren't you? You're like a dog worrying a bone. Give the boy a chance, El! He's still processing everything that's happened. Doug's right – feelings can mean anything.' She paused. 'Now listen. I've got something to tell you.'

'What?' Eleanor asked ungraciously.

'Don't sound so bloody interested,' Sam grumbled. 'Maybe I should talk to you tomorrow, when you've calmed down a bit.'

Eleanor was chastened. 'Sorry, sorry. I'm listening. What's happened?'

'Rob's been having an affair.'

Eleanor opened her mouth and shut it again promptly as an image of a rain-soaked Rob standing outside that odd shop sprang into her mind. 'Did I hear you properly?' she asked. 'Rob's having an affair?'

'Yes,' Sam said miserably. 'There's someone else. And she's got a kid.'

'Bloody hell.'

'Understatement of the year. He's four years old! Can you believe it?'

Eleanor didn't know what to say. 'I always thought ...'

'Yeah,' said Sam. 'Me too. I thought we were in it for the long haul. I had no idea, El. Not an inkling. I feel so stupid.'

'When did you find out?'

'He told me last night. Just blurted it out.'

'When's he going to leave?'

Sam snorted in derision. 'He's not. Or so he says. I might have something to say on that, though.'

'I don't understand.'

'The affair finished a long time ago, apparently,' Sam explained. 'He's been sending maintenance for the kid but he hasn't had anything to do with the mother for ages. He only sees her when he visits the child.'

'What's his name?' Eleanor asked unnecessarily.

'Andrew. Rob wanted me to know all about it because he needs more money now, for schools and what have you, and he didn't want me to get suspicious.'

The arrogance of the man was breathtaking. 'Why? Have you got a joint account, or something?'

'We were just about to open one. We've been talking about getting a place together and pooling our resources. He didn't want me to be checking bank statements and wondering about the outgoings. And he wanted to start with a clean slate.'

'How very noble of him.' Eleanor didn't know a less worldly person than Sam and she couldn't conjure up a mental picture of her friend checking bank statements. 'So let me get this straight. Rob thinks things can just carry on as they were?'

'Yep. With the added benefit of me paying towards the upkeep of his bastard offspring.'

'When you put it like that, it's a no-brainer. Throw him out,' she advised.

'But I still love him!'

'Ah. I thought you might say that. I sympathise. I know how you're feeling, Sam. I've just been through something very similar, don't forget. One man, two women.'

'But you haven't got a kid to contend with.'

Eleanor ignored the last comment. 'If Rob says everything's finished with the mother – do you believe him?'

Sam was silent for a moment. 'Yes, I think I do,' she said eventually.

'So all you need to get your head round is Rob having an affair five years ago.'

'He said it didn't last long,' Sam agreed.

'And it hasn't been threatening your relationship all these years, has it?'

'No-oo, I don't suppose so.'

'The question is: can you forgive him?'

'I'm still thinking that one through. But even if I can,' she hurried on, 'I won't forget.'

'No one's asking you to,' said Eleanor. 'Rob knows that. But do you love him enough?'

'Enough to be a part-time stepmother?'

'That'll be part of the contract, I suppose.'

'I'm going to have to sleep on it. What if we want kids of our own some day?'

'At least you know Rob's capable.'

Sam burst out laughing. 'I feel a bit better now,' she said, more seriously. 'God, we're a right pair, aren't we? Why do we let them get away with it?'

Chapter Thirty-four

Eleanor was deep in a troubled sleep, a rather too realistic struggle with Nick segueing seamlessly into a scene of Shakespearean misunderstanding and confusion featuring Daniel, Angie, and, unaccountably, Julian, when her alarm shocked her awake. She surfaced from the turmoil with the relief of one whose death sentence has been recently commuted and turned the clock face towards her.

It was some minutes after 5 a.m., she was already developing the sort of headache she knew from experience would hang around for hours, and another day in Paradise beckoned.

She wasn't looking forward to work today; she was expecting there to be a post-mortem about Nick and his skulduggery and her involvement with him was bound to be a point of avid discussion throughout the newsroom.

She'd just have to develop a very thick skin.

She turned on the television to see what delights awaited her this morning – it was always interesting watching the office from home; it made her feel a bit like a voyeur – and was delighted to see that an unexpected but significant announcement had thrown the news schedules into confusion.

A reprieve.

As she showered she felt guiltily relieved. The thought that intruded selfishly but insistently was: There is a God. And He's just knocked the Pagets' story off the front page. Hopefully forever.

For an early morning, the newsroom was buzzing. The excitement was tangible and infectious. The UK24 newsroom was no different from any other in shrugging off all sensitivity when someone famous died, particularly when that death happened in suspect circumstances. The alleged suicide of a world-famous film star – her body had been found on the terrace of a grand hotel on the Croisette in Cannes, wearing nothing but a pair of Louboutins – was a strange and tragic event. It was also an absolute gift, all the better for being completely unexpected.

'This story will run and run,' someone commented unnecessarily. 'Well, until the inquest, anyway. Anyone know when that'll be yet?'

'It's being fast-tracked, if that's the right expression,' Ashok said. 'Sometime tomorrow, I think. They'll want to find out whether she fell or whether she jumped.'

'Or was she pushed?' Eleanor asked darkly. 'God, how awful.'

When she booted up her computer and logged on Eleanor discovered that the deceased, Ginnie Applegate, had a history of depression and that none of her entourage could say with any certainty where she'd been prior to the fall, or who she'd spent her last evening with.

As she absorbed this news her mobile beeped; a text message from Daniel. *Off 2 France 4 Ginnie story ... Pagets forgotten – hurrah!* it said, comically replicated her own thoughts. He told her that he was booked on the next flight from Heathrow and he didn't know when he'd be back.

A surge of relief that he was still speaking to her was swiftly followed by a sharp spike of jealousy piercing her chest.

France. Angie was in France.

Her mind galloped off like a spooked pony. He might meet up with Angie and they might fall in love all over again ... She pulled back on the reins. Get a grip, girl; Cannes was hundreds of miles from Paris.

Belle must have also heard the story before she left the house. She was dressed head to toe in black, including a small veil that covered her eyes.

'What do you reckon?' Ashok asked. 'I think she's got a look of Jackie Kennedy about her. At JFK's funeral.'

'No,' Eleanor disagreed, shaking her head. 'More like a refugee from *Bleak House.*'

'What are you like?' said Belle, overhearing. 'I'm not even *in* character today. It would be disrespectful, trying to upstage poor Ginnie.' She looked thoughtful for a moment. 'I'll probably stay in black until the funeral,' she added. 'Then I'm outta here.'

'Something to look forward to, I suppose,' said Ashok absently.

'Ashok!' Belle squealed.

'That didn't come out right.' Ashok frowned at her. 'What do you mean, you're out of here? Are you going on holiday, or something?

Belle nodded eagerly. 'Better than that. I've been offered a place at the theatre school I told you about. After that, the world's my lobster. By the way,' she whispered conspiratorially, 'just in case you were thinking about it, I don't want a big send-off.'

'No,' said Ashok, shaking his head. 'I wasn't thinking about it.'

Belle frowned at him. 'I never know whether you're joking or not,' she said. 'Something I won't miss. Anyway, the karaoke night for my birthday will be my leaving do as well, providing this dog and pony show is over and done with by then.' She looked over her shoulder. 'Don't tell Julian yet. He's got enough on his plate today.'

'Oh, speaking of Julian,' Ashok turned to Eleanor, 'he wanted to see you as soon as you got in. Sorry, I forgot to give you the message.'

'You wouldn't think we were in the communications

business, would you?'

She walked towards Julian's office but she could see through the window that he wasn't there. She went in anyway and perched on his chair arm to write a note letting him know she'd obeyed his command. As she leaned over to stick the pink square to his computer screen, she noticed a copy of an email sitting on top of a pile of papers. She recognised the sender.

She glanced guiltily at the door, but there was no sign of Julian. She scanned the message quickly; it had been sent from Nick's Blackberry and was mercifully brief. '*Everything going according to plan. How much longer do I have?*' it said. She checked the date: last Wednesday.

Her headache was giving everything a fuzzy edge. In its befuddled state her brain refused to co-operate. She couldn't make sense of what she was reading but she knew it was important.

She left the office and walked round the corner, almost bumping straight into Julian coming the other way.

'Ah,' he said. 'Just the person. Come into my office.' She followed him obediently. 'Close the door.'

A cold wave of anxiety swept through her as Eleanor took the chair he indicated, mentally preparing an excuse in case he noticed any disruption to his desk, though the office looked as if a burglary had been committed anyway. She waited, her mind muddled with possibilities.

'This is a bit awkward,' Julian began. 'But just to let you know, Daphne has gone in to bat for you. She's at a meeting on the top floor as we speak.'

'*Gone in to bat*,' Eleanor repeated stupidly. 'Sorry, I don't understand.'

'The execs are considering your position,' Julian explained. 'From what I can gather, it's all to do with your mishandling of the Paget situation. Your lack of judgement over this whole business.'

Eleanor's jaw dropped open. 'Sorry? *My* lack of judgement?'

Julian ignored her. 'They think the entire debacle has brought the news channel, and by association, the entire station, into disrepute, exposing us to unnecessary risk, yadda yadda yadda, the whole nine yards. You have to admit, Eleanor,' he added, 'you did act rather rashly. It was a bit outside the brief.'

He was so flippant he sounded like he was reading from a textbook on how not to deliver bad news. He seemed to be taking a sadistic pleasure in it. Eleanor fought a rising flush of indignation. How dare he blame her for everything? She'd been acting on *his* instructions, but he was making it sound as if she'd ignored his advice. She opened her mouth to protest but he interrupted her.

'I thought I'd better warn you,' he said dismissively. 'I'll let you know what happens.'

She turned to go, but he called her back. 'You have to admit, Eleanor, it was a pretty thin premise.'

'But you agreed to it!' she protested. 'If it was such a daft idea why did you give me the go ahead?' She thought furiously for a moment. 'Was it my fault because I didn't check everything properly?' she asked. Julian shrugged. 'Won't they want to see me, at least?' she asked. 'Hear my side of the story?'

'Not necessarily. Depends on the verdict. Guilty until proven innocent is the way it usually goes in these situations, which doesn't give you much scope. I had to give them a stack of information. The Pagets' passports not being checked, stuff like that.'

Eleanor stared at him in disbelief.

He held his hands up, palms out in defence. 'I had to do it, Eleanor. I'm sorry. I couldn't lie to them, could I? You and Belle are in it up to here.'

'But Belle had nothing –'

'She managed to lose the passports, didn't she?' he

asked.

'No! She ... she ... I don't ...' she petered out. She realised didn't have a coherent thought in her head. She needed to think.

Julian looked up from his screen. 'Like I said, I'll let you know. We'll need to tie up the ends, but we can bury that little nugget in one of the overnight bulletins.' He turned away and began typing as if she'd already gone.

Eleanor was in shock when she left the office. She berated herself for been too gullible; she hadn't seen this coming. Her opinion of Julian was undergoing a rapid re-evaluation. Just last week he'd been so supportive when she'd told him how things had turned out but now she didn't think she'd trust him with a coffee order.

She was considering this turn of events when she passed Ashok on his way back to his desk.

'Is everything OK?' he asked. 'You look like you've just been handed your P45. Though on second thoughts, you'd probably be running round the newsroom shouting with glee, if you had.' He peered at Eleanor's face. 'Is this about the Paget business? I read the paper on Saturday – it was brilliant. Don't worry, things have moved on; it'll just get buried. Nobody's interested any more. This news about Ginnie Applegate has knocked everything else off the schedules.'

'But Julian is blaming me for everything. He's just told me the execs are having top level discussions about what to do about me and my,' she wiggled her fingers in the air, '"mishandling of the situation". I am deeply depressed.'

'What a knobhead that man is sometimes,' Ashok said. 'I thought it had turned out quite well for us. What's he on about?'

Eleanor pressed her lips together in an effort to stem the threatening tears. 'I did make sure everything checked out,' she mumbled. 'I wasn't negligent. I did my job properly. So did Belle.' She looked at Ashok miserably.

'But if push comes to shove, I don't think he'll support me.' She sighed. 'I've been thoroughly shafted. I suppose everybody knows by now?'

'No, no one knows anything. Ginnie's made sure of that,' Ashok explained. 'Look, I've had run-ins with Julian before. He always comes up smelling of roses and leaves the innocent party to pick up the pieces. You aren't the first,' he added comfortingly. 'And you'll not be the last, either.'

'I thought I could trust him,' Eleanor said.

'That was your first mistake.' Ashok looked round furtively. 'Julian can be a bit of a snake in the grass. He can also be very petty. You always need to watch your back, or he'll drop you right in it.'

'He already has,' Eleanor moaned. 'I thought we were all in it together. When we talked to Daphne, everything was agreed. I thought –'

'Between you and me,' Ashok interrupted, 'I've heard that he's been in trouble with Daphne. Maybe this is his way of getting back in her good books.'

'But she's been hauled upstairs to explain everything,' Eleanor wailed. 'She's there now.'

Ashok tapped his watch. 'Of course she's there now. She's always there this time on a Monday morning. It's when the execs have their regular weekly meeting.'

Eleanor absorbed this information. 'I'd forgotten about that. I'm not thinking straight this morning. Is he just winding me up?'

'Not quite,' said Ashok. 'He's just doing what he does best, offloading the blame.'

Eleanor debated briefly whether to let Ashok in on her suspicions. 'Look, I shouldn't be telling you this –'

Ashok's eyes widened. 'What's happened? Tell me.' He patted Eleanor's hand. 'It's OK. You can trust me.'

'Come with me.' Eleanor opened the door to the adjacent ladies loo and pulled a surprised Ashok in behind her. She checked the cubicles before speaking. 'I think Julian knew about Nick's con trick,' she said. 'I think he's been in on it from the start, but I can't prove it.'

Chapter Thirty-five

She felt slightly better by the time she got back to her desk and pulled out her mobile to call Sam.

'It's all my fault,' Sam wailed down the phone. 'If I hadn't suggested that Nick was planning a con, you wouldn't have thought of it and –'

'Of course I would,' Eleanor snapped. She tried not be offended. 'I'm not that stupid. It didn't happen just because you thought of it. Anyway,' she added. 'It doesn't matter. Seems they want a head on a spike, and it's going to be mine. What am I going to do? I know I've said it before, but this time I will have to resign before they sack me.'

'You're overreacting,' Sam said. 'They just need a scapegoat. They won't sack you. This is just a misdemeanour, not instant dismissal stuff.'

Eleanor could hear a scratching noise and realised that Sam was tapping the phone with a fingernail, a sure sign that she was thinking. 'Are you doing anything tonight?' Sam asked eventually. 'Rob's coming back to clear the rest of his things out tonight. I don't want to be around.'

In the midst of her own worries, Eleanor had forgotten all about Sam's decision. 'Sorry, I've been such a selfish friend recently. Are you OK?'

'I'm fine. It's just, I can't live with ... with the knowledge of the affair. It's not just the kid. Though I know I wouldn't be able to play happy step-families with them when he visited. It's just not me, El. Best cut my losses.'

'You're probably right. Bloody men. Talking of which, if you come to me, be warned: Dad's still hanging around like a bad smell on the landing.'

Sam snorted with laughter. 'It's quite depressing, really. Are they all the same? Anyway, regardless of what the cheating bastard's been up to, I actually still like Doug. And he might be able to advise.'

'Doubt it, but OK, see you at mine around eight. We can get a takeaway.'

Daphne rang through later that morning and asked Eleanor to pop by when she was free. Not quite the royal command she'd been expecting, but she was nervous, nonetheless.

'I just wanted to touch base,' Daphne said when Eleanor knocked and walked into her office. 'Let you know how things are.'

Eleanor's stomach plummeted. 'And how are they?' she gulped. 'Things?'

'Absolutely fine. The article on Saturday did the trick. Took the heat right out of the situation. I must say that Daniel of yours is a very capable writer.'

'Yes, he is,' said Eleanor, seizing on the diversion proudly. 'He's just been sent to Cannes to cover the Ginnie Applegate mystery.'

'Excellent,' said Daphne. 'Well, onwards and upwards, then.'

Eleanor had been dismissed without so much as a raised eyebrow. 'But ...'

'Is there something else? Only we've all got a lot on today ...'

'I just wondered ... Julian said ...' She stopped short of telling Daphne about Nick's email.

Daphne eyed her sympathetically. 'Don't take everything Julian tells you as gospel,' she said. 'Sometimes he gets a bit carried away with the sense of his own importance.'

'Oh. So, I won't lose my job?'

Daphne sighed. 'Of course not. That was never going to

happen, Eleanor, and I'll take Julian to task if he's given you that impression.'

'No, not really. He didn't ...' Why she was defending Julian she had no idea, but it seemed the sensible option under the circumstances.

'There's nothing for you to worry about,' Daphne carried on. 'You put us in a difficult situation, but you got us out of it very smartly. It must have been tough for you. Now, learn from your mistakes and get on.'

'And what about Belle?'

'What about Belle? I don't know anything about Belle. Was she involved?'

'Er ... no. No, she wasn't. I was just ... Never mind.' Eleanor smiled stupidly. 'As you say, onwards and upwards.'

By that evening Eleanor and Sam had both reached the same conclusion but neither knew what to do with the information. Over a takeaway pizza Eleanor told Doug about her meetings with Julian and Daphne that morning and the email she'd seen on Julian's desk.

'Sounds to me suspiciously like he's most been in it from the start,' he father announced. He pursed his lips in concentration. 'It would explain why he's suddenly withdrawn his support; he's trying to distance himself.' He looked from Eleanor to Sam pointedly. Both were nodding in agreement. 'But getting him to admit it will be difficult. The email doesn't prove anything, by itself,' he said. 'But I bet there's more.'

'If he's got any sense, he'll delete all copies, hard and electronic,' said Sam. 'So you need to get him to confess.'

Eleanor was thinking about Julian's demeanour that morning. 'I thought he was, well, not a friend exactly, but –' She paused for a moment. 'I actually told Daphne it wasn't his fault,' she said indignantly. 'I took all the blame. The man's a weasel.'

'You can't trust anyone these days,' Sam exclaimed.

'Thinking back,' Eleanor said, 'Julian acted really strangely throughout the whole search thing.'

'What do you mean?' Doug asked.

'Well, he was either absent altogether and knew nothing about what was going on, which I find really weird, because someone from the newsdesk would definitely have called him, unless he was completely off the radar. Like visiting the Pope or something. That's just the way things work.'

'Didn't you tell me he had the flu?'

'Yes, but he made a remarkable recovery in a couple of days and said he hadn't known what was happening. It's just a bit convenient, you know? He can't have been that ill to be back at work in two days, so why wasn't he watching telly or something? He's usually on the newsdesk's back all the time on his days off. Phoning every five minutes with helpful suggestions.'

'So you think he was somewhere else?'

'Possibly. But where?' Eleanor thought some more. 'And other times, when I was nervous about giving him updates, because things weren't moving very quickly, he didn't seem remotely concerned. Almost like he knew what I was going to say. Oh, and one time, he made a big thing about having to calm Daphne down because she got agitated about everything.' She paused. 'But she didn't. So that could have been a Julian invention.'

They were both staring at her expectantly.

'Do you think Nick was telling him everything?' Doug asked.

Eleanor nodded. The idea occurred to her that Julian might even have been spending time with Nick when she wasn't. She let it go unspoken.

'Hmm,' Sam was musing. 'It's all a bit coincidental.'

'But that would explain why he was so reluctant to go along with Daniel's idea,' Eleanor carried on. 'He took a lot of persuading. And he wouldn't go and see Daphne for me. He made me go myself. She would have rolled over for him, but it was a real struggle for me to get her on my side. And then she told *me* she had a right job convincing Julian, even after he'd given me the OK. It's all a bit odd.'

Eleanor could feel herself getting nearer the truth. 'And finally, Belle couldn't find the Pagets' passports, presumably because they'd never been in the building in the first place. I remember he didn't seem particularly surprised when we couldn't find them. He knew they weren't there because he knew the Pagets had them. He had a dig about that this morning. About me not checking my sources properly.'

'What a bastard,' said Sam. 'Looks like he was happy for you to be the collateral damage.'

Eleanor nodded. 'And don't forget Belle. Though Daphne said he never mentioned her. Anyway, it won't matter to her. She's off at the end of the month. Going to be an actor.'

For some reason, Eleanor suddenly recalled the morning a few weeks ago when she'd found out that she hadn't got the presenter's job she'd been angling for. News reporting needed more gravitas, Julian had said. At the time she'd been ridiculously grateful to him for sparing her feelings – she'd never have put herself in the gravitas bracket – but today's events put a whole new complexion on that failure. She was beginning to think that misogyny wasn't his only problem.

Chapter Thirty-six

Julian was absurdly drunk. He was standing close to the small stage in the karaoke bar, in reality a darkened recess off the main saloon, waving a glass of wine around and singing along loudly and badly to the tune currently playing on the machine. He swayed dangerously, narrowly missing a waitress carrying a tray of drinks; the manoeuvre unbalanced him and he dropped clumsily to his knees, spilling the wine.

'I've never seen him this bad,' said Ashok.

'I don't think I care.' Eleanor slipped off her jacket and joined him at the table.

'He's been at it since early doors,' Ashok continued. 'Now he's getting embarrassing.' He stood up. 'I'd better go and help.'

A comical fight ensued, with Julian trying to shake Ashok off. 'Come on, Julian,' he grunted as he wrestled the bigger man to his feet. 'Come and sit down. You're drowning everyone out.'

Belle was watching Julian closely. 'If he ruins my send-off I'll never forgive him,' she hissed. 'Can you talk to him, Eleanor?'

'Why me?' she asked, horrified. 'He won't listen to me. Anyway, he hates me. He hasn't given me the time of day since Monday.'

'Oh please,' Belle begged. 'Just tell him he's being filmed, can't you? And that he'll be all over YouTube if he doesn't behave.'

Belle and Ashok returned to the karaoke stage where they were up next, murdering 'Islands in the Stream'. A rather subdued Julian sat down heavily next to Eleanor. He put his head in his hands and moaned gently.

'Are you OK, Julian?' Eleanor asked, fearing the worst. She moved her chair fractionally round the table and out of projectile vomiting range.

'Just singing along,' he slurred. 'I don't know this one very well.' He leaned over to whisper in her ear. 'Sorry about that, er, that earlier fracas,' he apologised. 'I tripped on the carpet.'

Eleanor bit down an acidic remark about taking inebriation to new depths and searched for a more neutral comment. 'You seem a bit tense, Julian, is everything all right?'

He looked at her forlornly and took a deep swallow of wine. 'Not sure, really,' he confided. 'Are you going to sing? I seem to remember hearing you have a lovely voice.'

'I might, later on. I think I need a drink first.'

'Don't we all?' He nodded and made an expansive gesture with his hands and almost consigned the fresh round of drinks to the floor. 'I think …'

He seemed to be about to impart a nugget of information, but was having difficulty marshalling his thoughts. 'I think I've just been had, Eleanor,' he announced eventually.

'What do you mean?' she asked frostily.

'I mean,' he said with the careful enunciation of the very drunk, 'I mean that he's out to ruin me.'

Eleanor thought she understood but she needed to hear it again, just to make sure. 'Pardon?' she asked. 'Who's out to … I didn't get that last bit; it's so loud in here.'

Julian looked round furtively. 'Keep it down,' he said testily, even though the noise level was so high Eleanor was relying on reading his lips. He tried with difficulty to focus both eyes on her at the same time. 'Can I trust you?' he slurred.

'Of course you can,' Eleanor replied, crossing her

fingers behind her back. She thought he was going to burst into tears of self-pity. 'You'll have to explain everything,' she said. She didn't think she'd get another opportunity to hear this. 'From the beginning. Let's go outside for a minute, so I can hear you better.'

Julian nodded and struggled to his feet. He followed her out of the back door and propped himself against a drainpipe. 'I was in it from the start,' he began.

She blinked but said nothing.

'I can see you're shocked, and I'm sorry. Sorry about everything.' He trailed off and Eleanor sensed that he was struggling.

'Go on,' she encouraged.

He took a deep breath. 'I've been a bit of a naughty boy this last year,' he began. 'Ever since I came to UK24, in fact. You see …'

Belle burst through the back door at that moment. She eyed the pair of them curiously. 'Oh, there you are. Come on, Eleanor,' she tugged excitedly at Eleanor's sleeve. 'Your turn.'

'I don't –'

'No excuses,' Belle cried. 'It's my birthday and we've got Johnny ready with the camera and everything. Come on,' she urged. 'What're you going to sing?'

'I don't know yet. I haven't thought. Julian was just –'

'Never mind about Julian! You two can talk as much as you like at work. This is playtime!'

Eleanor couldn't bear to leave when she was so near the truth, but Julian just shrugged and took another slug of his drink.

'It'll keep,' he muttered, looking glassily at Eleanor. 'I'm not going anywhere … probably ever.'

Eleanor spent the next few minutes flicking though the karaoke selection book. After the tantalising snatch of conversation with Julian she was finding it hard to concentrate. Belle had gathered a crowd together and they waited expectantly as Eleanor walked onto the stage and took the microphone.

'What're you going to sing?' someone shouted.

'"Set Fire to the Rain"', Eleanor decided.

There was a smattering of applause as the first bars sounded and Eleanor prepared herself. The room fell silent apart from the distant clamour of the kitchen. As soon as she heard the music, all her previous reluctance dissolved. The events of the past week had done nothing to dim her voice and she allowed herself to be transported by the music. She didn't even notice Johnny filming every second. She didn't want to stop singing. The music was everything.

During the instrumental middle eight, her thoughts wandered to the rather different type of music she'd had to face at work recently. She never wanted to face it again. She pushed the thoughts way and concentrated in the song's crescendo. As the final notes died the spontaneous applause was almost an intrusion. She looked fondly at the upturned faces of her colleagues, all watching her with rapt attention. This was what she wanted. The music. The audience. The adulation.

'Sing us another one,' Ashok shrieked. 'Otherwise you'll have to listen to me again.'

She smiled. She was just getting into her stride. Her suggestion of "Someone Like You" was greeted with murmurs of appreciation; she programmed the machine and waited for the lyrics to appear on the screen. She didn't need them, she knew the tune and the lyrics off by heart. She hummed along to the introduction, all thoughts of Julian, Nick, even Daniel, vanishing in the euphoria of the moment.

Eventually, she realised she shouldn't hog the limelight completely. She had to let someone else have a chance, so she reluctantly left the stage, promising an encore later, and walked back to the table where Julian had returned. She was torn; she didn't want her moment of glory ruined, but she was desperate to hear what he had to say. And he was going to tell her everything, come what may. He seemed to have sobered up remarkably and was now drinking sparkling mineral water.

'That was very good,' he said when she sat down. 'You should do it professionally, never mind all this telly business.' He indicated a table away from the stage. 'Let's go over there. I can't hear myself think in this racket.'

They moved to a table in the almost deserted bar. 'Anyway,' he carried on without further preamble. 'Where was I? I need to get this off my chest,' he added dismissively. 'I can't live with it any longer.'

Eleanor was suddenly incensed. Anger bubbled up inside her as the injustice of the situation crystallised in her mind. Julian obviously thought that confession was good for the soul; that by unburdening himself he could absolve himself from all blame. She clamped her mouth shut and started counting up to ten.

She struggled to remember what he'd said already. Something about being a naughty boy. She recoiled from the image that sprang to mind. 'What do you need to get of your chest?' she asked coldly, regaining control of her temper.

Julian clunked his glass of water against her wine glass. 'I'm an alcoholic, Eleanor,' he said bluntly.

'An alcoholic?' she repeated flippantly. 'I'd never have guessed.' The word reverberated inside her head as its implications gradually dawned on her. 'Really? An alcoholic?'

'Is there an echo in here?' Julian asked, looking around. 'Shh, will you? I don't want the world and his wife to know. Yes, an alcoholic. In recovery, if you can believe it. I've been trying to stay sober, I even joined AA,' he carried on. 'Did the twelve steps and all that, but when I started at UK24, it all went to rat shit. I fell off the wagon.

Big time. And I haven't managed to scramble back on.'

Eleanor stared at him. 'Does anyone know?' was all she could think of to say.

'Daphne's always known,' he admitted. 'We go way back, as you know. When I applied for this job, she was completely against my appointment. She didn't tell the rest of the panel, which was loyal of her – some would say stupid – but she was overruled anyway. Seems I was a very popular choice.'

Get on with it, Eleanor thought. Never mind blowing your own trumpet. 'Going to AA was Daphne's personal condition,' Julian carried on. 'She said she'd make my life a misery if I didn't agree. I wanted to get clean, so it wasn't a problem. It was the push I needed.'

'So what happened?' Eleanor prompted.

'The usual, I suppose. The job. The pressure. The socialising. You know what it's like, Eleanor. All those nights in the pub. It's expected.'

She nodded, not unsympathetically. 'I know.' She'd always found it difficult to keep up with the drinking habits of some of her colleagues and mostly she didn't join them on their sessions. Julian was no different to the rest of them, he was just more vulnerable. Drinking mineral water all evening just wasn't an option with this crowd.

'Daphne soon saw what was going on,' he continued. 'Too many lame excuses for absences don't get past her for long. She insisted I get help. In fact, I'm ... I'm ...' he faltered, wiped his face with his hand and took another drink of water. 'Sorry, this is difficult to say. I don't even know why I'm telling you, but I, I wasn't all I should have been over this Nick business. I think you deserve an explanation.'

Eleanor tried not to let her surprise show. Her anger abated slightly. She waited. 'I won't say anything,' she promised.

'I know, I know.' He smiled wanly. 'That time I told

you I had flu? I was at The Priory.'

'That explains a lot. I thought it was odd that you hadn't kept up with the story.'

He nodded. 'Television was allowed, I just wasn't in a fit state to take anything in. And the time before that, that week's holiday in the south of France? I was at the Priory that time, too.'

'I wondered why you didn't have a tan when you got back. I thought it must have rained the whole time,' Eleanor giggled despite the seriousness of the conversation. 'Sorry. It's the wine. Oh, sorry.'

He waved her apologies away. 'Anyway, the crux of the matter is, I'm on a final warning. Daphne's lost patience and unless I get some therapy, I'm out.'

Chapter Thirty-seven

'The trouble is,' Julian carried on, 'therapy is very expensive and I've run out of money.'

'Won't the company pay?' Eleanor was surprised. 'I thought UK24 was quite humanitarian about these things.'

Julian laughed harshly. 'They are. And they have been. Only the well's run dry, so to speak. You only get so many chances, Eleanor, before everyone's patience runs out. Anyway, you can probably guess the rest. I need to get some money together.'

'Well, don't look at me, I'm –' With a sudden flash of clarity, Eleanor could see what was coming next. 'Oh.' She decided to play along. 'What about the bank?' she asked brightly. 'Surely you earn enough for –'

'Bad credit history.' Julian shook his head. 'This is an expensive habit,' he added mournfully. 'Too many loans, too many credit card applications. So, no joy there.' He laughed. 'When you came to me with the Pagets' story, it was like I'd been handed a lifeline. I was weak. It was easy. I couldn't resist.'

Eleanor thought back to the first conversation she'd had with Julian. He hadn't been very keen at all, until she'd suggested a donations line. Then, she remembered, he'd suddenly got very animated. 'You hatched a little plot to keep the money?'

Julian nodded. 'Once I'd figured out what was really going on.'

'How did you get Nick to agree to cut you in?'

'Oh, he played right into my hands.'

'How?'

'That business about the Pagets' passports. Nick

couldn't produce them, got very defensive when I pushed him. I smelled a rat. Which is more than you did,' he added.

'Thanks,' she said dully. 'And?'

'I sort of indicated that it wouldn't be the end of the world if he couldn't find them. We understood each other. I leaned on him and he caved in.'

Eleanor was putting all the pieces together. 'So you promised to smooth the path with Daphne, to keep her sweet and organise everything, even though you knew there was a double cross at the end, in return for a cut of the money?'

He nodded again. 'I was so angry with you when it all fell through.'

'I know.'

'You backed me into a corner. I had to go along with you or it would've looked too suspicious. There wasn't any option. I thought Nick understood. In fact, when I realised that there wouldn't be any money at the end of it, I even asked Daphne for an ex gratia payment for him, for keeping us all amused during the summer.'

'You didn't?' Eleanor was incredulous. 'What did she say?'

Julian dismissed the question with a weary wave of his hand. 'You can guess. The problem I've got now, though –'

'Never mind the problem you've got now.' Eleanor's anger was simmering again. She had to shout to hear herself above the cacophony of Belle and Ashok's singing. 'What about my problem?' she asked angrily. 'What about dropping me right in it? You as much as told me I was going to lose my job. How am I –?'

Julian had the grace to look guilty. 'Daphne was the only one I said anything to. Promise. And she sees right through me. You'll be OK. She won't hold anything against you.' He shrugged, back on track. 'No, my problem —'

'He's threatening you, isn't he?'

'What makes you say that?' Julian squinted at her. 'What else do you know? What's Nick been saying?'

Eleanor shook her head. 'Nothing,' she said. 'Obviously he never mentioned anything about his arrangement with you. I didn't suspect anything until the end. I just happen to know that Nick can be a bit, well, persuasive, when he wants to be.'

'What's he done to you?' Julian asked sharply. 'If he's —'

'Nothing. He's done nothing.' She took a breath. 'My dad arrived just in time.'

Julian groaned. 'The bastard. I'm so sorry, Eleanor. I had no idea.' He looked at her mournfully. 'I still don't know what I'm going to do.'

'This hasn't got you off the hook, Julian,' she said, in a flash of bravado that surprised even her. 'I know you probably had it in for me because I ruined your plans. I can understand that. But I didn't know about your involvement and I'm still smarting about being hung out to dry when all I did was try and warn you.'

'I've said I'm sorry. What more do you want?'

Visions of presenting her own programme flashed into her mind briefly. She could hold him to ransom, make ridiculous demands, but that would make her no better than Nick.

'I can't give you an answer to that, Julian,' she said. 'Not at the moment. I've had too much to drink. And anyway,' she nodded to Belle who was now standing behind Julian, making frantic singing motions above his head, 'my public awaits.'

She got up from her seat and touched Julian's shoulder. 'It's my time now. Everything else can go to hell.' She took the microphone from Belle and walked onto the stage.

Doug was packing an overnight bag, preparing to drive to Skipton when Eleanor staggered downstairs nursing a hangover of gargantuan proportions. She went immediately to the kitchen and drank a large glass of water.

'Where are you off to?' she asked groggily.

'Home,' Doug said. 'I hope.'

'What does Mum say about that? Have you asked her?'

'Last night,' said Doug. 'When you were out enjoying yourself.' He indicated the empty glass in Eleanor's hand. 'It looks like you had a good time.'

Eleanor nodded carefully. Any rapid movement of her head resulted in a horrible feeling of nausea that was difficult to control. 'Rather a lot of drink taken,' she admitted. 'I had a great time, though,' she added. 'I was singing nearly all night, except when –' She broke off, remembering her conversation with Julian. Renewed anger flooded through her.

'Except when …?' Doug prompted.

'Julian confessed,' she said bluntly. 'You were right.'

'Really?' Doug asked, the question heavy with understatement. 'What did he say?'

'Told me everything. I'm sworn to secrecy, obviously, but you don't count. He's been involved from the start. In fact, he says he saw through Nick straight away. He got in on the deception in return for a cut. He needed the money for therapy.'

Doug's eyebrows shot up. 'Therapy?'

'This must go no further,' Eleanor said unnecessarily. 'He's an alcoholic.'

'Hah!' said Doug. 'I knew it. I knew it had to be drink, or a woman. Or a man. Why else risk your career and your livelihood?'

Eleanor looked at her father appraisingly. 'Why indeed?' she muttered.

'So, what happens now?' Doug asked, oblivious to the irony. 'Has he still got a job?'

She nodded. 'Hanging on by his fingertips. He's only there now because Daphne's protecting him, but he's on his final warning.'

'And nasty Nick just fades away into the sunset, nothing more to be said?'

'Ah. No, not exactly. He's threatening Julian with exposure if he doesn't pay up.'

'Priceless! So, what's he going to do?'

'No idea. I told him I'd give it some thought, but I haven't come up with anything just yet.'

'It'll be all bluster,' Doug advised. 'Nick's very young and naive. He doesn't know how the world works. It's too late,' he carried on. 'The bird has flown. No one will be interested now. Especially after this bizarre Ginnie Applegate story. The world's moved on. Julian should just call his bluff.'

'Maybe I'll suggest that,' Eleanor said. 'What time are you going?'

'Anytime now.' He paused. 'I'm a bit nervous, to tell you the truth. D'you think she'll be OK? Your mum, I mean.'

'I don't know, Dad. She's given you lots of chances before. I wouldn't bank on a warm welcome, put it that way.'

'She's never actually thrown me out before, you know. Maybe that was what she needed. Something cathartic.' He pulled the zip on his bag and slung it over his shoulder. 'I don't expect this to be permanent,' he warned. 'This is just a preliminary foray back into her good books. So don't bother changing the sheets on my bed. I'll probably be back.'

Eleanor smiled thinly. 'You're always welcome.' She was about to close the front door when she remembered. 'Have you got Mum a present?' she asked. 'And I don't mean some horrid freeze-dried roses either.'

'What do you take me for, Eleanor?' He patted his bag. 'All sorted.'

'See you soon, then,' she said. 'Let me know when, if, to expect you. And thanks for … for … well, just thanks,' she finished.

'Glad I was there, poppet.' Doug slammed the car door and drove off in a cloud of blue smoke. I hope he gets there, she thought. That doesn't sound too healthy.

She checked the street nervously. Sensibly, she knew Nick wouldn't be back, but now her father had gone, she felt strangely vulnerable. It was an uncomfortable feeling. She went inside and called Sam.

'What about this Ginnie Applegate business?' Sam asked excitedly, referring to the news just announced that Ginnie didn't die where she'd been found. 'It's getting more and more bizarre isn't it?'

'Daniel has gone to Cannes to report on it.'

'Oh, so you've spoken to him since …?'

'No, just a few texts, But at least he sent those. I thought I'd blown it – again.'

'Don't be daft,' Sam said confidently. 'He'll be back. Especially now that Angie's out of the picture –'

'We don't know that.'

'For all intents and purposes, I was going to say, if you'd let me finish.'

'Sorry, sorry. Anyway, are we still on for tonight? My hangover needs topping up.'

Faced with a free afternoon before she joined Sam at her local wine bar, Eleanor packed her bag and headed for an hour's torture at the gym. The exercise might help her hangover.

She hadn't been in the room for five minutes when Nick's father walked in.

Their eyes met over the cross trainer and Jim's slid

away from hers guiltily. She watched as he walked away, but not, surprisingly, out of the gym completely. He took up a position in front of the wall of mirrors and began rhythmically lifting weights and grimacing at his reflection.

Eleanor finished her session on the machine and took a long swig of water from her bottle before lying down on a mat to start her stomach crunches. Almost immediately Jim approached. 'Can I still be your mat mate?' he asked uncertainly.

'Please yourself,' said Eleanor ungraciously. But she moved across and made a space for him.

'I had no idea,' Jim said, in between grunts. 'Nick never told me.'

Eleanor knew without doubt that he was telling the truth and she appreciated what this conversation was probably costing him. But she couldn't bring herself to relent, not just yet. 'Hmm,' she grunted in reply.

'The first I knew about it was when my sister showed me the paper on Saturday. I was shocked.'

'Really?' Eleanor asked sarcastically.

'You've got to believe me,' Jim said. 'You know I wouldn't do a thing like this. And if I'd known what he was plotting, I'd have stopped him.' He abandoned all pretence at finishing his stomach crunches. 'I'll be having a cuppa by the pool, if you want to join me afterwards,' he said, getting up and grabbing his towel.

Chapter Thirty-eight

Eleanor finished her circuit, refusing to allow thoughts about Jim to intrude on her workout. After the final session on the treadmill, where she walked furiously uphill for fifteen minutes and worked off some of the aggression she felt mounting, she headed for the showers and flushed a layer of antagonism down the drain with the soapy water.

She chose her customary hot chocolate from the vending machine, and joined Jim at the poolside.

'Well?' she asked coldly. 'Have you got anything else you want to get off your chest?' She took an experimental sip of the scalding liquid.

Jim shrugged half-heartedly. 'Honestly, Eleanor. Like I said, I had no idea. I still can't believe it. I brought him up to be ... well, honest and hardworking. I don't know where this has come from. He must have gotten into bad company.'

'That's no excuse and you know it, Jim! He almost cost me my job. He might still. I trusted him.'

'Yes, I know and I feel really bad about it,' Jim replied. 'Is there anyone I can speak to, on your behalf, like? Tell them it wasn't your fault?'

She shook her head, almost smiling. 'Live by the sword, die by the sword. I'm old enough to know the risks, Jim. I just didn't reckon on them being so close to home.'

He looked at her, puzzled. 'What do you mean?'

'Didn't he tell you? Obviously not.' She watched the swimmers in silence for a while. 'Nick and I had a ... a sort of, well, a relationship, really.' She laughed shortly. 'I'm not surprised he hasn't told you. Probably rather embarrassed.' She paused. 'Like me, I suppose.'

Jim was staring at her. 'He hasn't told me anything, Eleanor. Not about the con trick, not about your relationship, nothing. In fact, I haven't seen hide nor hair of him since this whole thing began.'

'Didn't he keep in touch when he went off?'

Jim shook his head emphatically. 'Not a word. I saw one of his reports when I was having some lunch in a pub last week, but I don't watch UK24 at home. I don't watch a great deal of television, full stop. I tried to get in touch with him, but his phone was switched off. Then the piece in the paper was a total shock.'

Eleanor drained her paper cup and threw it into a waste bin. She stood up and gathered her bag and fleece, hunting for her car keys in the pocket.

'I'm not blaming you, Jim,' she said as she turned to leave. 'So there's no need to feel embarrassed about meeting me at the gym. I won't hold it against you. But if you've got any sensitivity, you'll make sure I don't see Nick here again.'

Jim nodded. 'Of course,' he said. 'It's the least I can do, providing *I* ever see him again,' he added sadly.

'There was just one other thing,' she said, wheeling round and leaning across the table. 'Keep this to yourself, and I'm sure you will when I tell you. Nick is trying to blackmail one of my colleagues.' Jim look suitably shocked. 'If you do see him in the near future, tell him he's on a hiding to nothing.'

'I will if –'

But Eleanor had already left.

Back at home she tried getting hold of Daniel on his mobile. She needed to build some bridges and pithy texts wouldn't do.

The phone went straight to voicemail and she left a message. Maybe he was in a press conference, she thought. Or some other situation where he had to turn his mobile off. Like Ginnie's funeral, perhaps. But it was too early for that. The inquest hadn't even been scheduled yet and anyway, the funeral would be in England.

She tried several times throughout the afternoon, followed by some instant messaging. She decided against leaving any more voicemails. She didn't want to come across as too needy, but the fact remained that this was rather strange. Journalists always kept their phones switched on. On a whim, she tried his home number in case he'd come home earlier than expected. The phone rang before going to answerphone.

By seven o'clock she had to admit that she was getting worried.

'I don't know what to think,' she said to Sam over the first glass of wine. 'He never turns his phone off, unless –'

'Maybe he's avoiding you,' Sam deadpanned.

'Joke!' she cried when she noticed Eleanor's forlorn expression. 'Maybe he's just run out of juice.'

Eleanor tried to ignore her. 'If I can't get through by tomorrow morning, maybe I should call Gwen. She'll know what's happening.'

'Poor woman, hasn't she got enough on her plate?' Sam pointed out. 'I mean, she's just lost her home and her fortune in rather embarrassing circumstances. You don't want to worry her unnecessarily, do you?'

'So how do I find out, then?' Eleanor picked up her glass and tasted the wine.

'Ah, that's the fate of the other woman.'

'I'm not the other woman!'

'Yes, but it's a similar situation. You're just a friend. Daniel could be dead, but no one would call you. You don't count. You're sidelined.'

Eleanor stared at her friend. 'You don't think …?'

'No, of course I don't! Relax, will you? I'm just pointing out the disadvantages of your position. Did he put you down as next of kin on his passport?'

'I doubt it. It's a bit soon. Why would he?'

'Just saying …'

The waitress delivered bowls of peanuts and kettle chips and Sam fell on them as if she'd been saving the week's calories for this moment. 'I haven't eaten all day,' she said, stuffing crisps into her mouth. 'I'm absolutely starving.'

'I could call the newspaper,' Eleanor carried on, unconcerned.

'You could look on the internet. Oh,' Sam wiped her fingers on a paper napkin and fumbled in her pocket, 'just a thought. Doesn't Daniel tweet?'

'Of course he does! I forgot about that. I'll have a look when we get home.'

Sam pulled out her iPhone. 'You can do it now,' she said, pressing buttons. She handed the phone to Eleanor, shaking her head. 'You are such a dinosaur. When are you going to get one of these?'

Eleanor scrabbled about in her bag for her reading glasses. 'When they come with a fold-out screen,' she said testily. 'How am I supposed to read this teeny writing?' She took the phone and scrolled through Daniel's latest Tweets. 'There's nothing since Thursday night,' she said. She looked up at Sam. 'I don't know enough about this. Do people Tweet all the time?'

'Daniel would,' Sam said, nodding. 'If he was following a big story.'

'So this is suspicious?'

'It is rather.'

Eleanor frowned as she continued scrolling back and forth. 'He doesn't say anything about being out of contact. He's not posted anything since five o'clock on Thursday. That's very odd.'

First thing on Sunday morning, Eleanor checked Daniel's

Twitter feed, his Facebook account, and the newspaper website. Not a word. No mention either of a serious accident befalling one of *The Post*'s reporters. She tried calling his mobile but the recorded message still said it wasn't possible to connect her call. Did that mean the phone was turned off, or that the battery had died? She couldn't remember. Had she ever known?

There was still no reply from his home phone so she decided to call Gwen at the London flat.

'Hello?' Gwen's voice was guarded. 'May I help you?'

Eleanor forced some gaiety into her voice. 'Hi Gwen, it's Eleanor. How are you?'

Gwen's voice relaxed. 'Oh, hello, Eleanor. How nice to hear from you.'

'How are things?' Eleanor asked cautiously. 'I ... I saw in the newspapers...'

'Oh, that,' Gwen laughed. 'Old news. We knew it was coming, we were ... prepared, shall we say. No, I thought you were calling about Daniel.'

Eleanor's heart stopped. 'What about Daniel? Is anything wrong? I haven't been able to get in touch.'

'Haven't you heard? No, obviously you haven't.' Gwen paused for a maddening moment. 'He's been in an accident.'

'Oh my God,' cried Eleanor. 'In France? How is he? He isn't ...?' She was aware that she was gabbling.

'Calm down, dear,' Gwen reassured her. 'He's OK. Well, he's out of danger, anyway.'

'"Out of danger?"' Eleanor parroted. 'Why what's happened?'

'He was involved in a traffic accident,' Gwen said. 'Got hit by a car. He's got a broken collar bone and a few fractured ribs. They thought that one may have punctured a lung, but they've revised that diagnosis. There's some internal damage, but they don't think it's too serious. I'm so sorry, dear, I should have called you. But Daniel insisted I didn't bother you.'

'Jesus Christ. Is he still in Cannes? In hospital?'

'He is at the moment. But not for much longer.'

'Maybe I should go?' Eleanor asked. 'Only …'

'No, there's no need to go to those lengths. Grace is bringing him back once he's stabilised.'

'Grace?' It seemed the whole world was on the continent. 'Is she in France too?'

'Of course. It's the film festival. Felix can't miss Cannes. She flew them down there last week.'

'Thank God for that.' Eleanor breathed a sigh of relief. 'I could meet them at the airport,' she added desperately. 'Go with them in the ambulance, save Grace a trip. Which hospital will they be taking him to?'

Gwen hesitated. 'Oh. I don't actually know. I didn't ask. But no matter, Angie will ring when he's settled.'

Eleanor heard the name as if from a great distance. She had the odd sensation of being enveloped in a thick fog, which her thoughts couldn't penetrate. 'Angie?' she repeated. 'What's she –? I thought she was in Paris.'

'She was,' Gwen continued. 'Daniel told me what had happened. I can't say that I approve, but what a stroke of luck, though. Angie was in Cannes when Daniel had his accident. She went with him to the hospital.' She paused for breath for a long moment during which Eleanor's imagination took flight.

'I'm not quite sure what she was doing there,' Gwen continued. 'I hope she's not –' Eleanor heard a bell shrill in the distance. 'Sorry, Eleanor, there's someone at the door. I'd better go and see who it is. Hopefully not more creditors,' she joked. 'I'll ring you this afternoon. I should have a clearer picture by then.'

Eleanor put the phone down and tried with difficulty to process what she'd just heard. It just didn't make any sense. Had the accident involved Angie? Had she run Daniel down? Why did she happen to be in Cannes when she was supposed to be in Paris? And what did Gwen suspect?

All manner of improbable scenarios ran through her head; none seemed remotely plausible.

She had no choice but to wait impatiently for an explanation.

Chapter Thirty-nine

Gwen called a few hours later with an update. Daniel was now back in England and he'd been taken to the Charing Cross Hospital in Fulham.

'Is he in a fit state to receive visitors?' Eleanor asked.

'I hope so,' Gwen said. 'His father and I are going to pop in after lunch. I'm not sure about Angie's movements. She hasn't said.'

That name again.

'If you're thinking of going,' Gwen continued. 'Why don't you go this evening, spread the visitors out a bit so we don't overwhelm him?'

Eleanor didn't think she could wait that long. 'Yes,' she agreed. 'That's a good idea. I'll do that.' She looked at her watch. Seven o'clock would leave a decent interval. Maybe six. 'What about Grace?'

'She's had to go straight back to Cannes. Poor girl's hardly slept. That Felix is a real slave driver.'

Eleanor put the phone down. She tried unsuccessfully to watch a TV programme about the Middle Ages, then flipped through the magazine supplements of the Sunday papers. She was too distracted for the crossword or Sudoku. She fed Mabel, made herself a sandwich which she couldn't eat, then went into the garden and pulled up weeds for an hour.

At five o'clock she left the house for the hospital.

A lone male orderly was manning the nurse's station. Eleanor enquired about Daniel's whereabouts and was politely directed to a side ward.

'He's sedated,' the nurse advised. 'It's unlikely he'll

wake up for a while. Try not to disturb him, the pair of you,' he added.

Puzzled, Eleanor opened the door he'd indicated and tiptoed inside. Daniel was lying asleep, covered in a sheet and hooked up to an array of drips and monitors. His unshaven face was badly bruised but otherwise he appeared unhurt.

'Eleanor?' The woman sitting by the bed was very pale, with dark circles under her eyes. She was bizarrely dressed for the circumstances, in a pretty pink dress sprigged with tiny crimson flowers, and matching sandals. Her brown legs were bare and her arms were covered in goose pimples. Eleanor realised that she must have stayed with Daniel since they'd arrived. She wondered why Gwen and Peter hadn't invited her back to their flat for a shower, or at least loaned her a warm cardigan. After the split relations must be as cool as the air conditioning, she assumed.

Angie put down her magazine and stood up. 'Hi,' she whispered.

'Hi Angie,' Eleanor whispered back. She couldn't help herself. 'What are you doing here? I thought you were in Paris.'

Angie looked as if she hadn't slept for a long time and her speech was clogged. She coughed to clear her throat. 'Sorry. I came back with Daniel,' she mumbled. 'He's been in an accident.'

'I know,' Eleanor said. 'But how are you involved? What ... what are you doing here? Is Daniel going to be all right?'

'Daniel will be fine. He's asleep at the moment.'

'I can see that, thank you. Have you been here long?'

'I came in with Daniel.'

This was testing Eleanor's patience but she could see that Angie wasn't in a fit state to answer any questions. She persevered for a few more minutes.

'What do you mean, you came in with him? Were you in the accident too?'

'I saw it happen.' Angie put her hand across her face to stifle a yawn. 'Sorry, I haven't had much sleep. I'm rather tired.'

Eleanor decided to give her the benefit of the doubt. 'But why were you in Cannes in the first place?' she persisted. 'Daniel told me you were in Paris.'

'I was. I was with Jean. Do you know about Jean?'

Eleanor nodded.

'Of course you do. Daniel would have told you. Anyway, we were …' Angie yawned massively 'Sorry. I must go and get some coffee. I think I saw a machine in the foyer. Would you like one?'

She scrambled around for her bag. 'Oh, shit, I've only got sodding euros.' She looked pleadingly at Eleanor. 'Have you got any change?'

She tiptoed off, leaving Eleanor in an agony of expectation. She gazed down at the sleeping Daniel. He looked so vulnerable, but there was obviously something going on that she wasn't privy to yet.

Angie came back clutching two paper cups of black coffee. She gave one to Eleanor and sipped the other. 'Sorry, I forgot to ask about sugar. You must be wondering what's happened,' she added with remarkable understatement.

'Just a tad,' Eleanor admitted. 'I can't join the dots. You're going to have to tell me.'

Just then the nurse barged in. 'I have to check his vitals,' he informed the two women.

'Has he woken up yet?' Eleanor asked.

'Just once, for a short time when his parents were here, then he went back to sleep. But actually, that's a good thing under the circumstances. He'll need a while to recover from the trauma,' he explained. 'All his requirements are being catered for in the drips. He'll wake up when he's ready.'

Eleanor didn't share the nurse's lack of concern.

'But what about ... what about bedsores?'

'He's not Sleeping Beauty!' he exclaimed. 'He won't be asleep that long. And even if he was, we'd turn him regularly.'

'Oh my God,' Eleanor moaned. She looked at Angie for support, but she seemed to have fallen asleep across the end of the bed.

'You might want to take your friend to the canteen, or the visitor's lounge,' the nurse said, indicating Angie's slumped figure. 'I'd rather she had a kip in there.'

She helped Angie to her feet and hustled her out of the door. She turned to the nurse. 'I'll be in the canteen,' she said pointedly, 'if anything happens.'

The walk in the fresh air to the canteen had the desired affect and Angie was considerably more talkative by the time they got there. They bought pastries and more coffee from the man behind the counter. Eleanor would not be put off any longer. When they were sitting down, she asked Angie what she'd been doing in Cannes and how come she'd just happened to be there when Daniel was knocked down.

Angie looked at her through narrowed eyes. Eleanor couldn't work out if this was because of fatigue or intrigue. 'It's all a bit complicated,' she began.

'I'm sure I'll understand if you give it a try,' Eleanor said caustically.

'Hmm,' said Angie, nodding. 'Well, where to begin?'

'At the beginning,' Eleanor snapped. Her patience was stretched taut. She smiled. 'Daniel said you went to Paris to see Jean,' she prompted. 'So why were you in Cannes?'

'I'll have to start before then, if you're going to understand.'

Eleanor rolled her eyes. 'I'm all ears. Why don't you start with Paris?'

'All right.' Angie shifted uncomfortably on the hard seat. 'I wanted to see if the old attraction was still there. With Jean. He'd been in touch, you see.'

This bald admission almost took Eleanor's breath away. 'And was it?'

'You don't understand, Eleanor,' Angie moaned. 'I didn't want to hurt Daniel but I had to know.'

'You'd been seeing Jean, hadn't you? In London?'

Angie stared at her. 'How did you know? Daniel couldn't have told you. He ... he didn't know, did he?'

He would've done if I'd told him, Eleanor thought. 'No, I saw you. In Soho.'

'Fuck. But you didn't tell Daniel?'

'No.'

Angie smiled gratefully. 'That was good of you. At the time I didn't want him to know what I was doing. I wasn't sure of my feelings. And then Jean left London. Went back to Paris.' She put her head in her hands. 'Oh, I don't know, Eleanor. It's all such a mess.'

Eleanor's dislike of Angie threatened to come to the surface. She took a sip of coffee to swallow it down. 'So, you followed Jean to Paris to patch things up. Is that how it went?'

'Not quite. By the time I got there I realised something.'

Eleanor's stomach jumped into her throat. 'What? That you loved Daniel more than Jean, after all?'

'No,' Angie said quietly. 'I realised that I was pregnant.'

Jealousy lanced through Eleanor's heart like a hot knife through butter. 'Jesus,' Eleanor breathed. She didn't want to hear the answer but she asked anyway. 'And who's the father?'

Angie looked quite tragic. She shook her head. 'I don't know.'

'Can't you at least narrow it down?'

'Of course I can!' Angie suddenly snapped. 'I'm not a tart, Eleanor, regardless of what you might think. It's Daniel or Jean. There's no one else.'

'Thank God for that. But you don't know which? Can't you work it out from the dates?'

'I'm not a fucking almanac!' Angie hissed. 'I don't keep a diary. I was sleeping with them both, obviously. I didn't take a vow of chastity.'

'Sorry.' Eleanor felt chastened. She realised would have done the same thing, when she was seeing Nick, if Daniel had given her any indication …

'So what are you going to do?'

Angie shook her head miserably. 'I don't know.'

'But you never intended to have any kids,' Eleanor reasoned. 'Have you considered, you know, getting rid of it?'

'That's the thing, Eleanor,' Angie whispered. 'When it came down to the wire, I knew I couldn't do it.'

Putting her envy aside Eleanor saw a troubled young woman who didn't know which way to turn. But she also realised something else: Angie was definitely different. There was something almost ethereal about her. She seemed to glow, as if she was lit from inside, which had nothing to do with her round-the-year tan and everything to do with an inner radiance.

Angie was looking expectantly at Eleanor. 'I never thought this would happen to me, Eleanor. I was always so careful. But it has, and everything's changed, everything's a different colour, brighter somehow. I can't explain it very well, but it's as if everything in my little world has tilted. And it's never going to be the same again. But I do know that I can't do this by myself. If he'll have me, I'll stay with Daniel.'

Chapter Forty

When she looked back on that whispered conversation, Eleanor would see it as a turning point. She knew, with absolute certainty, that Daniel would embrace fatherhood, even as he might rail against the injustice of the ambush. The child she was carrying may not be his, but Angie would always be in his life.

The thought depressed and angered her in equal measure but she had no time to reflect; she'd been expecting Doug to arrive back from Skipton while she'd been at the hospital. But it was her mother who knocked on the door shortly after Eleanor arrived home. Her suitcase was sitting on the path behind her and she was carrying an incongruous blue plastic carrier bag.

'Thank goodness you're here,' Sylvia said. 'I had visions of eating my takeaway on the doorstep.'

Sylvia looked totally different. Her hair had been restyled and highlighted, she'd lost weight, and she was wearing a designer outfit that flattered her new figure.

'You look fabulous,' Eleanor said. 'But didn't Dad give you his key? I gave him the spare.'

'I haven't told him where I am,' Sylvia replied. She held up the bag. 'Would you like some? I've got sweet and sour prawn balls, deep-fried tofu, and egg fried rice.'

Eleanor grimaced. 'Don't worry, Mum,' she said. 'I'm not terribly hungry. I'll grab a bowl of cereal in a while.'

'Anything wrong, lovey?'

'No, nothing in particular,' she prevaricated. 'How'd it go with Dad?'

Sylvia walked past her through the house to the kitchen where she put the bag down on the counter. Eleanor followed, dragging her suitcase. 'Not as well as he was hoping, I think,' she said. 'I didn't feel like talking. I got the impression he would rather have been anywhere else.'

'Why d'you say that?'

'Oh, I don't know. He seemed on edge all the time.'

'That's unlike him,' Eleanor observed. 'Are you sure?'

Sylvia looked at her defiantly. 'I really don't care, Eleanor. I've had enough. I'm enjoying my freedom. Seeing my girlfriends. Your dad didn't think I had any.'

No, Eleanor thought wryly; you gave most of them up when you married him. The ones he hadn't had affairs with. 'Well, good for you,' she said.

'Anyway, I'm going on holiday. Would it be all right if I stayed a couple of nights? I'll be off soon.'

Eleanor suddenly rediscovered her appetite. 'No problem. Are you sure there'll be enough for me?' she asked, indicating the takeaway.

Sylvia nodded. 'Plenty. I'll get some plates.'

Over their meal Eleanor brought her mother up to speed on recent developments. 'Daniel came back from Cannes yesterday,' she explained. 'On a stretcher.'

'Goodness. What happened?'

She held up a hand. 'There's more. Angie was with him.'

'Your father called her a gold-digger. What was she doing with him? He said you –'

'I know what I said. I was wrong, or only partly right, put it that way.' She took a bite of prawn ball and continued. 'She was on holiday in Antibes with the new man, Jean, when Ginnie Applegate threw herself off the hotel balcony.' She paused while Sylvia poured lager into two glasses. 'Things weren't going too well with Jean, for reasons I'll explain later, otherwise it'll get too complicated, so for a bit of light relief, she popped along the coast to see what was happening.'

'I predict a coincidence,' said Sylvia between

mouthfuls of rice. 'Do go on,' she urged. 'This is getting interesting.'

'It was a bit of a coincidence,' Eleanor agreed, 'but she insists she didn't go looking for him. Daniel doesn't usually write about celebrity deaths, however bizarre, and she says she wasn't expecting to see him. Anyway, as luck would have it, there he was, on the other side of the street.'

She took a large swig of lager and helped herself to more tofu. 'This is actually quite nice,' she said. 'I've never had it like this before. I usually avoid it because it looks like congealed snot.'

Sylvia pulled a tortured face. 'Do you mind? I'm eating. Anyway, carry on,' she said. 'This is like something out of *Desperate Housewives*.'

'You can guess what happened next. Angie shouted to him across the street, Daniel stepped into the road in surprise, and got knocked down by a passing Maserati.'

'As you do,' Sylvia laughed. 'How very appropriate.'

Eleanor looked at her sternly. 'Mum! He was quite badly hurt. The car was going too fast. He broke his collar bone, some ribs, and there were some internal injuries too.'

'Sorry,' she apologised, assuming a suitably crestfallen expression. 'So he was shipped home and Angie came with him? Why didn't she go back to the other fella?'

Eleanor shrugged. 'I asked the same question. She said she felt responsible, but there's a bit more to it.' She stood up. 'I'll get some more lager then I'll tell you the rest.'

They were silent for a while, finishing off the food.

'That's better,' Sylvia said eventually, patting her still-flat stomach. 'Do you want to tell me the rest now?'

Eleanor nodded. 'This is where the added complication comes in.'

'Hang on. Go back a bit. How do you know all this? Have you been to the hospital?'

'Yes, I was there earlier. You see, I was a bit worried. I

couldn't get in touch with Daniel; he wasn't answering his phone or texts, so I spoke to Gwen and she told me about the accident and that Grace had flown him home. She told me where Daniel had been taken so I went this evening. Angie was there too. I didn't get to speak to him, though; he was asleep the whole time. But Angie gave me the full story.'

'And the complication?' Sylvia prompted. 'Come on Eleanor, the suspense is killing me.'

'Angie is pregnant,' Eleanor announced. 'And she doesn't know who the father is.'

'Why doesn't that surprise me? Are there many candidates?'

'Just the two. Daniel and Jean. Unfortunately, Jean doesn't want anything to do with the idea. And Daniel is unconscious and hasn't given his opinion yet.'

'What do you think he'll say?'

'This is where it gets difficult, Mum. You know Daniel. He'll want to do the right thing.'

'What? Even if the child's not his?'

'I'm sure he'll take a paternity test if Angie asks him to, but I'm not sure she will. Jean has already refused, and he's said that even if it was his without doubt, he still wouldn't be interested. It wouldn't fit in with his life plan.'

'And you don't think Angie will …?'

Eleanor shook her head. 'It's too much of a risk. She's changed, Mum. She's already told me she wouldn't contemplate getting rid of it. She wants a father for her child. Pregnancy does strange things to a woman, apparently. She needs Daniel. I'm not sure she'll tell him that he's not the only potential father.'

'Daniel isn't that stupid, though. He'll know that Jean is in the running as well, won't he?'

'No, the timing's all wrong. He doesn't know that Angie had been seeing Jean on the sly.'

Sylvia was incredulous. 'Has she?'

Eleanor waved a dismissive hand. 'Yes, I saw them together in Soho. She's admitted it to me, but not Daniel. And I haven't told him. Anyway, can you see him abandoning Angie to cope alone?' She shook her head. 'He just wouldn't do it.'

'And that leaves you ...?'

'Quite,' Eleanor said miserably.

'Don't be so pessimistic, darling!'

Eleanor looked at her mother bleakly. 'Pessimists are never disappointed, Mum.'

Sylvia touched her hand across the table. 'Did you tell him? About, you know, what we talked about?'

'Yes, no, er ... sort of.' She gave a short laugh. 'Just after we'd talked, I wrote him a letter, told him everything. But I couldn't give it to him.' Eleanor grabbed her bag and pulled out a folded sheet of paper. She handed it to her mother. 'First draft.'

'Do you mind if I read it?' Sylvia smoothed out the page.

Maybe it was the lager; maybe it was Angie's news. The letter didn't seem to matter any more. Eleanor shrugged. 'Whatever.'

Sylvia put on her very stylish reading glasses and began to read in silence. She nodded as she read, offering the occasional comment. When she'd finished, she laid the sheet down on the table and took off her glasses. 'It's very good,' she said eventually. 'You should've let him read it. It says everything he needs to know.'

'But after what'd just happened, what good would it do? It'd only make him feel guilty. He'd be caught between a rock and a hard place. It wouldn't be fair.'

'And what would be fair to you?' Sylvia asked gently. 'You always do this, Eleanor. You never put yourself first. What makes Angie worth more than you?'

'After all they went through together with his drug problem, they've got a bond. I haven't got that. And besides, she holds the trump card. She's having his baby.'

'She doesn't even know if it's his, for God's sake!' Sylvia exclaimed. 'Has she even hinted to him that there might be some doubt?'

'Not yet. He's been unconscious, remember?'

'She's operating under false pretences. Until she comes clean, all bets are off.'

Eleanor had never heard her mother talk like this before. 'Where did that come from?' she asked.

Sylvia smiled archly. 'It's a new friend. A man of the turf.'

'Jesus wept,' Eleanor moaned. 'Be careful, won't you?'

'Eleanor, darling, I've spent most of my life with a man who's gambled with my affections. I'm not likely to fall for that sort of spiel again.'

'You haven't lent him any money, have you?'

'Of course not! He's very wealthy.' She laughed gently and started to clear up the remains of their meal. 'It's just a bit of fun, darling. I'm not planning a future with him. Anyway, you've changed the subject. I don't think you should give up hope just yet,' she carried on. 'Daniel loves you. We both know that. He's just not very good at expressing it. I'm certain he won't go back to Angie after everything he's said.'

Eleanor swallowed the remains of her drink. 'He won't see it that way, Mum. He won't think he's got a choice.'

Chapter Forty-one

The next morning Eleanor walked into the newsroom bright and early. Several people waved and smiled, which was odd. Not that her colleagues didn't wave and smile in the normal course of events, but this was 6 a.m. Half of them were still asleep.

Ashok grinned at her as she sat down. 'It's all happening,' he said.

'What is? Has someone admitted chucking Ginnie off the balcony?'

'Not Ginnie,' Ashok said. 'That's old news. No, I'm talking about the next big celebrity.'

'Will you stop talking in riddles, please?' Eleanor snapped. 'It's far too early and I've got a lot on my mind.'

'I bet you have.'

'What are you talking about? Has Nick Paget gone and –?' She realised just in time that no one apart from herself and Daphne knew about Nick's blackmail attempt.

'What's he done now?' Ashok asked. 'I thought he was off the scene altogether.'

'He is,' Eleanor said hastily. 'So what do you mean? And why have I got so many emails? Look. There's hundreds.'

'That'll be all your fans,' he said.

'What fans?' Eleanor frowned. 'Have I just walked into a parallel universe, or something? I don't understand a word you're saying.'

'You'll soon find out. Just read a couple.'

'There's too many. Maybe I'll just delete the lot of them. It's probably all spam anyway.'

Ashok shrugged. 'Up to you. But I don't think you

should delete them without looking at them first,' he advised. 'They might be important.'

She peered closely at the subject lines of the emails. 'They're all about somebody's performance and how they're going to be famous.'

'Told you.'

'Oh, and now look!' Eleanor groaned, indicating her screen. 'What is happening today?'

Ashok came round the desk and read the electronic message that had popped up informing Eleanor that her mailbox was about to exceed its limit. 'Oh, that just means that your mailbox is full of clutter. You'll have to clear it out before you can receive any more emails.'

'I can read, thank you,' she said sarcastically.

'There's probably a lot more stuff backed up in the system,' Ashok said. 'You don't know what might be waiting for you.'

Something in Ashok's tone made Eleanor pause. She went to her *Deleted Items* box and immediately emptied the cache. Then she did the same with her *Sent Items*. This freed up a surprisingly large amount of space and she made a mental note to do this at least once a week in future.

Well, if she still had a job after today she would.

'Thank you,' she said. 'Now I can get some work done.'

'There'll be no time for that,' Ashok said. He grinned across the desk.

'What the hell are you on about?' Eleanor asked suspiciously. 'You sound like you know something I don't.'

'Maybe I do,' Ashok teased. 'Open an email, any email. You'll soon find out.'

This was getting beyond a joke. She opened an email at random, subject: *Your Performance*. She didn't immediately recognise the address, but it contained a link to YouTube. She looked up furtively; expectant faces were watching her all around the newsroom. She followed the link and watched in horror as a tiny version of herself burst into life on her screen. Embarrassed, she turned the sound down abruptly. She cringed. She'd never seen herself singing before and it wasn't a very edifying experience, particularly so early in the morning.

'You knew all along, didn't you?' she asked Ashok pointedly.

Ashok nodded sheepishly. 'Belle told me. She sent me the link.'

Julian had sidled up and was watching over her shoulder. 'You've been discovered.'

Eleanor's heart sank. 'What do you mean? Has Daphne –?'

'Didn't I say you'd make the big time?'

'Oh, I see. I thought you –' She suddenly realised what he was talking about. 'What?'

'The power of the internet,' he said. 'All that publicity. Someone's bound to see you and offer you a multi-million pound deal and the rest will be history.'

Eleanor snorted. 'I don't think so. Life's not like that. Well, mine certainly isn't. Things like that just don't happen to people like me.'

'It could be you,' Julian persisted, pointing his finger at her like a Lottery advert. 'You never know.'

Someone else talking in riddles, she thought.

He'd walked off before Eleanor could ask how things were. Julian didn't look as if he was too worried about finding the fortune that Nick was demanding for his silence. One good thing about being terminally drunk, she thought. Must be a lot like Alzheimer's: every day full of constant surprises.

She scrolled through the sea of emails, searching for something that might be to do with work, rather than her supposed fame. She was amazed at how many messages there were, and the sheer number of fans she'd managed to amass over one weekend.

She turned on her mobile. She'd completely forgotten that she'd switched it off in the hospital the previous evening. It beeped constantly while it downloaded multiple text messages. Most of them from Sam.

WTFRU??? Call me. You are going to be MEGA!! The messages went on until the inbox was full. Not again, Eleanor thought. What is happening to my life?

She cleared all the messages and speed-dialled Sam. 'Hi, it's me,' she said.

'Where have you been?' Sam almost screamed down the phone. 'I've been calling for ever! This is really big, Eleanor. You're going to be famous!'

Sam eventually calmed down enough to tell Eleanor that the talk on the internet at the weekend had been about her, Eleanor Jane Wragby, soon to be recording star extraordinaire. 'They absolutely love you!' Sam exclaimed. There's bound to be a deal in this somewhere,' she added. 'Belle has been fantastic!'

'Belle? What do you mean? I'm sorry Sam but –'

'How soon they forget,' Sam intoned mournfully. 'Belle, your ex-colleague, remember? She posted your karaoke session on YouTube and sent the link to her entire address book, by the looks of it. You're an overnight success!'

Well, at least that explained the overflowing inbox, Eleanor thought. 'Why would she do a thing like that?' she asked.

'You need to look on YouTube and read what Belle said, and all the other comments. But in case you don't believe me, or can't be bothered to look, she said that she owed you big time for her break into acting, and this was her way of saying thank you. Plus, she didn't want your talent to go to waste. She's even set up a Facebook page.

You've had thousands of hits already!'

Eleanor was silent.

'I wonder if she's got any contacts in the recording industry.' Sam carried on. 'Are you still there, El? What're you going to do? This is so exciting! El? Eleanor?'

'This is crazy,' Eleanor said. 'I can't think about it now. It's overwhelming. Sorry, Sam, I'll talk to you later,' she added, and ended the call.

She was in shock. What *was* she going to do? This was a turn of events she had never anticipated and she didn't know how to deal with it. She started to check her emails. Sam had probably been exaggerating.

Halfway down the first page of unopened messages were two from Belle.

The first was a profuse thank you for introducing her to Tommy Trivia, or Marcus as he was usually known, and how much she was looking forward to starting her acting career. There was also a reference to how much she appreciated Eleanor's defending her in the Pagets' passport row. A drunken Julian had told Belle that she had much to be grateful for. Tosser, thought Eleanor.

The second was slightly more circumspect. Begging Eleanor's forgiveness, Belle listed the A&R people she had sent the recording to. She hoped that something would come of one of them and wished her the best of luck in the future.

'What's A&R, Ashok?' Eleanor asked.

'Doesn't it mean Artists and Repertoire? Something like that. It's the people who scout new talent for record labels. Why?'

'Belle's sent a recording of my karaoke performance to every A&R person on the planet, by the look of this list. How does she know so many?'

'She knows a big noise at some music outfit. I forget which.'

'Why don't I know this?' Eleanor asked.

'She kept it pretty close to her chest,' Ashok said. 'I only know because I met him briefly at a party once. Nice bloke. Some poncy name.'

'None of them have contacted me yet. Mind you, I haven't read most of my emails. But I don't suppose anyone will.'

'Give them time,' said Ashok. 'Never say never.'

She continued scrolling through the pages of adulation. A person could get addicted to this, she thought as she read. It could quite turn your head.

She could hardly contain the mounting exhilaration. It was bubbling up inside her, threatening to overflow in a great, shrieking howl of glee. She felt like running around, laughing and screaming. She clenched her fists to prevent them waving madly in the air.

Calm down, she told herself. It probably won't amount to anything. Calm down and think peaceful thoughts.

How could she stay calm? This was the most extraordinary, exciting, enormous thing that had ever happened to her. She wanted to run in front of the studio cameras and shout it out for everyone to hear.

Instead, she shuffled some papers about on her desk; she went to grab a cup of coffee, as if she wasn't wired enough without extra stimulation; she twiddled with her mobile, and finally settled down to updating some diary entries on the computer. The repetitious nature of the task had the initial effect of stilling her rampaging thoughts but inevitably her mind slid off to less prosaic matters.

When her mobile beeped with a text message a few minutes later, she was feeling so blasé she almost ignored it. She checked the sender and opened the message immediately. *Daniel's awake*, it read.

Her heart bulged into her throat. All thoughts of fame and fortune fled. Hoping that Angie was in a part of the hospital where she could receive calls, Eleanor quickly keyed in her number. It was a rather crackly line but she could just hear Angie through the static. 'How is he?' she asked.

'Not too bad,' Angie said. 'I'm in the canteen.'

'Have you …?'

'I haven't had a chance. He's only just woken up and anyway … I don't know how to broach the subject,' she added. 'But I've got to do it soon.'

Me, me, me. Only ever one thought in her head. It's not all about you, Eleanor thought crossly. She took a deep breath. 'You should let him recover a bit first,' she advised. 'Then he'll be stronger and it won't be such a shock.'

'Maybe you're right.' Angie hesitated for a moment and Eleanor could hear panting.

'Are you all right, Angie?' she asked. 'Only you don't sound too clever yourself. Have you been back to Gwen and Peter's?'

'They invited me, but, honestly, I'd rather stay here.'

'Have you had something to eat? You must think about the baby.'

'I know, but I haven't got much of an appetite. The suspense is killing me, Eleanor. I have to know what he wants to do about …'

She sounded so weak Eleanor had a sudden vision of Angie being admitted to the hospital herself. 'Shall I come this evening?' she offered. 'I could come after work. That's if you don't think I'll be intruding.'

'Would you?' Angie asked weakly. 'I was going to ask … Only … I don't know what he's going to say. Would you be with me when I tell him? Please? I couldn't bear it if he didn't want to know.'

Eleanor looked blankly into the distance. She could think of a thousand places she'd rather be, but nothing else about today could possibly faze her. 'No problem,' she said. 'I'll be there about seven.'

Chapter Forty-two

For the rest of the morning Eleanor hardly had time to think about Daniel.

There were many presumptuous emails from total strangers offering to represent her in any forthcoming negotiations about recording contracts. Most were badly constructed and overly familiar and none had revealed any noticeable sympathy for her lack of experience in the music business. She had deleted most of them before her telephone rang yet again.

'Good morning,' the male voice enquired formally. 'Am I speaking to Eleanor Wragby?' He didn't sound like the excited teenagers of the morning's emails.

'You are,' Eleanor responded in kind. 'To whom am I speaking?'

'I'm so sorry,' the man apologised. 'I should have introduced myself immediately. My name is Gregory Symmington. Greg, for short.'

Public school, from the accent, Eleanor thought wickedly. 'How can I help you?'

'I've just seen your performance,' Greg explained. 'I represent Blah Music and I'm very interested in your version of "Jar of Hearts", and the others, of course,' he added.

'My –?' Eleanor had been unable to resist watching herself on YouTube several times, but she hadn't seen the song she'd chosen as the finale to her karaoke session. It had gone down better than she'd expected, attracting a large group of drinkers from the main bar.

'Oh, that,' she laughed. 'It's getting a bit cheesy now, isn't it?' she explained by way of mitigation. 'But it's still a crowd pleaser, and it suits my voice.'

'Admirably,' Greg agreed.

'But how have you managed to see that?' she asked. 'It wasn't posted on YouTube as far as I'm aware.'

'No, it wasn't,' he admitted. 'I've been looking at the recording that Belle Fenton sent me. Much better quality, and quite frankly, I've been playing it all morning.' He laughed softly. 'I must admit that when I first received it, I groaned. I thought, here we go, another wannabe with a dreadful voice. But I know Belle very well, and she wouldn't send me rubbish.' He paused and Eleanor waited impatiently. 'There are obvious similarities to Annie Lennox in your voice,' he continued, 'but there's also some Madonna and – betraying my age a bit here – undertones of Karen Carpenter. It's quite the loveliest thing I've heard for a long time. Perfect pitch, too, I think?'

'I ... er ... yes ...' Eleanor was completely taken aback. Here was someone who knew something about music, actually saying that he liked her voice. Loved her voice. She felt a blush of pleasure warming her cheeks and tears stung her eyes. 'Yes,' she stammered. 'I have. I've sung all my life.'

'Do you do any song writing?'

'A little. I used to do much more, just for myself, you know. But work ... it kind of gets in the way, doesn't it?'

'It does, it does,' Greg agreed. 'And do you play any instruments?'

'Just piano.'

'Good, good.' It sounded as if he was taking notes, or ticking boxes on an application form. 'Anyway, I think we could make something of you, Eleanor.'

After the fraught proceedings of the previous evening, his words were like healing balm.

'Do you really?' she asked. 'Are you sure?'

'Absolutely. I would consider it an honour if you would

have lunch with me, to discuss things,' he continued, sending shivers of excitement down Eleanor's spine. 'How does your diary look tomorrow?'

'I ... well ... let me check.' She didn't hesitate. 'Actually, tomorrow will be fine.'

'We'll go to La Caprice, shall we?' Greg asked. 'I'll book a table for one o'clock.'

She put the phone down and continued to stare at it for some moments before registering that Ashok was snapping his fingers to attract her attention.

'Have you heard the rumour about Julian?' he asked.

Eleanor smiled and nodded. Ashok continued speculating but she wasn't listening; his voice receded and gradually became indistinguishable from the general background hum. She pulled out her mobile and speed-dialled Sam. There was something to look forward to after all. She would emulate Scarlett O'Hara and think about Daniel and Angie another day.

Julian wasn't at the weekly planning meeting at 11 a.m. His absence was noted with several raised eyebrows but no comments were made. The talk was all about Ginnie Applegate's funeral, which was arranged for the following Friday.

Fraser, promoted from runner to newsdesk assistant, was a devoted fan and he was particularly astringent in his summing up of the situation. 'No one has come forward to claim responsibility for this atrocious act, so poor Ginnie might have to be buried in unconsecrated ground,' he declared histrionically. 'Without benefit of clergy.'

'That's really medieval,' someone said. 'I don't think that happens any more.'

'Makes no difference,' Fraser argued. 'Catholics still think suicide is wrong.'

How bizarre, Eleanor thought. What a small world.

After the meeting she walked reluctantly round to

Julian's office. Better to beard the enemy in his office than await the inevitable summons.

The small space looked as if it had been hurriedly vacated; there was an expectant air about it, as if it was waiting for its next occupant. Eleanor shivered.

The desk was almost empty, with just a small heap of papers piled with geometric precision at one corner; books and files had been cleared away and the computer screen was blank. Julian's laptop case and jacket were both absent. Neither, in themselves, a cause for concern, but still ...

She asked Fraser, but he didn't know. Already she missed Belle, the eyes and ears of the newsroom underground. 'You don't think he's ... you know ... been told to clear his desk?' she asked. 'I saw him earlier this morning, but now he's disappeared.'

'Never mind Julian,' Fraser cried. 'What about you? What about all this coverage you're getting?'

'I still can't believe it,' Eleanor said, shaking her head. 'It's madness. Absolute madness.'

'Enjoy it while you can. Do you think it'll lead to something?'

'I have no absolutely no idea.'

'Early days, though, isn't it? Give it time.'

'Yeah, yeah.' She put the conversation with Greg to the back of her mind. 'Anyway, what do you think's happened to Julian? Has he resigned or was he pushed?'

'Probably neither,' Fraser said. 'Someone said he might be doing a tour of the regions. He does that from time to time, doesn't he?'

Eleanor shook her head. 'I've just been in his office. It's like the *Marie Celeste*. He's taken everything with him. If he's only on a jolly, why didn't he tell anyone? And why isn't there anything in the diary?' she persisted, looking across the desk at Ashok.

'I'm not the bloody oracle.' He shrugged. 'We can only

guess.'

She was silent for a moment. 'Maybe he has gone. But one thing's for sure: if he's left under a cloud, we won't be told. We'll just be introduced to his successor.'

Her phone was ringing when Eleanor got back to her desk. It was Daphne, requesting her presence. Her heart sank. An interview with Daphne could take the gloss off a day as surely as paint stripper.

When Eleanor arrived at her office, Daphne wasn't alone.

'Take a seat, Eleanor,' she invited. 'Julian and I were just talking about you.'

She tried to keep the surprise out of her expression. In her mind, she'd already consigned Julian to the past.

'Julian was just telling me how helpful you've been over this Nick Paget business,' Daphne said.

'Oh?' Eleanor tried to sound non-committal.

'You'll have heard about the second blackmail attempt, I suppose? How nasty Nick is trying to extort money from Julian?' She nodded towards Julian, who sat with his head bowed. 'Obviously, he's not going to pay. And neither are we. We've been advised to sit it out.'

'Yes,' Eleanor agreed. 'I said the same –' She stopped abruptly. 'Sorry.'

'No, carry on. We'd like to hear your views. Julian also tells me Nick assaulted you.'

Eleanor glared at him. She'd hoped he'd keep that little titbit to himself. 'Well, it wasn't quite like that,' she stuttered. 'Nothing actually happened.'

'But you did advise Julian to call his bluff?'

'Did I?' She looked at Julian for support but none was forthcoming. 'Why? What is this?' Buoyed by the many messages of support she'd received that morning, her anger rose to the surface. Suddenly she had nothing to lose. 'Are you trying to blame me?' she demanded. 'Is this the collateral damage you didn't want to mention?'

'It's of no consequence,' Daphne said calmly. 'Julian has already tendered his resignation. Which we've accepted,' she added.

Eleanor frowned at Julian but he wouldn't meet her eyes. 'The question now,' Daphne continued, 'is who will replace him?' She looked pointedly at Eleanor and waited for a response.

'I've no idea.' Eleanor gestured towards the newsroom. 'There must be quite a few contenders in there.'

Daphne was still gazing at her, one eyebrow raised speculatively. 'You're aware that we utilise the SS system here at UK24?' she asked.

Eleanor had no idea what she was talking about. An image of Daphne wearing an SS uniform and goose-stepping around the place sprang into her mind. She shook her head. 'No, sorry, I've never heard of it. What is it again?'

'Suggesting Successors,' Daphne explained patiently. 'Traditionally we always look favourably on any potential successor whose name has been put forward for the post by the outgoing incumbent.'

There must be a less tortured way of expressing that, Eleanor, thought, but she got the drift. She looked at Julian, who pulled a face and shrugged.

'You didn't?' she asked. 'You can't be serious. You can't have suggested me?' Eleanor couldn't believe it. 'I don't have anywhere near enough experience for that position. Besides, I –'

'Besides what?' Daphne asked.

'Well, nothing, actually, I … I …'

'I told you, Daphne,' Julian interjected. 'Didn't I say her head would be turned by all this publicity?'

Eleanor almost laughed. 'What publicity?' she asked defensively. 'Anyway, how do you know about that?'

Daphne didn't seem to have heard. 'You certainly impressed us with the way you dealt with Nick and his con trick,' she carried on. 'Julian has nothing but praise for you. I can see you going a long way. We've been thinking for a while about reorganising Home News; you'd fit perfectly into the new structure.'

Eleanor was silent for a moment. 'I'm flattered to be considered,' she said eventually. 'But it's ridiculous. I'm not cut out for this kind of job. Do you really think I am? I'm better at sorting things out, not ... not a ...'

She ground to a halt. The offer was just an appeasement; something to make her feel better. It couldn't be anything else. It would probably be rescinded tomorrow. But it was nice to be asked; she may as well bask in the glory for a while. 'Well, if you think I'm up to it,' she said eventually, 'I'll think about it. Can you give me the new job description?'

Daphne smiled. 'Good girl. I'll send the new spec. through. There's no rush,' she said mildly. 'Though I'd like an answer by the end of tomorrow.'

'Tomorrow?' Eleanor shot a glance at Julian and got up to leave. 'Right, I'd better go and start thinking.'

By the end of the afternoon, she'd come to the conclusion that it was, in fact, April 1st, and an enormous joke was being played out at her expense. Of course she couldn't take Julian's job. Nor would she want it. There would be too much pressure and not enough time to ...

It struck her quite forcibly. If she took Julian's job, she would have to give up singing, and she was only just starting. The morning's activities had confirmed that there was a future to be grabbed, however short-lived it might turn out to be. She knew now that that was the job she really wanted, and judging by the amount of positive encouragement she'd had today, the vision had moved from the realms of pipe dream to possibility.

She took her time drafting a polite email to Daphne. She would send it tomorrow, so it would look as if she'd given the proposal some serious consideration. Then she pinged off a quick text to Sam, gathered her stuff, and left for the hospital.

Chapter Forty-three

Angie was still sitting beside the bed, dressed in the same clothes she'd had on the day before. Purple shadows under her eyes accentuated her sharp cheekbones; she'd obviously kept another sleepless vigil.

'Hi,' Eleanor said. 'How are things? You look like you need some sleep.' She gestured towards the empty bed. 'Where's the patient?'

'He's gone for a walk,' Angie replied. 'He's feeling much better. Still a bit stiff.'

'Have you –?'

Angie shook her head. 'No, not yet. I was waiting for you.'

'Oh. What about Gwen and Peter? And Grace? Are they expected?'

'No, they've been and gone about an hour ago, thank God. I didn't fancy saying anything in front of them. They've been cool enough as it is.'

'Angie,' Eleanor began. 'I've been thinking. Are you really sure you want me here? I mean –' She broke off as Daniel limped into the room, wearing a hospital gown covered by an ancient paisley robe that must surely have belonged to Peter.

He smiled guardedly, his eyes flicking nervously from Eleanor to Angie. 'How lovely to see you,' he said. 'Angie didn't tell me you were coming.'

'We wanted to surprise you,' Angie said cheerfully.

Daniel arranged himself gingerly on the bed. The bruising on his face had blossomed into a jaundiced yellow and he had angry scratches across his forehead and along his jaw. 'I can hardly breathe with this lot on,' he joked, indicating his torso, which was tightly wound with bandages. 'I think it's what's holding me together.' He turned to Eleanor, his face suddenly serious. 'Has Angie filled you in on what happened?' he asked.

'Oh yes.' Eleanor nodded. 'I know everything,' she added meaningfully. She raised her eyebrows at Angie. 'But I think Angie may have something else to tell you.'

They turned to Angie expectantly. She seemed to shrivel like a salted snail under the glare of their combined spotlights.

'Yes, well,' Angie began. 'Well, the thing is ...' She took a deep breath. She leaned over and started to plump the pillows behind Daniel's head. 'Are you comfortable? Can I get you another pillow, or do you want a drink? You need to keep yourself hydrated –'

'Angie,' Daniel moaned. 'I'm drugged up to the eyeballs. I'll be asleep again in a minute if you don't get on with it. What's going on? Eleanor, do you know what this is about?'

'Yes, I do, but I think it should come –'

'OK,' Angie said suddenly. 'Daniel, I'm pregnant.'

The only sound breaking the ensuing silence was the distant beep, beep of a heart monitor in a neighbouring room.

'You're what?' Daniel asked stupidly. He looked quizzically at Eleanor. 'What's she talking about? These pills are really messing with my head, El. I thought she said *pregnant*.'

'She did.' Eleanor looked at Angie who seemed on the point of tears. 'She is.'

The joyous expression that briefly illuminated his face squeezed Eleanor's heart. She'd been right. He wouldn't deny this child.

Daniel turned to Angie. 'I thought you didn't want any children. We've always been so careful. You'd always said –'

'I know what I've always said, Daniel,' Angie snapped, 'but it was an accident. It changes everything.'

'How long have you known? I mean, did you know before you went to see Jean?'

Angie nodded, staring at the floor and shuffling her feet like a small child. 'Sort of,' she admitted. She took an audible breath before she spoke again. 'I did a test the day before I went. It was positive. They're pretty accurate these days, but I already knew.'

Daniel took some moments to digest this information. He looked at Eleanor as if he couldn't comprehend what he'd just heard. He fumbled for her hand across the sheet. 'I don't know what to say. I mean, I, we …'

Eleanor gripped his fingers. She gazed back at him, willing him to utter the words that would confirm her place in his life.

'So,' he said eventually. 'We're going to be parents?'

Eleanor held her breath, looking towards Angie, waiting for the fateful admission.

It never came.

'We are,' Angie said defiantly.

When Daniel spoke, he turned Eleanor's already topsy-turvy world upside down again. 'Right.' He looked from one to the other. 'We need to think about this,' he prevaricated. Then he seemed to exclude Eleanor completely as he addressed Angie directly.

'We'll need to make plans. You can't go back to France now, can you? You'll have to stay in England, at least until the baby's born.'

Angie smiled and moved towards the bed. She bent and kissed Daniel on the forehead. 'Thank you,' she said. She stared knowingly at Eleanor over Daniel's head. 'I knew you'd be happy when you got over the shock.'

It was as if she had ceased to exist. Daniel had accepted his fate without a murmur. Maybe the drugs really were messing with his mind, but Eleanor didn't think so.

Disillusionment stung her like a whiplash, her earlier elation subsiding like a collapsed soufflé. She felt crushed and wished herself a million miles from the claustrophobic little room. Tears sprang into her eyes and she ducked her head on the pretence of a sneeze to hide them. Daniel didn't seem to have the slightest suspicion that the child might not be his.

She already knew that she wouldn't be the one to tell him. She refused to be cast as the jealous usurper, the unwelcome bringer of bad news. She'd known that Daniel would feel a financial responsibility towards any child he assumed was his, but she hadn't projected her thoughts forward to this development. He was actually inviting Angie back into his life without any hesitation.

She coughed discreetly and at last Daniel turned to face her. 'I think I'll be heading off now,' she said. 'You two have lots to talk about. I'll get out of your way. I'm glad you're feeling better.' She picked up her bag and started for the door but Daniel grabbed her hand.

'Don't go,' he said. 'I'm sorry. I'm still a bit shell-shocked.' He patted Angie's arm. 'Would you give us a couple of minutes, please?' he asked.

They watched as Angie smiled uncertainly and left the room.

'This doesn't mean anything, Eleanor. Just be patient,' he said, taking her hand. 'We can still be together. It'll just take a bit longer.'

'How can you say that?' she demanded. 'You're going to be a father. I'm not ready to be the wicked step-mother.'

'It's early days,' he soothed. 'Who knows how you might feel?'

She snatched her hand back. 'Daniel,' she said exasperatedly, 'you don't even know –' She stopped herself. 'I know what I want, and this isn't it. It would never fit with … It would never work.' She stood up and began pacing round the room. 'I haven't even begun to tell you what's been happening to me.'

His brow furrowed. 'What do you mean?'

She didn't want to tarnish her news by telling him when his mind was so obviously elsewhere. She wanted him to celebrate with her, be excited for her. Not this. She shook her head furiously. 'I'm not telling you now. It's too important to me.' She looped the strap of her bag over her shoulder. 'I think I should go now. Give you both some space.'

'Eleanor, I never meant …'

'No, I don't suppose you did,' she said sadly. As she walked out of the room she had no idea whether she would see him again.

Chapter Forty-four

Lunch was going rather well. Eleanor accepted another glass of champagne and smiled benignly across at Greg. She could definitely get used to this.

'So, what do you think?' Greg asked. 'Can we get you into a recording studio quite soon?'

Eleanor nodded. 'I've got some annual leave to take. I don't want to –'

'Of course not.' Greg nodded. 'We need to hear more of you before you burn any bridges. Best not give up the day job just yet. ' He smiled and held up his glass in salutation. 'But I don't have any worries. Personally, I think we're on to a winner. Cheers.'

Eleanor glowed. She soaked up the admiration like a parched plant. 'Do you see me with any, you know, any accompaniment?' she asked. 'Or are you only interested in à cappella?'

'Both,' said Greg promptly. 'We should exploit your whole range, which I expect to be considerable. Some songs will suit an unaccompanied voice, others not.'

Greg was obviously very well known. Several people she vaguely recognised stopped and chatted to him on the way to their tables. Occasionally he introduced her to some luminary from the music world. 'You'll get to know all these people, eventually,' he said. 'But not just yet. If you'll allow it, I'll be your filter for the moment. There are some very unscrupulous people around.' He scrutinised her face. 'But you already know that, working in television, don't you?'

'Indeed I do,' she agreed. 'But there are some absolute gems, too,' she carried on. 'Belle, for instance. I would never have had the nerve to send you that tape on my own.'

'Thank goodness for Belle,' Greg smiled. 'I'll thank her properly next time I see her.'

'Oh. I didn't realise. Are you …?'

Greg grinned. 'She's my sister. Well, half-sister, actually. Different fathers, hence the dramatically different surnames.' He laughed. 'As I understand it, it was you who wangled Belle her big break with Marcus whatisname, wasn't it? She's still over the moon about that. She'll go on to great things, too.'

Eleanor's stomach plummeted. 'You're not just doing this because of that, are you?'

Greg burst into laughter. 'Aha! Belle warned me you'd probably say something like that! Of course I'm not.' He assumed a serious expression. 'Eleanor, I wouldn't make the offer I've just made because you did my sister a favour. I see it as an investment. But the bottom line is, this is all about money, believe me.'

She relaxed, hugging herself with glee. She could hardly believe this was happening to her. And it was too late to back out now. The die had been cast and she was about to do something she'd never done before: she was going to face an unknown and uncertain future, comfortable in the knowledge that whatever happened was in her hands and however it panned out, she would be worthy of it. 'That's all right then. I hope … I hope I live up to your expectations,' she said.

She didn't bother going back to work. It was hardly worth it, she told herself. Let them wonder who was wining and dining her. Pleasantly full of champagne and good food, and with Greg's words ringing in her ears, she leant her head against the window and dozed as the tube train trundled homewards.

Daniel was sitting beside Mabel on the doorstep when

she turned down the path.

He struggled to stand up as she approached and her heart lurched as it always did when she saw him. He swayed as he got to his feet and she put out her arms to catch him. 'What are you *doing*?' she demanded. 'You shouldn't be here. You should still be in hospital.'

'I discharged myself,' he said. 'I had to see you. They said you weren't at work and your mobile was switched off and … and …'

'Shut up and come in,' Eleanor commanded, unlocking the door and ushering him inside. 'Sit down before you fall down. You look done in. Thank God I came home when I did.'

'I do feel a bit woozy,' he admitted. 'I thought I'd be OK.'

She bustled off into the kitchen and prepared tea, spooning sugar into Daniel's mug.

'I don't take sugar,' he moaned when he sipped it.

'I know. It's good for shock.'

'I don't –'

'Drink it, please,' she encouraged, trying to keep the concern out of her voice. She made him comfortable on the sofa with cushions and a throw. Mabel had sidled into the room and was sitting below the television with her tail curled neatly round her feet, watching the unfolding events with curiosity.

Daniel grimaced theatrically as he sipped the over-sweet tea. 'Ugh.'

'Don't be such a baby. You are an idiot,' Eleanor said. 'Why did you come? Why today? Couldn't it have waited a few days until you were feeling better? What if I hadn't come home? What would you have done?'

Daniel waited patiently until she paused for breath. 'Gone home, I suppose.'

'But what's happened? Has Angie –?'

'If you'd just let me get a word in edgeways,' Daniel

said mildly, 'I'll fill you in.'

'Sorry.' Eleanor sat down. She turned her mug nervously in her hand. 'So ...?'

'It's been quite an interesting few days,' he carried on. 'Angie eventually came clean about the baby. The father, I mean. It has to be Jean's; the dates fit. I was in Frankfurt when ... She was a bit economical with the truth at the hospital. But you already knew it was a possibility, didn't to you?'

Eleanor nodded. 'She mentioned something ... I didn't know what to think.'

'I was in Frankfurt,' Daniel repeated. 'And Angie was ... well she was already seeing Jean behind my back.' He paused, took another sip of tea. 'Anyway, she's gone back to France to sort things out with him. He's had a bit of a change of heart, apparently. Seems he's quite interested in seeing his dynasty continuing after all. He still wants a paternity test, but I guess that's his right.'

'And how do you feel about it all?'

'I'm glad she told the truth. It puts everything into perspective.'

Eleanor nodded. 'So what are you going to do now?' She was holding her breath; she wasn't sure she wanted to hear the answer.

Daniel took his time replying. Eleanor waited, silent, as he took another gulp of tea. 'Angie made me realise what I stood to lose,' he said eventually. 'Again.'

'Oh.'

'She was very grateful to you, actually,' he carried on. 'She thought it would be easier for her to leave, now that you're back on the scene.'

'But I'm not "on the scene",' Eleanor murmured.

'Oh yes you are.' Daniel pulled her towards him delicately. 'Angie's actually a very wise woman. She knew how I felt about you. She said it had been perfectly plain the moment she stepped into the kitchen that day you came to lunch at the flat.'

Eleanor blushed. 'Was I that transparent?'

'Only to another woman, apparently. I didn't see it at the time. I was too caught up with the idea of making Angie the centre of my life, a life-long thank you for saving me.' He laughed. 'It took me a while to wake up, I admit. It was probably the knock on the head that did it.' He leaned forward and kissed her tentatively on the forehead. 'When she said she was leaving, I admit I was a bit shell-shocked for a while. Then she reminded me that what I'd always wanted was right under my nose, if only I could see it. I'm sorry it took me so long.' He kissed her again. 'But I got there in the end.'

Eleanor's heart was beating so fast she felt breathless. 'I'm sorry you had to hear it at all. I was as shocked as you when Angie told me everything.' She relaxed in his arms. 'I just couldn't bring myself to tell you. I thought it would make me look a bit, well, you know …' she smiled to herself, 'a bit what-did-I-tell-you?'

'As if,' Daniel said. 'You didn't arrange for her to restart an affair with an old boyfriend. Lucky she chose a rich man,' he laughed. 'Ouch, that hurts,' he moaned, clutching his midriff.

'Hasn't she still got the engagement ring?' Eleanor asked mischievously. 'She could sell that and live in luxury for a while, I suppose.'

'Actually, she's given that back to me.'

'No!' She sat up and looked at him. 'I don't believe you.'

Daniel squirmed about and pulled a familiar jeweller's box out of his pocket. He showed her the solitaire, nestling on its velvet cushion. 'Look.'

Eleanor stared at him.

'Don't you want it?' He offered her the box.

She didn't know what to say. 'Are you –?'

'I'm teasing you,' Daniel laughed. 'We'll sell it and get

you another one.'

'But it's an heirloom,' she protested. 'You can't –'

'Who needs heirlooms?' Daniel asked. He hugged her carefully to his side. 'Let's get something modern, something that suits you, not my ancient old granny.'

Eleanor was so accustomed to convincing herself that life was all about wanting what you've got rather than getting what you want that she was having trouble accepting the possibility that she might actually achieve what she really, truly desired.

She relaxed against him. 'All right.' She kissed his cheek. 'Talking about family, how are they both, by the way?'

'Happy as Larry, by all accounts,' Daniel said. 'Dad's already started accumulating his next fortune. They're living in the London flat full-time these days, and Mum is loving it. I think she's relieved that she doesn't have an enormous estate to run any more.'

They lapsed into silence, Eleanor careful not to put any pressure on his injuries, but edging closer to him and enjoying the feeling of being encircled in his arms.

Mabel jumped onto the sofa and insinuated herself carefully between them, as if she knew instinctively that Daniel was injured. She curled up and purred contentedly.

'So where were you today?' Daniel asked eventually. He bent and kissed her head. 'No one at UK24 seemed to know where you'd gone. They were very mysterious when I rang. What were you up to?'

'Actually, I was out to lunch,' she replied, trying to keep the excitement out of her voice. 'With a man from the music trade. He offered me a recording contract.'

Daniel sat up gingerly and held her at arm's length. 'A what?'

'A recording contract.'

'That's brilliant!' He held her face in his hands and smiled widely. 'You dark horse, you.'

'It all happened when you were away, or in hospital,' Eleanor explained. 'And I haven't had a chance to tell you.'

He folded his arms and sat back carefully. 'Well, you can tell me now.'

'And finally, some good news.' The presenter smiled into the camera as a very flattering studio photograph of Eleanor appeared on the screen behind him. *'One of our own, Eleanor Wragby, the dedicated news researcher recently exonerated in the Nick Paget blackmail story, has just signed a major recording contract with Blah Music.*

'Eleanor had successfully kept her amazing singing talent under wraps until a friend posted her incredible performance at a local karaoke night on YouTube.' The portrait was replaced with some grainy footage of Eleanor singing in the bar. *'In the best tradition of the overnight sensation,'* the presenter continued, bending the truth slightly, *'her astounding singing voice was heard by a talent scout, and the rest, as they say, is history.'*

Women's Contemporary Fiction

For more information about **Maggie Cammiss**

and other **Accent Press** titles

please visit

www.accentpress.co.uk

For news on Accent Press authors and upcoming titles
please visit

http://accenthub.com/

Printed in Germany
by Amazon Distribution
GmbH, Leipzig